Also by Sheila Dyan

Love Bites

Beach Book

Sheila Dyan

CORONET BOOKS
Hodder and Stoughton

First published in 1994 by Hodder and Stoughton
A division of Hodder Headline PLC

A Coronet paperback

British Library Cataloguing in Publication Data

Dyan, Sheila
Beach Book
I. Title
813.54 [F]

ISBN 0-450-60598-1

Typeset by Keyboard Services, Luton

Printed and bound in Great Britain by
Cox & Wyman Ltd, Reading

Hodder and Stoughton Ltd
A division of Hodder Headline PLC
338 Euston Road
London NW1 3BH

To see a World in a Grain of Sand
And a Heaven in a Wild Flower,
Hold Infinity in the palm of your hand
And Eternity in an hour.

– from *Auguries of Innocence*
by William Blake
circa 1800–1803

FOR MY CHILDREN
WINIFRED AND BRIAN

and

MY SISTER, LINDA

Acknowledgements

To Sam Kirschner, for his confidence, encouragement and definitive criticism,

To Carolyn Mays, my eagle-eyed editor for her skill and understanding,

To Liz and Jim Trupin, of JET Literary Associates, Inc., for their continuing belief, support and other kindnesses,

To Octavia Wiseman at Abner Stein's, for her interest and support,

To my Family and Friends, for their love and patience,

I am most grateful.

WITH LOVE, I THANK YOU ALL

CHAPTER 1

White

Against the perfect silver-gold disk of the full moon, the young woman turned slowly on the slim cord binding her ankles, holding her aloft two hundred feet above the shore. Blood pounded in her ears. Her stomach weighed upon her heart. Opening her eyes, she saw the diamond-peaked black sea tossing and churning above her, the lucid sky below. As she moved, her buttocks flashed in the moonlight, her white breasts peeked out from behind her arms crossed against her chest. Her red hair hung down from her head like a flag.

She was imagining a cocoon about her, a metamorphosis within. Hanging from the silken thread, she could feel her body expanding, pushing out wings as she transformed before her inner eye.

'Now,' she said aloud.

Grasping the cord, the man in the balcony above pressed it to his left and then released it. The woman swayed back and forth slowly, excitement growing in her as the to and fro of her flight played havoc with her equilibrium.

'Faster, *faster*,' she cried.

The man pushed the rope.

Spreading her arms outward, she moaned softly. Waving her gossamer wings, she smiled as she felt her insides lighten, open.

'Yes!' she called.

Although not particularly young or large in stature, the man was wiry, agile and strong. He would hoist the *petite* woman up over the rail and into his arms. She'd flutter against him, allow him to carry her to his bed where he'd hold her arms out from her body.

'What beautiful wings. What a beautiful butterfly,' he'd say to her while another woman tied her wrists to the bedposts with forest-green silk scarves. The man would then mount her, pinning her to the bed.

They'd played the game so many times before, it had become ritual. But this time, barely having time to spread her wings, let alone fly, Marjorie Applebaum was falling, stark naked, on to the boardwalk below, passing Alison Diamond lying half asleep on her balcony.

. . . I was sitting on the beach under my white umbrella, constructing the final scene of a novel on my laptop computer, a fiction inspired by a tragedy at my seashore apartment building that had occurred just two weeks before. A young woman named Marjorie Applebaum had died in a mysterious fall from a balcony on to the boardwalk below. The investigation into her death, her probable murder, was still going on as I created my own solution from shreds of fact and rumour surrounding the unfortunate event. As was my custom, I borrowed the real names of the people and places that inspired my fictitious account, names that would change with a few key strokes once the story had taken on a life of its own.

I pushed a few keys to save what I'd written in the secret files of *Beach Book-91*. The computer whirred for a moment and then the screen went blank.

As for my own story, I should start at the beginning, or, if not at the very beginning – there really are so many beginnings in real life – at least the beginning of that summer month in my life that included the death of Marjorie Applebaum, a beginning not too far removed from Marjorie's end, in time, locale, and perhaps even state of mind – which is to say, reeling.

Colourful umbrellas dotting the shimmering sand two hundred feet below were spinning like solar powered pinwheels, or so it appeared to me as I reeled in a vertigo that was only somewhat assuaged by the steadying sound of the surf beyond the burning beach. I felt like I was falling in a dream ... in slow motion ... from a high precipice through a thickened, heated ether. The whirling disks of red, blue, green rushed to me as I leaned towards the sea, as my heart rushed to my throat, when suddenly I caught my body upright from its cant and blinked my eyes, disrupting the illusion, setting the colours back into place – vibrant tiddlywinks on a vast white canvas.

It was unusual for me to be at the seashore during the week. I'd awakened in my centre city Philadelphia apartment that crispy warm Thursday late in July, 1991 feeling restless and lightened, as if gravity's grip had slipped a bit and I was in danger of rising from the earth and being engulfed by the empty, endless sky. So I decided to deviate from the strict research and writing schedule I necessarily imposed upon myself (structure necessary to the seemingly unstructured life of a free-lance writer) and start my yearly month-long vacation at the Ivory Tower Condominium, in Atlantic City, a few days early.

The Tower is actually just south of Atlantic City, in the

small town of Kent. But, to me, all of Absecon Island, the thin, ten mile phalanx in a finger of land pointing south-east from New Jersey's fist, is *Atlantic City*.

With its broad white beaches and glistening surf, beachside boardwalk and amusement piers, lodgings from rooming houses to grand hotels, and homes from white clapboard bungalows to pink stucco mansions, Absecon Island in the summers of my childhood was a sun-warmed sanctuary of innocence.

The advent of casino gambling in Atlantic City, however, was transforming. The once subtle skyline gave way to a jagged line of towering casinos, a thin veneer of concrete, steel and lights that had sprouted – overnight, it seemed – out of the seeds of greed, planted by the ambitious in the backyards of the poor and elderly. And more than just the skyline had changed. The climate had cooled.

But approaching the island via the Albany Avenue Bridge between waves of prickly marsh grass and redolent green-grey waters that July morning, the present faded as the briny smell of the sea enveloped me, took me back to summer vacations at my grandmother's house *down the shore* on a beach block in Kent, the block since consumed by the Ivory Tower Condominium, where, perhaps not so coincidentally, I now owned an apartment. I recalled sultry days on the beach with the smell of salt and Coppertone oil, the feel of salt and sand, the taste of salt and cherry Popsicle, of pistachio fudge and lemon salt-water taffy. It all came back to me with the smell of the sea.

Just over the bridge a beautiful green marble woman surrounded by sixteen Doric columns welcomed me. The Greek Temple Monument, a great round anachronism of Indiana limestone and slate, is the hub about which the main roads converge. To the left of the Monument is The

City; to the right The Suburbs, from Chelsea to Longport. It wasn't until I was grown that I'd learned that the green lady was *Liberty in Distress*, rising from a pile of dead, a memorial to Atlantic City's World War I martyrs. The child in me remembered the Monument as a carousel.

Veering, as usual, to the right, leaving The City and its vices to others, I drove slowly down Atlantic Avenue. One block to the left was the ocean; a few blocks to the right the bay. Attempting to keep in sync with the string of timed traffic lights trailing to the horizon was a diversionary exercise that slowed and regulated my inner being like digitalis regulates the heart. When I turned towards the ocean at Ascot Place, I was startled into the present, as always, finding my grandmother's home supplanted by the twenty-storey white marble apartment building, the Ivory Tower Condominium.

Waiting for the elevator, I evoked the past from within, remembering my grandmother's three storey white stucco home with its Escheresque maze of front and back stairways, its white porches and thick wooden balustrades. It was up a steep flight of white-washed concrete steps to the huge, sun-washed front porch where someone was always on the rocking chair or in the hammock slung catercornered from the beams, and then through the front door into a world of musty oriental carpets and dark, overstuffed, slightly mildewed furniture. It was a world where no one felt a need to condition the air, so the morning heat and humidity often fogged glass panes and mirrors, and evening breezes and insistent surf enticed sleep through open windows. It was where my grandmother indulged me and my cousin Evy, and where cousin Larry played Monopoly with me on rainy days.

At the Ivory Tower, I rode up seventeen floors in an air-conditioned elevator of brass and mirror, to a long, air-conditioned hall, to an air-conditioned apartment where grass mats covered most of the white tile and pickled wood floors, and light oak framed the pink and blue pastel batik covered furnishings.

Following a ritual, I opened the two sliding glass doors in the living room to the wraparound, corner balcony, and the sliders to the balcony in the master bedroom. Then I walked out and around to the front balcony overlooking the beach. I closed my eyes – eyes that are decidedly green in the city and blue at the shore – and summoned the hot sun and salty breeze of my grandmother's porch.

Standing on my balcony, before I was overtaken by vertigo, I was six again, and the choices of the past thirty-four years were yet to be made. Standing in the warmth of the past, I didn't consider how life could have turned out, only how it had been when I was a child in Atlantic City. It was sweet innocence.

My apartment at the Ivory Tower had been purchased in 1984 with a portion of the proceeds from the sale of my large, refurbished estate home in the suburbs years before, a sale that had at the time enabled me to buy my centre city Philadelphia apartment. The suburban property would have been the bulk of my divorce settlement, had Carl and I divorced in 1976. Carl, an obstetrician, would have gotten his pension fund, his office building, and some other investments. It was, as they say in the divorce trade, equitable.

He was leaving me because he wanted passion, he had told me, passionlessly. Repeating the word *passion* over and over in my head, I had tried to remember how it felt. He tried to tell me how it felt as he related how he had found passion in the arms of Starr Hamilton, our nineteen-year-old baby-sitter, whose affair with Carl had begun shortly after she'd seen him about a urinary tract infection a few months earlier. He'd taken a catheterised urine specimen, in his office, after regular hours, a procedure that had caused her to moan.

'Am I hurting you, Starr?' he had asked.

'It doesn't exactly hurt,' Starr responded.

'Are you uncomfortable?' he asked.

'It's not exactly uncomfortable.'

'I think I should do an internal examination to determine what's making you, shall we say, uneasy,' he said, withdrawing the catheter, slipping two fingers into her giving young body.

'Oooh,' she moaned again. 'Don't stop.'

He didn't.

'Stop,' I implored as Carl recalled the details, insisting that he needed to share the experience with me . . . that he'd wished that I had been there, it had been so exciting . . . that maybe –.

'Stop,' I said again.

He did.

Failing to have the ideal marriage, we attempted to have the ideal divorce, drawing up the papers with the help of one attorney . . . quietly . . . agreeing that there'd be time enough after the separation to explain things to friends and family.

But our intent to divorce never came to public disclosure. Two months to the day after telling me that he was going to leave – the day before the settlement papers were to be signed – Carl suffered a heart attack while playing racquetball. Unfortunately, he was playing with Phil the psychiatrist, not Lou the cardiologist, Carl's usual Tuesday evening racquetball partner. Carl ended up dead on the court with a psychiatrist pounding frenetically on his chest, tearfully yelling in his ear, '*Death is an existential*

experience – you don't have to die! Don't you fucking die!!'
And I ended up getting it all.

'*A loving husband and father,*' the rabbi said of Carl at
the funeral, drawing honest tears from me. It's true that
Carl hadn't been a great husband, but he didn't deserve to
die, I thought. And my son, Shel, at three, didn't deserve to
lose his father.

Considering the circumstances, I thought it best to
consider myself a widow.

Peering down at the colourful umbrellas of the Tower
beach fifteen years later, thoughts of Carl's death, of Shel's
imminent departure for college, had brushed by me,
nudged me from peace, and I had wondered where the time
had gone. It was dizzying the way time passed, I thought,
feeling that in the rush I must have missed a lot. Watching
the tiny people below visit from umbrella to umbrella,
undoubtedly carrying tales like bees carry pollen from
flower to flower, I felt that I was too far away, too high up,
and I began to reel.

Dismissing my dizziness to the height, the bright, the
humidity – humidity, I had heard, could do strange things
to one's sinuses – I breathed deeply and closed my eyes
against the glare of the sun. Luminous disks were etched
into the black of my inner eye. Then again, I thought as the
disks faded and the black overwhelmed me, it could be a
brain tumour.

Sixteen years as a free-lance medical writer had left its
mark. I was a walking encyclopedia of medical trivia and a
victim of *a little bit of knowledge* plagued by hypochondria.

If I die from a brain tumour, who'll take care of Shel? I
wondered, breaking out in a cold sweat. Leaving the
balcony, I tried to call my son. When his answering
machine informed me that neither he nor his four

housemates were in, I left a message informing him that I was at the shore apartment.

Shel was my *raison d'être*. His birth had given confidence, constancy to my life; I had given my life to him. And now he was about to leave for college. He was about to leave me. By renting a house for the summer with his friends, though not a mile away from the Tower, he was practising.

I changed from jeans to shorts, smeared my exposed skin with number fifteen sunscreen, donned a wide-brimmed straw hat, and started off for the deli where Shel worked.

Contrary to my non-ambulatory habits in Philadelphia (finding the air too close, the concrete too hard, the traffic and lights a bother) I loved to walk on the boardwalk – the straight, uninterrupted, five and a half mile herringbone path of wood along the beach. The warm salty wind in my face, I barely felt the blocks slip by, until, giving in to a desire to feel the burn of hot sand beneath my feet – just for a minute, I told myself – I pulled off my sandals and descended the nearest stairs to the beach. There the everyday world faded in the penetrating glare of the sun off the sand, the low, insistent roar of the surf and wind. Alone behind crowds of people clustered around the life-guard stands like iron filings around magnets, I sank to the sand and breathed in the salty essence of the seashore. For a moment I was six again. Stretching out, my hands behind my head, my hat over my face, I rode over waves of heat into a dream . . .

Shel was in a rowing-boat behind my large, diesel-powered yacht. He was only a few yards from me, rowing furiously, but the distance between us was growing. On the bridge of my craft I fumbled with the gears attempting to reverse, but I was confused by the controls and succeeded only in increasing my forward speed and my distance from Shel. I ran down to the deck and tried pulling the myriad ropes of what was now a sailing-boat in an effort to slow the vessel, but the wind blew harder, filling the sails, and Shel was growing smaller and smaller in the distance. I turned to go below deck to find maps of the sea, but there were no stairs on what was now a small raft. Shel continued to row against the current that was pulling him from me. And then I was standing on a cold, darkening shore at sunset, straining to see the speck on the horizon that was Shel. Just as the last light of the sun was swallowed by the sea, so was he.

. . . I woke suddenly. A singular, massive cloud had covered the sun, and the cool breeze washing across me had left goose bumps in its wake. Arising, I brushed myself off and returned to the boardwalk just as the sun burst forth from behind the cloud, dropping a comforting blanket of warmth around me.

At the deli, I was told that Shel worked the evening shift that Thursday and Friday, so I bought a pastrami special on rye, three cartons of yogurt, a quart of one per cent milk, all-fruit strawberry preserves, and English muffins, and walked back to the Tower at a brisk pace, the warm breeze now at my back.

As soon as I entered my apartment, I checked my answering machine. Its little red light shined steadily indicating that I'd received no calls in my absence. I uncomfortably considered my son among the missing.

Settling on to the front balcony with my laptop computer, I retrieved the *Beach Book-91* directory, and then, from there, the *Notes* file – the single file in that directory – and found only the title, *Notes*, etched in blue on an otherwise blank white ground.

I stared skyward. 'Whale,' I said aloud, eyeing a large

cumulus cloud. 'Poodle,' I said moments later. Then, 'Crab. Bat. Filet of sole,' I said, laughing at my fey description as the flat-iron shaped cloud fragmented into ... 'Fish cakes!' I exclaimed, amusing myself further, waiting for ... inspiration? More likely waiting for Shel's call ...

Alison Diamond stared skyward. 'Whale,' she said aloud, eyeing a large cumulus cloud. 'Poodle,' she said moments later. Then, 'Two poodles mating,' she said, reeling in a sudden swell of passion.

... Letter by letter, word by word, my fingers clicked the keys, as I attempted to eke out the beginnings of what was to be a quick reading novel with a seaside venue and the usual erotic bent for which I – or, more specifically, Sloan I. Diamond, my alias, my alter ego – had become known in seven volumes of fiction published in as many years. In May I'd promised my editor the first draft by September 1. It was July 25 and I'd written nothing but my usual working title page:

BEACH BOOK-91
by
SLOAN I. DIAMOND

Although considered a successful non-fiction writer – my byline (Alison Diamond) appeared at least monthly in national or local magazines and newspapers – my real success was in my fiction, which sold quietly and steadily over the years, building a credible, loyal readership, though no one but my agent and editor, not even Shel, knew that Sloan I. Diamond and Alison Diamond were one and the same, separated only by anagram ...

* * *

Pricilla Perkins, television chef of local renown, would never pull a pot roast from the oven again without feeling the surge of sexual excitement tear through her body.

. . . So began *Appetizers*, the title story in my first book of the same name, a collection of short stories with first encounters of the sexual kind as its theme. I wrote the story in less than three days, catching the attention of a New York agent to whom I'd sent it on a whim. The rest of the nine stories in that slim volume also came easily, and, when completed, the collection was picked up by a publisher of paperback books. Six more books followed in yearly succession.

After *Appetizers*, I used the working title *Beach Book* for each new novel, an idea that came to me when someone told me that *Appetizers* was great beach reading. I intended to write the perfect beach book, while on the beach, each summer thereafter. Sitting on the beach or on the balcony of my apartment during my month down at the shore, I'd let the sea wash over my imagination – an imagination full of the seeds of characters, plot, and venue gleaned from experiences of December through July (personal, vicarious, and imagined) – suffusing it with new lives. This year, however, the story eluded me. I was stuck in the mire of ennui known as writer's block. Feeling sterile, creation was beyond my grasp, inspiration a toehold I was unable to secure. My head felt like my mouth felt when I woke up in the morning, stale and lifeless. My brain was logy, sodden with creative juices gone rancid. I wanted to hang my imagination out in the sun to dry, to crisp up.

I tried again . . .

Alison Diamond stared skyward. 'Whale,' she said aloud,

eyeing a large cumulus cloud. 'Poodle,' she said moments later. Then 'Two poodles mating,' she said trying to remember passion.

. . . I pushed the keys to save the paragraph in the *Notes* file, hoping I'd use it, if not in this story, in some other one. An inveterate literary pack rat, I held on to even the most meagre issue of creative thought. For the past eight months, however, I hadn't written anything worthy of saving for more than a few days.

When the whirr of the computer stopped, the screen went blank, along with my mind.

Now, a blank screen (or page) to a writer is like a blank canvas to an artist, a roll of blank film to a photographer, the dawn of a new day. It's both dreaded and embraced as an opportunity to fill, to fulfill. It's anathema to a writer who's blocked.

I turned my computer off and went back into my apartment to shower. As I undressed before the full length mirror in my bedroom, I wondered if an orgasm would get me off the mark. It had been weeks, maybe months since my last – by my own hand, that is. Years since I'd been with a man. Is that possible? I wondered with some alarm. Where have I been? What have I been doing all this time? Leaning forward, I gazed at my reflection in the mirror. An unfamiliar woman stared back at me. Beneath a thick mass of dark curls fine lines etched weariness on a pallid face. *Smile lines . . . bad light . . . lack of sleep*, I tried to soothe myself, rationalisations that could account for the dark shadows beneath my eyes, too. Yes. Definitely bad light. And then a glimmer caught my attention. A flicker in my hair as I turned my head. I grasped at the sparkle, but it eluded me. Turning my head back slowly I grasped again, this time taking hold of a silver thread. A swift yank delivered me of the odious harbinger of decay. But what about all those brown spots on my chest? I didn't remember being so freckled. One speck stood out, on the crest of my collar bone, on the left. It was darker than the rest. *Melanoma*! I thought, my heart racing, remembering in a flash the poor prognosis of that insidious skin cancer, the disfiguring surgery, the horrid chemotherapy, the painful end. But it's even around the edges, and flat, and really dark brown, not black, I observed, standing closer to the mirror. An age spot, then, I concluded, momentarily relieved and grateful for my reprieve. Then *age spot* registered, imparting a subtler, though just as sure, glimpse at my mortality.

Blinking, I stepped back from the mirror and allowed the airbrush of distance to soften the evidence of aging, but it did little to slim my thighs, which appeared definitely less toned than I had remembered. Am I losing it? I wondered, running my hands up the sides of my thighs. The skin puckered as the underlying fat globules bumped together. I placed my hands above my left knee, squeezed tightly, running them upward. The skin drew taut. The small pocket of fat on the inside of my knee disappeared and my thigh grew magically younger. Maybe liposuction, I mused. Only if the fat could be osmosed through the skin, without cutting, without blood, without life-threatening anaesthesia, I thought, remembering some of the details of an article on cosmetic surgery I'd written for *Staying Healthy* magazine.

I'll have to learn to live with the ravages of age, I conceded silently, releasing the spongy flesh, wondering if, in fact, men, in the heat of passion, notice firm thighs, or only *thighs*. And what about breasts? Once breasts are naked, do they register with defining adjectives, or simply as *breasts*? Cupping my breasts in my hands, I gave them a

14

gentle lift. Not bad, I thought to myself. Then I let them drop and, standing round-shouldered, with my tummy thrust out, I said aloud, 'Who am I kidding. I'm forty.'

Under the stinging points of steaming shower water, I recalled the orgasm I'd considered and attempted to trick myself into believing someone else's hands were soaping my body. It didn't work. Like my daydreaming character in my obstructed story, I couldn't remember what passion felt like.

I rinsed off quickly, bounced from the shower and vigorously rubbed myself dry, pretending that it really didn't matter, that I just wasn't in the mood. How many times, I wondered, had I said that to my husband – *'It's okay. It really doesn't matter.'* But impotency felt different on myself. It really *did* matter. I felt barren, vapid, dry. Old. And abandoned. I couldn't believe that Shel hadn't called.

I ate a late dinner in front of the television that evening, and then went wearily to bed at ten leaving my balcony door in my bedroom open, hoping that the cool evening breezes had stilled my neighbours' air-conditioners. No such luck. But for the crash of a mighty wave now and then, the constant hum of the nearby units drowned out the soothing, rhythmic sound of the surf.

I awoke with a start about three-fifteen Friday morning. Actually, I awoke with a spin. I'd been dreaming that I was riding The Greek Temple Monument carousel, whirling around and around the green lady, when my stomach suddenly swallowed my heart and I awoke in a cold sweat. I rubbed my eyes and tried to steady myself internally, but I felt as if my brain was caught in a cosmic eddy, straining to spin off on its own. My heart pounding, I jumped from my bed and was relieved to see my drawn but unfragmented image in the bathroom mirror. After gulping down a glass of water, I splashed cold water on my face and changed my sweat-dampened nightshirt. The whirling sensation abated somewhat. Probably a stomach virus, I considered, or maybe something I'd eaten. *Pastrami poisoning*! I thought. Or maybe it was the mayo. *Botulism, Listeriosis, Salmonella*, I considered, sure for a moment that I'd never see the morning. *Air*, I thought, stepping out on to the balcony.

A full moon reigned over an agitated surf; the breezy night air was warm and cool at the same time. Shivering, I stepped back into my room, pulled on a sweatshirt, then returned to the balcony and walked around to the front. I laid back on a lounge and stared at the lady in the moon, finding comfort in her familiar company. Ever since I could remember, the lady struck the same glamorous, amorous pose in the lower right sector of the shimmering silver-gold disk: her head resting back, her lips slightly parted, she looked as if she were awaiting a kiss.

Snakes ... dragon, I thought as a series of long, thin cirrus clouds passed in front of my wistful lady. And then, the drone of air-conditioners, the drum roll of the surf, perfect black speckled with brightly coloured dots as I drifted on the sea in half-sleep, until I woke with a start, feeling something had rushed by me. Disorientated, I opened my eyes. *Buzzed by a sea gull*, I thought, ascertaining my presence on my balcony, not considering that birds don't fly at night. Without another thought, I closed my eyes and was sucked back into a dream of another night ... in the back seat of my parents' car, on the Tacony Palmyra Bridge, on my way from Philadelphia to Atlantic City. Then I was standing on the bridge looking down at the river. And then I was falling. The moment I hit the forbidding dark surface, I woke up, my heart pounding.

Looking out at the black sea, its evanescent peaks glistening silver in the moonlight, I felt immersed in it, chilled by it, and I went back to my bed, gravity pulling at every cell in my body.

A few hours later I awoke feeling tired and still off centre. I was irritable and impatient with my morning newspaper, unable to concentrate on the words. The beginning of Alzheimer's, I quickly diagnosed. And I had a headache. Maybe just sinuses after all, I down-graded my condition. I consumed two aspirin tablets along with my muffin and coffee before sloshing on sunscreen, pulling on a bathing suit and sweatshirt, and slipping into a pair of rubber flip-flops. Then I left my apartment with my beach bag over my shoulder, looking forward to the sun burning away my weariness.

Leaving the beach elevator at the ground floor, I made my way along the dingy grey hall, past the wall of mail boxes, past the janitor's closet and the door to the pool area, to the street exit. Leaning my full weight on the heavy door, I almost tripped as it swung open abruptly, throwing me into the blinding light of a brilliant day that already had the feel of a scorcher. I breathed the salty air deep into my lungs and held it there for a moment, trying to make it a part of me. Then, oblivious to all around me, I walked a few yards up the street, up the ramp to cross the boardwalk, and down the stairs to the beach, where I kicked off my flip-flops before stepping on to the still cool sand. Halfway between the boardwalk and the ocean, I stopped at a mountain of aluminium tubing and colourful canvas. 'Apartment 1701,' I told the young man in the wraparound mirrored sun-glasses standing nearby.

He fished my low beach chair and white umbrella from the neat stacks and followed me to a bare spot away from the life-guard stand, where he planted the umbrella in the sand and opened it. 'Have a nice day, Mrs D.,' the young man said. 'You know, you've got the only white umbrella on the beach,' he added. 'Let me know when you want to trade it in for something a little spiffier.'

When he walked away I moved the chair from under the umbrella into the sun and folded into it. I didn't want to talk to anyone. It was still early, nine-thirty, and I knew I'd have at least an hour by myself before the parade of people began to fill the space around me. Maybe enough time to doze wrapped in the warmth of the morning sun.

Just as I began to feel the tension drain from my body, I heard my name called, and every muscle in my body contracted anew.

'Alison! You're up early. And what are you doing here on a Friday?' It was Robin Crystal.

'On vacation. Thought I'd catch some quiet time before the daily headlines,' I replied, referring to the usual grapevine of gossip that trailed from umbrella to umbrella throughout the day.

Robin didn't take the hint. Tossing a small towel on to the sand, she sat down in front of me. 'I thought your vacation started tomorrow. Not that I'm complaining. I'm glad you're here. So, do you think she jumped?'

'Jumped? Who jumped –'

'Marjorie. They found her on the boardwalk at five-thirty this morning. Stark naked. I think she jumped.'

'Marjorie Smith?'

'Marjorie *Applebaum* Smith. Actually, Marjorie Applebaum these days. I'd heard she's been really odd – I mean odder than usual – since her husband's departure last summer with Tiffany Kaufman. You know, the shrink's wife . . . from the eleventh floor.'

'Tiffany Kaufman?'

'Oh, you know Tiffany. The one with the Barbie Doll hair and the gorgeous green eyes. A terrible flirt . . . and hopelessly stuck-up. A real bitch, I've heard.'

'Marjorie's a bitch?' I said, having heard only snatches of Robin's diatribe.

'No, no. Tiffany. Susan Kravitz – the lawyer's wife from the tenth floor, the one who wears the thong bathing suits and shouldn't – well, she told me she'd heard that when Tiffany left her husband she didn't even have the decency to face him. Would you believe she left him a note?'

I looked at Robin blankly.

'Oh, I told you all this last year when it happened. Don't you remember?'

'Vaguely. But what about Marjorie?'

'Dead. Splat on the boardwalk. Didn't you see the area cordoned off by the police . . . all the people milling around – I mean, honestly, Alison, don't you notice *anything*?'

'They think she jumped? From where?' I asked, looking around.

'*I* think she jumped . . . from her balcony–'

'That's right above mine!' I exclaimed, remembering with a chill the vague sensation of a large bird swishing by me as I lay half asleep on the balcony just hours before.

'So. What do you think? Suicide?'

'I have no idea. I hardly knew her,' I replied, thinking about Marjorie, the delicately coloured young woman with straight, light-red hair sometimes pulled into a ponytail, sometimes into two bunches like a little girl, and sometimes simply hanging down, pushed back behind her ears. She had almost no nose, her very large round eyes were less than exciting for their washed out green-grey colour, and her eyelashes and brows were almost too light to notice, especially by the end of the summer. Although thin, she was shapely, with a tiny waist and breasts large enough to

19

bounce when she walked. But if anything was particular about Marjorie Applebaum's appearance it was her mouth – highly-coloured *blow* lips that contrasted sharply with her otherwise pale complexion. Men thought Marjorie's perpetually puckered mouth was sexy. Whenever I looked at Marjorie straight on, I thought of coming face to face with a fish.

'*Nobody* knew her very well,' said Robin. 'She was so quiet. Like a mouse.'

Marjorie, like me, had been an aberration in the summer seashore community of weekday widows. We both worked in Philadelphia during the week and came to the shore on the week-ends along with the week-end husbands. Also, we were single, while most of the other summer regulars at the Tower beach – those who lived in the Ivory Tower Condominium for the summer – were married, except for one or two divorcees and a few full-time widows – those whose husbands had actually died – like Brenda Forrester, for example. Brenda's husband had died of a stroke after finding out that Brenda had been having an affair with a life-guard, so the story goes, and, the story goes further – perhaps too far for credulity – the life-guard happened to be her husband's son from a previous marriage. All this Robin had told me. She'd heard it from Myra Richter who was best friends with the next-door-neighbour of the second ex-husband of Mr Forrester's ex-wife, who swears to its veracity.

'Of course, it could have been murder,' Robin said of Marjorie's death.

'Murder! What makes you say that?'

'Well, if she didn't jump –'

'So you *don't* think she jumped?'

'I didn't say that. I was only laying out the possibilities.'

I slumped low in my chair and closed my eyes behind the

large dark glasses I'd retrieved from my beach bag
emblazoned with the logo of The Philadelphia Orchestra.
My head was still fuzzy, my world askew. I found it difficult
to concentrate on the tragedy, Robin, or the curious events
of the early morning hours. It was all I could do to keep a
nascent panic from exploding beneath my heart.

'*He* could have murdered her,' Robin said after a
moment.

'Who's *He*?' I asked, lost.

'Her husband, the Hunk.'

'What do you mean?'

'He married her for her money, right? So maybe he
murdered her for her money.'

'About your premise, Robin –'

'Why else would he marry her?'

'More interesting is why she married *him*,' I replied
abstractly.

'Don't be so naïve, Alison. That's the easy part. She
married him for his body.'

'I can't believe an intelligent woman would marry a man
for his body,' I said, falling into the conversation.

'That doesn't surprise me.'

'Well, it's a neat package,' I said, ignoring her comment.
'Maybe a little *too* neat?'

Robin peered intently through half-closed eyes. 'I don't
know,' she murmured.

'You don't know what?'

'Maybe it *is* a little *too* neat. The truth is, I can't figure
how Marjorie managed it all.'

'All what?'

'*All* of it. She seemed so . . . I don't know . . . so mousy,
and yet she managed to acquire a high-powered job, a
condo in Kent, an apartment in Philly . . . the Hunk – well,
until he left, that is.'

Images started flashing through my head. Images of Marjorie, of her husband, Doug. I pictured Marjorie in a free-fall, her reddish hair sticking straight away from her head, her mouth opened wide in a scream – a fat chocolate-glazed doughnut.

I was so distracted, '. . . *ready for Chicago?*' is all I heard Robin say. 'What was that?' I asked.

'I asked if Shel was ready for school?'

'Getting there,' I answered tersely.

'And are *you* ready, now that he's almost out of the nest?'

'I don't know. I . . . I'd rather not talk about it,' I said impatiently, remembering that I didn't want to talk; I especially didn't want to talk about Shel.

'You okay?' Robin asked. 'You seem awfully edgy this morning.'

'I didn't get much sleep last night. I woke up in the middle of the night feeling . . . I don't know . . . dizzy.'

'You mean the room was spinning?'

'No. The room was still. It was more like my head was spinning. And I felt headachy and a little nauseous.'

'Sounds like you slept on a boat. Maybe you should see someone? There's a lot of stomach flu going around.'

Bolstered by Robin's innocuous and thoroughly rational explanation, I sat up and studied my summer friend. A visual pun, Robin looked like her name. Slight, high-waisted, with a prominent chest and chicken thin legs, she was built like a bird. She even walked like a bird, fast, her bent elbows flapping up and down with each step. And she held her head high, her straight, slightly pointed nose directed skyward, her round, dark eyes always on the alert below a cap of close-cropped brown hair that flared red in the sunlight. She appeared confident, in control . . . controlling.

'You're probably right. A virus,' I said.

The sun disappeared behind a cloud and I removed my glasses, exposing the dark circles around my eyes.

Turning her head slightly to her right, Robin peered at me askance, heightening her bird-like image. It was an idiosyncratic gesture arising from a deafness in her right ear – sequela of childhood mumps. 'You do look beat, Alison. And I've been babbling on, haven't I? Well, I'll just let you get some rest,' she said, jumping up, pulling her towel with her.

'When is Elliot coming down?' I asked, sorry I'd asked the instant it was out of my mouth. Elliot Crystal, Robin's husband, and an obstetrician/gynaecologist, showed up faithfully every week-end he wasn't on duty, which was three out of four, and one night during the week.

'Either late tonight or tomorrow morning,' she answered, sitting back down on her towel. 'I spoke to him last night and he said he may have to cover for one of his partners tonight, but I hope he doesn't. I've really missed him this week.'

I recognised the longing in Robin's voice. It was lust.

We fell silent as the sun emerged from the other side of the cloud. I put my glasses back on and laid back in my chair.

Lust. Yes, I remembered lust. Vaguely. Like the pain of childbirth, I remembered feeling it, but not how it felt. Mercifully, I decided.

CHAPTER 2

Blue

The Ivory Tower Condominium is like a small town. And, as a small town in one place is in many ways like a small town anywhere else, at the Ivory Tower Condominium everyone knows everyone else's business, or some version of it.

Most of the year-round residents, occupying about one-third of the two-hundred-and-some units, are senior citizens, and are generally pool dwellers in good weather. The younger owners, who are seasonal residents – surfacing in a sporadic fashion on winter week-ends, and moving in for the summer the last week in June (when their young children leave for overnight camp) – prefer the beach. During the week, until near the end of August (when the children come home from camp) the umbrellas of the Tower beach shade mostly women – thirty to fifty-something – and an occasional husband on vacation. Older teenagers who aren't at school, on trips, working at camp or in the city often rent bungalows a few blocks inland with their friends and work in the supermarkets, shops, and restaurants, and as pool and beach life-guards. They work hard, party hard, and visit their moms for dinner when they're short on cash. Most wouldn't be caught dead beneath the colourful umbrellas of the Tower beach.

Although the pool dwellers and beach dwellers rarely mix socially, the grape-vine forms the ties that bind them. The young hear of the horrors of gallstones and strokes and thank God that they're too young to know of such things; the old hear of the horrors of convoluted love affairs, and thank God that they're past such things. Not that the seniors don't occasionally have their own *affaires de coeur*. There was, for example, Mrs Emma Chankin, known as 'The Shark'.

At seventy-two, Emma Chankin was slim and trim, a widow with upswept blonde hair and china-blue eyes that hadn't faded with age. She always wore make-up, including porcelain pink lipstick and wonderfully drawn light-brown eyebrows (her own sparse brows, which she used to pluck out in any case, had vanished years before).

Ever alert to the medical infirmities of her elderly married lady friends, she'd bring cooked meals to those who were bedridden ... and kind words to their worried husbands. And of course there was the well worn shoulder she offered following the funeral and through the period of mourning. In her fifteen years at the Ivory Tower, Emma had out-lived her husband and three other gentlemen friends. At the time of Marjorie's death, Mrs Chankin was living alone, but looking.

Gossip about Emma Chankin's exploits was considered top priority, as was the death of Marjorie Applebaum. Affairs after sixty, like deaths before thirty, are like that.

By eleven o'clock the pool dwellers were speaking of nothing else even as cards slapped and Mah Jong tiles clicked, and beneath every beach umbrella speculation about the details of Marjorie's death was foremost. Well, almost every umbrella. I, for one, was entrenched in the details of Marjorie's life. That is, the life of Marjorie Applebaum as seen through the eyes of Sloan I. Diamond, a version which, from what I've seen and heard in my life, was as valid as any other.

It was with a surge of inspiration that I'd retrieved my laptop from my apartment after Robin finally left my umbrella for another's, and, sitting on the beach on Friday morning, wrote my own history of Marjorie Applebaum. I probably knew as many facts about Marjorie as anyone else on the beach, and certainly more than most people in the world, I reasoned. I'd heard this and that from one or another over the past year or two to be able to piece together a plausible story, maybe a story more plausible than any number of other versions. Perhaps more plausible than the 'real' story, if anyone knew what that was.

It's said that there are as many sides to a story as there are participants. That's an understatement. In fact, there are as many sides to a story as there are story tellers. And the truth? It's relative, and often not recognised by those closest to it.

And the story of Marjorie Applebaum, the mousy little girl who'd died early that morning, came to life for me as I formed it on the white screen under the file-name *Blue* for Marjorie's blue umbrella . . .

There was no question – Marjorie Applebaum, who spent summer week-ends at her grandmother's apartment in the Ivory Tower, had been flirting in a deliberate, albeit awkward, manner with Doug Smith, the sun-tanned, sun-streaked sandy blond hunk in the little red bathing shorts and red tank top, as he watched over swimmers from his white throne on the Tower beach. It was the summer of '88, the summer Marjorie had been hired by Gerston Montgomery, a major accounting firm in Philadelphia, after passing her CPA exam. And what with her impressive new salary and her move from her mother's suburban apartment into her own apartment in a regentrified area of Yuppie dwellings around the Philadelphia Museum of Art, Marjorie was feeling pretty good about herself, good enough to still her usual discomfort around anyone who in any way interested her, and flirt with the man so many others admired from a distance.

Although intelligent, organised, and extremely competent, Marjorie was shy and had spent most of her life quietly. Through her teen years she had few friends and rarely dated, while inwardly seething with romantic expectation, often erupting in spates of dreadful poetry, purple passages of lusty longings, long before she understood lust for what it was.

Of course she'd experienced the hot, damp quickening of pubescent lust, and naturally took it for love. It was when Corky Ross – the boy next door – leaned against her as they sat on the living room floor of her parents' home listening to a Rolling Stones album, their backs pressed uncomfortably against a brass and wood cocktail table. She was twelve.

Although it was only sixty-eight degrees in the drafty old house, Marjorie was hot. Her skin burned, her body creases grew damp. She didn't dare look at Corky, so she wasn't aware that he wouldn't look at her, either. Then, without warning, he lifted a gangly arm and let it fall awkwardly across her shoulders. Marjorie's heart stopped ... and then started with a triple-beat, at triple time. Shifting her eyes to the left, she saw khaki clad knees sticking up as high as her eyes and she remembered sitting cross-legged on the floor in front of Corky in his living room a few days before. Wearing a white sweatshirt and chino pants that hung loosely on his long, bony body, he had sat with his back against an enormous yellow and white striped wing-chair. His knees had been drawn up then, too, and spread apart, and when Marjorie looked at his face between them, her eyes couldn't help but follow the line of his lanky legs down to his crotch. The distinct impression of something heavy hanging within the folds of his pants, pressing against the worn ecru cloth, unsettled her. This image Marjorie recalled as Corky's oversized hand alit tentatively on her right shoulder, the surprising smell of hoagies emanating from his armpit. Oblivious to her surroundings, she sensed only the odour of oiled onions and the feel of heavy wet heat on her shoulder. She couldn't imagine that she was going to be kissed; the only knowledge she'd had in these matters was what she'd seen in the movies, and in the movies she hadn't learned about the oniony perspiration of teenage boys. But, seemingly out of nowhere, Corky's huge, beaked nose came towards her, then all went voluminously black as his overly-ample lips met hers and she floated in space on the softest sensation she'd ever experienced, a sensation that seemed to last well into forever . . . and then they sat stone still next to each other, staring straight ahead at the stereo turntable spinning around and around, her left shoulder in his armpit his hand melded to her right shoulder, neither aware of the world around them as they reeled in the gathering storm of lust.

It was a feeling she invoked over and over long after Corky left that afternoon, a parting that was stiff and permanent, although she didn't realise it for the longest time, insulating herself in the memory of Corky's kiss, resisting implications of his absence from anywhere that she was. After a while, however, she began to think of him in the past, and she understood that she and Corky had 'broken up'. She hadn't the faintest idea why, or even when; she wasn't even sure *what* had broken up. But the memory of Corky's kiss was branded into Marjorie's gut and she promised herself that the feeling it had stirred in her – which she was sure was love – would be her standard, that the man she married would make her feel that way.

It was a feeling she carried with her through junior high school, where all her romances were on the silver screen of the Main Point theatre . . . and into high school, where her big romance with Ken Leiber – a tall, blond cheerleader with a broad, vacant smile – was as imaginary as those at the Main Point. Nonetheless, Marjorie attended all sports events during her sophomore and junior years just to watch Ken in tight white pants and a white crew neck sweater emblazoned with an orange 'V' for Valley High, as he belted out cheers and caught his partner, Sarah Bainbridge, in his arms. Ken graduated a year ahead of Marjorie, but that didn't stop her from dreaming about him, dreaming of how his kiss would make her feel the way Corky's had. Nor did it stop Marjorie from hating her classmate, Sarah Bainbridge. Marjorie sought redress in a small, mean way – dishing out rumours at the lunch table about Sarah and others on the squad. And so a friendship became a sordid affair, a week out with the flu became an abortion. By graduation, Marjorie felt avenged as the rumour sharks vied for a place next to her at lunch.

Marjorie's college heartthrob was Mitch 'Moose' Glover, who she met in her sophomore year when he asked her for help in their statistics class. Marjorie was only too eager to oblige. After all, being on a football scholarship, Moose was considered a big man on campus. Indeed, Marjorie couldn't believe he had asked *her* for help. The fact was that Moose hadn't missed the adoring gazes of the little girl with the big pale eyes, the puckered, puce lips – the smartest girl in the class.

Marjorie helped Moose through two semesters, studying

with him once or twice a week at the library, always bringing offerings of microwave popcorn or brownies. He was grateful; she was lustful. After he'd walked her to the women's dorm, she'd go to her room on the second floor where she'd make love to herself, pretending her touch was his; he'd go to the fourth floor where he'd make love to Stephanie Hanover, the star of the school's theatre group.

Then one evening, aware of Marjorie's crush on him, and all too aware of himself, Moose kissed her. The touch of his lips – her first kiss since Corky Ross – sent a charge through her body. But then he stuck his tongue in her mouth. It was fat and rough and tasted of soured chocolate. Marjorie's body stalled. Attempting to will herself to feel the way she had imagined she'd feel, she clung to Moose and allowed his tongue to chase hers around her mouth until she began to feel, instead, the panic one experiences when, upon turning the ignition key in a car, the engine doesn't turn over – her engine wasn't turning over. And she remembered Corky's kiss while she made love to herself that night, and how it had made her feel like her engine had exploded.

After that disappointment, which she took as a personal affront, Marjorie became unavailable for tutoring and confided to the campus gossips that Moose Glover was not only dumb, but impotent.

The summer of 1988, however, Marjorie was filled with self-confidence as she flirted shamelessly with Doug Smith at his life-guard stand, managing to get his attention.

Nice tits, he thought, listening with half an ear to Marjorie telling him of her grandmother's condo at the Tower, her new job. But mention of her salary drew his full attention to the pale young lady with the ribboned bunches, looking very much younger than her twenty-five years.

Now, besides being a life-guard, since his graduation

from high school two years before, Doug had been waiting tables at The Silver Sail restaurant and taking courses at the community college. He dreamed of getting out of his parents' contentious home and becoming a lawyer, but he secretly despaired that the closest he'd ever get to the bar was the one at the Sea Gull Tavern on the corner, where his father had taught him all he knew, among which pearls of wisdom was that it's just as easy to love a rich girl as a poor girl.

'So, you do pretty good for yourself. You have a boyfriend here?' Doug asked, his eyes quickly scanning her face, noting her blow lips, and falling back on her perky breasts.

'No. I'm free at the moment,' she said, not mentioning that, except for her brief affair with the football hero at college, she'd been free since she was twelve, when she and Corky had *broken up*.

'Maybe we can have a beer sometime,' Doug suggested.

So one night they had a beer (his treat), and then, the following week, they had dinner (her treat), and then, the night after dinner, a movie (his treat) – a movie from the video shop that they took to Doug's parents' home.

'They're away for a week visiting my Aunt in Michigan,' he explained to Marjorie as he showed her around the small, two-bedroom home a block from the bay in Chelsea. While watching the movie, Doug put his arm around Marjorie, and the touch of his hand on her shoulder made her head swim in the memories of Corky Ross. And when he kissed her, she was twelve again and feeling, again, the hot rush of sexual awakening.

He was, that night, no more impressive than any handsome young man of twenty, which was impressive enough for Marjorie, not having made love to any man before. He was hot and quick; she was impressed by her ability to incite him to such passion. He'd fallen asleep leaving Marjorie panting for orgasm; pressing close to him, making love to herself, pretending her touch was his, she was impressed with *his* ability to incite *her* to such passion. And so the brand of Corky Ross's lips was supplanted by the brand of Doug Smith's dick. Marjorie Applebaum was his . . . forever.

When Marjorie and Doug eloped at the end of the summer, Marjorie's widowed mother was relieved that she didn't have to prepare a wedding. Marjorie's grandmother, however, was appalled, being of the firm opinion that life-guards were not for marrying. 'This will be the death of me!' she threatened her only grandchild, proceeding to make good on her threat the following night, dying of a massive stroke in her sleep, leaving the apartment to Marjorie.

With Marjorie's help, Doug scraped through four semesters at Temple University in Philadelphia, retiring in the summers to the Ivory Tower and the life-guard stand.

It was assumed by the ladies under the colourful umbrellas of the Tower beach that Marjorie had inherited her grandmother's money as well as the apartment, in that she certainly wasn't supporting that apartment *and* the one in Philadelphia with her earnings as an accountant, and, Lord knows, they buzzed to one another, the Hunk wasn't capable of providing much beyond . . . well, they *all* knew what he was best at providing.

In fact, Marjorie's grandmother had left an account to cover the expenses of the condominium unit for only a year, long enough for Marjorie to sell it. The remainder of her estate, which wasn't as much as everyone had imagined, was left in a trust for Marjorie's mother. But, despite the fact that Marjorie had spent summer week-ends in her grandmother's apartment only to escape the heat of the city and her alcoholic mother, and to assure herself a piece of her grandmother's post-mortem pie (Marjorie was fair and burned easily, she disliked the shelly, agitated surf, and she was intimidated by the ladies beneath the colourful beach umbrellas who seemed to have it all), she kept the apartment and sat beneath her blue umbrella every week-end, relishing the lustful glances of her neighbours when Doug was about. Suddenly the envy of the Tower beach ladies, Marjorie felt she could have anything she wanted – and she wanted it all, confident that she'd figure out how to pay for it later.

. . . Saving what I'd written with a few keystrokes, I knew I'd created the first bone of the skeleton of my story. After defining the rest of the characters, I'd fit them together – the head bone connected to the neck bone . . . and so on – fill it in with the organs of plot, the sinew of conflict, the flesh of imagination and fancy, and then cover it with a skin of new identities. It was like playing God.

I'd just put my laptop in its protective pouch when Jason Pearl and Pete Shapiro, two of Shel's housemates, found me.

'Uh, hi there . . . ,' Jason greeted me, avoiding my name, as, like many young men of his age, he didn't know what to call mothers of friends. Fathers were easy – it was Mister or Doctor So-and-so. But mothers . . . well, that was different. Even though I'd told Shel that his friends should call me Alison, they continued to stumble over Mrs Diamond, skip over Alison, and land on *Uh*.

'Hi, guys,' I said, looking around for my son. 'Isn't Shel with you?'

'He was,' Pete answered, 'but we sort of lost him. We thought maybe you saw him.'

'No. But if you find him, let him know I'm here, will you?

Apparently he didn't get the message I left on your answering machine yesterday.'

The boys shuffled their feet, then Pete whacked Jason in the arm. 'I *told* you to tell Shel his mom called,' he chided his friend.

Jason blushed. 'Sorry, Uh ... I guess I forgot,' he directed to me, avoiding my eyes.

'No problem. Just let him know you saw me. Okay?'

'Sure,' Pete called to me as he and Jason started walking up the beach towards Atlantic City.

Robin, who'd been engrossed in conversation with Marty Steiner (one of the few full-time husbands on the beach) under his green umbrella, walked over to me, holding her sandals and beach bag. 'Want some lunch, Alison? It's one-thirty.'

'Is it that late? I've been wrapped up.'

'So I see. What happened to your nap? I thought you didn't feel well,' Robin said.

'I'm feeling a little better. This is just some stuff I had to take care of, and I thought it would take my mind off my body.'

'Well, I'm going up to make a sandwich. Can I make you one, too? I've got corned beef in the fridge,' she offered.

'Sounds good. By the way, have you seen Shel? His friends were looking for him.'

'Haven't seen him. But I saw Carole Pincus – she's married to that creep ... the fertility specialist.'

I raised an eyebrow.

'Oh, I told you about Carole's husband. He carried on an affair with his office manager, *for years* –'

'Right. And his wife found out ... and he fired the office manager ... and now his wife works in the office to keep her eye on him,' I filled in.

'Right,' she confirmed.

'Except during the summer, when she's down here. Nice arrangement . . . for him,' I added.

'For them both. But that's another story,' Robin said.

I didn't press for details.

'So Carole told me that she and her husband spend lots of winter week-ends here, and that this past February she saw Marjorie getting on to the elevator with a man,' Robin continued seamlessly. 'Carole said it was Jeffrey Kaufman, the shrink.'

'So?'

'Alison, you have absolutely no imagination.'

'Maybe not,' I conceded, thinking that the stories I made up paled next to the ones Robin was always re-inventing.

'By the way, I was also talking to Marty Steiner. He said Maggie's in the city taking care of their daughter and granddaughter. They're sick with a stomach flu. So I was probably right about your malady.'

'Whatever it was, it seems to be passing. In fact, I'm starving.'

'You do look better. But I'll tell you, Marty doesn't look too good. He seemed very upset about Marjorie.'

'Were they friendly?'

'I didn't think so. But you never know. Marty's kind of a horny old guy –'

'Oh? Now you're going to tell me Marty Steiner and Marjorie were having an affair. You just finished intimating that the shrink was having an affair with her. *You* certainly have an imagination, Robin.'

'And *you* are naïve.'

'I'm *hungry*. How about lunch?'

'Okay, so maybe I get a little creative sometimes,' Robin allowed. 'I'll go create some sandwiches.'

As Robin headed for the boardwalk, I put my sun-glasses back on, walked to the ocean's edge, and stood almost motionless looking up and down the coast for a sign of my son as the foamy green water washed over my feet. I'd been picturing him drowning in the surf . . . swimming out too far, going under with a cramp . . . being knocked down by a great wave, unable to surface . . . wading into an undertow, being dragged off into the depths . . . when the lapping water eroded the sand beneath my feet, sinking my heels, throwing me off balance, dispelling my morbid musings. I walked further into the surf, splashed salt water on my face and then returned to my umbrella where I sank to the soft, warm sand, unable to decide whether to bake in the sun or read in the shade, whether to eat a peach or wait for Robin's sandwich . . . whether or not to cry, for a reason that seemed to elude me along with my ability to make decisions.

CHAPTER 3

Yellow

Saturday morning was clear and breezy. Looking over the top of my *Esquire* magazine, I saw Robin stop to talk with Jeffrey Kaufman under his yellow umbrella on her way from her umbrella to mine.

'Guess who *I* just introduced myself to?' Robin chirped, standing before me moments later.

'The question isn't *who?*, but *why?*' I replied.

'The time, Alison. I forgot my watch,' she said, sitting down on my towel in front of me, 'and I told him to join us.'

I raised an eyebrow.

'Poor guy is probably feeling pretty bad today, what with Marjorie's tragic demise ... after what Carole said ... about him and Marjorie,' she explained.

'You asked him for the time?' I questioned, incredulous.

Robin was quiet for a moment and then she asked, 'You don't suppose Doug will move back into Marjorie's apartment ... with Tiffany ... Jeffrey's wife? You know, Marjorie's divorce wasn't final, so Doug will probably inherit it. That would be awful, don't you think? After all, Marjorie may be gone, but poor Jeffrey Kaufman's still here,' she went on.

'Actually, I heard that Tiffany left for the city,' I dropped.

'Oh?'

'A policeman was at my apartment asking questions this morning –'

'The police? At *your* apartment?'

'A Lieutenant Fiori. He said he was going to question everyone in the building.' Pause. 'So why did you all of a sudden decide to introduce yourself to Jeffrey Kaufman?'

'He knows Elliot. Apparently Elliot's referred some patients to him at the clinic,' she answered.

'I see,' I said, seeing I wasn't going to get anywhere. 'Anyway, Lieutenant Fiori told me about Tiffany's leaving the shore.'

'Do you think the Hunk went with her?'

'I don't know. I haven't seen him since last summer.'

'Oh, he's been around. I saw him a few beaches up last week.'

'Guess he decided it was politic to get posted on a different beach when he and Marjorie split.'

'That's if he knows what *politic* means. Anyway, what else did the lieutenant ask?' Robin continued her inquiry.

'He wanted to know if I saw or heard anything unusual the morning Marjorie died.'

'Which of course you didn't.'

'Well, actually I was out on the balcony around three or four yesterday morning. That's when I had that dizzy spell I told you about. I was getting some air and I dozed off on the lounge.'

Cocking her head to the right, Robin leaned closer to me. 'You mean you were out there when Marjorie fell?'

'I guess so.'

'Did you tell the lieutenant?'

'Of course.'

'What else did you tell him ... I mean, what did you see?'

'Nothing. I was sort of asleep, and something woke me, like something whooshing by me ... a bird or something ... or maybe I dreamt it.'

'You saw Marjorie fall right past your balcony!'

'I didn't see –'

'You're probably the only witness!'

'Robin, I didn't *see* anything, I –'

'What did he say?'

'He said I was probably the only witness.'

'There!'

'Well, well. Look who's coming,' I said, spotting Jeffrey Kaufman walking slowly towards us, beach towel in hand.

'Looks like he's coming to meet you, Alison,' Robin said, finally tipping her hand. 'By the way, did you find Shel yesterday?' she quickly changed the subject.

'No. But he called this morning. We're going to have brunch tomorrow.'

'Ladies. Mind if I join you?' said Jeffrey as he approached.

'Alison, this is Jeffrey Kaufman.'

Smiling, I reached up to shake the hand of the fuzzy man standing in front of the sun, then watched as he spread his towel on the sand and sat down facing me.

'However do you do that?' Robin asked Jeffrey, who had twisted his legs into a lotus position.

'Took me a while,' he said. 'A client taught me. Now I find it very comfortable. Keeps my back straight.'

It can't be true, I thought to myself, watching him, unable to imagine Marjorie Applebaum with this short, slightly chubby, hairy man with the greying reddish beard,

curly brown hair and warm brown eyes. *Nobody* could have
– not if they'd ever seen her with the Hunk.

I had most of it drafted in my head by the time I left the
beach at noon to grab a sandwich and buy lox and bagels for
brunch with Shel the next morning. It was the improbability
of a relationship between Jeffrey and Marjorie that
generated the flow of memories, unconnected facts,
seemingly inconsequential observations, all the little things
that make up a life if one has a mind to put it all together.
Not that how one person puts it together is the same as how
another would put it together, and certainly not necessarily
the same as what actually was from the perspective of the
subject, but a reasonable portrayal of a life, as close as any
other might get to the truth. Unlike death, with its own
unequivocal truth, life is a matter of perspective, with
everyone re-inventing everyone else, and themselves. 'The
facts' of life should be taken with a grain of salt. 'Fiction',
on the other hand, holds a grain of truth, often coming
closer to life than The Facts. At least fiction is pinned down
to a single, concrete story, not open to the whims of
forethought, afterthought, and conflicts of emotional
interests.

   After a visit to the deli I settled on to my balcony with my
laptop and constructed Jeffrey Kaufman's life story under
the file heading *Yellow* . . .

Jeffrey Kaufman had been listening to other people's
problems since he was a kid, when his best friend told him
everything, like the time he put a fat, black water bug in his
sister's bed and his mom made *him* sleep in *her* bed *without
changing the sheets*! Jeffrey told him he deserved it. And
the time he forgot to tell his mom that his grandmother had
called, and that his grandmother died that night, and he

was sure that somehow it had been his fault. Jeffrey told him it wasn't. After a while other guys told him stuff. And by the time Jeffrey was in high school he was writing an advice column in the school newspaper, when the girls, too, wanted to talk to Jeffrey. It appeared he was a born caretaker, so it surprised no one that Jeffrey Kaufman became a psychologist. In fact, Jeffrey became a psychologist in an attempt to learn how to get others to take care of *him*.

It was a surprise to everyone that he remained single until he was forty, although it wasn't for lack of trying. Jeffrey dated a lot, and the women liked him. They loved to talk to him . . . about their problems with other men . . . the ones they couldn't talk to but loved to fuck. And Jeffrey would listen. But when his passion overpowered his patience and he'd press for more than confessional sessions, he'd be dismissed with, 'You're a really special person, but we can't continue this relationship.' It happened so many times he jokingly told a friend that he had a theory that all single women read the same *how-to* book on breaking up.

Tiffany Pennock, the woman he would marry, was a client. And, although it's not considered professional for a psychologist to date a client, these things do happen.

Tiffany sought Jeffrey's help after the man she'd been dating for several months suddenly dropped her with no more of an explanation than, *You're a really special person, but we can't continue this relationship*. This she wailed to Jeffrey amid the forest of plants in his home office in the Germantown section of Philadelphia. Already too familiar with those onerous words, Jeffrey flinched imperceptibly, sure then that *all* single people read the same book.

'. . . And just the week before he'd told me he loved me!

It seems that all my relationships with men end this way,' Tiffany cried to Jeffrey, confirming his hypothesis.

After a few sessions, Tiffany told Jeffrey of her penchant for unavailable men, confessing that the ex-boyfriend was married, as were all of her boyfriends since her divorce three years before, except for two could-be converts – a priest and a gay violinist – who wouldn't be.

As Tiffany became comfortably settled into their sessions, Jeffrey became uncomfortably unsettled by the stunning blonde with the alabaster skin and the most intense green eyes he had ever seen. Oz came to mind when he looked at her – the emerald city of Oz, tinted in fantasy and wonder. He eagerly explored how she perceived the world through those beautiful green eyes.

'Deceitful! Treacherous!' she screamed at him in his office one Tuesday afternoon, a few months into her therapy. She was looking particularly beautiful sitting in the soft feather chair facing his great leather rocker, her natural golden hair curling around her delicate oval face. 'Men are all the same!' she screamed. 'But one day it'll be my turn.'

'What will you do when it's your turn,' he asked, professionally probing her fantasy . . . with more than a tad of personal curiosity.

'Take what I want, and leave when *I'm* ready!' she answered, tears of rage falling to her folded arms.

So, it's not that she didn't warn him. But his skin was afire.

'Tiffany,' he rasped through a dry throat. 'Tiffany, I think you're very angry,' he tried.

When she looked up at him, he was startled to see that her left eye was the palest of blue.

'My lens!' she cried, startled by her sudden blurred vision. 'I lost a contact lens!' And she examined her lap before descending to the floor in search of that tiny bit of emerald green. 'Please help me,' she entreated Jeffrey, who dropped to his knees and began patting the oriental carpet with Tiffany. 'Do you see it?' she asked, looking at Jeffrey, whose face was inches from hers . . . who could see nothing but that one clear blue window through which he felt he could look into Tiffany's soul and was all but swept away by the depth of her vulnerability. Only his practised professional stance kept him from leaning towards her, kissing her.

'Our time is up,' he said, glancing at the clock on his bookcase behind her chair, standing up, hoping his pants were baggy enough to conceal his otherwise hidden passion.

Tiffany, too, stood up, smoothing her skirt. 'Please call me if you find my lens,' she said.

'Of course,' Jeffrey replied, fighting to regain his composure.

'And I'll see you next week?' she asked tentatively, sensing something awry.

'Well . . . actually . . . I'll call you tomorrow morning and let you know what we'll do,' Jeffrey answered even more tentatively.

'You're going to cancel our sessions, aren't you!' Tiffany flared in a panic.

'No . . . it's just –'

'You are! Why?'

His composure slipping away once more, Jeffrey couldn't lie. 'I'm sorry, Tiffany. You're a really special person, but we can't continue this relationship,' he said, ruing his unfortunate choice of words even as they fell from his mouth.

Stricken, she picked up her pocketbook, raced past Jeffrey through the air-lock of doors, the empty waiting room, to the red brick path outside.

Jeffrey sat down on Tiffany's chair and stared at the intricate pattern of the red, navy and camel carpet until his eyes tripped over a spark of green. Picking up the lens, he held it in front of one eye. Through it the world appeared bright green and badly warped.

As he sat bewildered, looking through the lens, Tiffany was looking through her tears at the rear-view mirror of her car where she imagined her imperative crystallising in its blurry image. In a moment, while Jeffrey Kaufman sat lamenting the loss of control of his life, Tiffany Pennock, with newly applied mascara, blush and lipstick, was on her way up the red brick path, determined to take control of hers.

Six years later – the summer before the death of Marjorie Applebaum – Jeffrey Kaufman sat silently beneath his yellow umbrella on the beach of the Ivory Tower Condominium with his wife, Tiffany. Theirs had been a short and passionate courtship marked by long sessions of love-making following marathons of talking. After six years of marriage they neither talked nor made love very often, but Jeffrey was content. Like a man who settles into a very hot bath with an interesting book and hardly notices the slow cooling of the water, occupied as he was by the lives of others, Jeffrey had paid little attention to his own.

Robin Crystal dropped her sand chair next to Alison's on that July Sunday in 1990. 'Have you noticed how the Kaufmans don't hold hands any more?' she queried.

'No. But I'm sure you have,' Alison replied, not looking up from her copy of the *Atlantic*.

'Oh, I have, indeed. You know, you should pay more attention to your neighbours, Alison.'

'I don't have to, Robin. You manage to tell me everything I need to know, and a lot I don't need to know.'

'Well, if that's your attitude, maybe I shouldn't tell you what goes on while you slave away in the city,' Robin teased.

'Okay,' Alison said, closing the magazine and resting it on her outstretched legs, 'I'll bite. What juicy bit of gossip have you managed to dig up?' she asked, picturing her bird-like friend scratching around in the sand for worms early in the morning.

'Well,' Robin started, 'I'm sure you remember when the Kaufmans practically made love on the beach . . . from the time he got here Friday night until he left Monday morning.'

'So?'

'So, they hardly even talk to each other any more.'

'Robin, they *have* been married for a few years and –'

'Well, rumour has it that during the week, when he's in the city, she and Marjorie Applebaum Smith's gorgeous life-guard husband –'

'Oh, come on Robin. Tiffany's old enough to be his mother.'

'But –'

'It's absurd. I can't imagine how you come up with some of these stories.'

'And I can't imagine how you view the world. All spit and polish, I suspect. Well, believe me, there's a lot more spit than polish in this world, Alison.'

'And you try to make life sound like one giant intrigue, Robin. But as far as Tiffany Kaufman and Doug Smith are concerned . . . well, they're just not all that interesting,' Alison insisted.

'To you, maybe. But, for what it's worth, I was in the basement waiting for the elevator, and when the door opened, there they were … *very* close together. They jumped apart, but not fast enough.'

The following Thursday, after his two Friday morning clients had cancelled and, coincidentally, the Friday afternoon class on handling rejection he was teaching at The Philadelphia Couples Foundation was also cancelled, Jeffrey Kaufman decided to surprise his wife by coming to the shore on Thursday evening instead of Friday, arriving at the Ivory Tower about six. His apartment was empty. Mildly disappointed by Tiffany's absence, but greatly appreciative of the peace, he waited for her on the balcony, watching the sun set, the moon rise over the surf. At nine o'clock he left to get a sandwich at the deli. Stepping into the elevator, he smiled and nodded to Marjorie Applebaum Smith who was leaning against the rear brass rail, her arms folded in front of her. She appeared somewhat distressed, returning Jeffrey's nod but not his smile. She, too, coincidentally, had tried to surprise her spouse with a long week-end, but ended up being surprised when she found her apartment empty at six-thirty. Jeffrey held the door for Marjorie as they left the building, and it soon became apparent to him that they were walking in the same direction.

'Out for a walk?' he asked, catching up to her.

'Dinner, actually,' she replied tersely.

'Me, too,' he said, adding quickly, so she couldn't ignore him, 'my wife isn't home yet, and I was starving so I decided to grab a sandwich. Care to join me?'

Now, as in any small town, although Jeffrey and Marjorie hadn't been formally introduced, they knew of each other. He knew she lived on the eighteenth floor and was a week-end wife as he was a week-end husband, that her name was Marjorie and she was married to the Hunk –

as his wife referred to the well-built life-guard – a man who, according to rumour, was having an affair, but Jeffrey didn't know with whom.

Marjorie knew he was a psychologist named Jeffrey who lived with his wife, Tiffany, on the eleventh floor, and she'd heard that Tiffany was having an affair, but she didn't know with whom.

'By the way, I'm Jeffrey Kaufman ... and you're Marjorie Smith,' he said, extending his hand.

'Marjorie *Applebaum* Smith ... and, thanks, I hate eating alone.'

Although but five minutes away from downtown Atlantic City, with its casinos, lights and crowds, its edge of danger, its lack of charm, the streets of Kent were comfortable and warm, slow-paced and friendly. And the walk to the deli in the salty moist night air inspired camaraderie and relaxation of tensions and pretensions.

By the time Marjorie and Jeffrey were seated in a window booth and had ordered Reuben sandwiches, root beers, and a side order of fries to share, they'd forgotten their own missing spouses and each was silently wondering if he/she knew that his/her wife/husband was having an affair.

After a time, Marjorie said, 'It's funny the way we're sitting here – just like on a first date. And I was thinking how glad I am to be married and not have to go through *First Dates*.'

'I know what you mean. Dating isn't much fun when you're single.'

'But it's fun when you're married?' Marjorie teased.

'That's not what I meant,' Jeffrey replied, blushing, meaning exactly that.

'So how long have you been married?' Marjorie asked.

'Six years.'

'Your first?'

'Yes. I took my time –'

'And waited for the best,' Marjorie finished his sentence for him.

Shocked by the incongruity of her assessment of his feelings and how he actually felt at that moment, Jeffrey let Marjorie's remark fall embarrassingly on the table between them like splattered gravy.

'How long have you been married?' Jeffrey asked after an awkward pause.

'Almost two years. My husband is a life-guard here during the summer and goes to school in Philadelphia the rest of the year. He wants to go to law school.'

'Sounds like your husband's quite the renaissance man,' Jeffrey said.

Marjorie's non-response was telling to a man with Jeffrey's training.

'Of course, I've learned in my business that things aren't always the way they seem,' he continued, trying to mop up his splattered gravy, but, in fact, merely smearing it.

Their positions and mutual discomfort thus firmly established, Jeffrey smiled. 'I suddenly feel like I'm on a first date,' he said, breaking the tension.

'Would you like it to be?' Marjorie ventured.

'Maybe,' Jeffrey confessed, although until just a few moments before, the idea of seeing another woman hadn't occurred to him.

They gazed at each other across the table in the warmest possible manner, their half-eaten Reubens growing cold and crusty. When their fingers met at the french fries, Jeffrey pulled his hand back as if he had received an electric shock. Brazenly standing her ground, Marjorie dragged a fry through the once neat blob of ketchup on the side of the plate and brought it to her mouth.

Aroused by Marjorie's defiance, but nettled by guilt, Jeffrey looked at his watch. 'Can you believe it's almost eleven? Tiffany's going to be furious with me,' he said.

Marjorie pushed the fry into her mouth and licked her fingers ... slowly ... causing Jeffrey to blush. 'I guess we should go,' she said, surprised and pleased by her noticeable effect on the good doctor.

Insisting on treating, Jeffrey paid the bill, and they walked back to the Tower briskly, without a word between them. Once inside the lobby, Jeffrey dashed towards the elevators just as a door was closing and lunged at the UP button. The door opened, revealing Doug and Tiffany standing at opposite corners in the back of the small car. For a moment, all were nonplussed, staring from one to the other, silently attempting to sort out the puzzle until Tiffany broke the uncomfortable silence.

'Jeffrey, what a nice surprise!' she said, sidling next to her husband as he and Marjorie entered the elevator.

'It was supposed to be a surprise for dinner. But when you didn't come in by nine I went out to get a sandwich –' Jeffrey started to explain.

'And what an incredible coincidence that we should all end up in the same elevator at the same time!' Tiffany interrupted, eyeing Marjorie.

'Actually, Marjorie and I had dinner together. We met on the elevator coming down,' Jeffrey sputtered out.

'A likely story,' Tiffany teased, still flustered. 'I went for a walk on the boardwalk. I was missing you.'

Her alibi established, all eyes fell on Doug.

'And I ran out for cigarettes,' he jumped in, pulling a new pack from his breast pocket, holding the exhibit up for all to see, 'but I somehow ended up at a casino,' he finished, executing a bad boy smirk.

'Don't you want to know why *I'm* here tonight?' Marjorie asked her husband.

'Well, I guess you wanted to surprise me, too,' Doug replied.

'Surprise!' Marjorie snapped, glaring at him.

Doug stepped over to Marjorie and put his arm around his wife as the elevator stopped on the eleventh floor.

'See you on the beach,' Tiffany said with forced gaiety as she and Jeffrey stepped out.

But the door didn't close. As Tiffany and Jeffrey disappeared around the corner, Marjorie and Doug looked at the panel of unlit numbered buttons on the wall, and then at each other.

'Nobody pushed our floor,' Marjorie said, the pieces to the puzzle suddenly falling into place.

'Guess I forgot,' Doug said.

'Guess you were both getting off on Tiffany's floor.'

'Marjorie –'

'Guess you thought I was some kind of idiot!'

'But –'

'Guess you better find somewhere else to sleep tonight!' Marjorie spewed, pushing Doug out of the elevator.

Doug watched the door close and the indicator count to eighteen, then pushed the DOWN button and waited, trying to decide whether he should get drunk at the Sea Gull Tavern, or go to a casino. It was a tough decision.

Once in her apartment, Marjorie stood on the balcony staring at the moon. He may not have been the brightest, or the most sensitive man in the world, but Doug Smith was *her* husband. And the thought of losing him, of not having his rock hard body in her bed – of it being in someone *else's* bed – crushed her heart. Overwhelmed, she laid down on the lounge and soothed her pain with a loving hand ...

pretending her hand was Doug's. No ... not Doug's ... Jeffrey Kaufman's, she fantasised, remembering his kind eyes, his caring manner ... the way he blushed when she licked ketchup off her fingers.

As Marjorie comforted herself beneath the full moon while thinking of Jeffrey, several floors below Tiffany was comforting her husband, Jeffrey, beneath that same silvery orb, while thinking of Doug.

At nine-thirty the following Monday morning, Marjorie called Jeffrey at his Germantown office to arrange for an appointment to see him – about a marital problem, she explained.

'I can see you tomorrow at four, Marjorie. It's my last appointment of the day, so I can give you all the time you need,' he said without hesitation, remembering the way she had licked the ketchup off her fingers.

Not very professional, he thought, after putting the phone down, leaning far back in his desk chair, chewing on the eraser of a pencil. Seized with guilt, he considered that it wasn't really going to be a professional visit. *She's just a friend who needs advice*, he thought. *I'm not even going to charge her*, an idea that made him flush with anticipation, a reaction that made him feel even more guilty. *God! I can't believe this*, he thought. *She's not even pretty. Now my wife ... my wife is pretty*.

And Jeffrey tried to remember Thursday night, when his pretty wife made love to him on the balcony. It was exciting. But he was soon thinking about making love to Marjorie Applebaum Smith.

Jeffrey's ten o'clock client was short-changed on Tuesday as Jeffrey was short on concentration in anticipation of four o'clock. His eleven o'clock client was kept waiting as Jeffrey was forced to relieve his burgeoning lust when he developed an erection by the mere act of attempting to urinate between clients, after which he felt a need to jump into the shower before seeing his client, and whilst lathering his member gave in to a compulsion to relieve himself again, startling himself, never having performed so well before – and Marjorie Applebaum Smith wasn't even in the room.

By four that afternoon Jeffrey was running almost thirty minutes behind, and Marjorie sat impatiently in his waiting room, thumbing through old *People* magazines and listening to the radio set just high enough to drown out most, but not all sounds coming from his office. One or two bumps, thumps, and laughs filtered through the strains of DeFalla's Fire Dance. Finally, voices grew loud enough to be distinguished, signalling the end of the session, and the door opened. Into the waiting room stepped a couple smiling enigmatically, followed by Jeffrey whose burnt orange silk shirt was partially hanging out of the back of his designer jeans. He appeared quite disordered as he ran a hand through his tousled hair. Marjorie wondered what could possibly have been going on in that room.

'Yoga,' Jeffrey told Marjorie after she'd settled into the chair across from his rocker. 'They're an interesting couple. Always trying to come up with new ways to relate to each other. This month it's Yoga, and they were showing me some of the exercise positions. I'm afraid I'm not as agile as I'd like to think I am.'

'You tried it?'

'Sure. Want to see my lotus?' Jeffrey asked, leaving his chair, pulling off his loafers and sitting on the floor before Marjorie. He attempted to cross his legs into the lotus position. 'This is where I have a little trouble,' he said, laughing as his feet kept slipping off his thighs.

Marjorie laughed with him, kicked off her sandals and joined him on the floor. Scrunching her long, full, khaki skirt up to her thighs, she deftly twisted her legs into a perfect lotus.

'Very good!' Jeffrey praised, aroused by the sight of her bare legs. He imagined the rest of her bared in that position. Taking a deep breath, relaxing his posture, Jeffrey tried to be appropriate. 'You're going to have to show me how to do that. My clients will be very impressed,' he said.

'Do you end up on the floor with *all* your clients?'

'What brings you here today?' Jeffrey asked in his best professional manner, ignoring her question.

'Do they teach you that in school – how to achieve a conversational hair-pin turn?'

'You said you wanted to discuss a marital problem,' he turned again.

'Yes,' Marjorie said, giving in. 'My husband ... well, Doug's having an affair ... and I told him to leave.' And Marjorie broke into deep sobs, surprising herself at the depth of her pain, forgetting for a moment why she had come – for revenge, not confession.

Jeffrey leaned forward but said nothing.

'I guess I knew my marriage wasn't perfect, but I wasn't prepared for how I'm feeling.'

'How are you feeling?'

'Betrayed, unwanted, unattractive.'

'I'm sorry, Marjorie. What can I do to help?'

Make love to me here, with Tiffany's picture on your desk, she thought. 'Just be my friend,' she said, reaching out to take his hand.

The touch of her hand sent a familiar shock through him, but this time he didn't pull away. 'I'll be anything you want me to be,' he said, giving in to the incredible warmth that had overtaken his body. Swallowing a sudden flood of saliva, he tried to talk, but found his mouth had gone dry.

Marjorie, who couldn't believe how easy it was going to be, leaned forward and pulled Jeffrey to her with one hand. With the other, she pulled up her skirt, revealing the fact that she was not wearing underpants.

Even as Jeffrey was sucked into the tempest of lust swirling about them, he couldn't believe that they were going to do what they were going to do. But that day in Dr Jeffrey Kaufman's office they did it on the floor, on the sofa, and then, finally, on the big leather rocker, with Marjorie astride Jeffrey.

'Want to play rodeo sex?' Marjorie asked, playing contemptuously on an old joke, kissing him on his nose, his chin, rocking slowly to and fro.

'Whatever you say,' Jeffrey answered trustingly, ready for anything as long as it included penetration.

Slipping him deep into herself, Marjorie wrapped her arms around his shoulders. 'Do you and Tiffany ever do it this way?' she asked.

Passion robbing him of his powers of speech, Jeffrey just shook his head.

Marjorie tightened her grip, put her cheek against Jeffrey's and whispered in his ear, 'Too bad. Doug tells me that Tiffany loves it this way.'

She was able to hold on for about ten seconds before Jeffrey managed to throw her off and get to his feet. Assaulted by a myriad of emotions – disbelief, hurt, anger at Tiffany, at himself, at Marjorie who had rearranged herself impudently on his rocker – Jeffrey stared down at her with an open mouth and tear-filled eyes.

'It's true, Jeffrey. My husband is your wife's lover,' Marjorie said, trying to enjoy his pain, hoping it would assuage her own.

'How long have you known?' he asked.

'Since Thursday night in the elevator.'

'The elevator?'

'I confronted Doug over the week-end . . . he told all . . . I told him to leave,' she ticked off in a most offhanded manner, although the tears in her eyes belied the callousness of her words.

Jeffrey stared at Marjorie with eyes that focused inward. He was thinking of the full moon over his balcony. Feeling suddenly exposed, Jeffrey turned from Marjorie to pull on his jeans, ignoring his shorts. His unfilled condom dangling from his hand, he slumped down on the sofa and closed his eyes. 'I can't believe I didn't know,' he whimpered. When his eyes opened a moment later, they fell on the clock above the bookshelf across from his rocker. *Five-fifty-five – hour's up*, he thought automatically, as if what had transpired had been only a matter of time.

It was a tough week for Jeffrey as anger and guilt sparred with him – one, two . . . one, two. By Friday his psyche was black and blue, he was emotionally anaemic from loss of self-esteem. Wanting to explore his feelings, think through his reactions, assess the psychic damage before he confronted Tiffany, Jeffrey had avoided talking to her all week by letting his answering machine screen his calls. Tiffany called Wednesday morning. He didn't return her call. She didn't call again. His ride to the shore Friday night was fraught with anxious renditions of his intended conversation with her. Even as he drove up to the Ivory Tower, he wasn't sure if he would be indignant or understanding, confrontational about her sins or confessional of his own, if he would ask her to leave or beg her to stay. In the elevator, somewhere between the first and eleventh floors, all sins seemed to balance out and Jeffrey approached his apartment with assuredness in his step and forgiveness in his heart. Mentally applauding himself as self-therapist, Jeffrey entered his surprisingly dark home and switched on a light.

A note was propped against the small Lalique nude on the white marble table in the foyer: *You're a really special person, Jeffrey, but we can't continue this relationship. Tiffany.*

. . . While the computer saved my progress, accepting what I'd written unconditionally, I reflected upon my motives. Surely I didn't know Jeffrey Kaufman well enough to speculate upon his life; I'd barely met the man. But he was familiar, nonetheless. He struck me as a type. An unfair view, perhaps, but that was the truth of it.

Another truth was my view of the only other shrink I'd ever known, Philip Krausen, with whom my late husband had been playing racquetball when he'd had his fatal heart attack.

Like Jeffrey, Phil married late. In fact, when Carl and I'd known him, he was still single. He'd had an unusually close relationship with his mother, visiting her almost every day. It was five or six years ago that I saw her obituary in the newspaper, and, just a few months later, Phil's wedding announcement.

And Phil, like Jeffrey, was nice, in a sweet, soft way . . . a man easily overwhelmed by passion . . .

'Alison, I know this is wrong, but I can't hide what I feel,' he'd cried to me not two months after Carl had died. It was in his office, at his home in Merion, where he'd invited me to come to talk with him, after his regular office hours, about Shel's behaviour.

Phil was one of Carl's few friends. He'd known Carl for years before Carl and I'd met. They worked at the same hospital, and they played racquetball together when Carl's regular racquetball partner, Lou Sommers, was unavailable – like the night Carl had died. Carl and I socialised with Phil at hospital dances and cocktail parties, and occasionally we went to a movie and dinner with him and a date. He was quietly handsome, deeply intelligent, and flatteringly attentive to me.

Like the time with the figs. We'd seen a movie in an art theatre, in which a man – it may have been Michael York, or Alan Bates – was eating a ripe fig in a most lascivious manner, explaining to companions how the inside of a fig resembles the sex of a woman. The scene aroused me. At dinner after the movie, Phil ordered ripe figs for dessert, an innocent act in itself. But he pierced the final section with his fork and held it out for me to eat. 'No thank you, I can't eat another bite,' I said, dousing his playful gesture in priggish disregard. My rejection sounded ungrateful, obtuse. *Why did I do things like that!* I thought to myself when I saw the sparkle leave his beautiful green eyes, the fleshy fig dropped upon the plate untouched. Maybe because I didn't know how to flirt. Maybe because I understood, at some level, that Phil's motives were deeper than mere flirtation.

It was Phil who came to tell me that Carl had died on the racquetball court. He helped me with the funeral arrangements, and guided my words to Shel about the loss of his father. He came every night the week following Carl's death, making a special effort to talk with Shel, to help him deal with his loss. After that he called every other day or so to see how things were going, if we needed anything, if I wanted to talk. One Sunday he took Shel to the zoo, one evening he took us both to dinner. Twice I invited him to my home to have dinner with Shel and me. He was gentle and supportive. And although I never displayed false grief, I never told him of Carl's and my plans for divorce, either. I told myself it would have been disloyal. It was, in fact, self-serving; I was attracted to him, but felt afraid of getting too close to him – maybe because I was attracted to him.

That evening in his office, the evening I came to talk about Shel's regressive behaviour – wetting the bed, temper tantrums, and the like – Phil seemed tense, distracted. I asked if another time might be better, but he insisted I stay. After assuring me that Shel's behaviour was well within the normal range of grief reactions for a young child, and that time and hugs would ease him back to the bright, happy youngster I knew him to be, Phil asked me about my life, about how I was coping. Before I had a chance to answer, he was telling me how he viewed me – strong and confident, full of grace, he said – how he admired me. And then he opened his glass-doored bookcase, taking from it a small volume of poetry. In his hands, the book fell open to a well-turned page. Offering it to me, he said, 'This makes me think of you.' And I silently read the poem by e.e. cummings that began, '*somewhere i have never travelled, gladly beyond/any experience, your eyes have their silence:*' and ended, '*(i do not know what it is about you that closes/and opens; only something in me understands/the voice of your eyes is deeper than all roses)/nobody, not even the rain, has such small hands*'.

He loves me, I thought, my face burning, my icy hands closing the book. I stared at the cover, not daring to look up, but feeling his gaze upon me, reaching into me. That's when he sat beside me and said, 'Alison, I know this is wrong, but I can't hide what I feel.' Looking up I saw his face close to mine and reason deserted me, resistance vanished. And then we were on the floor, pulling at our clothes, at each other's clothes, until skin's hunger for skin was satisfied, the demand for union accomplished. Locked together, we drew from each other reserved passion that had suddenly become vital sustenance. Those few moments became eons as we became each other's universe, being all, meaning all.

Alas, intensity of that magnitude is short-lived, ending in a new world, like the Big Bang . . . or a vaporised one.

Overwhelmed by passion before the act, Phil was overcome by guilt after. 'I'm so sorry, Alison . . . I never meant . . . Carl was my friend . . . we can't ever do this . . . this was so *wrong* . . .' he'd stammered on and on as he twisted from my embrace, wrestled with his clothes. And then, 'Oh, my God, I've lost a contact lens,' he cried, falling to his knees. With refocused determination he explored the intricate design of the oriental carpet for an aberrant sparkle, a glossy bump, while I, confused and hurt, dressed and headed for the door. 'Phil –'

He looked up, startling me with his schizoid glance – one eye was blue, the other green. 'I'm sorry, Alison . . . you're a really special person, but we can't continue this relationship,' was what he said.

. . . It was about four o'clock when I headed back down to the beach, still thinking about Phil. I'd never heard from him after that evening, although I'd written. I hadn't dared to call. The whole matter had made me feel intensely guilty, although I wasn't sure what I was guilty of, and I wrote to tell him of Carl's and my plans to divorce, so he'd know that he hadn't betrayed a friendship after all, that I hadn't been unfaithful to a husband barely cold, a letter that was as self-serving as my initial rejection of full disclosure had been, a letter that was never answered.

Several years later I went to see Woody Allen's movie, *Hannah and Her Sisters*. A rueful smile crossed my lips when Hannah's husband seduced her sister with a poem. The line, '*nobody, not even the rain, has such small hands*', stretched boldly across the giant screen, and I wondered if all men on the make read e.e. cummings.

. . . Within moments of my arrival at the beach on Saturday afternoon, Robin sat down beside me smiling from ear to ear.

'So?' she asked enthusiastically.

'So, what?' I questioned back.

'So what did you think of him?'

'Of who?' I asked, being deliberately obtuse.

'Of Jeffrey, of course.'

'He seemed nice enough,' I said, pushing away my bitter memories of Philip Krausen. 'So where's Elliot?' I asked, changing the subject. 'I thought he was coming down today.'

'When I went up for lunch there was a message from him on the machine. He was called in to help his partner with deliveries. Elliot has one of the biggest practices in the city, you know. And he's very loyal to his patients. He'd never leave them in the hands of a resident.'

'That's very nice.'

'Yep. He's really a very special guy,' Robin said affectionately.

'Will he be down later?'

'God, I hope so. I'm horny as anything.'

'Don't worry. You'll survive,' I said with a nip of meanness, a twinge of jealousy stinging me.

'Oh! Look who's the expert. So tell me, Dr Ruth, when was the last time you –'

'Come on, Robin! That's not the point,' I said, growing annoyed, although more at myself, than Robin.

'So what *is* the point?'

I pulled a bunch of large black grapes from my beach bag and popped one into my mouth. 'Here, try one. You'll like it,' I said, pitching a grape at my friend . . . my happily married, happily lustful friend.

Sailing past Robin's hands, the grape landed in the sand. 'Thanks a lot!' Robin said, picking it up. After carefully wiping away the grains of sand, she bit into it and grimaced. 'Sour skin . . . but very sweet inside,' she said.

'Like some people I know.'

'Must you get philosophical . . . or is it psychological? Anyway, getting back to what's important, sex is necessary to your well-being. Try it. You'll like it.'

'Well . . . I hear Doug's available.'

'God, you're so cynical, Alison.'

'Maybe,' I said, now feeling guilty about my momentary jealousy of Robin . . . not to mention what I'd just done to nice Jeffrey Kaufman in *Yellow*, the revenge I'd exacted on Phil Krausen by proxy. 'But I'm really a *grape* big sweetie at heart,' I added, feeling just a little sorry for myself.

'Yeah. I know,' Robin replied, comprehending perhaps better than I the slight quiver in my voice, the sudden glisten in my eyes. 'So . . . when does Shel leave for school?' she asked.

CHAPTER 4

White

After setting out lox, bagels, crunchy raw veggies, and strawberry cheesecake for myself and Shel – who was expected at eleven – I sat on the balcony with the *New York Times* magazine a little after ten on Sunday morning and started to work on the crossword puzzle. I quickly put it down, however, when my stomach knotted and my heart raced as my internal gyrocompass seemed to go askew. Prickling in a cold sweat, I went into the apartment, turned on the television, and focused on the screen. Oddly, it helped. 'Hello!' Shel called, entering the apartment minutes later.

Jumping from my seat, I greeted my son with a hug and kiss, but, as usual, he finessed out of my embrace, and my lips landed on the edge of his ear. 'You're too old to kiss your mother?' I asked in what was more of an affectionate rebuke than a question.

'God, you're short!' Shel exclaimed, side-stepping my dismay, flattening his hand on top of my head.

'I'm five-four,' I defended my stature.

'No way!'

'I'm not wearing shoes.'

'You're a shrimp.'

I smiled at the familiar repartee as I walked into the kitchen to retrieve butter and cream cheese from the refrigerator. It was a game we'd played ever since Shel was tall enough to look over my head. I understood it was an adolescent mix of insecurity and pride that kept it going, that along with Shel's impatience for growth was a sense of anxiety about growing up, about being bigger than, more powerful than his mother. If he were the more powerful, who would take care of him, he who was no longer a child, but not yet a man?

'So how's life treating you, Shel?' I asked, sitting across from my son at the table, enjoying the perfect Greek line of his nose, the sculptured fullness of his mouth, the beauty of his large, graceful hands as they built a mountainous sandwich, incredulous, as always, that this handsome hulk was a part of me – my baby.

'Great,' Shel answered, intent on layering cream cheese, salty lox, thin slices of Bermuda onion and tomato on an onion bagel.

'How's the job working out?'

'Great.'

'Do you like your house?'

'It's great.'

'Do you like living with the guys?'

'Yeah. They're great.'

'Don't you miss being here?' I fished.

'Nope.'

'So much for the care and maintenance of a mother's ego,' I stated without hope for contradiction.

'You should be happy, Mom. My room is clean . . . no food in the living room . . . no wrestling matches on TV . . . peace and quiet,' he said before chomping into the giant sandwich.

'I'm delighted,' I replied, contradicting my gut, whose sudden wrench signaled that the last thing I wanted was the peace and quiet of an empty nest. 'I'm happy for you. Just remember, before the summer is over, we have to get you ready for school.'

'No sweat, Mom. I've got it all under control,' Shel managed to say through a full mouth.

I sighed and bit into my sandwich, my perception of Shel swinging like a pendulum between the child and the man, knowing that he was capable enough to have everything under control, but doubtful that, in fact, he did. 'Are all the forms filled out?' I probed.

'All done, Mom.'

'Do you know what clothes you need to buy?'

'Chill out, Mom. I'm totally organised,' he said smiling, popping a black olive into his mouth. 'How about the lady who took a dive from the top of the building a couple of days ago?'

'Shel! That's horrible!'

'What'd I say?'

'It's the way you said it.'

'Wasn't that the lady with the mouth?' Shel asked, puckering up his lips ... pushing the olive pit through them with his tongue.

'If you mean Marjorie Applebaum, yes. And don't be gross.'

'What a waste. Police been around yet? The paper said they're going to question everyone at the Tower.'

'Saturday morning.'

'Yeah? What'd you tell them?'

'That I might have heard her fall.'

'No shit!'

'Shel!' I reacted perfunctorily, not really caring that my son's speech was peppered with four-letter words, but feeling that I *should* care, at least make an attempt at discipline.

'Come on, Mom. Did she jump?'

'I don't know, Shel. I was half asleep on the balcony. I thought I dreamed something went by me. But, actually, it could have been Marjorie. It's a horrible thought.'

'Cool! Mom's a star witness! She was pretty young, wasn't she?'

'Younger than me.'

'*Everybody's* younger than you.'

'Thanks. I really needed that.'

'It's okay. You don't look too bad for an old lady.'

'What is this, mother bashing day?'

'Jason thinks you're a fox.'

'Oh?' I sat a little straighter in my chair. 'Really? Did he tell you that?'

'Uh-oh. Here we go. I'm sorry I said anything.'

'You brought it up. I'm just curious. So what did he tell you?'

'Not to worry, Mom, all the guys still consider you a Milf.'

'A what?'

'Milf – as in Mothers I'd Like to Fuck.'

'Sheldon Diamond! I'm shocked!'

'Sure, sure. *Everything* shocks you. Tell me you've never heard of Milfs before.'

'So . . . what guys?' I asked, ignoring his comment.

'You didn't know the Tower beach was Milfville, right?' he asked, ignoring my question.

'Milfville!?'

'God, you're naïve!'

'About what?'

Shel stuffed the last of his sandwich into his mouth and began building another.

I took my coffee mug into the kitchen for a refill. 'About what, Shel?' I asked again.

Silence.

Setting my filled mug down, I reached across the table and pulled a lock of my smirking son's curly brown hair that was already streaked reddish-blond by the sun.

'Don't touch the hair! I hate it when you do that.'

'So tell me.'

'Tell you what?'

'Why do you think I'm naïve? . . . And which guys think I'm a . . . you know –'

'You don't know *anything*,' Shel teased.

'Like what don't I know?' I insisted against my better judgement.

'Like I'll bet you didn't know that Mrs Pincus had an abortion last year,' he said quietly, smoothing cream cheese off the edge of his bagel.

'A what!'

'An abortion.'

'Where did you hear that?'

'From the father.'

'Excuse me?'

'The father of the baby – or should I say the em-bry-o – and I don't mean *Dr* Pincus . . . even though he is – ahem – a *fertility* specialist. Ah, sweet irony.'

'This isn't funny, Shel. Now, who do *you* think the father is?'

'*Was*, Mom. And let's just say he can fuck but he can't vote.'

'Shel!'

'What? I'm just saying it like it is. And, trust me, she's not alone.'

'Alone at what?'

'Taking advantage of young flesh,' Shel baited me, flexing his carefully nurtured biceps, smiling broadly, exposing perfectly aligned, post-orthodontic teeth.

'Your teenage hormones are rotting your brain, Shel.'

'Pass the veggies . . . please?'

'Well, I don't know about all this,' I said, although a vague memory of the beach boy winking at me clicked into sharp focus.

'I rest my case. You don't know *anything*!'

'Do you want this cheesecake on a plate or on your face?' I threatened.

'Don't throw it! Sorry!'

I cut a slice of cheesecake for Shel and one for myself, ate the strawberry from the top, and then, 'So who else preys on adolescents around here?' I asked casually.

'Hah! You *do* believe me, don't you? Well, you'd be surprised.'

'Surprise me.'

'Hmmm. Let's see. How about Mrs Forrester?' Shel said, looking to the ceiling.

'I don't believe it.'

'I told you you'd be surprised.'

'Brenda Forrester? Who was the guy?' I asked.

'I'm not at liberty to say,' Shel tantalised me.

'WHO, Sheldon!'

'Maybe one of the guys in my house . . .'

'Pete?'

'. . . maybe not.'

'Jason?'

'I cannot break a confidence.'

'I don't believe it. I can't believe intelligent, grown women are seducing children.'

'Children? Mother, please. And I wouldn't call it

seduction,' he said, starting on the cheesecake.

'What would you call it? And just what do you *know* about it?'

'I listen.'

'You *listen*?' I asked my man-child, trying to picture him another way . . . a way other than my son.

'I give great ear, Mom,' Shel said, turning an ear to me, flicking it with his finger.

'Mmm. Milfs.'

'You like that, don't you?' he asked, laughing.

'I don't think I want to hear any more about this,' I said.

'Milf, milf, milf,' he needled me, reaching across the table and mussing up my hair.

'Don't touch the hair!' I threw back at him. I eyed my son with an expression of mock annoyance, grateful that he could talk to me about anything, while at the same time feeling that he often told me more than I wanted to hear – and wondering if he'd even told me the half of it.

Sipping my coffee, I pictured Shel at eleven, and remembered what seemed to me our seminal conversation of sexual enlightenment – *my* enlightenment about *his* sexuality. He'd been sitting across from me at the dinner table, just as he was now, when he dropped, 'I really like Dr Ruth.' 'And what do you know about Dr Ruth?' I'd asked with a practised nonchalance. 'She's neat. Last night was great,' he said through a mouthful of broccoli. 'Really? What was it about?' I asked. 'The big O! Organs and orgasms,' he answered. 'More mashed potatoes?' I punted, wondering just how much he knew about orgasms, remembering the explanation I'd offered when he was five and had asked how it *felt* when *sperms ejected*. I had said, *It's kind of like a sneeze in your penis* – an explanation I'd heard from a friend, who had seen it in a book. Shel had laughed, and pretended to sneeze, and then asked if elephants *ejected* from their trunks, too – a wonderfully creative misconception, I thought.

But Shel wasn't five any more, or eleven. He was eighteen and possibly – whether I wanted to believe it or not – sexually active. So I was troubled by my son's revelations. I worried that he could get hurt ... he could get sick ... I wondered if he used protection ... if he was *really* doing these things. It was times like this that I rued the absence of Shel's father. A father's word on such matters would sound more authoritative, I thought, feeling that Shel thought me to be over-protective, not to be taken seriously.

'I certainly hope your horny friends use condoms,' I tackled the situation, careful to avoid implicating him. 'You know, it's a dangerous world out there now, Shel. It's not like –'

'Hey, Mom, worry not,' he cut me off, starting in on an animated recitation of a poem that had gone around school. '*My friend Robbie Rubber says, before you cock it, blanket that rocket ... Don't be silly, wrap your Willie ...*'

'Okay, okay! I get the point,' I interrupted.

'*... If you're not going to sack it, go home and whack it ...*'

'I've heard enough,' I shouted over him.

'*... It'll be sweeter if you wrap your peter ...*'

Giving up, I sat back and let him finish.

'*... Don't be a loner, wrap your boner. And always remember,*' he concluded, raising his eyebrows and a forefinger, '*No glove, no love!*'

Applauding slowly, I projected an indulging smile.

'Still worried, Mom?' Shel asked.

'Only about the state of the art of poetry,' I quipped, relieved for the moment, thinking that I taught him well, even without a man in the house.

'Great cheesecake,' Shel said, scraping the last from his plate with his fork.

'Have some more,' I offered, already cutting another slice.

I watched him attack the second piece of cake as I sipped my second cup of coffee, my heart swelling just at the sight of him; it almost burst as I thought of more and more dangers in the world from which I was becoming less and less able to protect him.

'Do you think you would have married Dad if you hadn't gotten pregnant with me?' he asked out of nowhere.

'Of course,' I said immediately, without a thought, responding to something deeper in Shel than his sudden curiosity about *my* life.

'I figure you must have been two months gone when you guys married,' he continued his inquiry.

'Your father and I loved each other very much, Shel, and . . . well, you would have happened sooner or later . . . so you happened just a little sooner,' I said, not weighing the veracity of my words, attempting only to quiet whatever fears Shel had about his place in the world, in my world, wondering how long he'd been thinking about it, why he brought it up just then. 'What brought this up?' I asked.

'Just a passing thought.'

'A passing thought? Like a Mack truck passing a skateboard. What are you thinking about?'

'I guess it would've been easier for you if I hadn't been born, wouldn't it?'

I was stunned. How could he have so misunderstood my love for him, my support – my whole life, I thought, nonplussed.

'So you should be glad I'm going away. You'll have

some time to yourself for a change. Maybe you'll even meet some guy and get married again.'

'Shel, I –' I started, but was unable to continue as a rush of conflicting thoughts and feelings choked me with tears.

'Check it out! Mom's going to cry!' Shel said, trying not to show his embarrassment for my display of emotion. 'God! What did I say?'

'Nothing. It's just that I don't want you to feel you have to go away for *me*. You're the most important, the most wanted person in my life . . . and I love you . . . and I can't believe you have feelings about yourself like this –'

'I'm not thinking about *me*, I'm thinking about *you*, Mom.'

'You don't have to worry about me. That's not your job. I'm your mother. I worry about *you*. No matter how old you get, Shel, you're still my baby.'

'In case you haven't noticed, I'm a big boy, Mom,' he said shyly. 'I can take care of myself. Honest. I'm eighteen. You don't have to defend me any more. Hey,' he exclaimed, turning wilfully chipper, 'I could be defending *you* . . . I could be defending our whole country!'

I wanted to answer him, to tell him that the world wasn't his responsibility, that *I* wasn't his responsibility, but I couldn't say a word as I imagined young boys going off to war . . . tearing themselves away from their mothers . . . babes in the woods, the jungles, the deserts of conflict. It was more than I could bear. 'War is not a joke, Shel!' I scolded.

'Lighten up, Mom. I'm teasing. I'm just going to college, not boot camp,' Shel said.

A smile found its way through my pout. Shel could always make me smile in spite of my distress. There was nothing my son ever said that didn't affect me, change me, bend me towards his perspective as I bent towards him to love him, to protect him. I sometimes wondered if it would have been the same with a daughter, or if it would have been the same for a father. Moot issues. We were mother and son, and there's a special bond between mothers and sons that has to do with the specialness between women and men. Being both mother and father to Shel for so many years, I'd tried to ignore that specialness, to neuter myself in his eyes. I didn't consider that perhaps I had neutered myself in my own eyes only.

'I'm going to be fine, Mom. You don't have to worry about me. I'll be a great success. I'll make you proud of me,' Shel spouted over his cheesecake, seeming to understand my silence, shouldering the onus of responsibility the way children tend to do when their parents are in pain . . .

The evening following his father's death, Shel hugged me hard. '*I'll* take care of you, Mommy.' He was three.

Holding him close, rocking him gently, I replied, 'No, sweetheart. I'm your mommy, you're my little boy, and *I'll* always take care of *you*,' sure that my attitude would suffice.

. . . It didn't, of course. I was aware that Shel grew up feeling a burdensome responsibility for me, especially when he saw me tired, or ill, or – and this was the worst – alone . . .

'Won't be home for dinner tonight . . . studying with the guys . . . big maths exam tomorrow. Can you drop me at the library?' he had asked one night when he was about fifteen.

'You have to eat,' I'd chided him.

'I won't be hungry. I ate at four,' he replied, the smell

of Kraft macaroni and cheese still clinging to him.

'Okay. I'll stop in at the diner for a quick bite by myself after I drop you off,' I said, feeling proud of myself for allowing him his awful teenage eating habits.

'Why don't you call a girlfriend,' he suggested. 'I don't want you to eat alone.'

'Don't be silly, I don't mind –'

'On second thoughts, maybe I'll have time to eat with you before I go to the library,' he said, taking control.

... And now it seemed he was trying to protect me again. He didn't want me to be alone once he left for school.

'Shel, I'm already proud of you,' I said, regaining control. 'I've always been very, very proud of you.'

'Well ... you don't have to worry about me,' he repeated, embarrassed by my praise. 'Your little boy's all grown up,' he said, coming around to my side, throwing pulled punches at my arm, not understanding that I was worried *because* he was all grown up.

I stood up and threw my shoulder into my son, a move he countered with his shoulder, encouraging a further exchange of bumps and pushes serving as surrogate hugs. *Not quite grown up*, I thought, reaching up and managing to kiss him quickly on the cheek.

'Do you want to take the rest of the cake back to the house for the boys?' I asked.

'Sure,' he said, scooping up the creamy cheesecake and carrying it into the kitchen where he carefully wrapped it in plastic and then in foil, the way he had seen me wrap his lunch box goodies when he was a little boy.

'Love you,' I called to him as he walked down the hall towards the elevator.

'Of course!' he answered, turning his face to me, flashing a candidate's smile, filling me, as always, with pride. But the words unsaid stung me, deflating me.

Later, on the beach in front of the Ivory Tower, I smeared number twenty sunscreen around my eyes, number fifteen on the rest of my face, and number ten on my body before sitting in my sand chair in the shade of my white umbrella. Looking around, I spotted Robin sitting alone under her pink umbrella. I called to her, waving my arm high above my head.

'How do you feel, Alison?' Robin asked, dropping her chair in the sun in front of me.

'Fine, now,' I replied, suddenly remembering the dizziness I'd felt that morning, and that it had gone as mysteriously as it had come.

'How was brunch?'

'A trip!' I said.

'How's that?'

'Do you have ten hours?'

'Try me,' Robin challenged, settling into her chair, offering her face to the white, hot sun, stretching her legs out on the warm, white sand.

'He wants me to get married.'

'Oh? Where did that come from?'

'I think he doesn't want to leave me alone when he's off to school.'

'That's so sweet that he's so concerned about you.'

'It's not actually about me, Robin. It's about him. He feels responsible for me. It's a heavy load.'

'That's a bit unfair, don't you think? Give him a little credit.'

'I'm not being unfair at all. It's the way it is, and I give him lots of credit. I'm the selfish one here. I feel I didn't do my job right. He shouldn't feel so responsible for me. I should have found him a father.'

'You make it sound like you stayed single deliberately.'

'Maybe I did. Maybe, for some reason, I avoided getting involved on purpose.'

'Now you're being too hard on *yourself*. What possible reason –'

'He is a sweet guy, isn't he? But don't tell him I told you. He'd kill me.'

'He'd love to know you say such nice things about him.'

'I know that but . . . *he* doesn't. Kids are like that.'

'He's not a kid any more, Alison.'

'That's what he keeps telling me. And, in a way it's true. But, as his mother, my perspective is a little different.'

'Your perspective on everything is a little different, Alison. That's what I like about you.'

'By the way, ever hear the term *Milf*?'

'You mean as in Mothers I'd Like to Fuck?'

'Ah. And I suppose, then, you're also familiar with the rumours about their affairs with our children?'

'You mean tales of the Milfs and the great horny ones?'

'So how come I don't know these things!?'

'You never asked.'

'Very funny. Am I the only –'

'Alison, you're usually only here on the week-ends . . . and, to tell you the truth, I often get the feeling that you'd rather not hear a lot of gossipy stuff.'

'So what are you saying, I'm some kind of priss?'

'Not exactly, but –'

'Well, I found out this morning that my son knows more about what's going on around here than I do. It was very embarrassing . . . not to mention shocking.'

'Well, there you are. You're shocked. Nobody else around here is shocked. So what exactly did he tell you?'

'He told me that Carol Pincus had an abortion last year...'

'Ah.'

'...and that one of his housemates was seduced by Brenda Forrester–'

'Not surprising.'

'Oh?'

'So who?' Robin asked tilting her left ear towards me.

'That's what I asked Shel. He wouldn't tell.'

'The real question is, why did he tell you any of it.'

'Well, we were talking and–. Actually, I'm not sure.'

'Uh-oh. Guilt.'

'What do you mean?'

'Alison, brace yourself; he was probably talking about himself.'

'Never!'

'Remember when you were looking for him Friday afternoon. And his friends couldn't find him?' Pause. 'Do you remember seeing Brenda on the beach?'

'It's not possible!' Pause. 'Do you think so?'

'It's possible.'

'But Brenda Forrester! She's probably ten years older than *me*. What would he want with someone older than me?'

'Sex. With anyone, anywhere, any way. He's eighteen, remember? And she's nothing if not intriguing.'

'But she's so *old*.'

'She doesn't look it, Alison. And, besides, do you think a horny teenager sees beyond a beckoning finger? Remember the movie *When Harry Met Sally*? Harry's comment about unattractive girls? like he wanted to nail them, too? We're talking raging male hormones here, not a beauty contest.'

'But *Brenda Forrester*!'

'I'd kill for her legs.'

'Wouldn't we all,' I admitted wistfully.

'Want some ice-cream?' Robin asked, spying the veteran ice-cream vendor walking in our direction, bent under the weight of the bulky white ice-box slung over one shoulder.

'Fudgsicles here! Get yer fudgie-wudgies,' Bill cried out as he walked. A familiar cry, and a familiar face to the beach regulars in Atlantic City and Kent.

'Not really. My stomach's a little off. Actually, my head's still a little off balance.'

'I thought you said you were better.'

'I was, until now.'

'I'm no shrink, but I think it's all in your head – figuratively speaking, that is. Look, I may not have kids, but I've read enough to know that you're a perfect example of the empty nest syndrome.'

I listened with growing annoyance as my friend analysed me – body and soul.

'. . . You have to let him go, Alison. You'll see, Shel'll be fine. *You're* the one who's going to need some TLC and –'

'Robin,' I finally interrupted, having heard quite enough, 'you couldn't be more wrong. Shel and I have a very healthy relationship, and I'm completely willing to let him go. I've raised him well and I expect he'll do well in school and in whatever career he chooses,' I defended myself pedantically. 'We've always been open with each other Robin, so I'm not expecting any surprises.'

'You mean other than Brenda Forrester?'

I conceded Robin's point with tears.

'I'm sorry, Alison. I didn't mean –' she started, jumping up, heading towards me.

'No, no. It's okay,' I said, waving her away. 'You're

right. I'm upset about Shel. About his leaving.'

'I could be wrong about your dizzy spells, though. Maybe you should see a doctor,' Robin said, red-faced with concern.

'I'll be fine.'

'By the way, the police were up at the apartment this morning,' she said in an attempt to distract me.

She succeeded. 'Oh?' I asked, pulling myself together. 'Was Lieutenant Fiori there?'

'Yes, with another officer. An older man. But Fiori did all the talking. Asked a lot of questions about Marjorie. I really didn't have anything to tell him.'

'Are you kidding? How about Marjorie's affair with Jeffrey Kaufman, and Marjorie's affair with Marty Steiner?' I attacked, surprising myself as well as Robin who blushed again.

'Well, it's really just rumour, Alison. I didn't think I should involve anyone without proof. If it's true, the police will find out soon enough.'

The score evened, I turned the conversation. 'So what else did Lieutenant Fiori have to say?'

'Nothing much. But I got the distinct impression that he's interested in you.'

'Honestly, Robin –'

'He asked if I knew you. Said you may have been the only witness, that you seemed like a really bright lady. Loved the idea that you're a writer, and said that he'd probably have to talk with you again.'

'Why would he tell you all that?'

'Well, maybe I started it.'

'What did you say?'

'Maybe I told him that I knew you had been on your balcony Friday morning, and that I thought it had upset you . . . being alone and all.'

'Why would you say a thing like that to him?'

'He brought your name up first. And he did ask if I knew you. He's really cute, you know ... and kind of sexy.'

'And young.'

'Not really. I think he looks younger than he is. And I don't think he's married, Alison. He wasn't wearing a ring.'

'Well, from now on I wish you –'

'Whoa! Look who's coming,' Robin said, nodding to my left, where Jeffrey Kaufman could be seen walking towards us, chair in hand.

'Good afternoon, ladies. Want company?' Jeffrey asked as he approached.

'Sit, Jeffrey,' Robin commanded.

'What a fantastic day! I can't remember a clearer sky,' he said, dropping his chair next to Robin.

'Rob, have dinner with me tonight?' I questioned my friend, rudely ignoring Jeffrey for no reason that I could fathom.

'Aren't you going back to the city tonight?' Robin asked.

'No. Remember? I'm on vacation.'

'Jeffrey, would you like to join us tonight?' Robin asked, determined.

'Sure. Actually, I'm on vacation, too. Six weeks – until the end of August,' said Jeffrey.

'You can leave your clients for a month and a half? Elliot would never leave his patients for that long,' Robin said with a touch of pride.

'I usually can't, either. But I got lucky this year. And speaking of the good Doctor Elliot, when can we expect to see him?'

'Yes, Robin. Where *is* Elliot?' I echoed.

'It's a long story,' Robin sighed. 'Bottom line is he's not coming this week-end.'

'I'm so sorry, Rob,' I sympathised. 'I know you've missed him this week. Will he be down before next week-end?'

'Maybe on Wednesday,' she answered, watching her big toe trace a question mark in the sand.

Even in the best of marriages, I thought. *Questions*.

CHAPTER 5

Pink

Assailed by images, answers to questions, I left Robin and Jeffrey on the beach and retreated to my balcony with my laptop where I quickly began creating my version of the life of Robin and Elliot, a life I was somewhat privy to, having known them for six years. Of course the fiction I would write would be based on the impressions I had formed about the 'facts' Robin had chosen to relate to me, in whatever context she felt appropriate at the time . . .

Robin met and married Elliot Crystal during Elliot's senior year of medical school. Though tall and dark, he wasn't what most would call handsome. He was, rather, heavy boned and craggy, and surprisingly meek for one so large.

They appeared an unlikely couple, strikingly different, not only physically, but in demeanor; Elliot was ponderous, while Robin was flighty – like a bird. But they seemed to complement each other, sharing a passion for one another, and for the salty air and pearly sand of the Jersey shore. Summer week-ends they'd drive to Atlantic City to picnic on the beach and stroll hand in hand along the ocean's edge, invigorated by the cool grey-white foam slapping at their ankles.

Walking in front of the Ivory Tower Condominium, they never failed to be captivated by the covey of colourful umbrellas, the aura of calm there, unlike the beach a few blocks to the South, which resembled a kindergarten playground, or the beach a few blocks to the North, where the boom boxes of the teenagers challenged the roar of the surf. But they never chose to sit on the Tower beach, finding themselves unable to intrude on its tacit privacy.

And then one summer Elliot declared prosperity and he and Robin bought an apartment on the eighth floor of the Ivory Tower. The first thing they did after settlement was select a beach umbrella from the dozen or so that stood in a corner of the Tower's storeroom like a bunch of giant lollipops. On their first official beach day at the Tower – the third Saturday of August, 1985 – the beach boy retrieved the singular pink umbrella, now labelled, *Crystal, apt. 807*, from his stack, and followed Robin and Elliot to the centre of the Tower Beach, where he plunged it into the sand. 'Have a good one!' he said, leaving the Crystals to settle in.

'Well, we're here,' Elliot said, setting the labelled chairs they brought from the city under the umbrella. He then donned his sun-glasses, reached for a plum and his copy of the *Journal of the American Medical Association*, and sat in his chair a happy man.

Robin moved her chair into the sun and began scanning the immediate area. It was a hot, dry day, and the glare of the sun off the white umbrella a few yards to her left momentarily blinded her. 'Elliot, would you toss me my sun-glasses?' she asked the bulky figure. Getting no response, she walked over to her husband's chair. 'Elliot,' she started to reprimand him, but, finding him sound asleep behind his magazine, sighed and retrieved her glasses from the canvas beach bag herself. Walking back to her chair, Robin spotted a young woman about her own age sitting beneath the white umbrella eating a cherry popsicle and looking out to sea. Robin walked over and introduced herself to Alison Diamond, who'd been wondering where her son, Shel, was.

'Are you here for the summer?' Alison asked, after welcoming her new neighbour.

'*I* am. Elliot's an obstetrician in Philadelphia. He'll be down week-ends – well, most week-ends.'

'I'm going to be here mostly on week-ends, too, but I'm on vacation right now, so I'll be around for another week. Would you like to sit? I have a towel –'

'Thanks,' Robin said, dropping to the warm sand in front of Alison, just outside the shade of the umbrella. 'Elliot's asleep already – poor guy's had a tough week. Is your husband with you?'

'I'm a widow –'

'Oh . . . I'm so sorry.'

'Thanks, but it's been nine years,' Alison said. 'I'm here with my son, Shel. He's twelve. He was down by the water a few minutes ago, but he seems to have disappeared.'

'I haven't seen any kids at all.'

'He probably went down a beach or two to find someone to play with. Would you like to walk with me? I'd feel better if I knew where he was.'

And the two walked towards Ventnor in search of Shel, talking the informational chit chat of new found friends.

Alison told Robin about her free-lance writing, and the barest details of her late husband – 'He was an obstetrician, too,' she said. Robin told Alison of her work teaching handicapped children, confiding that they were likely to be the only children she'd ever have.

Children had been the common thread running through both Robin's and Elliot's individual and collective life designs. Both their careers revolved around children, and having children of their own had been a given, an assumption based on their naïve belief that you grow up, get married, have children and live happily ever after. But as the years in special education taught Robin, and the years in obstetrics taught Elliot, conceiving and delivering a relatively normal child is not always the easy, natural process they had expected.

'Children should never be taken for granted,' Robin said to Alison as they walked.

Nodding in agreement, Alison grew more anxious as she found no sign of Shel in the crowds they passed.

'We tried so hard,' Robin continued, quite comfortable by then in Alison's presence, unaware of her companion's unease. 'It's really ironic, because the first few years we were married we didn't want to have a baby. Elliot was still in training and we couldn't afford a family. So we were compulsively careful. You won't believe this, but we actually used double condoms at first – Elliot wouldn't let me take the pill. Resident doctors are so neurotic. They hear all the horror stories. Anyway, when we decided it was time to start a family, nothing happened.'

Alison looked over to Robin, wanting to say something appropriate. 'I'm so sorry,' was all she could muster, feeling tenuously balanced between nosy and politely interested. She wasn't even sure Robin heard her, as Robin continued talking, describing her odyssey through the halls of the fertility experts.

First there were the daily temperature chartings and the ejaculations by appointment. 'You can't imagine the havoc that played with our sex life,' Robin related to a somewhat surprised Alison who was feeling her balanced attention slip towards voyeurism. 'I'd call Elliot at the hospital to tell him my temperature had spiked and that he should come home ... immediately. Of course, he was always in the operating room, or the delivery room ... and then when I'd finally get through to him he'd be annoyed ... and when he'd come home we'd try to make love but we'd be so angry with each other it would be a disaster. And sometimes when we really wanted to make love we'd have to wait for the *right time*. We *used* to think it was *always* the right time to make love!'

Alison laughed, although she was growing ever more uncomfortable with such intimate details from a near stranger, and ever more anxious as they walked further and further from the Tower beach without sighting Shel.

'And then there were the tests. I can't tell you how painful it all was, psychologically as well as physically,' Robin continued, well-entrenched in her case history. 'Elliot had sperm counts, I had endometrial biopsies, x-rays of my ovaries and tubes – you know, they blow air up your tubes and–. Well, it wasn't pleasant. And, after all that, they found nothing wrong,' Robin said to Alison, who was beginning to feel that something was very wrong.

'We even tried artificial insemination,' Robin was saying. '... And there I was with my legs up in the air and ...'

By then, however, Alison's attention was focused on the search for her own lost child, her eyes darting this way and that as panic quickened inside of her. Squinting at the horizon, she felt as if she were peering through the wrong end of a telescope and finding the sea and sky swirling together in a great blue-green eddy swallowing up birds, fish, and little boys out for a swim.

'... but my ova weren't receptive during those gold-plated invitationals, either,' Robin continued, looking to

Alison. But before Robin realised Alison was no longer listening, a splash of cold water on their backs announced the arrival of Shel and an end to her story.

. . . The phone rang. I put my computer down and ran into the apartment to answer. It was Robin. She'd worked her way into quite a funk over Elliot's absence, and was calling to cancel dinner that evening with me and Jeffrey.

'I'm just not good company, Alison. You understand, don't you,' she said.

'Of course, but I really think you'll feel better being with people. I wish you'd come.'

'I don't think so.'

'Well, then, do it for me. I'd rather not be alone with Jeffrey Kaufman. It'll be like a date, and I don't want to put him in that position.'

'You mean *you* don't want to be in that position.'

'I mean I don't want *either* of us to be in that position.'

'God, Alison, you make a date sound like a visit to the dentist.'

'Sometimes I think dentists are less painful.'

'That doesn't surprise me.'

'Robin, something's up. I can hear it in your voice. What's wrong?'

'I'm just upset that Elliot's not coming down.'

'That's all?'

'Maybe the Marjorie Applebaum stuff got to me.'

'What does that have to do with you?'

'Nothing, I guess. It's just that –. Nothing.'

'Try again, Robin,' I said gently, sure that there was something she wanted to tell me.

'Well, do you remember last summer when I told you about Marjorie playing up to Elliot on the beach?'

'Vaguely. You saw her talking to him . . . if that's what you mean.'

'Well?'

'Well, what?' I asked.

'Nothing, really. I guess I'm just being neurotic. Look, let's just have dinner tomorrow night. Okay?'

'Okay,' I said, deciding not to push it. Far be it from me to try and convince someone else not to be neurotic.

After hanging up, I returned to my balcony and my computer . . .

By the summer of 1990, Robin and Elliot had given up hope of having a child . . . and Elliot had all but given up sex. Or so it seemed to Robin, who was becoming alarmed at her husband's waning passion. It wasn't that he loved Robin any less, but once their passion had become a proving ground for procreation, their failure to procreate precipitated his failure to perform. Passion, however, like all energy, does not simply dissipate, it changes. Elliot became passionate about his work. As for Robin . . . well, she found that news of other people's passions insulated her from her own.

It was on a sticky, hot, overcast Saturday afternoon near the end of August that Marjorie Applebaum stopped at the Crystals' pink umbrella to introduce herself to Elliot, who was sitting alone, and to ask the time. He informed her that it was two-twenty, and she informed him that she knew his wife, Robin, and that it was astonishing – and unfortunate – that they hadn't met until that moment, and that she had always admired him from afar – '*You appear so . . . well, so primitive,*' were her exact words, words that affected him deep in his gut, where his manhood met his heart. And when Robin returned from her rounds of the umbrellas, Elliot asked about Marjorie Applebaum – 'Isn't she married to the life-guard?' Sensing danger, wondering why Marjorie Applebaum, who had never made a social overture to *her*, would stop to talk with her husband, Robin didn't tell him of Marjorie's husband's recent departure with Tiffany Kaufman. 'Yes' is all she said, closing the subject. Elliot, however, was intrigued by Marjorie's leech-like lips.

Baking beneath the sun behind his copy of *The Journal of Obstetrics and Gynaecology*, he tried to imagine what Marjorie's lips might feel like sucking on his own ample mouth. And as he began to fall asleep he remembered the time he saw a live leech in an aquarium when he was eleven, and how thoughts of the creature sucking its way up the glass wall of its watery home had excited him sexually, and how, when he told his best friend Mark about it – 'It made my prick hard,' he had said – Mark told him he was weird. But he didn't care if he *was* weird as he lay awake in bed rubbing himself, engrossed in a fantasy of a large, lascivious leech.

On Sunday morning, while Robin flitted from one umbrella to the next, Elliot was once more visited by Marjorie, who was again in need of the time, offering in exchange a half of her peach. Elliot's salivary glands gushed when he bit into the juicy, sweet fruit. As he watched Marjorie devour her half, every other gland in his body began to pump. *It's not that she's pretty,* he thought, *but there's something . . .* , understanding that she chose to visit him when Robin wasn't there, but not really understanding, and not recognising availability and attention for the aphrodisiacs they are.

He was genuinely surprised when early Monday morning he received a phone call in his Philadelphia office from Marjorie Applebaum. He thought he understood when she requested an appointment to see him about an annoying gynaecological problem, but he didn't really understand, a fact that was evidenced by his irritation when she insisted that she see him soon – she was uncomfortable, she said – and at the end of the day – she couldn't miss any work, she said. But out of kindness, neighbourliness, and perhaps a certain *je ne sais quoi* in her voice, he agreed to see her the next day, Tuesday, at five-thirty, momentarily forgetting that the office closed at four-thirty on Tuesdays.

'Ooh, ooh, uuh, ooooh,' moaned Marjorie Applebaum as she lay splayed upon Elliot's examination table beneath a flimsy, light-blue paper gown and sheet, while Elliot's large, but gentle fingers probed her internal organs from within and without.

'I'm sorry if this is uncomfortable,' Elliot apologised, taking her articulations as involuntary expressions of discomfort rather than premeditated signals of passion. 'That's it,' he said, withdrawing gloved fingers from her body, standing up and stepping to Marjorie's side. 'And you'll be happy to hear that I can't find anything wrong, Marjorie. Certainly nothing to explain your pressure-like symptoms.'

'Elliot, I'm so afraid of cancer –'

'Marjorie, please, believe me, I see no evidence of anything at all –'

'My aunt died of breast cancer, and –'

'Your breasts are perfect, Marjorie, no lumps, no bumps, just about as perfect as breasts can be,' Elliot tried to assuage her fears, suddenly aware of how perfect her firm, smooth breasts, in fact, were.

'Maybe you should examine them again . . . just to be sure –'

'Marjorie, trust me, there's nothing –'

'Please. Indulge me. I'm so frightened.'

Elliot, being a truly compassionate man, acquiesced and pulled aside the paper gown. 'If it will make you feel better . . . but, I'm sure –'

'Oh, it *will* make me feel better, Elliot, I –. Oooh, Elliot, my nipple is so sensitive,' she crooned to the good doctor as he squeezed the deep pink bud to be sure no fluid was lurking within.

As much as Elliot tried to remain objective, distanced, the sound of her voice stirred him, the feel of her skin excited him. It had never happened to him before, this sexual connection to a patient, although he had examined hundreds of women, many much more attractive than Marjorie. Aroused and confused, Elliot fled from the room in an attempt to regain his composure. 'I'll be right back, Marjorie. You can get dressed,' he said as he disappeared down the hall to the powder room.

While Elliot splashed cold water on his face, Marjorie wiggled into a more comfortable position on the examination table, pulling the paper sheet higher up her thighs, allowing her knees to spread even further apart while her heels remained nestled in the metal stirrups.

Elliot returned to the examination room after giving Marjorie what he thought was ample time to dress. 'Ready, Marjorie?' he asked, knocking lightly on the door, which was slightly ajar.

'Yes, Elliot.'

Entering the room, Elliot was surprised to find Marjorie still up on the table. He stammered an apology and was about to turn away, to walk back out, when Marjorie called to him. He froze.

'I think I know what the problem is, Elliot,' Marjorie said, extending her hand to him, causing the paper gown to separate in the middle, once again exposing a perfect breast.

Elliot tried to avert his eyes, because, although he looked at breasts all day long, every day, this breast was different. It was not just an anatomical structure of fat and glandular tissue, sometimes prone to cystic formation, occasionally invaded by cancerous growth, it was a living, throbbing amphora of sexuality. It winked at him, called to him from its tiny eye/mouth. It begged to be caressed. Trembling, breaking into a sweat, Elliot obeyed.

'It's okay, Elliot,' Marjorie whispered, reaching up to wipe the beads of perspiration from his forehead with her fingers. And then she ran a salty fingertip along his lips, sliding it into his mouth to meet his tongue.

Elliot practically swooned as he fought a desire to place his own finger between Marjorie's leech-like lips.

'I need relief, Elliot. It's been so long ... I'm all congested,' Marjorie said, pulling the sheet from across her thighs, exposing the rest of her.

Elliot stared at Marjorie through tears of panic. 'What should I do. I don't know what to do. I have to go,' he sputtered, pushing her hand from him. But he stood fast next to the table, a dark mountain of fear and desire, trembling, perspiring, his heart pounding so hard he could hear it in his ears.

'Help me, Elliot. Surely you understand ... all that pressure ... feeling like you're going to explode ...'

His erection straining against his pants, Elliot understood.

'Here, Elliot,' Marjorie said, her hand drawing his eyes downward towards her silky rust triangle as she touched herself. 'Touch me here.'

On anxiety starched legs, he walked to the front of the table, stood between Marjorie's legs and watched as she stroked herself. With one hand he reached out to touch her, with the other he touched himself through his clothes.

'Yes, *yes*,' Marjorie called to him as he caressed her. The sight of her orgasm triggered his own. But even before his spasms had ceased, Elliot was overwhelmed with guilt. He rushed to the powder room once again, turned on the tap, and stood hunched over the basin with his eyes closed, the sound of the rushing water filling his ears as he tried to catch his breath, to still the waves of nausea closing his throat.

There was a rap at the door, and Marjorie's voice. 'Elliot? Are you okay?'

Elliot squeezed his eyes shut tighter and breathed deeply.

'Elliot?'

'I'm fine, Marjorie. I'm fine.'

'I'll wait in your office, okay?'

'Fine, Marjorie. I'm fine,' he said before burying his face in hands full of water. Looking up, he stared at himself in the mirror. 'I'm an animal,' he whispered.

Back in Elliot's office, Marjorie picked up a picture of Robin from the desk and grimaced. 'Jealous bitch,' she addressed the photograph. 'You were all jealous. And who knows how many of you seduced my Doug while I was in the city.'

'Marjorie, I –' Elliot started, walking in.

'Elliot, I was just admiring this picture of Robin. She looks so sweet and –'

'Marjorie, I'm so sorry. I don't know what got into me. I never intended –'

'Oh, Elliot, I'm not sorry,' Marjorie soothed, walking towards him.

But Elliot brushed by her, scooting behind his desk to the safety of his chair.

Sitting across from him, Marjorie continued, 'You've done something special for me, Elliot. When Doug left, I

died inside. Now you've made me feel alive again.'
Marjorie pulled a tissue from the box on Elliot's desk and
dabbed at her eyes.

'I don't know what to say. I –'

'Don't say anything, Elliot. We'll consider this our little
secret. Trust me. I'll never speak of it to anyone.'

'But, Marjorie . . . I don't want you to get the wrong idea.
I love my wife . . . I never intended . . . it's not what you
think –'

'Not another word, Elliot. I understand.' Marjorie
paused and lowered her head, but raised her eyes to meet
Elliot's. 'Thank you, Elliot. I'll never forget how you
touched me.'

Elliot squirmed in his seat, turning his eyes from hers to
the picture of Robin and then to the plastic model of the
female reproductive organs on the table behind Marjorie,
wondering what Marjorie meant by the word *touch*, finding
himself once again aroused, back in the examination room
touching Marjorie's glistening vulva. Dispersing the day-
dream with a visible shake of his head, Elliot stood up. 'I've
got to go, Marjorie. Rounds at the hospital –'

'Of course, Elliot,' Marjorie agreed, standing, opening
her pocketbook and pulling out her keys. 'Oh . . . Elliot,
how much do I owe –'

'No! Marjorie, no. You don't owe me anything.'

'But –,' Marjorie tried, retrieving her wallet, opening it.
'Oh, dear. How embarrassing! I seem to have left the
house without any cash. Will you take a cheque?'

'Marjorie, I said no,' he said, completely mortified at the
idea of taking money from her. 'Consider it professional
courtesy . . . or neighbourly courtesy . . . you're a neighbour . . . a friend –'

'You're such a dear, Elliot. Actually, since you're being
so nice about this . . . well, I just realised that I need cash to

pay the parking lot. This really is embarrassing . . . but do you suppose you could lend me –'

'How much, Marjorie? How much do you need?' Elliot asked, taking his wallet from his pants pocket, ripping a fifty dollar bill from it, and then another. 'Is this enough? I mean, you shouldn't drive around the city without any money.'

Marjorie took the two bills from Elliot and tucked them in her wallet. 'You are *such* a kind man. I'll pay you back soon, I promise.'

'Don't worry about it. Just consider us even . . . after what happened and all . . . and –'

'Well, I've got to go, now. I have an engagement,' Marjorie said, cutting Elliot short. And she walked out of his private office, out of his suite of offices.

Elliot followed her to the hall and watched as she walked to the elevators, waited with her back to him until the lift reached their floor, and then turned to blow him a kiss.

In the elevator, Marjorie leaned against the back rail and watched the numbers above the elevator door tick off *3 . . . 2 . . . 1 . . .*

'SHIT!' Elliot exploded, shutting the door to his waiting room. Sitting on a sofa, he let his head fall back acutely and stared at the ceiling. Tears ran from the corners of his eyes into his ears. 'I'm an animal,' he whispered with remorse . . . but not enough remorse to wash away the feel of Marjorie Applebaum's satiny flesh from the tips of his fingers.

'I don't know what it is,' Robin confided to Alison beneath her white umbrella the following Saturday morning, 'but something isn't right with Elliot.'

Alison, who'd been listening only half-heartedly to Robin's stream of consciousness about her reflections on one neighbour or another, opened her eyes and focused on her friend. There was a different quality to Robin's speech when she spoke of personal things. Unlike Robin's comments on others' lives, comments on her own life were quieter, more thoughtful.

'Something's happened this week, Alison. I don't know what, but I know something's happened to Elliot.'

'I don't understand, Robin. Do you mean physically, or what?'

'I know this sounds odd, but I don't *know* what.'

'So what makes you think anything's happened?'

'The way he sounds on the phone. We're very close, and I can tell when something's disturbing him.'

'Maybe he's just tired. Has he been up with a lot of deliveries?'

'No, no. It's not that. He seems distracted. He couldn't wait to get off the phone when we spoke last night. Usually on a Friday night when he's facing a week-end alone we talk a long time on the phone. And sometimes we even play.'

'Play?'

'You know . . . *play*.'

'Give me a hint.'

'*You* know . . . phone sex.'

Alison bit her lip over Robin's candid disclosure.

'Oh, God! I've embarrassed you, haven't I?'

'No, of course not. You just take me by surprise sometimes.'

'Yes you are embarrassed, Alison. You're blushing!'

'*Now* you're embarrassing me. So get on with it. So last night Elliot had to get off the phone quickly and you feel rejected.'

'Elliot didn't *have* to get off the phone. That's the problem. He *wanted* to get off the phone. Of course I feel rejected! Something's happened.'

'What?' Alison asked impatiently.

'I don't *know* what. I *told* you that.'

Both ladies closed their eyes and the conversation stopped.

'Do you do that often?' Alison broke the silence a few minutes later.

'What?' Robin answered coolly.

'The phone thing . . . with Elliot.'

'Now and then. Have you ever done it?'

'No.'

'You should try it. You'd like it.'

'Well, I haven't had much opportunity. Actually, I've never given it much thought.' Pause. 'Shel brought it up once.'

'That doesn't surprise me.'

'Well it surprised me . . . that I heard about it from my baby.'

'He's not a baby.'

'Anyway. He's always teasing me about dating, and . . . well, he once said that I'd never let any man closer to me than the telephone . . .'

'That doesn't surprise me.'

'. . . and,' Alison continued, ignoring Robin's comment, 'that's when he went into this long story about a friend who had a long distance telephone relationship with a girl for almost a month last year – she was a freshman in college somewhere out west. And how it ended when his father got the phone bill and his friend had to get a part-time job to pay it off. But that it was worth it because it was the best sex he'd ever had. Probably the *only* sex, I told him.'

'And what did Shel say?'

'I don't remember.'

'Alison, trust me, high school boys do it.'

'That's what he said.'

'I'm not surprised.'

'I'd rather not think about it.'

'That doesn't surprise me, either.'

'Will you kindly stop being not surprised.'

Silence.

And then, 'I'm beginning to think that . . . well, maybe Elliot's having an affair,' Robin said quietly.

'Elliot? An affair? Robin, you don't really believe that, do you?'

'I don't know what to believe.'

'He acts weird for a week and you imagine he's having an affair?'

'It's not just that . . . not just that he's acting weird this week.'

'What else?'

'He's been . . . well . . . impotent. It's been months now –'

'But you said . . . the telephone –'

'That's different. We can do *that* . . . but that's all we've been doing. At first I thought it was the baby thing –'

'The baby thing?'

'Okay. The *infertility* thing . . .' Robin said, irritated at Alison's apparent insensitivity.

Alison sunk back in her chair and squeezed her eyes shut. She wanted to bite her tongue off.

'. . . but now I'm beginning to think maybe there's someone else.'

'Oh, no, Robin. I'm sure there isn't anyone –'

'Now what could you possibly know about *that*?' Robin snapped.

By the following summer Elliot's guilt, along with his impotency, had attenuated with each successive act of infidelity with Marjorie Applebaum. Not so Robin's worries. And the week-end following the death of Marjorie

Applebaum threw Robin further into the throes of suspicion and self-doubt when Elliot failed to show up at the Tower, presenting one excuse after another. By Sunday evening Robin was in a definite funk and called Alison to cancel their dinner plans.

. . . I hit the save key on my laptop and listened as the whirring sound assured me that my narrative – fictitious answers to real questions – was being recorded in a file marked *Pink*, under the *Beach Book-91* directory.

Yes, I thought, for the second time that day, *even in the best of marriages. Questions.* In real life, however, questions weren't so glibly answered. And sometimes it appeared there were no answers. I firmly believed, however, that every question in life had an answer.

There'd been questions in my marriage, which, I'd assumed, was neither the best nor the worst of marriages. Of course, I'd had little to compare it to. Few of my friends (who were few in number to begin with) had married, and Carl and I never socialised with those that had. In fact, we'd hardly socialised at all, outside of some functions associated with Carl's practice, and the occasional evening with Phil Krausen. Why was that? I now wondered.

It could be that our first year together was spent adjusting to a precipitous marriage, and preparing for and having a baby – Shel, a wonder that totally absorbed our second and third years in a sense of awe and fulfillment. During our fourth year, Carl was adjusting to the deceit of adultery, and I to the loneliness of it. And then Carl died. Perhaps that's the answer. Perhaps not.

Perhaps it's also the answer to the question of the paucity of conjugal socialisation – our lovemaking, that is. At the time I assumed that our spare sex life was normal, believing Carl when he'd said I was 'over-sexed'. It seemed to go along nicely with my father's assessment of 'overly sensitive' and 'over-emotional'.

'Don't you love me?' I'd asked Carl one night when Shel was two months old, and I was restless, and we hadn't made love since months before Shel was born.

'Of course I love you,' Carl had answered. 'I wouldn't have married you if I didn't love you. Not after thirty-four years of bachelorhood.'

It's interesting how answers often provoke more questions.

'Why did you stay single so long?' I'd asked.

'I took my time and waited for the best,' he'd replied, kissing me on the forehead.

I don't recall whether it was his chaste kiss or his answer that made me feel unworthy of both, I only remember the burn of shame. Looking back, perhaps a more truthful answer would have been that he'd waited for the most naïve.

As I sat staring at the blank computer screen I wondered why I'd been so naïve. According to my son, and to Robin, I was still naïve. I wondered, too, if that were true, if that were possible. Naïvety, after all, implies a certain innocence, and I certainly didn't consider myself innocent. I was forty, a single mother out in the world of dating (if only occasionally), and, although known as Alison Diamond the medical journalist, I was also Sloan I. Diamond, writer of popular, but questionably proper fiction. Surely I'd lost my innocence long ago. How long ago was another question, one I pondered as I created a line of ????????s on the blank screen before putting my laptop aside and dressing for dinner with Jeffrey.

CHAPTER 6

White

Contrary to Sunday's late news weather predictions, Monday turned out to be a perfect beach day. The hot July air had given way to a cool sea breeze that blew away the early morning haze along with every cloud. I'd allowed myself the luxury of sleeping late, so by the time I finished my morning coffee and slipped into a bathing suit it was almost ten-thirty. Peering down at the beach from my front balcony, I watched the laser show of sunlight flashing off the surf. On the brilliant white stage below, only a few colourful umbrellas were set, the characters were just beginning to take their places.

Monday mornings at the beach were usually quiet. Spouses and guests had left for the city or elsewhere, apartments were being straightened, pantries re-stocked. I especially enjoyed Monday mornings, and this Monday in particular, because, for the first time since Thursday, when I'd played hooky from work, I felt centred. No headache, no queasiness, no dizziness. My head was as clear, as uncluttered as the sky. Secure in my relief, I gazed down at the beach, searching for the pink disk that was Robin's umbrella. It wasn't there. I could just make out Jeffrey's dark body spilling over his lounge a foot or two in front of his yellow umbrella, and I thought about the evening before – the hard shell crabs and seasoned french fries at Barney's Steampot, and the long walk on the boardwalk back to the Tower . . .

Barney's was located in downtown Atlantic City – that is, just two blocks inland from the tinselled coast of casinos that I never entered, considering the glitz and din of those gambling establishments offensive to eye and ear and painfully disruptive of my childhood memories of Atlantic City.

Although the area surrounding Barney's had changed – adjacent buildings had been torn down or boarded up – inside was still a noisy, warm place of gathering for the long-time residents of the area, both seasonal and year-round.

'Did you come to Atlantic City when you were a child?' I had asked Jeffrey while wrestling a crab claw.

'All the time. Mom would pack a picnic and we'd leave early in the morning, and sit on the beach up by Convention Hall, near the public bathrooms.'

'I've never quite got the hang of these things,' I said, twisting off the long spindly legs of the crab before me, searching for a morsel of something edible.

Jeffrey laughed and pulled my plate across the table. 'Like this,' he said, cracking the creature in half, gleaning chunks of meat from the split carcass with a small fork.

'You make it look so easy.'

'Did you say your son is leaving for school soon?' Jeffrey asked.

I plucked an oyster cracker from the glass jar in the middle of the table and topped it with Barney's famous extra hot horseradish. Stuffing the whole thing into my mouth at once, I couldn't answer Jeffrey's question. When tears began to run down my reddened face we both laughed and I thought the question was forgotten.

'Alison, I want you to know that if you ever want to talk to me, about anything, I'm a good listener,' Jeffrey said after we were composed, and I understood that the question wasn't forgotten. 'Listening is my business, you know.'

I picked silently at my crab.

'Most of my clients aren't crazy ... just going through some tough changes.'

I continued to pick.

'Some are even people you know ... from the Tower,' he continued, trying to win my confidence.

I bit. 'Like who?' I asked.

'Well, you know I can't name names, but one couple was having a bad time when the husband retired, and I'd like to think I had some part in helping them through it. You know, losses, even happy ones like retirement or sending kids to college, can cause all kinds of unexpected complications.'

'I know, Jeffrey, but I'm fine. Really,' I said, trying hard to believe it.

After dinner and more small talk spiced only with the horseradish, we walked home. Ever mindful of the old days, I was always disappointed when I walked past the movie-set skyline of new buildings on the boardwalk. The small shops, and grand hotels of the old days had given way to the outlandish architecture and tacky presence of the casinos.

'Remember how the kids hung out on the boardwalk in front of the Chelsea and the Ambassador?' I asked Jeffrey.

'And the old people who sat in the rolling chairs parked along the rail? Well, they seemed old at the time. I guess a lot of them were our age,' Jeffrey added his own memories.

The wicker chairs resembling giant baby strollers pushed by strong, quiet men had disappeared from the boardwalk for a while, having been replaced by electric carts and trams. But they'd made a comeback in recent years, painted white and pushed by aggressive boys who shamelessly intimidated elderly boardwalkers for business. What I remembered most about the chairs, however, were the rides in them with my cousin Evy, and my grandmother, who, on even the warmest of evenings, wore an ancient mink coat that reeked of moth balls.

'Did you go to Steele Pier?' Jeffrey was asking as I emerged from my musings, a question that threw me back again.

Extending more than a city block into the Ocean, the Steele Pier was a city in itself, holding something for everybody. One fee admitted you into the main building with its several movie theatres, ballroom, and stage shows where famous performers made their rounds.

Also on the pier were amusement rides, and game arcades where we lost our allowance to the lure of stuffed animals as big as ourselves. And there was the diving bell that carried groups of people, like seeds in a pomegranate, to the floor of the ocean to view the flora and fauna of the briny deep. When I was about eight, Evy's twin brother Larry persuaded me to take the short journey in the bell, promising a Jules Verne adventure of glassy water and exotic, technicolour fish. I remembered feeling smothered by the people packed closely in the iron sphere, and all I saw through the dirty windows was murky water and strands of green slime. All I experienced was panic. Larry taunted me for days after the bell's trip was cut short by my cries of terror.

A less traumatic memory was of Steele Pier's legendary

diving horse. Poised on a tiny platform sixty feet above the water was a horse mounted by a beautiful lady. I remembered the crowds of people tightly packed on the wooden deck supported by pilings coated with slippery algae, tiny crustaceans and smelly tar. I remembered the emcee, and his long introduction, about the thrill and the spectacle, the danger and the courage. I remembered how impossibly long the wait to the good part seemed . . . and how short the good part was. It was breathtaking, watching the horse leave the platform. And then it was over in a splash, barely before it had begun. When I was a child, I felt that way about a lot of life's promises. As I grew older, I found that things didn't go much differently, except that the introductions got shorter.

I remembered the freak show along a corridor in the main building – a woman with a beard and the skin of a reptile, a man with half a face, a man the size of two men – victims of nature's cruel sense of humour. I remembered feeling horrified by them, and embarrassed by my horror.

And there was the funhouse – a building within the main building. The face of a laughing clown was mounted over the entrance to a long, narrow, twisty hall that faded into total darkness. Feeling our way along the hall like blind mice, we'd eventually find ourselves in one of the brightly lit perception bending chambers. First there was the room where everything, including the floor and ceiling, was tilted. Only the people were upright. But I always felt like the room was right and I was wrong. And there was the room of mirrors where I'd lose my sense of balance again, along with my sense of self as I vainly searched the distorting mirrors for a true image.

'Remember the funhouse?' I asked Jeffrey.

'The funhouse?'

'The one on Steele Pier. I had no idea when I was little

that it was a peek into life's bag of tricks.'

'You lost me, Alison. What I remember about Steele Pier is the smell of cotton candy and peanuts,' Jeffrey said, jumping over my morass of memories and back into his own. 'It was like a summer-long circus. I used to get excited just seeing the long beams from the pier's arc lights sweeping the sky.'

'My cousin Larry used to tell me and his sister Evy that they were searching for planes that were coming to bomb us. We believed him.'

'A bit sadistic, wasn't he?'

'Aren't all little boys?'

'Do you think so?'

'Some big boys, too.'

'Should I take that personally?' Jeffrey asked with a sheepish smile.

'No, no. I'm sorry, Jeffrey. I don't know why I said that.'

'So, tell me more about your family.'

'There were just my parents, my grandmother Ellis – my father's mother – and my cousin Evy's family.'

'Are you close to your parents?'

'They live in Florida. I don't see them very often, which makes them crazy, but keeps me sane,' I said coolly, a reaction I thought ironic, considering my father's opinion of my emotional constitution – that is, bordering on hysterical – having little grasp of his own emotions, let alone mine. The only child of adoring, if fearful parents who were unaware that they couldn't protect me from everything evil in the world, let alone from themselves, I was always well scrubbed, if misunderstood.

'So I guess you're not close,' Jeffrey said.

'No . . . yes . . . Actually, I don't know why I said that. It's not that we aren't close, it's just that I don't think my parents understand me. My psyche's a bit clichéd, isn't it?'

Jeffrey smiled.

'I felt close to my grandmother when she was living, but she died years ago.'

'She understood you?'

'Probably not, but she was non-judgemental.'

'Your parents are judgemental?'

'My mother, mostly. I guess she means well.' Pause. 'She's been especially vocal about my single status. "A woman needs a husband . . . a boy needs a father," she says. Actually, she says it almost every time I speak to her. I don't even talk to her about my social life any more, because, if I mention a man, even casually, she's ready to send out wedding invitations.'

'Sounds like a nice Jewish mother.'

'I suppose . . . ,' I agreed half-heartedly, understanding that there was a lot Jeffrey didn't understand, but unwilling to get into it, probably not really understanding myself. '. . . But I was telling you about my grandmother. I remember the summer weeks I spent with her in Atlantic City as the most carefree of my life. We'd sit on the sun porch after lunch and watch the sky. I wasn't allowed on the beach for an hour after I ate. She was afraid I'd go into the water – cramps, you know. Anyway, she'd point out the different kinds of clouds, then I'd imagine them to be all kinds of things, and she'd make up the most wonderful stories.'

Jeffrey laughed. 'The romantic's Rorschach test. I did that when I was a kid.'

'I still do.'

'How about your cousins?'

'I don't see them,' I said, turning sullen.

'Well, I can understand why you're not interested in cousin Larry –'

'And you don't even know the half of it.'

'Oh? What became of him?'

'I'm not sure. He got into some kind of trouble in high school, although I hadn't seen him for a couple of years. Cheating on a test, I was told. And then he was sent to a military academy. Again, that was what I was told. I'm sure it wasn't the truth. My family was big on secrets. There were rumours in my school about a boy who'd been expelled from another high school for doing naughty *things* to little girls. I don't know why I'd thought it was Larry at the time, but I clearly remember thinking that.'

'And Evy? It sounds like you were friends,' Jeffrey said after a moment.

'Evy's dead.'

'I'm sorry.'

'When she was fifteen, she jumped from the Tacony Palmyra bridge late one night in the middle of February. It was below freezing. It was horrible,' I related quietly, precisely.

'Why did she do it?'

'I don't know. She was with an older boy. They were coming back from Atlantic City, from our grandmother's summer house – Evy had taken my aunt's key. Apparently they'd gone there to be alone. Evy was, well, she was a little promiscuous. At any rate, on the way home she made him stop in the middle of the bridge. She said she was going to throw up. But she didn't throw up . . . she jumped.'

My heart was pounding by the time I'd finished relating the story, and I must have looked pretty shaken because Jeffrey put his arm around me.

'What a terrible story,' he said. 'I'm so very sorry, Alison. I didn't mean to upset you by asking so many questions. It's not really my business. Occupational hazard, I suppose.'

I smiled at his concern.

'I'm sure it was a big loss for you, but it was . . . what . . . twenty? twenty-five years ago? That's a long time. And time heals all wounds,' he soothed.

'Not all,' I said, pulling away from him.

'Why do I get the feeling that something else is upsetting you, something more recent?'

'Like what?' I asked obtusely.

'Like another loss, perhaps?'

'Like . . . my son's leaving for college at the end of the summer,' I confessed.

. . . Looking down at Jeffrey's yellow umbrella the following morning, I remembered telling him how surprised I was that I was so upset about Shel's leaving, and that I'd been getting these odd dizzy spells and that Robin had suggested that maybe they were psychosomatic . . . and I smiled as I remembered his smile of indulgence at Robin's unprofessional opinion . . . and how he tactfully hadn't commented.

The yellow disk blurred as tears suddenly welled up in my eyes, and then the whole beach blurred. And as centred as I'd felt only a moment before, I now sensed my gyroscope shifting, tilting, the world spinning out around me in a kind of ellipse. The yellow disk shot up and struck me in the eye – or was it a beam off the surf? – and I reeled backwards, stumbling on to my lounge. My heart racing, my skin burning, I laid back for a few moments staring at the sky, trying to focus on a puff of cloud resembling a fairy tale castle. I wanted to be on that cloud, beyond my spinning world. Feeling the bite of panic, I left my balcony, threw a sweatshirt and shorts over my bathing suit and took to the supermarket, to keep busy, to be amongst busy people, to outrun my anxiety.

By the afternoon, having relaxed somewhat, I went to the

beach to salvage what I could of the perfect day.

'Thanks,' I said to the young man who planted my white umbrella in the sand. As I pressed two quarters into his hand, I thought he gave my hand a slight squeeze. But before I had a chance to consider the gesture, Robin appeared, oiled and red from an hour in the sun, and covered with a light dusting of sand deposited by gusts of cooling sea air.

'It's been positively gorgeous, Alison,' she said. 'Where've you been?'

'Shopping.'

'On a Monday? your favourite beach day?'

'I know. But I was feeling a little off this morning.'

'Dizzy again?'

'Yes, but it's gone now,' I lied, hoping the sickening feeling, like an evil imp, would leave me if I ignored it.

'You really *should* see someone.'

'I will. But I'm fine now, really.'

'So. How was dinner last night . . . with Jeffrey?' Robin asked, settling herself on the warm sand in front of my chair.

'We went to Barney's for hardshells. It was crowded and good, as usual –'

'I'm not really interested in the restaurant review, Alison. How was Jeffrey?'

'What do you mean "*How was Jeffrey?*"?'

'You know what I mean. Was he a good date?'

'He wasn't a date. We were *all* supposed to have dinner together, but you finked out.'

'I was in a funk.'

'I know. So how come you weren't home when I called you when I got in from dinner?'

'I was visiting the Steiners.'

'Isn't Maggie in the city?'

114

'Uh-huh. I just stopped in to see Marty. I guess I needed company.'

'And we wouldn't do?'

'That was earlier . . . when I didn't want company.'

'Well, you're chipper enough this morning. What did you and Marty talk about?'

'Actually, I spoke to Elliot.'

'He called this morning?'

'Last night, about midnight.'

'He's coming down?'

'Not until the week-end. But we had a very satisfying chat.'

'A little phone sex?' I asked without thinking.

'Alison! I can't believe that came from your lips!'

'God! I'm sorry, Robin. I only meant –' I started to explain, knowing that I couldn't really explain how I'd mixed her up with the fictitious Robin in my story.

'My dear, you've been holding out on me.'

'Well, I haven't had any personal experience, but –'

'Why not?' Robin asked, definitely teasing.

'It's not one of my great ambitions in life, Robin.'

'Alison, pardon my bluntness, but don't you ever get horny?'

I was nonplussed by Robin's bluntness.

'Well, in any case, I thought of you this morning,' Robin continued without waiting for my answer. 'I was looking through one of Elliot's medical magazines – a special issue on human sexuality – and I read about some futurist who predicted that by the year 2020 you won't have to date to get sex, you'll be able to buy a sex robot.'

'And you thought of me?'

'Think about it, Alison. We both know how you love to date.'

'Well, by the year 2020 I'll be too old to be horny.'

'Alison, you're *never* too old – look at Chankin the Shark.'

We both laughed and then fell quiet.

Covered with varying degrees of sunscreen, I laid beneath the comforting heat for another hour or so, buoyed by the rhythmic sounds of the sea, drifting in and out of rememberings . . .

Don't you ever get horny? echoed in my head as I remembered how horny I was for months after my husband had died, and how hot showers, cold showers, and rabid sessions of masturbation – followed by inexonerable guilt – did little to alleviate my passionate longings. How odd that time was, I thought, considering my nearly celibate marriage. Or perhaps that was the 'why' of it. With Carl's death came at least the possibility of a normal sexual relationship with a man, although the idea of normal remained undefined for me. I'd written the first story of *Appetizers* during this time. In a way, I suppose one could view the entire collection as an attempt to define the boundaries of sexual relationships. The heroines of the stories were, of course, modelled after myself in my own *first* sexual experiences with various lovers (some real, but most figments of my imagination born of lust or curiosity, or both) written as if each time was *the* first time. Indeed, whenever I'd embarked upon a sexual relationship – actual or imaginary – it was from the perspective of a virgin.

I was in fact a virgin when Carl and I had our first sexual encounter, an encounter which immediately resulted in the conception of my son Shel, and, later, spawned the first story in *Appetizers*. The first paragraph of that tale, like the experience mirrored in it, is indelibly imprinted in my memory . . .

Pricilla Perkins, television chef of local renown, would

never pull a pot roast from the oven again without feeling the hot rush of sexual excitement tear through her body. Every time she'd glimpse the blue and white checkered pot holder mittens hanging innocently from their hook by the stove, she'd blush. For Pricilla, pot holders had taken on a whole new meaning.

... After I'd written them, the lines became a hot wire, their recollection evoking the confusing mix of apprehension, passion and guilt that I'd experienced the first time Carl made love to me. Although *I* was unrecognisable as Pricilla Perkins in the story (for one thing, my only success in the kitchen is my spaghetti sauce), I hadn't done much to disguise Carl. After all, he was already dead when I wrote it, so I figured my betrayal of our intimacy didn't matter.

Unfortunately the situation with David Lawrence, a man who I'd redefined in a later book, was otherwise. In fact, my relationship with David was *otherwise* in more ways than one. Because, though it wasn't my first relationship since Carl had died, it was the first that counted, and because, despite a couple of false starts at intimacy, like with Phil Krausen, by my second year of widowhood, sex with a man was the exception, not the rule.

I met David Lawrence at a Parents Without Partners meeting, which I'd attended at the urging of my mother. It was a *safe* place to meet men who were interested in family and looking for marriage, she'd said – *not* looking for sex, she'd meant. There were some very nice people there ... mostly very nice women. But David Lawrence, an attractive professor of archaeology, was there, too, and our subsequent year-long relationship – the longest relationship I'd ever had with a man either before or after Carl's death – ended up fictionalised in *The Patient Cried Wolf*, my novel about Leslie Dean, a commercial airline pilot suffering from Munchausen's syndrome, a psychiatric condition leading to unnecessary hospitalisations and surgeries – the last word in hypochondria. After falling in love with his psychiatrist, Dr Madelaine Lovejoy, Leslie takes her away to an island in the South Pacific. There he dies of Botulism poisoning when Madelaine, convinced he is having a relapse of his medical obsession, refuses to believe his symptoms are real. *'Were you breast-fed as a baby?'* are the last words he hears before dying.

Actually, the only part of my relationship with David that I borrowed for my book was a portion of our first sexual encounter, when I'd discovered the many legitimate surgical scars on his body. I was fascinated by those erose reminders of organs in revolution – his appendix, gall bladder, kidney, heart. I'd touched each one, kissed each one in a gesture of empathy, caring, a gesture that impassioned us both . . .

As Madelaine ran her fingers over the scars mapping his body, she was held in thrall by their depth, both physical and psychological. Her heart broke at the sight of those erose reminders of emotional trauma. Leslie carefully explained in vivid detail the history of each – the elaborate story he'd presented to the doctor, the tests, the diagnosis, the surgical procedure memorialised in the scar – while she interpreted his psyche through the gnarled, purple lines on his flesh. It was like reading Braille, she thought. Overwhelmed by his pain, Madelaine held him close to her, promising silently to take care of him, to protect him from further hurt, from himself.

'And now you,' Leslie said, pulling away from her. Whereupon he began a meticulous, but tender examination of her body, finding a myriad of tiny imperfections, pointing out each as his fingers discovered it. 'Here,' he said, taking her finger, touching it to a barely perceptible indentation left on her forehead by chicken pox. He then soothed her brow with his hand, kissed the tiny scar, licked it with his tongue. 'And here,' he said, guiding her finger to her right breast where he'd found another pockmark. He then caressed, kissed, tasted that delicately marred flesh. 'And here,' he said, slipping her hand over a pencil point of a mole on her right flank. 'You can't be too careful about moles,' he said, kissing the dark dot, gently nipping at the skin surrounding it. And he worked his way down and around her body to her navel – 'God's scar,' he called it – to her sex. 'Here,' he said, moving her fingers into that warm, moist flesh. 'A splendid wound. Feel how it swells . . . and weeps.'

Madelaine followed him into his fantasy as he bent over her to kiss, to heal her *wound*.

. . . Of course nothing about David was in my novel, except for the scars that I'd found so fascinating, so very attractive that I felt compelled to memorialise them. But David, close to hysteria, called me a few months after the book's publication, accusing me of attacking him at a most personal level, of embarrassing him before the world. He'd picked up a copy of the book in a hotel gift shop, in a strange city where he'd gone to lecture. When he'd read that very passage from *The Patient Cried Wolf*, he was struck by similarities between himself and Leslie, and it didn't take him long to decode the anagram of Sloan I. Diamond.

I'd tried to explain how Leslie was not him, how Madelaine was not me, how the plot and the characters were totally made up, and how I'd used that small piece of our time together because I'd been affected by it, that it had left impressions with me that had to do not only with our world, but with other worlds that had nothing to do with him. 'No one could ever know any part of it was you,' I'd insisted.

'But the scars!' he cried.

'Many men are scarred,' I said.

And how could I explain why I'd used the name *Leslie Dean*, which, like his own name, consisted of two first names. And, he'd carefully detailed, I'd used his initials, inverted.

'Surely an unconscious gesture, but not a distinguishing one,' I tried to explain, stung by conscience.

'And why did you make Leslie an airline pilot?'

'Because it was a far cry from an archaeologist.'

'But I have a pilot's licence,' he'd said, his voice cracking with the pain of disillusionment. 'Making Leslie a pilot was simply the final blow!'

Now that was pure coincidence – if coincidence can ever be pure. I never knew about his pilot's licence. In fact, when I'd known him, he was afraid to fly. 'You took trains anywhere you'd go to lecture,' I'd pleaded my innocence.

'I got my licence to cure me of my phobia,' he'd said. And then, 'I may be a little neurotic, but you made me into a freak.'

'Life isn't necessarily stranger than fiction,' I'd said, 'but it's certainly more ironic.' It was an off-hand comment that did nothing to ease his hurt, which hurt me . . . because I'd cared for him and couldn't imagine myself capable of hurting him. Yet I'd wounded him, and nothing I could say would erase that scar.

. . . Fantasy, like reality, can be a hazardous business, I was thinking as the crash of a great wave doused my rememberings and I opened my eyes to an ice-cream vendor standing above me, blocking my sun.

'One ice-cream sandwich,' he said, handing Robin the frozen block in exchange for a dollar.

'Have a nice nap?' Robin asked me. 'I'm off to do a few errands.'

'Guess I must have dozed off,' I said, stretching. 'I'm going to stick around for a bit. See you tomorrow.'

A few minutes later I was alone, licking the last of a fudge-bar from my fingers, when I heard my name called. Looking around, I saw Lieutenant Fiori heading towards me, jacket and shoes in hand.

'Mrs Diamond, I was hoping I'd find you here,' he said, stopping in front of me. 'The concierge at the Tower suggested you might still be on the beach. Can I talk to you a minute?'

'Of course, Lieutenant, is anything wrong?' I asked, concerned, but not too concerned to recognise my pleasure in seeing the Lieutenant again.

'I wanted to ask you about Friday morning . . . when you were on the balcony.'

'I thought I told you all I knew.'

'I know, and you were very helpful. But I thought maybe we missed something. I've talked to a lot of people since Friday morning, Mrs Diamond, and nobody seems to know anything. I'm kind of counting on you to help me get a handle on this case.'

'I don't know how I can help any more, Lieutenant.'

'Well . . . would you mind if I sat down?'

'Please,' I said, handing him a towel.

Setting the towel across from me, the Lieutenant sat down, laid his jacket and shoes next to him and turned up the sleeves of his shirt. 'Beautiful day, isn't it? By the way, I couldn't help but notice the laptop computer on your balcony the other day. Sure is a nice place to work. Great view. You should see my office. I don't even have a window.'

'I guess that's one of the biggest advantages of being a writer. I can take my work anywhere.'

'I saw an article of yours a few weeks ago in *The Inquirer* . . . about aspirin and heart attacks. I noticed it because my father's been on aspirin since his heart attack three years ago.'

'How do you know I wrote it?'

'I remember your byline. I notice things like that, sticks right to me. I don't know why,' he said, tilting his face towards the sun.

'So what can I tell you, Lieutenant?'

'Anything you can remember about Friday morning, or about Marjorie Applebaum. You told me that you didn't know her very well. Is that right?'

Sitting there in the afternoon sun, relaxed by the sound of the surf and the smell of salt, flattered by his attentiveness, I wanted to be his muse, so I almost told him the rumours linking Jeffrey and Marty to Marjorie, but all I said was, 'Right, I didn't know her very well.'

'Have you heard anything about her private life since her husband left? Specifically, do you have any knowledge about a relationship between Marjorie Applebaum and Dr Jeffrey Kaufman? He's a neighbour of yours.'

'No, I have no knowledge of such a relationship,' I said honestly, still choosing not to offer my knowledge of a *rumour* of a relationship. There was no need; obviously someone had already done that.

He paused, and then asked, 'Where else are you published, other than *The Inquirer*?'

'A few health and science magazines, and some women's magazines,' I answered, glad that he'd changed the subject.

'Anything coming up soon that I could look for?'

'I don't think you'd be interested in male pattern baldness,' I said, looking at his thick, curly black hair.

'Believe it or not, my father is almost totally bald. And during the summer he shaves off what's left. He looks like Kojak. And look at me. I have hair like my mother's. Funny, isn't it?'

'Actually, you inherit balding from your mother's genes, not your father's.'

'I didn't know that. It's what I love about this job, Mrs Diamond. You learn something new every day.'

'Glad I could help with something,' I said, surprised by a desire to run my hand through the Lieutenant's tangled mop.

'Well, I'd better be going,' he said, standing up, running his own hand through his hair, pulling the stray locks back, revealing a widow's peak. 'I'll let you know if I need to speak to you again. Is that alright?' he asked.

'Sure, Lieutenant.' And I watched as he walked away, towards the boardwalk, not understanding why he'd come, or what he'd accomplished, but expecting him to turn around and come back with just one more question, like the frumpy television detective, Columbo. He did, in fact, resemble the Peter Falk character, I thought, but taller . . . and younger. Although Fiori wasn't wearing Columbo's signature rumpled raincoat, his shirt was satisfactorily wrinkled.

I moved my chair around, out of the sun, sat back down, closed my eyes, and pictured Fiori's fingers in his hair . . . my fingers in his hair. I could feel the touch of his hand, the softness of his hair, and something inside me stirred. It was lust. Although surprised by its appearance – surely the Lieutenant wasn't my type – I was grateful. It made me feel alive.

Lolled by the heat, the sound of the sea, I tried to picture Fiori's arms about me, but I only got as far as his widow's peak floating somewhere above me, before I left the present. And then Ira Pressman surfaced in my memory . . .

I'd met Ira in the supermarket. At the condom display. It had been thirteen years since Carl had died, and three years since I'd had a physical relationship with a man – when I found myself standing in front of a rack of condoms while doing grocery shopping for my month-long vacation at the Ivory Tower. I hadn't thought about purchasing those pointedly male articles before, having left that responsibility to males, but I'd begun to preach in earnest to Shel about the need for safe sex (although I was sure my son, at sixteen, wouldn't need such information for . . . well, for a long time), and as I've always held hypocrisy in the highest contempt, I decided that I had to have condoms in *my* bedroom. Just in case.

It was a different world, I thought, contemplating the selection of condoms next to the aspirin and antacids, just an aisle away from the condiments, canned peas, and rolled filets of anchovies. When I was growing up, condoms were hidden behind the counters in drugstores. The buying of those sexually explicit devices had been a teenage boy's Rite of Passage – confronting the stern druggist (a dragon guarding his lair) a deed of bravery rewarded by the esteem of his peers and a badge of honour to moulder in his wallet. And no one called them condoms. They were rubbers.

So there I was confronted with a myriad of colourful boxes promising sensitivity, strength, security, amusing myself with the notion that men who advertised in the 'personals' columns probably plagiarised their ads from boxes of prophylactics. Smiling, lost in myself, I was startled by a man's voice: 'I'd give almost anything to know what you're thinking right now.'

My amusement turned to embarrassment as I attempted an unnecessary explanation of my presence in what I still considered to be a male domain. 'My husband died . . . you see . . . well, as a good Girl Scout, I must be prepared,' I sputtered to the tall gentleman who had addressed me.

'Isn't that a coincidence! I was a Boy Scout . . . a long time ago,' he replied, his warm, open smile easing my mortification, allowing me to bring him into focus, the attractive man with the jet black widow's peak.

'I'm sorry,' I apologised, 'I can't imagine what you must think of me. I was just –'

'And so was I. Need any help?'

'Well, there are so many, and I have no idea –'

Reaching up, he plucked two boxes from a hook and dropped one into my cart. 'I think you'll find these satisfactory. Scouts' honour,' he said displaying the Scouts' two-fingered hand signal. 'And if I can be of further assistance . . . ,' he added, offering me a business card retrieved from the pocket of his tweed jacket.

Smiling hesitantly, I took the card from him. 'Thank you, Ira Pressman, M.D.,' I said, reading from it.

'Any time,' he replied, extending his hand.

After a brief handshake, I smiled, then pushed my cart by him and headed for the fruits and vegetables.

It was at the deli counter that we met again. As I reached up to take a numbered ticket, his hand got there first. I turned and saw Ira Pressman standing behind me, smiling.

'You're number sixteen,' he said.

'Thank you again . . . but they're only up to number nine. I can't wait that long,' I said, although I had no pressing engagement. 'You take it,' I said, refusing the ticket Ira Pressman held out to me. I turned my cart and headed towards the cashier, not looking back.

For the rest of my month at the shore, my libido surged every time I sat at my make-up table, knowing that the little red box of condoms was in the drawer behind the myriad lipsticks and eye shadows (most of which I'd never used more than once), where I'd hidden it so Shel would never find it. Sex would blow in my face alone with the tiny clouds of glistening, transparent face powder that escaped the drawer whenever I opened it. The box may have been out of sight, but it was never out of mind. Nor was Ira Pressman, the Boy Scout from the supermarket. I'd placed his card as a bookmark in a copy of Philip Roth's *The Counterlife* that sat, half-read, on the table next to my bed. Every night before turning out the light I took the book to read, but never got further than Ira Pressman's card, which I studied carefully, touching the raised black lettering of his name as if it were a kind of Braille that would impart a knowledge of the man himself. Once, I had picked up the telephone and punched in his number. But I hung up without completing the call.

... It all seemed so long ago, I thought as I lay on the beach beneath the waning heat of the late afternoon sun three years later. Roth's book – which I'd loaned to someone – was long gone. The card, I supposed, had gone with the book. And whatever became of Ira Pressman? I wondered ...

Opening her eyes she saw him moving above her and she remembered the second time she'd seen him, which she'd thought was the first. It was in the emergency room of the hospital. She'd opened her eyes and seen the dark vee of his widow's peak, and then his brown eyes looking at her. There'd been an accident, he'd told her, and someone called him in when they found his card in her pocket. She hadn't recognised him, only the widow's peak seemed familiar.

Now, seeing his face tense with passion, she couldn't imagine ever forgetting even the smallest crease, the most subtle mark. Over the past four months he'd brought together the splintered pieces of her life, just as he'd stitched together the wounds on her body in the emergency room that night – a terrible night, but for the fact that it had brought him to her. She closed her eyes and saw him still as she felt him in her, bringing her closer to where she burned to be, where no man had ever taken her. She could taste it on the back of her tongue, feel its emergence from somewhere inside her. And she grabbed on to it's enormity with arms she didn't know she possessed; let it take her. She soared with it high above him and her locked in their compelling dance. Until, like a rocket, she burst into a billion glittering stars . . . each one falling silently back to earth, back to him.

. . . No. That's what became of him – my fantasy of him – in my newest novel, *A Stitch in Time*, published this past May. In it, a woman tortured by a distorted memory of the mysterious death of her husband suffers total amnesia after being knocked off a bicycle by a hit-and-run driver while on a retreat to St Maarten. She's tended to by a surgeon she'd met by chance a few days earlier. As he helps restore her memory, and her life, they fall in love . . . and, of course, solve a mystery.

I'd probably never know what really became of Ira Pressman.

Waiting for the beach elevator in the basement of the Tower about five-thirty that afternoon, I closed my eyes to ease a nagging ache behind them, a subtle sense of seasickness underlying my less subtle fatigue.

'You alright, dear?' a kind voice reached me.

Opening my eyes, I focused on Emma Chankin wrapped in a short, white lace beach jacket. 'Oh, yes. I'm fine,' I said, looking into her china blue eyes.

'You looked a little fragile there for a moment. I thought you might be ill.'

'Just a headache, Mrs Chankin.'

'You shouldn't let these things go, you know. You should see a doctor.'

'Yes. Thank you.'

'You know, dear, my apartment is just a couple of doors down from yours, so if you ever need me –'

'That's very nice, Mrs Chankin. But I'm fine, really.'

'I saw your son yesterday morning. What a handsome young man he's become. It's nice to see young people here, although I haven't seen much of him this summer.'

'He's living with some of his friends,' I explained, trying to be neighbourly, but wanting only to get to my apartment and stand under a very hot shower as my discomfort grew.

'He's about sixteen?'

'Eighteen.'

'My, my. So young to be off on his own. Young people today –'

The elevator door opened, and we stepped in. I pushed the button for the seventeenth floor and then leaned against the brass rail at the back of the lift, now acutely aware of my gyroscope wobbling around unsteadily inside me.

'And that poor young Marjorie. Such a tragedy. Did you know her?' Mrs Chankin asked.

'Only to say hello.'

'I can understand, you know. I've lost a husband and

three gentlemen friends myself, and there were days...'
she said, her voice trailing off for a moment. 'I thought
Marjorie might settle down with that nice Dr Kaufman. I
saw them together – well, I believe they were together – a
few week-ends this past winter. You know that Dr
Kaufman's wife and Marjorie's husband –'

'Yes.'

'I guess that's what you call *switchies* these days, isn't it?
Nothing's new, my dear. Just the names change. We used
to say what's good for the goose is good for the gander.'

I smiled abstractly.

'Are you sure you're all right? You look a little peaked to
me,' Emma said.

'I'll be fine, Mrs Chankin. I've been a little off centre
lately, probably stress,' I said, Emma's chatter about
Marjorie and Jeffrey not quite sinking in.

'Maybe you should see my nephew. He's a doctor ... an
internist. Very smart, and good-looking,' Mrs Chankin
said scanning me from head to toe. 'And also,' she said as
the door opened and we stepped into the hall, 'he's single.'

'Well, if I feel I need to see a doctor, I'll be sure to get his
name from you.'

'You shouldn't wait until you're really sick. His office is
only a few blocks from here. You'll like him. Maybe you
could have dinner with him. Being alone, he probably
never eats a decent meal. You look like you could eat a
little more, too. You're so thin! When you get old like me
you don't care about being so thin. Good mashed potatoes
are more important.'

'Mrs Chankin, you have a lovely figure,' I said, a
compliment Mrs Chankin waved away with her hand.

'Emma, dear. Call me Emma. It makes me feel young,'
the older woman replied with a laugh, walking towards her
door, pulling her keys from her bag. 'Now you take care of

yourself . . . and –. You know, I'm going to give you my nephew's number right now. Come in for a minute,' she said, opening her door, waiting for me to follow her into the foyer. From the drawer of an antique secretary she retrieved a card and handed it to me.

'That's very kind,' I said, taking the card from her. Running my fingertips over the engraved name, I read aloud, '*Ira Pressman, M.D.*'

Back in my own apartment, I propped the card up against a bottle of moisturiser on my make-up table and then stripped off my bathing suit before stepping into the shower. Under the steamy hot spray I thought about the staggering coincidence. It had been two years since I'd actually met Ira Pressman . . . less than two hours since, spurred by the sight of Fiori's widow's peak, I'd remembered him . . . wondered what had happened to him . . . and then there I was staring at his name on a card. One might have thought it the kind of coincidence that makes a good story but isn't possible in real life; but, in fact, it was the kind of coincidence that isn't tolerated in fiction, but happens in real life all the time.

Of course, I had no intention of calling him. In fact, I'd probably not see any doctor. I was feeling better already, just standing under the hot water. *Stress*. That was it. I was dizzy because of stress. A hot shower, a little dinner, a good night's sleep, I'd be fine.

Up early the next morning, I felt refreshed. After my coffee and a cool shower I sat at my make-up table to brush my hair and dab on a tint of lipstick-with-sunscreen before heading for the beach. I picked up Ira Pressman's card and ran my fingers over the raised print again, then put the card down and opened the drawer as far as I could. *It's still here, after all this time*, I thought to myself, not considering that there was no reason why the little red box of condoms wouldn't still be there. Prying the box from its hiding place, I wiped it clean of irridescent powder. Turning it in my hands, the little red box triggered long-forgotten memories . . .

My cousin Evy and I were up to no good again. Only the week before, during Evy's week-end sleep-over at my house, we'd been spanked and sent to bed after having been discovered rifling through my mother's jewellery boxes. The dozen or more cardboard boxes lined with cotton and containing the most sumptuous *faux* treasures, were, after all, lying in plain sight in the top drawer of my mother's dresser, a temptation too great for any young lady of seven or five with even a whit of curiosity. And Evy and I, at seven and five, were, if nothing else, curious. When my mother surprised us, our arms, ears, and necks were laden with silver and gold, beads and rhinestones. And we reeked of Shalimar, the open bottle of which lay on its side amidst several tinted glass atomisers, dripping its precious sweet contents on to the mirrored perfume tray.

And now, no lesson learned, we were up to no good again. This time we were in Evy's house, exploring Evy's father's drawers, which, I was finding, held far less interest than my mother's. But after pushing around the striped boxer shorts, white undershirts, and boxes of matches, I found, hidden behind two cartons of Camels, a little red box. Evy only shook her head when I held it out to her to identify, but she took it from me and secreted the prize past the great mahogany four-poster bed and into the bath-room, closing the door behind us. There we sat cross-legged on the cold tile floor where I watched Evy tear open with ease a foil packet from the red box, and was confounded by the odd white balloon found therein. Why

Evy's father would keep such a toy hidden in his drawer was a question I never considered; what intrigued me was its character. Unlike any balloon I'd ever seen, it was rolled up, and it was such a stupid colour.

It will never be known who first fit the mouth of a condom over a sink tap and turned on the water – or why – and Evy, who did just that, surely wouldn't be the last. In awe I was as I, accomplice to the crime, held the condom on to the tap, and witnessed with delight the capacity that small rubber thing had for expansion. Filling with water, the great whale of a balloon grew to occupy the entire sink basin, turning my delight to panic as the thing began to appear horrifically out of control. Evy had backed to the door, but I was trapped: I couldn't turn off the water without letting go of that which was expanding at a frightening rate beneath my hands, nor could I just stand there until it exploded right under my nose. I was spared further agony of that dilemma, however, when my tiny hands proved incapable of holding the thing's neck on the tap. As it slipped off, a gush of water spouted up evoking shrieks from us both. Jumping back in vain to avoid the drench, I grabbed Evy and we both slipped to the wet floor. It was Evy's father who heard the racket and opened the door to find us sopping wet, sobbing in each other's arms. The deflated condom lay in the sink, undeniable evidence of our misconduct. Dripping water and shame, terrified of repercussions, I fled the bathroom to hide under Evy's bed. I vividly remember squeezing by my uncle standing in the doorway, my face brushing his red plaid shirt, the one he always seemed to be wearing when I visited on week-ends. I remember it was faded and soft – probably from many washings – and it smelled distinctly of my uncle, the musty sweet and pungent odour of deodorant and sweat. Every now and then I catch a whiff of that same smell from a stranger in a movie or a crowd and it always makes me feel a little off, a little sick. I've read that smells, not sights or sounds, are the most evocative of the past.

When I was not quite twelve I learned of another male smell – the smell of semen – and more about rubbers.

Evy's brother Larry and I were alone, listening to records in his basement recreation room. He was fourteen, fat, and worldly-wise. He carried a rubber in his wallet. He told me so.

I'd heard of rubbers from my girlfriends at school, all of whom talked of them knowingly. The actual known facts were that boys carried rubbers in their wallets so they could have sex with girls and not get them pregnant, and that rubbers fit on their penises when they got hard. The unknowns were far greater – in number and import – for neither I nor any of my friends were privy to the mysteries of the male sex organ, nor had any of us, to my knowledge, actually seen a rubber. My literal imagination conjured an image of stiff little penises shod with rubbers, the kind that fit over shoes in wet weather. It was an odd conception, but, at not quite twelve, acceptable in the abstract.

'Do you want to dance?' Larry asked.

'Okay,' I said, getting up from the scarred brown leather sofa and allowing Larry to hold me in his short, chubby arms, unmindful of what a sight we must have been, as I was at least a head taller than he.

After we'd danced to something slow for only a minute or two, Larry asked, 'Do you feel my boner?'

Now, *boner* I understood. It was a *hard* penis. That was something all well-informed girls of not quite twelve knew, along with the fact that boys got boners when they danced with girls, and that sometimes boys put eye-glass cases in their pockets to pretend they had boners when they didn't.

133

Of course, a really smart girl could tell the difference. I, for one, had never felt a real boner, I had told my friends. All the boys I'd ever danced with wore glasses. But I'd seen a real boner. I'd seen my father's boner when I walked into my parents' bedroom one Sunday morning and found him standing next to the bed in his pajama top, his very long penis hanging down very straight. It looked hard. I was sure that Larry's boner would be much shorter than my father's because Larry was much shorter than my father.

I looked Larry right in his beady little eyes monstrously magnified by the thick lenses of his tortoise-shell framed glasses. 'You're such a liar,' I said.

'I am not.'

'Yes you are. That's your glasses case.'

'No it's not.'

'Yes it is.'

'I'll show you.'

'I dare you,' I challenged.

Much to my surprise, he stepped back, coolly unzipped his fly, reached in and pulled out his penis, which was not hard and looked very much like I had remembered it from the old days – when Larry was about six and we'd played together in the kiddie pool, in the nude, in Larry and Evy's back yard on hot summer days, under the watchful eyes of their father.

'That's not a boner,' I mocked.

'Do you want to see it grow?' he asked, unaffected by my jeering tone.

'Okay,' I agreed, now extremely curious.

And we both watched while the small worm lengthened, and fattened, and stiffened, and – wonder of wonders! – began to rise up like the flanged cobra of a snake charmer. This astounding and totally unexpected trick held me in thrall.

'Can you make it move?' I asked.

'Sure,' he said. And we watched as it twitched to and fro.

'Neat,' I said, truly amazed, gaining respect for my ungainly cousin.

'Do you want to touch it?' he asked with pride.

'Uh-uh,' I declined, feeling suddenly naughty, uncomfortably exposed. 'Put it back.'

'It won't fit now,' he said. 'I have to make it small again.'

'How do you do that?' I asked, incredible curiosity overwhelming my growing guilty fear.

'Well . . . you have to rub it hard until all the jit comes out, and then it goes down.'

I supposed something had to have filled up his little penis to make it so much bigger, so I tentatively accepted his explanation, although I wasn't clear on the mechanics involved. I also wasn't clear on the nature of jit. But I was clear on one known fact: if you got jit on you, you got pregnant.

'First put on your rubber,' I demanded, drawing from my quickly growing store of known facts.

Pleased with myself, I watched as Larry took from his wallet a vaguely familiar red foil packet that he deftly opened with his teeth, exposing the object that I suddenly remembered from my youth – the enormous water-filled white balloon that had deflated after spilling its bloating liquid. Yes, there was logic about.

And I watched as Larry unrolled the rubber over his boner with practised precision. Another mystery resolved.

'Okay. Now rub it,' he commanded.

I looked at him, wide-eyed. 'You do it,' I said.

'*You're* supposed to do it,' he said in an exacting tone that froze me. 'God! You're such a baby,' he said after a moment, understanding that I was not about to submit. Then, grasping his shodden organ, he stroked it as if he

135

were polishing the thing. 'See? Now you try it,' he tried again, this time in a more solicitous, but nonetheless intimidating manner.

'I don't want to,' I said, backing away.

'Come on, you'll see something *really* neat. I promise,' he entreated, stepping closer.

'Uh-uh,' I intoned, dredging up a memory of another of his promises – the wonders of the diving bell ... and the green slime I'd seen, the panic I'd experienced. Feeling frightened, vaguely threatened, I hid behind the sofa, until, concerned by the odd snorts and grunts issuing from my cousin, I put my hands over the top of the cushions and slowly raised my head until I could see him.

His knees slightly bent, Larry was standing motionless except for his hands, both of which were now engaged. His eyes were closed, his reddened lumpy face scrunched up in a most grotesque manner. And then he started to rock, while his clasped hands continued to polish at what was now an astonishing pace. He looked weird.

'Are you okay, Larry?' I asked nervously, wondering if he was having an epileptic fit, like the one Warren Robertson had in an American History class the month before. But Warren had fallen to the floor before he'd started his frenetic dance. Larry was still on his feet.

'Uh-huh,' Larry gasped in answer as he continued his frenzied exercise. He groaned and gasped and then stopped dead, letting out a most grievous wail. A glistening stream issued forth from Larry and landed with a splat on the seat back of the sofa, then dripped slowly down between the cushions.

'Larry? You okay?' I asked, again, alarmed, imagining that such a forceful expulsion must be very painful indeed.

He said nothing, but stood there holding his deflating boner.

'Should I get your Mom?' I asked, beginning to panic.

'NO!' Larry yelled.

I saw the rubber fall to the dark green vinyl tile floor. Rent, it was.

And as I watched Larry stuff his little penis back into his pants, I became aware of a spot of wet on my hand. 'Look what you did! It touched me! I'm going to get pregnant!' I screamed, pulling the sleeve of my cotton sweater down to wipe the wet from my hand.

'No you're not,' he said, unconvincingly, although, I hoped, at fourteen he had knowledge I didn't have at not quite twelve.

Momentarily relieved, I put my arm to my face to wipe the mist of fright from my eyes and was overwhelmed by an odour reminiscent of Clorox and the sea that I'd forever after associate with Larry and the way he'd made me feel that afternoon – vulnerable.

'Do you think I could have a baby?' I asked Evy that night in bed, after we turned the light out, while the radio was playing number six of the top ten, after lying in a cold sweat trying to summon the nerve to ask my cousin the question, hoping she wouldn't ask *me* any questions, thinking up answers to questions she might ask.

'No,' is all Evy said.

'Why?' I asked, heartened.

'Because you haven't gotten the curse yet.'

It was at that moment that the connection between the curse and babies – although still a little sketchy – became a 'known fact'. My aunt's explanation, which Evy had shared with me when she started to menstruate, had been, at the time, information far too abstruse to hold meaning for me.

'Oh,' is all I said. Awash in relief, I was now able to close my eyes and surrender to the suddenly overwhelming desire to sleep, a sleep, that, when it came, was filled with visions of Larry and a horde of his boyfriends armed with water pistols, chasing me menacingly from my home.

. . . 'I'm glad you finally called a doctor, Alison. I was beginning to worry about you,' Robin was saying to me on the beach an hour or so after I'd arrived.

'Well, to be honest, I'm not sure if I called him this morning because of my health or because I was curious to see him again,' I confessed, having told Robin of meeting Ira Pressman in the supermarket, but not about the condoms.

'It was a healthy decision either way. After all, it was a really bizarre coincidence, Ira Pressman being Emma's nephew and all. I'd say it's fate. You *had* to call him.'

'Well, this dizzy thing is getting scary, so –'

'So you don't feel guilty about making a date with him, right?'

'It's not a date. It's an appointment with a doctor.'

'Face it, Alison, Emma Chankin, at seventy-plus, is more with it than you are. Do you honestly think she gave you Ira Pressman's number to cure your headaches? She could have given you a bottle of aspirin.'

'I really looked sick when –'

'Let's be honest here. She's match-making, Alison, fixing you up! And you called Ira because you wanted to see him again.'

'But I really am dizzy –'

'No kidding. Just don't let Ira find out.'

'Very funny.'

'So Chankin the Shark comes through. You know, she'll probably be the first in line for that sex robot I told you about . . . if she's still alive that is. But for now I hear she's got her eye on Mrs Grossman's husband.'

'I didn't know Mrs Grossman died.'

'She didn't . . . yet. But she's been in a nursing home for months. Wait. You'll see. Emma will be fixed up before you are.'

'She does seem to have her ear to the ground, doesn't she,' I said, suddenly remembering the rest of our conversation in the elevator. 'In fact, she knew all about Tiffany Kaufman running off with Marjorie's husband last year, and she said that she saw Jeffrey and Marjorie together this past winter. She called it *switchies*! Would you believe that?'

'Of course! I told you they were involved.'

'But she called it *switchies*, Robin, don't you think that's priceless?'

'Right on the money, actually.'

'Well, she certainly shocked me.'

'As I've said more than once, you're painfully naïve, Alison.'

I feigned a pout.

'But charming, so it's okay.'

I sunk in my chair considering my friend's indictment.

'At any rate, I told you Jeffrey looked sad,' Robin continued.

'Do you really think I'm naïve?' I asked.

'And judgemental.'

'I don't mean to be.'

'That's part of your naïvety.'

'I don't mean to be naïve, either.'

'That's what makes you charming.'

'Tense, maybe.'

'You're tense?'

'Not me. I was thinking of Jeffrey. He could have been a bit tense, but he certainly didn't seem *sad* on Sunday night.'

'You charmed him, Alison. I think he likes you.'

Silence.

'Are you going to remind Ira Pressman that you met before?'

'Do you think he'll remember me?'

'So why do you think he's still single?'

'Do you think I've changed a lot in the last two years?'

'Did I know you then?'

'Do you want some ice-cream?'

'Sure.'

CHAPTER 7

Red

Leaving the beach around five-thirty, I found Shel waiting for me in my apartment. He was on the front balcony slumped in a chair, his sneakered (but unsocked) feet propped up on the rail. I didn't think he'd heard me come in, so when I came up behind him and kissed his forehead, it was he who surprised me, pulling a lock of my hair.

'Hey, Mom!' he greeted me. 'Catch enough UVs? You're going to wrinkle up, you know. Then I'll call you prune-face.'

'Hello, son. As always, it's a pleasure to see you,' I replied with a carefully measured dose of good-humoured sarcasm.

'Let's see. Any deep creases yet, or only fine lines around the eyes?' he said, swinging around and studying my face.

'I use number fifteen, and I sit under an umbrella,' I said, growing defensive, not able to maintain my sarcasm, still not smart enough, after eighteen years of being a parent, to know that I don't have to defend my actions to my child, and still not flexible enough not to take everything he said seriously.

'I ate the tuna fish in the refrigerator, and the grapes, and a muffin. Okay?'

'Of course. Is that going to be your dinner, or do you want to have dinner with me?'

'That's it. Got plans tonight. Just stopped in to raid your fridge.'

'Well, I'm glad you waited around to see me,' I said, sitting in a chair next to him, propping my feet on the rail next to his.

'So, how's work?' I asked.

'Great.'

'And your house-mates?'

'Great.'

'What's going on?'

'Nothing.'

'What are you doing tonight?'

'Not sure yet.'

'I thought you said you have plans?'

'With the guys. We're going to do something, but we're not sure what. Probably catch a movie or something. Maybe hit the casinos.'

'You're not allowed in the casinos. You're underage.'

'Not to worry, Mom. I've got ID.'

'Excuse me?'

'We all have IDs. Necessary equipment at the shore.'

'Well, if you get caught, don't bother calling me,' I said, picturing him in a jail cell, waiting for me to bail him out, get him an attorney, pay his fines. *I won't do it!* I averred silently, until I pictured the jail cell crowded with murderers, thieves, and drug addicts. 'Just stay out of trouble,' I said impotently.

'We just have fun, nothing serious. You want to see my ID?' he asked, reaching into the back pocket of his jeans.

'No thanks. Don't make me a part of this.'

'Oh, by the way, I found this in the elevator on the way up today,' Shel said, handing me a little red leather book about the size of a pocket telephone directory.

'What is it?'

'Don't know,' he said looking straight out to sea.

I took the book from him and leafed through it. The gilt-edged pages were titled with colours – YELLOW, GREEN, etc. – beneath which were lists of dates and monetary figures, all written in a careful hand with peacock blue ink. 'God. I haven't seen peacock blue ink since I was in junior high,' I commented, flipping through the book, when the first page became unstuck from the front cover. There, written on a printed line headed *This book belongs to*, was the name *Marjorie Applebaum*.

'Where did you say you found this?'

'In the elevator,' Shel said, still staring out to sea.

'This is Marjorie Applebaum's.'

'Oh, yeah?'

'I wonder how it got in the elevator,' I said, unease stirring up inside me.

'Beats me.'

'Is there something you're not telling me, Shel?'

'Right, Mom. I was having a passionate affair with Marjorie Applebaum, pushed her off the balcony when she threatened to tell my mom the prude, and grabbed the book for a keepsake when I left her apartment.'

Shel's clearly defensive reaction startled me, and I didn't know how to respond.

'So, you're sure you won't have dinner with me?' I said.

'Yep. In fact, I gotta go,' he said, jumping up from his chair. 'See ya later. Maybe you should give the book to the police. It could be a clue.'

'Love you, Shel,' I said.

And after tousling my hair he was gone.

I sat there for a few minutes staring at the notebook. He was right, of course. I had to give it to the police. Dismissing the ever so fleeting idea that Shel could in any way be involved with Marjorie's death by the mere fact that he suggested giving the book to the police, dismissing the ever so fleeting idea that Shel could in any way have been involved with Marjorie Applebaum by the mere fact that he made up that silly story about being involved with Marjorie Applebaum, I wondered why he'd been so defensive. And then I thought about the Milfs. And then I dismissed my thoughts.

I looked through the book again. Most striking was that, like my *Beach Book-91* manuscript, the little book was sectioned into colours. The colours of beach umbrellas? I wondered.

Picking up my computer, I brought the *Beach Book-91* directory on to the screen, and from that directory, the file marked *Pink*. At the end of the section, where Marjorie was in the elevator after leaving Elliot's office, I added a few lines . . .

In the elevator, Marjorie pulled a small red leather book and a peacock blue felt-tip pen from her pocketbook. At the top of a new page she wrote *PINK* in capital letters. On the first line she wrote *July 15 – $100*, put the pen and book back in her pocketbook, leaned against the back rail of the car and watched the numbers above the elevator door tick off *3 . . . 2 . . . 1 . . .*

. . . 'Bingo!' I said aloud.

For the first time since I started the manuscript I felt a most welcome rush of confidence. 'This is what I've been looking for,' I said to the air, 'a plot.' I saved the addition, put the computer on the table next to me, propped my feet up again and laid back in my chair, smiling.

After a moment, however, my smile faded as I grappled with the problem of how the little red book got into the elevator four days after Marjorie's death. *Milf* popped into my head again. I pushed it away. Not Shel. Not Shel and Marjorie. The idea was absurd. Not my Shel. He's just a baby.

And then I remembered what I'd said to Robin about Shel, that he seemed to know more about what was going on in the world than I did, that it was embarrassing, shocking, even. That he'd been talking about Brenda Forrester . . . about Brenda Forrester seducing young men. I remembered what Robin had said: '*Alison, brace yourself; he was probably talking about himself.*'

'Never!' I said aloud, sitting suddenly upright, beads of sweat forming on my forehead, nausea twisting the top of my stomach.

I tried to remember Friday afternoon when Shel's friends were looking for him. Where had he been? What had he been doing?

'*Sex. With anyone, anywhere, any way,*' Robin's words jumped out at me.

I forgot Marjorie Applebaum for the moment as the heightened sense of being that I'd come to know as writer's reality overwhelmed me. I reached again for my computer and started a new file: *Red* . . .

Brenda Forrester was a woman well into her forties, with a long, coal-black Dutch-boy hairdo, and a surprising hour-glass figure topped by large pointed breasts whose time should have run out years before. Friday afternoon she lay stretched out on a red and white pin-striped canvas lounge, lapping at a missile-shaped banana-fudge popsicle held provocatively above her upturned mouth. Shel sat on a towel next to her watching, mesmerised.

...No, I thought, not *Shel*. Shel's my baby. Sheldon. I'll call him Sheldon for now, I decided, going back to the manuscript and changing Shel to ...

Sheldon sat on a towel next to her watching, mesmerised, his mouth moving along with hers – like when one watches a baby eat. Brenda's eyes were closed as her lips honed the sweet missile, but she knew that Sheldon was gazing with glazed eyes and taut muscles. She turned to him, offering him a taste of her sweet. His tongue was already out.

'What time do you have to go to work, Sheldon?' Brenda asked.

'Not until five-thirty, Mrs Forrester,' he replied licking the cold, thick chocolate from his lips. 'I work until closing.' When she didn't respond he continued nervously, 'I'm waiting tables tonight. Sometimes I work the grill, but I prefer waiting tables because the grill gets so hot –'

'It is rather hot today, isn't it Sheldon? What time is it, dear?'

'I'd say it's about one,' he said confidently, looking at the position of the sun.

'How clever you are, Sheldon,' she said, lowering the dwindling popsicle into her mouth again and pulling the stick out clean. 'Are you clever enough to get us something to drink? I'm dying of thirst.'

At that moment, Sheldon wanted nothing more than to please Mrs Forrester – the sophisticated woman who always smiled and tipped him well when he waited on her table at the deli, and who had invited him to sit beneath her umbrella after meeting him at the water's edge quarter of an hour earlier.

Red

Sheldon had been walking along the shore with two of his house-mates looking for the perfect spot to settle, when he yelled, 'Cool down!' and the three dropped their stuff on the dry sand and dove into the surf. It was not as arbitrary a detour as it might have appeared, in that it was the beach where Sheldon's mother, Alison, sat beneath her white umbrella on the week-ends, so Sheldon had a preference – a quiet preference – for the air there. The water's edge of the Tower beach was a favourite temporary resting place for the summer boys in any case, being the home of the Milfs. That's what the summer boys called the meticulously groomed week-day widows of the Tower Beach – Mothers I'd Like to Fuck. So as far as his friends were concerned, it was business as usual when Sheldon decided to cool down just there. As Pete and Jason wrestled underwater, Sheldon rode a large wave to the shore, landing at Brenda's feet.

'Sorry–. Oh, hi, Mrs Forrester! Did I splash you?' he said, standing up, wiping the sand and salt from his eyes. Sheldon was over six feet tall, and the sun's glare obscured Mrs Forrester's vision when she looked up to match the face with the familiar voice.

'Is that you, Sheldon? Yes it is. Having a nice day?'

'Sure thing. Hot isn't it?'

'It certainly is. The sun's so bright I almost couldn't see your face way up there.'

Now, Sheldon, at eighteen and sharing a shore house with a group of his friends, was familiar with the territory. Not that he had had any personal experience with the Milfs, but he'd listened to enough torrid tales from his peers to be hep to, to watch for, to pursue the inviting glances, the coy opening lines, the subtle cues advanced by these women of the world – the lusty, lonesome ladies of Milfville.

147

So, when Brenda Forrester said, *It certainly is*, thus agreeing with him regarding the heat, he understood that she wasn't speaking only of the heat of the sun. And when she invited him to enjoy a cold treat with her, he understood that she wasn't referring only to something sweet to eat. *Ice cubes*, perhaps, he mused as he walked with her to her umbrella. He'd heard that some people use ice cubes in sex, although he wasn't clear on the particulars. Maybe she's kinky, he thought, remembering his friend Greg's description of the sex he'd had the summer before with a thirty-eight-year-old mother of three boys. She hadn't used ice cubes, but, Greg had related, she did this incredible thing with cherry vanilla ice-cream.

'Sit here, next to me, Sheldon,' Mrs Forrester had directed, indicating a place next to her chair, 'and watch for the ice-cream man.'

Sheldon's knees melted. He dropped his Nikes, spread his sweatshirt on the sand and sat down obediently, immediately, before he fell down. 'I heard someone jumped from the top of the building last night,' he said, trying to make conversation.

'Oh, there's Bill, Sheldon,' Brenda interrupted, spotting the vendor walking along the surf.

Jumping up, waving his arms above his head, Sheldon caught Bill's attention, who soon dropped his ice box under the red umbrella.

'What'll it be, folks? I got fudge bars, banana-fudge, cherry ice pops, lemon cups, and sandwiches,' he announced.

Sheldon chose an ice-cream sandwich and Mrs Forrester the banana-fudge popsicle.

'My treat,' Mrs Forrester said, handing Bill two dollars.

Sheldon ate his sandwich quickly and then watched Mrs Forrester slowly, suggestively, devour hers.

And now she was thirsty. And she had just told Sheldon how clever he was, so this was his chance to show her just how clever he could be.

'I'll run up to your apartment and bring you some water,' he said. 'That is if you don't mind giving me your key,' he added with a calculated respectfulness.

'I'll tell you what. Why don't we both go up and get a drink. Maybe something a little more than water. We really do need a good thirst quencher on a day like today,' Mrs Forrester said.

YES! Sheldon yelled in his head, clenching his fists. He congratulated himself as they walked together towards the boardwalk – unaware of his mother's presence not fifty feet from their path sitting with her eyes closed under her umbrella, unaware of her presence at the shore that Friday, because his house-mates hadn't told him of her Thursday evening message on the answering machine.

As he held the curbside hose for Mrs Forrester to wash the sand from her feet outside the Tower, Sheldon imagined the sight of her large pointed breasts naked, ignoring the lines in her face somewhat tempered by her three-year-old face lift, remembering what he'd heard – that women age from the head down – noting that Mrs Forrester had exceptionally shapely calves and ankles for a woman her age . . . for a woman any age.

Riding up in the elevator, Sheldon stared at the numbers ticking off above the door. At nineteen the elevator stopped and the doors opened. Although it wasn't necessary, Sheldon held the door until Mrs Forrester exited, then followed silently, watching her swank walk, her high-wedged beach mules clap against her heels. Inside the apartment, Sheldon stepped out on to the balcony while his hostess took a small crystal ice bucket from the bar and carried it to the kitchen.

'Scotch is all right, isn't it, Sheldon?' she called to him, returning to the living room, the bucket filled with ice.

'Oh, sure,' Sheldon answered, stepping back into the living room, although beer was usually as hard as he drank. He flushed at the sight of the ice cubes.

'Good,' she said, handing him a half-filled tumbler. 'To the heat,' she toasted, clicking her glass against his.

Sheldon flushed deeper with her *heat*. 'Nice apartment, Mrs Forrester. Great view,' he gasped nervously.

'Yes,' Mrs Forrester replied. 'Come, I'll show you the rest of it.'

Mentally tripping on her *come*, Sheldon gulped down a large mouthful of scotch, hastily deposited the glass on the nearest table and followed her obediently.

'This, of course, is the kitchen,' she said walking in one end of the galley kitchen and out the other end into the hall. 'The main bath, the guest bedroom . . .' she pointed out each room, saving the master bedroom suite at the end of the hall for last, '. . . and this is my bedroom.'

Fortified by the quick-acting scotch – or so he told himself – he walked by her and over to the open sliding glass door and out on to the balcony. The view, like the one in his mother's apartment, was of the coastline clear to Longport. 'This is really something,' he said, turning to the odd sound behind him.

It was a zipper. 'I'm just going to get out of this damp suit, Sheldon,' Mrs Forrester said, sliding the sleek black bathing suit down to her ankles and stepping out of it. Released from their support, her large, heavy breasts hung further down her torso than Sheldon had thought possible. This was, after all, his first 'older woman', and the only bare breasts he'd seen were in magazines and on less teenage girls than he bragged about.

'I'm not embarrassing you, am I?' she asked coyly.

'You've seen a woman change her clothes before, surely.'

'No. I mean yes, I have . . . and no, I'm not embarrassed,' he replied, his face visibly red through his dark tan.

Mrs Forrester took a deep breath and stretched erect, her coral-tipped fingers smoothing down the curves of her body while Sheldon's eyes followed those painted talons until they rested on a most intriguing sight – to wit, Mrs Forrester's fine, rounded mount of Venus, which was, well . . . *Bald!*, Sheldon cried out in his head, *her cunt's as bald as a baby's!*

'I'm going to shower, Sheldon, to wash off the sand and salt. Would you like to shower?'

Sheldon didn't move. He didn't say a word, but watched Mrs Forrester as she went about the business of carrying her bathing suit into the adjoining bathroom and dropping it in a white wicker hamper, taking two plush yellow towels from the linen closet and placing them on the vanity, reaching into the large, tiled, two-headed stall shower that was out of Sheldon's line of vision, and turning on the water. Now visibly aroused, Sheldon watched as the bathroom filled with steam and Mrs Forrester stepped out of his sight and into the shower, leaving him standing awkward and alone in the middle of the bedroom, wondering what to do next. He glanced around the room thinking, *Wow! If the guys could see me!* and imagined his friend, Jason, saying through a mustache of beer foam, *So what did you do then, dickhead?* Realising he had to have a better end to his story than running out of the apartment in terror and back to his buddies on the beach calling, *Hey, bozos! Wait'll you hear this!* – who were probably furious with him by now for disappearing without a word – which was exactly what he felt like doing now that his initial shock was dissipating, along with his erection, Sheldon boldly pulled off his sweatshirt and bathing suit and stepped into the misty shower where he was met with another shock. *She's as bald as a cue ball!* he cried again in his head, this time regarding her perfectly shaped, perfectly hairless head. And then he noticed her eyebrows – actually the absence of her usually heavily pencilled eyebrows that had washed down the drain. In fact, the woman didn't have a hair on her body. *Japanese geisha girls shave their bodies*, Sheldon thought, pulling to consciousness a memory of something he had read somewhere, thinking, *The guys are never gonna believe this!*

'Be a dear and wash my back, Sheldon,' Mrs Forrester said, in a languid tone that compelled Sheldon's hand up to meet the washcloth and bar of transparent amber soap she held out to him.

As he began to work the soap into a lather on the cloth, his eyes found the black wig perched on a shelf just outside the clear glass shower enclosure. Mrs Forrester had turned her back to him, awaiting his touch. Dutifully, Sheldon rubbed the cloth across her shoulders, and then down her spine, his eyes never leaving the disembodied mop of black . . . until he reached her buttocks. Lathering one cheek with the cloth, he ran his bare hand around the other, taking careful note of the surprising firmness of that soft flesh. Unlike her fallen breasts, Mrs Forrester's ass had held up well. Sheldon's erection returned with a vengeance and, overwhelmed with lust, he found himself clasped around Mrs Forrester's back, humping her thighs like a dog. His eyes closed, he felt Mrs Forrester turn in his grasp, her arms go around his chest, her pendulous breasts press against his stomach. He grabbed her bottom with his left hand and, with his right, steered himself into her. Her loud moan caused him to open his eyes, to be shocked all over again by her closed, lashless, browless eyes, her hairless head thrown back in unbridled passion. He wrapped his hands around her smooth pate creating the most unbelievable sensation in his fingertips, a feeling that seemed to run through his body and out the end of his penis like an electric current.

'Ooh, so quick. We'll have to do this again . . . soon,' Mrs Forrester crooned to Sheldon, who was now hanging on to her in a state of near collapse. Retrieving the soap Sheldon had dropped to the floor, Mrs Forrester proceeded to lather him from the ankles up, lingering on his now flaccid penis. 'Well, maybe not *too* soon,' she said, quickly soaping her own body.

After they rinsed, she turned the water off, pulled a towel from the vanity, and tenderly wrapped it around Sheldon. Then she wrapped one around herself and stepped out of the shower. Zombie-like, Sheldon followed her to the bedroom and laid down beside her on the king-size bed. He was asleep in an instant, but soon woke to another amazing sensation, that of Mrs Forrester's mouth tenderly wrapped around his newest, and most impressive erection. Opening his eyes, he saw the other end of Mrs Forrester swaying above him. *Dead clam!* popped into his head, as he remembered the description of a woman's shaved genitals from a dog-eared page in a Henry Miller novel. It was the first time he'd had such a clear view of a woman's hidden parts. He found it fascinating, the smooth, cloven mound of bare flesh. No, there was nothing dead about it, he thought, pulling the offering closer to him. Inhaling, he was overwhelmed by its subtly salty scent. His mouth was drawn to its dewy ruby warmth . . . and he thought of ripe figs, sun-warmed and velvety soft, as another heretofore buried memory emerged: a scene in a movie where a guy shows another guy how to eat a ripe fig, split open to reveal its moist red flesh – like a woman. It had excited him, but, at fifteen, he was mortified that his date might see the bulge straining his tight jeans.

There was no thought of embarrassment now, only gratification. Mrs Forrester tensed and cried out, and then a series of turns and flips left Sheldon on top, driving himself into her. Again the electric current when he locked his fingers across the top of her head. Opening his eyes before he dropped off to one side of her, he was startled yet again by the baldness of her, this time noticing for the first time the almost invisible line that ran around one ear, up to and around the top of her forehead and down and around the other ear – the faded evidence of her facelift. *It looks like her face was sewn on*, he thought with a shudder, remembering some weird science fiction movie he'd seen years ago at a Saturday matinée.

It was dull and quiet when he awoke, panicking as he tried to orient himself, to assess where he was, what time it was, what day it was! The glowing red digital numbers on the clock to the left of his face showed five-zero-five. A quick glance around the room reminded him that he was in Mrs Forrester's apartment, and that he'd spent a most unusual afternoon. 'The guys are never going to believe this,' he whispered aloud, jumping off the bed, on to his feet. He swayed slightly as a momentary hypotensive spell sent his head reeling. 'Whew! Gotta go . . . now!' he said, pulling on his bathing suit and sweatshirt. He picked up his Nikes and walked to the living room. There wasn't a sound in the place save the crash of the ocean coming in through the open balcony doors. Ascertaining that the apartment was empty, he relaxed and sat on an ottoman to put on his sneakers. As he eased his feet into the ugly black and white things that felt as though they had half the beach in them, he looked from table to lamp, from picture to vase until a flash of afternoon sun, reflecting off something on the desk, struck his eye. Curious, Sheldon stood up and gingerly picked up a bright one-hundred dollar golden gift coin from Tiffany's department store. He examined it, shrugged his shoulders and dropped it back on to the desk. Then he off-handedly picked up a little red leather book the size of a pocket telephone directory. Leafing through the tiny notebook, he found the gilt-edged pages titled by colours, and displaying lists of dates and monetary figures, all written in a careful hand with peacock blue ink. As Sheldon scanned the book, he heard the front door open, and swung around to see Mrs Forrester in the foyer walking towards him. He stuffed the little red book into the back of his bathing suit.

'You're awake!' Mrs Forrester chirped. 'I just ran down to the commissary to pick up some soda. Would you like something to drink . . . or eat . . . or . . . no, you're supposed to be at the deli soon, aren't you?'

Sheldon stood in the middle of the living room staring at Mrs Forrester, foregoing her great pointed breasts for a more compelling sight – her black eyebrows arching dramatically once again over her eyes to her black bangs. Blood was pounding in his ears, almost drowning out what she was saying, until *deli* made its mark, and he recovered his powers of speech. 'Right . . . yes . . . I really have to go. Uh, thanks for the drink and . . . uh . . . well, thanks.' And Sheldon moved quickly by Mrs Forrester, patting her lightly on the shoulder in an attempt to acknowledge their recent intimacy? familiarity?

Out on the street after a painfully long ride down in the elevator thinking, *Christ! I didn't use a condom. My mother would kill me!*, Sheldon called the deli from the first pay phone he could find to tell his boss he'd be a little late – an announcement taken with a show of annoyance, beneath which was an acceptance of the way it was for teenage boys at the shore in the summer, and ending with, 'Okay, but no more than twenty minutes or you're fired!'

Sheldon jogged to his house, entered the back door (which was always unlocked), ran to the bathroom to shower, where he stripped off his sweatshirt and bathing suit, throwing them on to the pile of dirty clothes in the corner. That's when he remembered the little red book – when it fell out of his suit and on to the floor. He picked up the book. *Gotta get this back to her*, he thought, his skin growing inflamed as visions of his visit with her flared before his eyes. He flicked through the book considering presenting it to her on the beach. *Hi, Mrs Forrester. Thought you might like to have this back. I found it in your apartment*, he rehearsed in his head. 'Right,' he said aloud. 'I just happened to find it . . . and, unbeknownst to me, it somehow got caught in my bathing suit. Sure. That's going to sound great.' He then considered dropping it on her chair while she was in the water . . . putting it in an envelope and dropping it in the mailbox . . . throwing it away. No solution, however, fulfilled his need to do the right thing and not get caught. He wondered if he should simply tell her the truth, an idea he dismissed as unthinkable. While thus contemplating the fate of the little red book, and flipping through its pages, he came upon a startling fact. There, on the inside of the front cover, on a printed line headed *This book belongs to*, was the name *Marjorie Applebaum*.

'Whoa!' Sheldon whispered, wide-eyed. 'Check . . . it . . . out!' but, pressed for time, he tossed the book on to the pile of dirty clothes, showered, dressed and raced on his bike to the deli.

Mr Fishbein met him at the door, pocket watch in hand. 'Sixteen minutes,' he said sternly. 'You're a very lucky young man.'

Mr Fishbein had no idea *how* lucky.

Red

* * *

. . . As I typed the last sentence, I felt excited, delighted with Brenda's kinky character, the set-up for a twist in plot. Although I didn't know yet *how* I'd get Marjorie's red book into Mrs Forrester's apartment, I was sure that placing it there was right, that a good explanation would emerge as I continued my story. But then I read through what I'd written from the beginning, and shame dampened my exhilaration. How could I imagine Shel, my son! in such a situation. And even if it were somehow even remotely close to some bizarre perversion of the truth, how could I write about it? What would people think of a woman who writes of her son in such a way? I wondered. What do *I* think? Am I perverted? No. Imaginative. Exorcising my deepest fears by exercising writer's licence, I argued with myself, knowing that, with a few keystrokes, Sheldon – already distinct from my Shel – would be reborn as Alan, or Joe, or Stephen. Then the entire episode would turn up in a foreign venue, in a novel context authored by one Sloan I. Diamond, so that every vestige of Shel would be lost.

Yet I blushed.

CHAPTER 8

White

Walking back to the Tower to shower and dress for my two o'clock appointment with Dr Pressman, Wednesday afternoon, a loud squawking pulled my attention towards two sea gulls squabbling on the beach beside the wooden stairs of the boardwalk. It was the smaller gull that seemed the aggressor, pecking at the other's beak, trying to push its own beak inside. It was after food, from its mother, I decided, remembering a wildlife documentary I'd seen on television, of a mother bird feeding nestlings, her beak stuck down their throats, regurgitating digested food. Rather overwhelming, I thought, facing all those gaping, needy mouths – mouths as big as their bodies – clamouring for attention, for sustenance. But, although the small sea gull wasn't fully mature, he (I assumed it to be male) was no longer a nestling, either. Too old, perhaps, to be fed by his mother who continued to struggle with her noisy offspring, running from him, but never too far. Finally, his lesson learned? giving up? sulking? the young bird walked away. It was the mother gull, then, who ran after him, squawking shrilly until her fledgling came back to her. The two continued their excruciating game as I climbed the steps and crossed the boardwalk. That's what happens when they grow up, when they're not quite grown up, I thought to myself, understanding that motherhood ... letting go ... is never easy, even for a bird.

'This dizzy thing is getting a little scary, Dr Pressman,' I told Emma Chankin's nephew in his office, Wednesday afternoon, having decided not to remind him of our meeting two years earlier, both disappointed and grateful that he didn't remember. In fact, I barely recognised the man when he greeted me, only the widow's peak of the former Boy Scout from the supermarket was familiar, and even that seemed different – steeper and greying.

'Let's just take a look at your eyes, Alison. Chin up, and look straight ahead,' he instructed, bringing his face close to mine, only the black ophthalmoscope in his hand between us.

While Dr Pressman peered deep into my eyes, I didn't breathe for fear of offensive breath due to extreme dryness in my mouth as a result of anxiety ... being examined by a doctor ... an attractive doctor ... an attractive doctor close enough to kiss.

'Looks fine, Alison. I can't see anything in your eyes.'

'A friend thinks it's all in my head,' I said to the widow's peak above the unfamiliar face.

'Perhaps it is – literally. The symptoms you've described often originate in the inner ear.' With this, Dr Pressman opened a tall, glass display case holding plastic, oversized models of organs – a macabre museum of the human anatomy. He selected the ear from the second shelf, brought it to me, and took it apart.

'Looks complicated,' I said, studying the delicate configurations.

'Here's the osseous labyrinth,' he lectured, pointing to the three bony cavities of the inner ear. 'And you can see the tiny semi-circular ducts of the membranous labyrinth within the osseous labyrinth ...'

I tried to follow Dr Pressman through the maze of medical jargon, but, although I'd written about *otitis media* – the bane of mothers of pre-schoolers – a few years before, I became lost somewhere in the semi-circular ducts. 'I see,' I lied.

'The bottom line is, it sounds like you're having a problem with your equilibrium ... your balance,' he said.

'I see,' I said, still unclear about the balance between mental and physical equilibrium.

When Dr Pressman finished his examination, he scribbled something on a prescription pad. 'I want you to get an MRI examination of your head – it's like an x-ray,' he said, handing me the slip of paper marked with his illegible scrawlings. 'My secretary will give you a pamphlet that explains the test. Will you be able to get to the lab this week?'

'Yes. I'm on vacation –'

A quiet rap on the door signalled the arrival of the technician who seemed to know by some sort of magic exactly when to appear.

'Barbara's going to draw some blood for a few tests. Now, call me if your symptoms get any worse, or if you have any questions, Alison. And I wouldn't be concerned. I don't think this is serious,' he added, in what seemed to me to be an attempt to put me at ease, which only made me feel more anxious, promoting a wave of heat to climb my chest and scorch my face. 'And please give my love to my Aunt Emma. She's becoming my best source of referrals, and my favourite – she only sends me the pretty ones,' Dr Pressman said, with a trace of a smile, on his way out of the door.

I tensed again, not sure if he was being patronising or charming. Embarrassed in front of the technician, I clutched my paper gown around me more closely and stared at the giant ear sitting on the end of the examination table.

Returning home about four, I found a message from Shel on my answering machine: 'Want company for dinner, Mom? Call me. I'm available. Your treat. I'm broke.'

Shel found me exceptionally pert when he arrived for dinner at quarter to six. 'You're acting weird,' he said.

'What's that supposed to mean?' I asked.

'I don't know. You're too happy. What's wrong?' He knew me well.

'Nothing's wrong. I'm happy because you're having dinner with me,' I said, taking the plastic tub of homemade meat sauce from the microwave, chipping away with a knife at the persistently frozen chunks afloat in the thick red sauce. After returning the tub to the microwave, I slathered softened butter and fresh garlic on Italian bread while Shel pulled a diet Pepsi from the refrigerator.

'We having spaghetti *again*?' he asked.

'What do you mean *again*? I haven't made you dinner in ages. And, besides, my spaghetti is your favourite –'

'Just kidding, Mom. I love to kid you. Your ears get so red,' he said, laughing, coming up behind me and rubbing my ears.

'Stop that, Shel! You're messing my hair.'

'Ooh, ooh, look who's worried about her hair! So

what's new at the beach, Mom?' Shel asked, sitting at the table with his soda.

'Actually, I wasn't at the beach today. I had an appointment,' I dropped, anxious to tell Shel about my illness . . . my possible tumour . . . my possibly imminent death.

'An appointment?'

'With a doctor.'

'A doctor? You sick?' he asked, trying to sound unconcerned.

'It's nothing . . . really . . . just a little dizziness.'

'So . . . who's the doc?'

'Mrs Chankin's nephew.'

'Chankin the Shark?'

'Shel!'

'So what'd he say?'

'He wants me to have an MRI – it's like an x-ray,' I echoed Dr Pressman, taking him at his word. 'He wants pictures of my inner ears . . . and my brain.'

'Maybe I should go with you,' he offered, now sounding as concerned as he looked.

'Thanks, but I can go myself.'

'What's he looking for?'

'I'm not sure, but it has something to do with my sense of balance,' I said, picturing a gyroscope tottering around in my cranium.

'Sounds scary.'

'Not really. The doctor said he didn't think it was anything serious,' I said, putting a steaming plate of spaghetti in front of Shel, and a napkin-lined basket of garlic bread in the middle of the table.

'Well, it'd be pretty serious if you lost your balance hanging over the balcony staring at clouds. You could take a dive like your neighbour . . . seventeen floors to the boardwalk ... *splat*!' he said, slapping his hand on the table for emphasis.

'That's grotesque, Shel,' I said, somewhat annoyed with his dramatics, but understanding all too well his need to play out his worst fears – his fear of losing me. 'But you don't have to worry about me falling over the balcony. The railing's too high,' I explained to my son unnecessarily, as if he were a child.

'Anyway, it looks like Marjorie might have had some help off her balcony,' I added, changing the subject. 'I heard – actually, I think I read it in the paper this morning – that Marjorie's balcony door was locked ... from the inside, so the police are considering murder.'

'Mystery and intrigue at the Ivory Tower!' Shel said, grabbing a slice of bread and plunging into his spaghetti while I served the salad. 'By the way, isn't Mrs Forrester's unit right over Marjorie's?' Shel asked.

'Now how would you know that, Shel?'

'I don't. I was just wondering–. Never mind.'

'You were wondering what? Tell me.'

'I was just wondering if maybe Applebaum could have gone off someone else's balcony.'

'Like Mrs Forrester's?'

'Right.'

'Where did *that* come from? Just what do you know about that woman?' I asked, thinking only of Brenda Forrester the possible child molester, not Brenda Forrester the possible murderess.

'Only what I've heard ... and I've already told you that. Remember? The Milfs?' he said, smirking at his plate.

'How could I forget?' I said with a flush, remembering, too, what I'd heard from Robin ... remembering what I'd written.

'You know, Shel, you can tell me anything, honey,' I

cajoled my son, sure that he wanted to tell me something
. . . like about the day he disappeared from the beach,
which to me was a lot more important than murder.

'*Anything*? Sure, Mom,' he said with an edge of
sarcasm.

'*Sure, Mom*, what?'

'Trust me. There are some things I couldn't tell you . . .
things you definitely wouldn't understand,' he said.

'*Things*? What kinds of *things*?'

'Guy things.'

'What kinds of *guy* things?'

'Like . . . well, like sports, for instance.'

'And?' I asked, sure that I hadn't missed a vital turn in
the conversation, that what was on my son's mind wasn't a
bawdy brush with baseball, an illicit tryst with tennis, a
close encounter with curling.

'*And*, what?'

'*And* what *other* guy things?'

'Well . . . guys.'

'*Guys*?'

'Yeah. *Guys* . . . as in men.'

'*Men*?'

'*Men* . . . as in *dates*. Remember dates? When was your
last date, Mom. I bet you can't remember,' Shel responded, shifting the interrogation.

Suddenly on the defensive, I stopped to think, searching for documentation. Since the kinky neuro-surgeon
Robin had fixed me up with the summer before – the one
who proposed making love to me while hooked up to an
electroencephalogram – I'd had only one date . . . *but even
that was six months ago*, I thought, straining my memory
for something to tell Shel. 'Just last Sunday!' I finally said,
remembering dinner with Jeffrey Kaufman, grateful now
to Robin for leaving us in a *date* situation.

'Oh yeah? Who?'

'Jeffrey Kaufman. He's a –'

'I know. The shrink. Last summer his wife ran off with Applebaum's husband – the life-guard.'

'You certainly keep up with the local gossip. I hope you do as well with schoolwork come September.'

He rolled his eyes. 'So how was the shrink?'

'He was very nice. We had dinner at Barney's.'

'Now don't forget Robbie Rubber,' he teased.

I rolled my eyes. ·

'Think he's material?' Shel asked.

'Material?'

'Husband material.'

'Okay,' I said, putting my fork down, looking intently at my son. 'Now, what's all this about?' I asked, aware that Shel had managed to evade my inquiry into Brenda Forrester – I didn't dare to think why – but feeling, too, that there was more to *this* conversation than an attempt to evade the other. 'Why are you suddenly so interested in my love life?'

'I'm always interested. I just want to see you happy. You know . . . taken care of.'

'I think I take pretty good care of myself. In fact, I've taken pretty good care of both of us for the past fifteen years. What makes you think I need someone to take care of me?'

Shel stuffed his mouth with garlic bread so he couldn't possibly answer my question . . .

'What makes you think I need someone to take care of me?' I'd asked my father.

Since Carl's death, nine months earlier, my parents had been uncharacteristically quiet about my life, my mother had even given up calling me on rainy days to tell me to

166

put regular shoes on Shel, not sneakers, which would get wet in the rain, and lead to a cold, sore throat, pneumonia. And I couldn't remember the last time she'd called to warn me of some grocery hazard – poison in the grapes, Botulism in the anchovies, Salmonella in the chicken. I supposed she was being sensitive. After all, I was a widow with a young child. I had enough to worry about.

Not quite enough, apparently, as that particular evening, after dinner at my parents' home, my mother escorted Shel off to the den to play dominoes, leaving my father and me at the table over coffee. 'Let's talk for a minute,' he'd said. And he started like this: 'How are you doing ... how's Shel doing ... do you need anything ... are you getting along all right ... do you have enough money? Your mother and I are worried.' And ended like this: '... You've been a brave little soldier ... but it's been almost a year, and you should start to think about finding someone to take care of you.'

That's when I asked, 'What makes you think I need someone to take care of me?'

Ben Shipman called the following week. He was the son and partner of my father's dentist. Recently separated – his wife had left him for the tennis pro at their country club after finding out about a six-month affair he'd had with his technician – Ben was trying to get 'back into life'. My father suggested he call me. 'You kids would be good company for each other,' he'd said.

We spent several evenings at some of Philadelphia's finest restaurants, where, between a glass of white wine and a pony of Drambuie, I was treated to four course dinners and non-stop whining – starting with escargot Pernod and the evils of his wife, moving to a tri-colour salad vinaigrette and the evils of divorce lawyers, then on to medallions of veal with baby veggies and the tribulations of single life, finishing with mounds of white chocolate mousse with fresh raspberry sauce and the difficulties Ben had finding himself and learning to like himself, which, by our fourth date, I was understanding all too well.

So I'm not sure why I went out with him again. And I'll never understand why, after our fifth date, I had sex with him – except that he was attractive, he smelled good, and I hadn't slept with a man since Carl had died (I choose not to count my crazed coupling with Philip Krausen, because I'd known him for years . . . because it was only once . . . because it was too soon after Carl's death . . . because it made me feel bad . . . *he* made me feel bad). Bottom line: I had sex with Ben Shipman because I needed someone to make me feel good . . . to make me feel like I counted. Maybe. More likely, I had sex with Ben Shipman because I was horny.

So, after that evening's dinner and whine, I invited Ben into my apartment and led him into my den/office. Sitting together on my dove ultra-suede love-seat, we spoke briefly of the fluoride-in-water controversy and bonding – teeth, that is – and then he kissed me softly, the way he'd kissed me at my front door after our last two dates. It was a nice, non-threatening kiss, a decent open-mouthed, no-tongues kind of kiss, a kiss that could have been the beginning and end at the same time, but for the fact that, quite by accident, while shifting position in an effort to avoid having my elbow stuck uncomfortably in his rib cage, Ben's left hand brushed ever so slightly against my breast. More specifically, his fingers grazed my nipple, a nipple that was quite bare beneath my pale taupe silk blouse. And that chance caress sparked a blaze of passion in me that surprised us both. Well, it surprised me. I'm not sure that men can be surprised by passion.

After, he rolled off me and said, 'Alison, let me take care of you.' Taking his limp hand in mine, I placed it on my yet unrequited body. 'Here, Ben, gently,' I said, not understanding. He'd already fallen asleep. When he woke warm and cocky a half-hour later, he nuzzled my neck. 'You've been brave to go it alone all this time,' he said. 'Let me take care of you.'

'What makes you think I need someone to take care of me?' I asked, finally understanding.

. . . 'Don't you think I've taken good care of us?' I asked my son, feeling my confidence slip under the indictment of my father's slight, Ben's conceit . . . Shel's silence.

'Um-hm,' Shel intoned through his full mouth, staring at his plate of spaghetti.

'You *don't* think so, do you?' I begged the question.

His eyes on his plate, Shel swallowed.

Before he had a chance to fill his mouth again, I demanded, 'Shel? Answer me . . . please.'

'Sure you take good care of us, but –'

'But what?'

'Well, in case you haven't noticed, there've been two adults in this household for a long time. And I kinda thought we took care of each other . . .'

I put my fork down and looked at my son . . . and wondered when he had grown up . . . wondered when *he* thought he'd grown up.

'. . . and now I'm going to go away to school . . . and . . . well . . . it's just that I'm going to be far away,' he said quietly, opening the door to his inner self just enough for me to be privy to more than Shel himself was probably aware of.

Far away, he'd said. Far away *from me*, he meant, and

he was worried about me, but he was worried, too, that *I* might find a new life and move far away from *him*. All at a time when he was straining to be free of me. All this I saw quite clearly when he said '*I'm going to be far away.*' Poor baby, I thought, remembering the sea gulls on the beach, fighting the desire to cradle him in my arms like the baby he once was. 'You *are* going to be far away, Shel. You're going to miss me, aren't you?' I said, reaching across the table to touch his arm ... his sunburned, muscular, very grown up arm.

'Don't touch the bod!' he cried in mock horror, pulling his arm away.

'Actually, I miss you already,' I confessed, my eyes misting.

'If you cry I'm not going to eat another thing,' Shel threatened, attempting to eschew emotion.

But I saw it in his face, a face I knew so well, so much better even than my own. And scooping up the almost empty basket, I jumped from my seat to fill it with the remainder of garlic bread warming in the oven ... saving his face ... savouring the painfully sweet moment of declaration of his almost shed tears, which I thought was about the closest I'd ever get to hearing that he loved me. 'Love you, Shel,' I said, pecking him on the cheek as I placed the filled basket of aromatic bread before him.

'I think I should go with you tomorrow,' he said commandingly, pretending not to notice my affectionate gesture.

'Thanks, Shel. I promise to call you if I get nervous about going alone,' I said, allowing him his eighteen-year-old sense of dignity.

When I closed my eyes that night contemplating Shel's dizzying complex of feelings, I quickly became aware of my own drifting sense of balance. It was as if the endless black behind my lids, an abyss of uncertainty, provided no focus for my inner eye. Again I remembered the gulls, and large, heavy tears fell from my eyes to the pillow, providing an anchor for my drifting soul.

CHAPTER 9

White

I awoke in the middle of the night with thoughts of The Tube. I hadn't exactly been dreaming, but as I became aware of wakefulness I also became aware of The Tube wrapped around my mind. I remembered the picture of the thing in the pamphlet. Kind of like an iron lung, I thought, but my head would be *inside*, and my legs outside. I imagined trying to move in the tube. It was confining. A mirror, I was told, would be above me so that through the magic of optics I would be able to see outside the tube, view the windowed booth where the technician would be sitting safely at the controls, away from the strong magnetic field that was doing only God knows what to the molecules in my body, in my brain. I imagined the mirror in front of me, close to my face, too close to focus on . . . and much, much too close for comfort. And I couldn't move my head and I couldn't move my arms, and the tube was ten feet long and I couldn't crawl out . . . and it was tight . . . and there was no air . . . and I yelled that I wanted to get out but no one heard me and the technician wasn't in the window and I was all alone in a tube twenty feet long binding me holding me suffocating me and I sat bolt upright in bed dripping perspiration.

I can't do this, I thought. *I'll never be able to do this.* And I got up and, mindful of my already upset stomach, took two non-aspirin pain relievers which undoubtedly would relieve only a non-headache. I turned on the television with the remote control, flipped through the channels and then closed my eyes as the crew of the starship Enterprise fought a tinselled alien whose computer synthesised voice threatened to fragment my already cracked composure.

Somehow, Thursday morning came. I called Dr Pressman at eight-thirty to tell him that I couldn't possibly go through with the test . . . that I was claustrophobic and wouldn't last thirty seconds in The Tube.

He told me to stop into his office . . . that he'd give me a tranquiliser. He also suggested I take a tape of my favourite music to the lab, that they'd play it for me through headphones. 'Actually, a lot of people have trouble with the MRI because of claustrophobia,' he said.

I felt less crazy when he told me lots of people were as crazy as I.

Sipping my coffee at the snack counter in my kitchen, I organised my day in my head, keeping in mind my two-o'clock appointment: first shower and dress; stop at Dr Pressman's office and pick up The Drug; stop at the library to look up The Drug in the Physician's Desk Reference – an encyclopedia of prescription drugs that could make you swear off prescription drugs – to make sure The Drug didn't have any untoward effects.

Untoward. That's medical terminology for *unfortunate*, and – doctors would have you believe – *unusual*, as in *a reaction that most people don't get, but more people get than doctors would have you believe, a reaction that is often worse than the symptom*, like when my neighbour, Jessie Gold, took a *mild* tranquiliser, to help relieve her crying jags associated with menopause, and she relaxed so much she peed all over the floor in the perfume department of Saks Fifth Avenue. It just poured out of her, she said, like the time her water broke when she went into labour with her second child, although that was in Bloomingdale's, in the china department. The profound relaxation of her urinary sphincter was an Untoward Effect of the drug, her doctor later told her.

On my way to the shower, I decided to first call the lab and ask about Untoward Effects of the MRI.

'None,' said the technician, who identified herself as Debbie. She explained how the MRI is a *non-invasive* technique and that, unlike the older and less sophisticated CAT scan, it doesn't require the injection of a dye that's been associated with allergic reactions.

Fatal allergic reactions, I remembered reading, making *death* an Untoward Effect of a CAT scan.

'How long does the MRI take?' I asked, although I'd read in the pamphlet that it takes thirty-five minutes.

'About thirty-five minutes,' Debbie confirmed. 'But if your doctor ordered an injection of gadolinium the test takes a few minutes longer.'

'Gadolinium?' I questioned.

'It's a naturally occurring element. It's on the periodic table.'

'So are arsenic and plutonium,' I countered.

Debbie didn't laugh. 'Well, it helps the radiologist see questionable structures more clearly. It's perfectly harmless. There's never been an untoward effect reported,' she said.

'Sorry to keep you waiting, Alison,' Dr Pressman said in his office, handing me a long white envelope. 'I think you'll find these helpful.'

'Thanks. And Dr Pressman—'

'Oh, and maybe you should get someone to go with you. The medication can make you sleepy. And call me when you're home. I'll be in the office until nine tonight.'

'... what's gadolinium?'

'Gadolinium? It's a naturally occurring element. It's on the periodic table,' he answered, echoing Debbie's words too closely for comfort.

'So are arsenic and plutonium,' I tried again.

He didn't laugh. 'Well, there's never been an untoward effect reported,' he further echoed. 'Although one lady claimed to lose her ability to read Tarot cards after having an MRI. You don't do cards, do you?' he added with a chuckle.

I didn't laugh. 'So, what does it do?' I asked.

'Well, it's a magnetic substance that makes your molecules spin a different way, giving the radiologist sharper pictures.'

One could only imagine the Untoward Effect of every molecule in your body spinning like tiny compasses at the north pole. I pictured the molecules in my body, in my brain, spinning off in millions of directions, colliding with one another. A body at war with itself; a mind in total chaos spinning into the vast universe of insanity. *An Untoward Effect of gadolinium*, some specialist would tell my weeping son, *it'll make an interesting scientific paper*.

'Don't worry. You'll be fine,' Dr Pressman said as a nurse handed him a chart and he turned to head towards an examination room. 'By the way,' he said, turning back to me, 'you look very familiar. I'm sure we've met before.'

'I don't think so. Dr Pressman—'

'Ira. Please.'

'. . . Ira. Did you order gadolinium for me?'

'It's up to the radiologist – if he feels there's something he wants to see more clearly.'

'The technician said it was up to you,' I challenged.

'Well, it's a call the radiologist has to make. He's the expert,' Dr Pressman replied.

'By the way, how long have they been using gadolinium?' I asked.

'About three years,' he answered, confirming my worst fears – that they were still collecting data.

At the first red light on the way to the library, I pulled the envelope from my pocketbook, opened it, and inspected the plastic-bubbled, silver-foil-backed cardboard container of two tiny white pills. A quick stop at the library provided valuable information that Ira had neglected to mention, including a long list of Untoward Effects that I decided to ignore so that I wouldn't be tempted to go into The Tube without benefit of something designed to kill my primitive instincts – like not doing something that terrified me. One tablet was the usual single dosage, the book informed me.

Returning to my apartment, I tried to call Robin. When she didn't answer, I went to the beach to look for her, but she wasn't there, either. Jeffrey Kaufman was.

'Alison!' he called to me, putting his book down as he stood up. 'You're all dressed. Going somewhere?'

'Yes. I was looking for Robin to take a ride with me. Have you seen her?' I asked, walking towards him.

'No. Can I be of service?'

'Well, actually it's kind of personal.'

'How personal?'

'I need someone to come with me and watch my molecules spin.'

'Well, now. That *is* personal. I don't think I've ever

177

gotten quite that close to anyone. Your place or mine?'

'Neither. But I can tell you that there's a mirror above the bed, a stereo system, cameras to capture the action, and an observation booth with a one-way mirror,' I answered, almost manic with anxiety.

'I'm yours! Is it The Inn of the Dove? The Boulevard Motor Lodge?'

'The Magnetic Resonance Imaging lab. I have an appointment at two. They want to look inside my head to see why I've been getting seasick on land. Maybe a brain tumour . . . or some exotic neurologic wasting disease –'

'Whoa there,' Jeffrey said. 'Sounds like the doctor gave you quite a scare. Listen, if you want me to come, I'd be glad to.'

'Thanks, but I think I'll call my son.'

'Well, if you change your mind –'

And then I caught sight of the book Jeffrey had been reading, *A Stitch in Time*, by Sloan I. Diamond. I'd been used to seeing my books on the shelves in bookstores and markets, but seeing someone actually reading it – seeing someone I *knew* reading it – held a different kind of satisfaction, a secret excitement.

'Enjoying the book, Jeffrey?' I asked, attempting utter nonchalance.

'It's a kinky medical mystery. Actually more kink than mystery,' he said, smiling.

'Well, there's really a lot more kink than mystery in the world, Jeffrey,' I said, suddenly smitten with an idea about the mystery of Marjorie Applebaum's death.

'Well, that certainly is a mysterious – and perhaps kinky – way of looking at life.' Jeffrey responded, confounded and amused. 'And, in answer to your question, yes, I'm enjoying the book.'

'Well, I gotta go and get zapped,' I said, my anxiety

breaking through the comforting wave of ricocheted praise.

'By the way, Alison, a friend of mine had an MRI last year for a ruptured disk and he said there was nothing to it, just a little close,' Jeffrey said, trying to be comforting.

A little close . . . *close*, as in tight, constricted, constraining, binding . . . , I thought, panicking. 'I gotta go,' I said to Jeffrey. And I fled the beach, trying to maintain my composure . . . at least until I reached my apartment, where I pushed one of the little white pills out of its plastic bubble through the foil backing, accidentally cracking it in half. After swallowing the two halves with a gulp of water, I called Shel at work to ask if he could take me to the lab after all – of course, he would – and then sat on my balcony, waiting to feel unanxious. About half an hour later, still feeling anxious, I decided to take another pill. Ira had, after all, given me two.

By the time Shel came, I was feeling . . . well, I was feeling very little. I might as well have been encased in bubble paper . . . softly but firmly held together . . . insulated from jarring sights and sounds.

'You okay, Mom?' he asked, finding me motionless on a chair on the balcony, staring out to sea.

'Fine, honey. I guess we should go,' I said, but not moving.

Shel waited a moment, then, shifting from one foot to the next, finally said, 'So, let's go,' his cross tone probably signifying growing concern more than impatience, for we had more than enough time to get to the lab.

Although he told me later how my lack of affect had spooked him, I wasn't aware at the time of him staring at my reflection in the mirrors in the elevator, where my disquieting silence was reflected over and over, until my image all but disappeared. 'We're going to be early,' Shel said, looking at his watch as we left the elevator.

I didn't respond.

'God, your car's a mess, Mom,' Shel said as the attendant drove up to the front door. 'Don't you ever wash it?'

Ordinarily I would have remarked about Shel's unwillingness to wash my car, but at that moment I felt no need to chastise him. 'It's okay. Just a little dusty,' I answered.

'We're *really* going to be early,' Shel said again as he drove towards the hospital.

'It's okay,' I said, feeling at that moment like everything *was* okay.

'Tell you what, Mom, we're going to get your car washed,' Shel said, turning precipitously off the road and into the Minute-Wash drive-in carwash, in what, I later realised, was an attempt to get me to react.

'Shel, what are you doing!?' I reacted.

'You've got to be good to your car, Mom.'

'But, Shel—. I can't believe you're doing this! We have more important things to do right now,' I said as Shel paid the man at the entrance, asking for *The Works*. '... It's such a waste of money. I could do it myself. Actually, *you* should do it for me! And why did you get the hot wax? You can never get that stuff off the windows,' I continued haranguing him as the car, cruising slowly through the tunnel, was squirted and rubbed and scrubbed, and then, beneath an arch of flashing red and white lights, coated with hot wax.

'Every now and then you've got to treat yourself, Mom,' Shel said.

In the waiting room of the MRI lab, I'd fallen back into myself when a tall, lean young woman dressed in white escorted me to the lab where everything was white – the walls and floor and ceiling ... The Tube encircled by its great, white, doughnut shaped magnet. Following the woman's instructions, I laid down on a white cot in the white room. Feeling unconcerned with what was going on, I was watching a short, chubby man, also in white, in the control booth through the window in the wall when the woman placed earphones on me and slid a kind of grate over my head – like a football helmet, I thought. I then felt the cot rolling backwards.

As I was swallowed head first into the belly of The Tube, a twinge of panic broke through my synthetic composure. But I closed my eyes, and a man's comforting voice came to me through the earphones: 'Are you okay?'

'Yes,' I said.

Then the music started, expanding my pinched world of stifling black into a vast universe of breezy space and brilliant sound. In a moment I was in the front row of the balcony in the Academy of Music looking down on The Philadelphia Orchestra playing the transcendent opening movement of Beethoven's seventh symphony.

Then the banging started, distracting me – loud metallic knocks, at first one or two, then a short series, then a barrage sounding very much like a jackhammer. *Street sounds*, I imagined, allowing the power of Beethoven to pull me back to the balcony where I was no longer sitting, but lying on a black velvet lounge, wrapped in a black velvet coverlet as light as sea foam, as the double dose of tranquiliser permeating my brain reached its peak effectiveness. The only thing in my mind was the music vibrating through me.

But on the downstroke of the slow, quiet second movement, I began to wander from the balcony. Floating through a tunnel, I found myself on the beach. Strangely, it was night. There was no moon lighting my way as I walked on impossibly warm, soft sand towards the umbrellas, luminous in day-glo colours, piercing the black of the night. And I sat next to Robin, who'd been alone on the beach until that moment. She was slouched down in her seat and appeared to be fidgeting with something between her legs, but I couldn't see what.

Robin ignored me for a moment. Then above the unusually loud pounding of the surf and the strains of Beethoven emanating from her portable radio, I heard my friend ask, *'Don't you ever get horny?'*

And then I saw what she was doing. She was masturbating.

I suddenly found myself transported to my marriage bed. My husband, Carl, was at work; three-year-old Shel was in nursery school, although it must have been night because it was oddly black beyond my bedroom window. It would be two hours until the minibus brought Shel home, I thought, lying in bed in the unlighted room. The radio was playing Beethoven's seventh symphony, and through an open window I heard the distant din of a jackhammer engaged in some nocturnal street repair. I felt bored, lonely ... and I itched, deep down inside me. Running my hands up my naked body beneath my black velvet comforter in an attempt to quell the odd prickling of my skin, I reached my breasts and began massaging them to the slow steady rhythm of Beethoven's largo. The familiar heat of lust swelled up in me. *Yes*, I thought, feeling at once deprived and depraved, remembering that I was alone, with no place to go, nothing to do but to stir my nerve endings into a seething frenzy of sexual excitement.

'Yes,' I admitted to Robin back on the beach in the middle of the night, under Robin's pink day-glow umbrella, *'Yes, I get horny.'*

'You should be good to yourself, Alison,' Robin said caressing herself unabashedly, a sight I found disturbingly exciting.

'It makes me feel guilty,' I said.

'I'm not surprised,' my friend responded.

'I'm not saying I never –'

'The body craves sexual release, Alison,' Robin lectured. 'And it's true that you can lust after one you love,' she said, alluding to her own dear but impotent husband, 'and you can lust after one you don't love,' she continued, alluding to the late Marjorie Applebaum's sexy husband, the Hunk, 'but it's also true that sometimes the sexual object is lust itself. Every now and then you've got to treat yourself,' she said.

I didn't answer.

'Alison, you look so tense. Let me show you how to relax. Watch me, Alison. It feels so good,' she said turning towards me, spreading her legs slightly as her hand – which had taken on the appearance of a bird in flight – fluttered against the naked flesh between them.

I watched with swelling excitement until an overwhelming sense of guilt made me look away.

'I'm getting excited, Robin. Do you think that represents a latent homosexual tendency?' I asked, matching Robin's physical candour with my words.

She laughed.

'Well, then, would you consider sex with a shower massage a homosexual act?' I asked, remembering my own trysts with the hand-held shower head many mornings after my husband had left for work, after he had left my bed, left me aching.

'Not unless another woman's hand was doing the holding – like Brenda Forrester.'

'Brenda Forrester?'

'Yes. The woman's obviously capable of anything.'

'That may be, but I could never have sex with any woman other than myself,' I said indignantly.

'Sometimes I'd rather do it myself than with a woman or a man. Like now,' she said, luxuriating in her strokes.

'Really? Do you think men feel the same way?' I asked, trying to overlook the bisexual implication of her comment, and her reference to Brenda Forrester.

'Well, according to a survey I read in ... I don't remember ... *Cosmo* ... *Playboy*, maybe ... most men said that, all else being equal, they'd prefer a prostitute to their own hand.'

'Why do you suppose that is?'

'Because a man needs to have his ego stroked along with his penis,' Robin stated with authority.

'I couldn't go to a prostitute; I could never have sex with a strange man.'

'I'm not surprised.'

'So what's a horny woman to do?' I asked, my body aching to be touched, to be fondled, to be released from its prickle, its tingle ... its itch.

'Have an affair.'

'There's nobody–'

'There's Jeffrey Kaufman.'

'Oh, no, I couldn't–'

'Then do what I do. It's so good. Watch me, Alison, watch me,' she urged fervently.

'I can't,' I said, turning nonetheless to her. 'It makes me feel so guilty–'

'Wait a minute,' Robin said, slouching further down in her chair, the now frenetic movement of her hand intensifying along with the approaching end of Beethoven's rousing third movement, until her back arched and she let out a most impassioned sound.

'There should be a place for women to go for therapeutic sexual release,' I said, desperately turned on, politely pretending to ignore Robin's orgasm, stressing the word *therapeutic*. My friend was, after all, a doctor's wife.

'Well, I attended a medical lecture recently by a sexologist who predicted that someday there'll be robots that can be customised to fit people's sexual needs. That should solve your problem,' Robin answered cheerfully after a moment, sitting up in her chair.

'Sounds expensive.'

'No doubt some enterprising man will set up a rental service of mechanical call guys.'

'That wouldn't be cheap, either ... and you'd have to make an appointment. How embarrassing.'

'Perhaps we should go into business, then. Something mass market ... inexpensive and immediate ... like a drive-in restaurant.'

'Or a drive-in carwash,' I jumped in. 'We'll call it *Minute-O*.'

'I like it.'

'The client drives into what looks like an ordinary carwash. Okay?' I chattered on, my sexual excitement momentarily rechanneled. 'Now, she gives the secret signal – she asks for The Works – and pays a little extra, so once through the first line of chamois scrubbing fingers, her car is elevated to an upper track where the front doors are automatically opened and mechanical arms slide the seat back into a reclining position . . .'

'That's good!'

'. . . Of course the client wears the required *loose outer garments and no underwear* . . .'

'Nice touch.'

'. . . and as the car glides along the humming electric track through the warm, dark, secret tunnel above the regular carwash, tiny little brushes and soft and hard things enter the car and touch her body in the right places, while sensual music plays in quadrilateral stereo.'

'Ravel's Bolero.'

'No. Not the Bolero. Too trite. Beethoven. Beethoven's seventh symphony,' I said, closing my eyes and listening to Robin's radio as the orchestra entered the powerful, multi-climactic fourth movement.

Like the tide responds to the phases of the moon, my body surged and ebbed to the measures of the music . . . and I found myself in my car, which was no longer beige, but black, with black velvet seat covers. I was on the upper track of the Minute-O carwash, and my body was being deliciously ravished by all manner of touching and probing things . . . causing me to swoon with pleasure. And then something hard and smooth slipped into me – the Orgasometer, an instrument designed to signal occurrence of orgasm by setting off an arch of flashing red and white lights on the track below.

Opening my eyes, I saw a mirror close to my face reflecting a small window through which a man was watching me. I fancied the mirror to be the rear-view mirror of my car . . . and the window, a peep hole in the carwash through which people watch their cars being scrubbed by robotic arms. I wondered if he'd paid extra to watch *me* get polished instead of my car. The idea excited me. I closed my eyes again, turning them inward as I listened to the orchestra filling the space my body didn't with what was now the conclusive paroxysms of Beethoven's multi-orgasmic symphony. I swelled to a climax just as the final bombastic chords of Beethoven screamed in my ears. Red and white lights flashed below me.

Bravo! Ludwig, I cheered silently to myself, wondering where the Maestro had dipped his pen while composing those gloriously passionate notes.

'We're going to bring you out now,' a disembodied voice reached me.

I felt myself moving along the track until I was out of the tunnel.

Disorientated, I opened my eyes and saw the odd couple standing above me. The stone-faced man – the voyeur from the carwash – was holding a tray; the woman, smiling, rolled the grate back from my face. 'Good morning!' she said. 'Are you okay?'

'Yes,' I managed to say with a thick tongue, though I felt dazed and warm from my erotic fantasy – an Untoward Effect of the tranquiliser, no doubt.

'Your test is normal so far,' the woman said, 'but the radiologist would like to have one more set of pictures. First we're going to inject you with this contrast material.'

I woke up. 'Contrast material?' I questioned.

'Gadolinium. It's a natural element. It's on the periodic table.'

'So are arsenic and plutonium,' I tried yet again, my mind suddenly sharp though my body felt like silly putty.

The odd couple did not laugh. 'It's non-toxic and non-allergic,' the woman said, sounding like a television commercial.

'How long has it been used?' I asked.

'We've been using it for three years now and we've never had an untoward effect.'

'Still testing it?'

'We'd like to give you this.'

'I'd prefer not.'

'We'd prefer you did.'

'I'd prefer not,' I resisted passively, understanding that passive resistance was the only resistance I was capable of at the moment.

'If the radiologist requests it after he sees the films, will you come back?'

'*After* he sees the films?' I questioned, wondering, *How could he tell he needs clearer pictures if he hasn't seen the films yet?* 'I'd like to talk to him,' I said.

'He's not here right now.'

'Call me if you need me,' I said, rising from the cot, feeling more centred than I had in days.

On the way home from the lab I was quiet, partly because I was still mellowed out by the tranquiliser, partly because I was still distracted by my erotic dream. Shel, on the other hand, was quite chatty, partly because he was relieved to see me safe and sound after he'd sat alone in the waiting room for almost an hour, partly because he was still disturbed by my flat affect.

He told me that he'd been thinking about the time, years ago, when I'd lightened my hair. He was about eleven. It was when everything about himself had been changing and suddenly the one touchstone in his life – his never changing mother – had changed. And he'd felt alone, disconnected from me, unbound from the world. An Untoward Effect of the bleach, I thought to myself.

It took me a few minutes – drugged as I was – to figure out that he was feeling disconnected from me once again. This time, however, the disconnection was mine, not his. It was pleasant – a nonchalance I wasn't used to. And I didn't mind it, this drug-induced detachment. But Shel minded.

'You know you're acting a little spooky,' he said.

'It's only the tranquiliser the doctor gave me. I'll be myself in a few hours,' I said in an attempt to ease his apprehension.

'Actually, it's okay, Mom. It's kind of nice having you so chilled out for a change. Maybe I should take this opportunity to tell you everything you've wanted to know about me that you've been afraid to ask.'

Now, ordinarily I would have jumped on this obvious ploy, this blatant invitation to pry into my son's life, to wheedle out of him the things that I wanted to know and he wanted to tell me, *But*. As in *But* he was afraid to tell me . . . *But* he thought he'd get into trouble . . . *But* he thought I'd be angry with him . . . disappointed in him . . . shocked. But I was so complacent sitting beside him in a drug-induced near stupor, that I just smiled and said, 'You know I'm always here to talk, Shel.'

Hardly a mental crowbar. In fact it pretty well nailed him shut.

The phone rang at nine o'clock that evening. 'Alison? It's Ira Pressman. When you didn't call I got a little concerned. Everything go okay this afternoon?'

'Fine. I took the pills. They worked. In fact, they worked so well I'm still feeling rather mellow.'

'Pills? You took more than one?'

'You gave me two.'

'No wonder you're still mellow,' he said, chuckling.

'Maybe you can give me some more when my son leaves for school.'

'Maybe we'll talk about it further when I see you again. I'll call you when I get the results of the test and we'll set a . . . an appointment.'

'Sure. And thanks for the call. I appreciate –'

'And I'm going to remember where we met.'

I sincerely hoped he wouldn't.

'Where were you yesterday?' Robin asked me on the beach Friday morning – an exceptionally hot morning.

'Getting my molecules spun.'

'Okay. So it's none of my business. But where were you?'

'Really. Getting my molecules spun. I had an MRI of my

head to see what's making me dizzy.'

'That sounds like a nice summer afternoon's entertainment.'

'Actually, it was. Sort of. Ira gave me a tranquiliser before I went, so I slept through the whole thing, and I had this incredibly erotic daydream,' I said without thinking.

'Oh?' Robin said, perking up. '*You* had an erotic dream? I can't wait to hear it!'

Looking at Robin, I couldn't help but picture her the way I'd seen her in my dream – with her hands between her legs – and I briefly thought about how people really had no idea how other people behaved sexually.

'What?' Robin said. 'Why're you looking at me so funny?'

'I was just thinking about my dream. It had to do with a drive-in carwash and Beethoven.'

'A car wash. Beethoven. I'm not surprised.'

'Something wrong with Beethoven?'

'Personally, in my dreams, I'd prefer Sting . . . in a drive-in movie.'

'Each to his own. By the way, where were *you* yesterday? I was at the beach in the morning looking for you. I thought maybe you'd drive me to the lab, but you weren't around . . . and you weren't in your apartment.'

'Oh, I stopped in to see Marty Steiner. I got to the beach about two,' Robin said, jumping up and hot-footing it towards the water.

I followed, quickly skipping across the burning sand, dodging bodies on blankets on the way to the icy water that soothed the soles of my feet but sent a shock through my body.

'So who drove you?' Robin asked, picking up a thread of our conversation.

'Shel.'

'How's he doing?'

'He's fine. But, as you already suggested, the question remains, how am *I* doing?'

'Okay. How *are* you doing?'

'You know, it doesn't get any easier,' I sighed.

'What doesn't get any easier?'

'Kids. Or should I say, *having* kids. When Shel was little, I thought that when he grew up things would get easier, that I'd stop worrying about him all the time ... about trying to protect him all the time. But now that he's grown up I worry *more* about him, not less.'

Robin silently indulged my sudden need to be neurotic, which was probably a backlash against my day of ultra-mellowness. Insanity: an Untoward Effect of sanity.

'When he started in school I was afraid he'd get kidnapped from the playground ... get hurt in a bus accident,' I went on. 'I hated going to a mall. He never wanted to hold my hand ... and there were so many people, so many weird looking people ... ready to snatch him up ...'

And I remembered a day at the mall when Shel let go of my hand and disappeared in the mire of legs and shopping bags. Frantically searching, pictures of police cars and newspaper headlines spinning through my head, despair racked my heart as I imagined a joyless, guilt-filled life in search of my baby, wondering every minute where he was, if he was hungry, frightened, in pain. I could hear his cries from the bowels of his captor's dungeon: 'Mommy! Mommy!' ... until, not ten seconds later I spotted his red snowsuit in front of the toy store four steps away. 'Mommy! Mommy! Look, train!' he was calling to me. Holding Shel in my arms, I realised for the first time, but not the last, how a lifetime of horror can be felt in an instant.

* * *

'. . . And car pools were a nightmare,' I continued my litany to Robin, not missing a beat, although my eyes had filled with tears. 'I never trusted another driver with him. And then *he* started to drive! I can't tell you about that agony. Every time he took the keys I was a wreck until he was home. I'm still a wreck when he drives. Of course, it's even worse if one of his *friends* drives. And half the time I'm not sure where he is . . . even if I know where he started out. At least when he was a baby I always knew where he was – he was where I put him! The only time he was out of my sight, the only time I could totally relax, was when he was safe in bed . . . asleep.'

'My sister-in-law isn't even secure when my nephew's asleep,' Robin said. 'She goes into his room several times a night to check on him . . . to make sure he's still breathing.'

'Oh, yes. I did that too. I guess all new mothers do that for a time.'

'My nephew is *ten*!'

'I guess that's carrying things a bit too far. But I can understand. I've been known to peek into Shel's room at two o'clock on a Sunday afternoon and listen for sounds of life, watch to see if his covers rise and fall.'

'Two o'clock? P.M.?'

'And then there's the sex thing,' I continued, bypassing Robin's shock over the sleep habits of teenagers. 'When I was a teenager I guess my parents worried about sex. Although, they shouldn't have; I was a terrible prude –'

'I'm not surprised.'

'You know, you said that to me in my dream.'

'*I* was in your erotic dream?'

'Don't worry. We just talked.'

'Chicken,' Robin teased, laughing.

'Where was I? Oh, yes. Sex. When the media was

warning about the epidemic of herpes and genital warts, I was happy that Shel was too young to be at risk ... that there was at least one thing I didn't have to worry about. So what happened? He grew up and I now have to worry about AIDS – Death: an Untoward Effect of sex. As I said, it gets harder, not easier. And they get weirder as they get older. You wouldn't believe some of the things he's been saying to me lately.'

'Like what?'

'Trust me. It gets harder.'

'But there's the compensation, Alison. Unlike husbands, kids appreciate what you do for them,' Robin said, inserting a bit of her own agenda.

'If they do they're careful not to let you know it!'

'But you *know* your kids love you.'

'Sometimes I wonder. Shel hasn't told me he loves me since he was three. So I worry that maybe I'm not giving him what he needs, that he's growing up resenting what I *didn't* do, that someday he'll need a shrink ... and he'll tell his shrink that he blames me for everything that went wrong in his life ... that he really hates me.'

'Maybe I'm lucky – not having kids – no labour pains, no worries,' Robin said unconvincingly.

'*Labour* pains? Labour is the *easy* part! It's the after-birth pains that get you. The doctor tells you they last a few days. Hah! They last a lifetime.' I sighed again. 'But, worries and all, Shel's the most important part of my life. I can't imagine what it would be like without him.'

'Well, Alison, you're about to find out. You'll see. Once he's settled in Chicago you won't worry so much,' Robin said, trying to close the subject, but, in fact, giving me more fodder for my neurosis mill.

'Surely you jest!' I said. 'I'll be a basket case. I'm already a basket case. The further away he gets the more I'll worry.

The less control I have, the more I'll worry. The more I don't know, the more I'll worry! The truth is, dear friend, that worry is an Untoward Effect of having children,' I finished, exhausted.

'Mmm.' Pause. 'So it's *Ira* now, is it? Anything brewing here that I should know about?' Robin asked, dropping the subject of children, picking up a different thread of our conversation.

'Nothing special,' I said, following her lead. 'And just what were you doing in Marty Steiner's apartment in the middle of the day?'

'Nothing special.'

CHAPTER 10

Green

I was perspiring at the edge of the surf telling Robin of the vicissitudes of child rearing. I had asked her what she'd been doing in Marty Steiner's apartment in the middle of the day, and she had answered, '*Nothing special*', when Marty emerged from a wave and landed at our feet.

'This has got to be the hottest day of the summer,' he addressed us, standing up, adjusting his small, revealing, black swim suit, wiping the salty water from his eyes, fluffing his curly hair with his fingers.

'Hi, Marty,' Robin crooned in a tone that I found unbecoming. 'Have you ever met Alison Diamond?'

'Of course we've crossed paths often, but I believe this is the first time we've been formally introduced. May I add that I'm sorry it's taken so long,' Marty said with a gallantry far above the call of a beach. 'My wife is an admirer of yours, Alison. She said she'd give anything to be able to wear a bathing suit like "that lovely young woman",' Marty flattered. 'Not that there's anything wrong with Maggie!' Marty covered the rest of the bases.

Squinting out the brilliant sunlight, I looked at the not

too tall, slim man with the steel blue eyes, the very white teeth. Although retired, he'd obviously retained all of his finely honed salesmanship, and then some. I didn't remember the days when Marty plastered his close-cropped, kinky hair flat across his head, when he didn't worry about the slight paunch spreading his always crisp shirts, when he wore oxfords. When I started noticing him, he had already retired. He'd let his hair go natural, worked out at a gym twice a week and was wearing Italian loafers. He was also looking younger than Maggie who was three years younger than he.

'When's Maggie coming back?' Robin asked.

'She should be here late this afternoon. This is the first time she's been away this long – over a week now. She was supposed to return from our daughter's home last Friday morning, but it was so overcast when I woke up that I called and told her to stay another day,' he said, directing his explanation to me. 'And then Susannah and my grand-daughter both came down with a stomach bug, so Maggie stayed to help my son-in-law.'

'Sorry to hear that,' I said. 'I hope they're on the mend.'

'Good as new. Nothing like a mother's love.'

'Just what we were saying, Marty,' Robin said.

'Anyone up for a walk?' he asked.

'No thanks,' Robin and I replied in unison.

'Maybe a little later,' Robin added.

'Friendly guy,' I noted when Marty had jogged beyond earshot.

'Very,' Robin agreed.

'And quite attractive.'

'I think so.'

'I had the distinct feeling he was coming on to you, Robin.'

'Surely you jest.'

'Didn't you once tell me that there was some talk about Marty playing around . . . that he had a mistress living in the Tower?'

'Tish Gordon . . . according to Ellen Katz, that is,' Robin hedged.

'And didn't you recently mention that Marty might possibly have been having an affair with Marjorie Applebaum?'

'I just said that he seemed inordinately affected by her death,' Robin answered reluctantly.

'And that Marty was a horny old guy?'

'All of a sudden *you're* into intrigues, Alison?'

'Oh. And all of a sudden there aren't any intrigues?' I teased.

'Look, Alison, there's no need to worry. Marty's all talk . . . and I've needed someone to talk to lately.'

'Careful, Rob,' I warned affectionately.

'Of what?'

'Just be careful.'

'Yes, mom,' Robin said, wading deeper into the water. 'Tune in again tomorrow for more from The Voice of Experience,' she mumbled just loud enough for me to hear over the sound of the surf.

'I heard that!' I yelled to her as she bobbed up and down in the rolling water.

'You were supposed to,' Robin yelled back.

I took three steps forward and then dove into an approaching wave to cool off just before Robin let out a sharp yelp. 'A crab pinched my toe!' she cried, fleeing the water.

Following her to my umbrella, I examined Robin's nipped toe.

'You can't be too careful about these little things, Robin.

If the skin's broken it could become infected. I don't want to scare you, but a severe case of cellulitis could become gangrenous, you know. You could end up losing a toe . . . or a foot,' I said, my hypochondria spilling on to my friend.

But finding only minimal damage – a small red dimple on her big toe – we stretched out to sun dry.

'By the way, that's what Shel said to me,' I said after a moment, picking up the conversation where it had left off at the water's edge.

'What?' Robin asked, having lost track.

'Shel said that I don't have much experience with men.'

'Well, you have to admit, Alison –'

'I'm not exactly a nun, you know.'

'I never said –'

'I have had my times.'

'Of course you –'

'And it's not that I don't *want* to date more. But . . . well, who is there?'

'There's Jeffrey Kaufman.'

Silence.

'There's Jeffrey Kaufman,' Robin repeated.

'I heard you.'

But what I kept on hearing in my head as I lay there was Robin saying, '*Oh, I stopped in to see Marty Steiner. I got to the beach about two.*' And what I kept seeing was Marty Steiner's steel blue eyes boring through Robin's bathing suit.

We fell silent beneath the hot sun as my imagination modelled the flesh of Marty's and Maggie's lives from the bones of 'facts' I had observed, or I'd interpreted from what I'd observed, or heard from Robin and others, one time or another, bones that would become part of the skeleton of *Beach Book-91*.

Back in my apartment, after gulping down a grilled cheese sandwich at my kitchen counter, I sat on my balcony with my laptop and started a new file – *Green* . . .

When Marty Steiner retired from the import-export business at the age of fifty-five, he and his wife, Maggie, became the youngest year-round residents at the Ivory Tower Condominium, where they'd been renting the unit from an investor for a number of summers.

The Steiners had one daughter, Susannah, who lived with her husband, Ralph, and their six-year-old daughter, Jennifer, in suburban Philadelphia, conveniently near the Steiner's French provincial home. Once Marty retired, sold his suburban Philadelphia home and moved to the Tower in the early Spring of 1990, it was not unusual for Maggie to spend a day or two at her daughter's home once or twice a month.

During the summer months, Susannah and her family also visited the Steiners at the shore, occasions when Maggie would lovingly cook for her family, build sand castles with her granddaughter, and tell her daughter of the rumoured adversities of her neighbours, stories she'd collected with the open arms and ears of a truly compassionate woman.

Marty would take long walks on the boardwalk with his son-in-law, Ralph, philosophising on politics and the stock market, bragging of his coups in the casino – advising Ralph, 'We'll just keep it between ourselves . . . women don't understand these things' – and reminiscing about the old days in the import-export business, when he'd travelled to Hong Kong, Thailand and India. Stories of his travels always included the other thing women didn't understand – other women. Ralph took Marty's struttings and crowings with a grain of salt as he did with most of what Marty said on these missions of male bonding, for although Marty was well-meaning and generous, he tended towards embellishment, the stories he told and retold seemed to grow in the retelling.

Until he met Tish Gordon, Marty had been, in fact, as faithful as most husbands. But for a lapse or two in exotic countries where reality became relative, Marty had strayed only in his mind. And, after thirty-two years of marriage, Marty and Maggie appeared content.

A good businessman, Marty was proud of his accomplishments. He was especially proud of the deal he'd made when he purchased the unit in the Tower. 'Two for the price of one,' he often bragged to his son-in-law while walking on the boardwalk. 'The guy was having financial problems and wanted to sell my unit along with two others he owned in the building. I told him I'd buy the three bedroom penthouse if he'd throw in the studio on the seventh floor. The market was soft . . . I had cash . . . he couldn't say no.' Ralph could only imagine how the deal had really gone, and where the money from Marty's subsequent sale of the seventh floor studio to a young lady with 'great eyes and a terrific smile' had gone. Ralph guessed the casinos had cost Marty a lot more than he'd revealed. He couldn't have dreamed what the lady in the studio apartment on the seventh floor cost him.

As far as Maggie was concerned, Marty's business deals were Marty's business. 'I don't understand all that, and I don't want to,' she'd tell her daughter. 'As long as there's money in my account so I can pay the household bills I figure he knows what he's doing.'

Marty thought he knew what he was doing when he'd imported his mistress, Tish Gordon, from Pittsburgh to work as his office manager in Philadelphia. Less than a year later, at age thirty-six, Tish retired along with Marty, moving into the seventh floor studio.

Tish did have great eyes and a terrific smile, even if she used too much make-up, a fault Maggie once pointed out to Marty in the elevator. 'That young woman is so attractive, don't you think?' Maggie had asked Marty when Tish got out on the seventh floor. 'It's a shame she ruins herself with all that make-up.'

It's true that over the years Marty had successfully deflected the charms of other women with the shield of marital love and the sword of middle-class morality, but Tish came to him at a vulnerable time in his life – when he was doing well. He had a loving wife that still inspired him to lust, many friends, and a business that had grown far beyond his wildest expectations. He was complacent. So his downfall was inevitable. For what is complacency if not an insidious form of hubris? Marty hadn't read enough Greek tragedies.

Another thing; Tish was more than just something different for Marty, she was unusual. Not that the affair hadn't started in the usual way, for it had.

Marty met Tish in Pittsburgh, two years before he'd retired. Tish was the office manager for one of his customers. One night, Marty took his customer and Tish to dinner to discuss business. A month later, Marty took Tish to dinner alone – his customer had a previous engagement, a charity event to attend with his wife. The following month, Tish took Marty to bed. Over the next four months, Marty made many trips to Pittsburgh – many more than usual, many without seeing his customer. The logistics of the affair proved somewhat difficult, because, in addition to hiding their relationship from his wife, Marty had to hide it from his customer, Tish's lover.

When Marty decided to surreptitiously bring Tish to

Philadelphia to work for him, he naïvely thought it would make things easier. Marty hadn't watched enough soap operas.

When Marty's customer found out that he had lost his office manager and mistress to Marty, Marty lost his customer – his biggest customer. Marty retired earlier than he had planned.

Now, Maggie met Jeffrey Kaufman two years after complaining to her daughter and her friends that she was feeling blue, bored, dissatisfied (not surprisingly, about the time Marty had met Tish). Suspecting menopause, Susannah had suggested her mother seek the help of her gynaecologist. The gynaecologist gave Maggie hormones and suggested she seek the help of a therapist. Maggie's friends suggested throwing pots.

So Maggie threw pots for a while in classes at the community college, which got her out of the house one night a week. But the glazed ashtrays, vases and fruit bowls that began to fill her house did little to fill her heart.

'Take up an instrument,' one of the ladies at the pottery class suggested when Maggie complained of her growing loneliness.

So Maggie took up the recorder at a music school in Philadelphia. Her scales could be heard far into the night. But the music that filled her home did little to fill her bed.

'Try meditation,' a gentle woman in her recorder quartet suggested when Maggie complained of her growing anxiety.

So Maggie learned to meditate at a Yoga club in Jenkintown, and she *Ommmed* into the wee hours of the morning. But the exercises that threatened to break her bones did little to break the silence at her dinner table.

So Maggie finally went to see Jeffrey Kaufman – who her gynaecologist highly recommended as being supportive

and non-threatening – who suggested that Maggie introduce Marty into their therapy sessions, and into her new
interests in an effort to bridge the growing gap in their
relationship. Jeffrey was, of course, unaware of Marty's
new interest.

Feeling secure in his relationship with Tish – who had
just moved to Philadelphia – Marty agreed to join Maggie
at her sessions with Jeffrey Kaufman and enthusiastically
embraced her invitation to throw pots. Maggie was
delighted.

Himself delighted at how well he was handling the
growing number of interests in his life, Marty took up the
recorder and played duets with Maggie.

And once Marty retired, and he and Maggie moved to
the Tower, Marty learned to sit cross-legged on the floor
with Maggie and *Om* his way to serenity – after a short visit
to the seventh floor.

At this point, Maggie was feeling pretty secure in her
relationship with her husband. So one day when she was
going to visit Susannah, and Marty suggested she stay
overnight with their daughter – 'It'll give you a little space
. . . You must feel stifled now that I'm home all the time,'
Marty had said – Maggie ended up staying two nights.

At this point, Marty was feeling pretty cocky about the
flexibility of his life, so when Marjorie Applebaum stopped
at his green umbrella to ask the time one day when Maggie
was in Pennsylvania, Marty ended up giving her a drink in
his apartment, and not long after that a private lesson on his
recorder, and soon after that a lesson in Yoga in her
apartment (her *second* lesson, it turned out, her first being
at Jeffrey Kaufman's office a few weeks before). And
Marty ended up on a page marked *GREEN* in Marjorie's
little red book.

It didn't take long for Marty's mistress, who had seen

more soap operas than Marty's wife, to catch on. Being the excellent manager that she was, Tish soon introduced herself to Marjorie Applebaum, and introduced Marjorie into a *ménage à trois*, which proved a satisfactory arrangement for all concerned. Tish held on to Marty, Marty held on to Tish and Marjorie, Marjorie held on to Marty's wallet and learned an unusual thing or two from Tish.

. . . *Yes*, I thought, as I hit the save key on the keyboard, *all kinds of possibilities here*. I listened contentedly to the whirr, and watched the screen go blank. But imagination can't be turned on and off as readily as a machine, and, staring at the blank screen, I felt unsated. For although a blank screen is anathema to a writer who's blocked, it's irresistibly seductive to a writer on a roll. I'd taken Marty from the mundane scenario of a long-time, outwardly happy marriage, to a tangled intrigue of sex, betrayal, and, possibly, murder. Where to go from here? Who to implicate next? I mused.

And as I stared at the blank screen, the image of a crab formed in my head, the crab that nipped at Robin, and I began to sketch with words a picture of the crab, as I imagined it had developed in Robin's head behind her closed eyes as she laid on the beach, her big toe throbbing . . .

When Robin felt her body drifting just off the surface of the towel in a beach sleep, she saw a huge crab floating on the turbulent, foamy water, its eight spindly appendages sticking out in nonconforming angles. But *this* crab had no huge claws with which to nip her. This was a most unusual crab, she thought.

Indeed. It had two heads. And it had breasts.

That's what Robin viewed in Marty Steiner's candle-lit bathroom, reflected in the mirror above the whirlpool tub: the image of herself laying back against Marty, nestled between his legs, their arms and legs akilter – looking very much like a most unusual, giant crab.

. . . Oh, horny, horny Marty, I thought. Naughty, naughty Robin. Wicked, wicked me. Normality, I mused, is but skin deep. Scratch the surface of any portrait and find a whole new cast of characters.

I saved the vignette in the *Notes* file, not sure yet what was to become of this new twist, this new kink in my story, not sure yet whether I wanted it filed under *Pink* or *Green*. And I couldn't help but wonder what I'd find crawling around under my skin, if I dared to look.

CHAPTER 11

White

Later Friday afternoon, I was on my back, rolling with the movement of the sea.

'You sure I can't interest you in something a little more colourful, Mrs D.?' I remembered the beach boy saying to me as he planted my white umbrella in the sand that morning. His words bobbed on my consciousness as I bobbed on the murky saltwater until a shrill whistle drew my attention to the present and I opened my eyes and swung vertical, sinking to the sandy bottom. I was in over my head.

Resurfacing, I saw a lifeguard standing at the water's edge far ahead of me, far to my right. He was blowing his whistle and waving his arms at me as if he was guiding a jet plane on to a runway. I swam in, letting a huge roller carry me the last few yards and dump me on the shore. After wiping sand and salt from my eyes, I saw a blanket of dark clouds sweeping shoreward from far out at sea, so I walked quickly back to my umbrella to catch what might be the last half-hour or so of sun before the entire sky was engulfed in black.

While basting myself with sunscreen, one foot up on my

chair, I saw the beach boy carrying Robin's pink umbrella back to the stacks. Although his eyes were hidden behind his wraparound mirrored sun-glasses, his mouth smiled as he passed me. Self-consciously settling into my sand chair, I closed my eyes and soon felt the heat draw consciousness from me like a blotter . .

'You sure I can't interest you in something a little more colourful, Mrs D.?' I heard a man say to me. Opening my eyes, I found myself lying on the beach at night surrounded by colourful day-glo umbrellas.

Looking much like a week-old mushroom, my dingy white umbrella barely emitted any glow, so I couldn't see who was talking to me. 'Who's there?' I asked, sitting up, feeling strangely edgy.

'It's me, Mrs D.,' the man said, thrusting his head into the dim light.

But all I could see was my own face – looking surprisingly young – reflected in his wraparound mirrored sun-glasses.

'What do you want?' I asked.

'The question is, what do *you* want?' the man answered.

'I don't know,' I replied.

'I have red, yellow and orange,' he said, reaching into a white ice chest, pulling out a colourful bunch of frozen fruit pops in the shape of unopened umbrellas.

'I'm not hungry,' I said, feeling an exaggerated gravity pulling at me. 'I'm really very tired.'

'Then let's take a nap. I'll rub your back,' he said.

I laid down and turned on to my side, and the young man laid down behind me. My eyes closed as I felt his fingers on my back. When he touched my buttocks my breath stopped. And then he put his hand between my legs. I opened my eyes and looked back over my shoulder, but I could see only the red plaid of his shirt.

White

You shouldn't do that, I protested silently, unable to open my mouth to speak, frightened by an unfamiliar excitement. But desire quieted my protest and I closed my eyes and rolled a tuft of green chenille beach towel between my fingers as I felt my body levitate beneath his touch.

. . . 'Alison? Are you asleep?' I heard another voice calling to me from a louder world.

'No . . . maybe,' I answered, opening my eyes to a darkening day, to Jeffrey Kaufman, to a vapour trail of an unremembered dream that had left me perspiring and chilled.

'You all right? You look a little pale,' Jeffrey said, sitting down beside me.

'What time is it? What happened to the sun?' I asked, sitting up and wiping my eyes, feeling uneasy. Disturbed.

'Almost four-thirty. Time to go in. Storm's coming,' Jeffrey answered.

The sky had been overtaken by heavy grey clouds, and gusts of wind filled the soggy air with skin-stinging whips of sand. I reached for my sweatshirt and pulled it on. 'Not yet, Jeffrey. I think I'll sit for another few minutes,' I said, looking out to the white-capped waves of the sea. But I became aware of a sensitivity of skin, an irrational sense of oppression wrapped about me. 'Actually, I think I will go in,' I said, feeling panicked, a need to leave. But I couldn't move until a bright flash and a loud crack of thunder sent us scrambling to our feet, grabbing shoes and bags.

We ran towards the boardwalk through sheets of rain. Chairs and umbrellas were left for the beach boy, but he'd already sought shelter in the basement of the Tower, waiting for the lightning, if not the rain, to stop. He was standing just inside the door when Jeffrey and I ran in. When I saw him, I remembered him in my dream asking, '*You sure I can't interest you in something a little more colourful, Mrs D.?*' and I flushed. But, his sun-glasses in his hand, his naked seventeen-year-old eyes were guileless. *He's just a baby*, I thought, the stifling mantle drawing tighter around me.

'There's nothing more dismal than a rainy day at the shore,' Jeffrey said in the elevator.

The dozen or so people crowded around us smiled in agreement.

When the car stopped at the eleventh floor, I touched Jeffrey's arm. 'How about a cup of coffee?' I offered, needing to be not alone.

'Sounds good,' he said, stepping back.

Once in my apartment, he said, 'I should have stopped to change out of these wet things.'

'These should fit,' I said, pulling a pair of Shel's bathing trunks and a sweatshirt from the pile of clean laundry on the dining table waiting to be folded. 'Pardon the mess, I was doing some laundry for my son,' I apologised before going to my room to change and blow my hair dry. When I returned, Jeffrey was standing in Shel's clothes folding Shel's laundry. A pot of coffee was brewing.

'Jeffrey, you don't have to –'

'No problem. I'm quite useful around the house,' he said. 'By the way, your answering machine is blinking.'

I pushed the button to retrieve the one message.

'Hi, Mom. This is your son. I'm hungry ... I'm broke. Feed me,' Shel pleaded from the black box. 'Six-thirty okay? Or do you have another date with the shrink? P.S. Is my laundry done?'

Mortified, I quickly wiped out the message as if I could

wipe out Jeffrey's memory of it, as well. 'Sorry about that,' I said to the air.

'I'm not,' Jeffrey said cheerfully.

I opened my mouth but no words came out.

'So, do you have a date with the shrink tonight?' Jeffrey asked.

'I don't know what to say,' I finally said.

'Say, "Yes."'

'But Shel –'

'Leave him some money to buy dinner. He'll be delighted. Trust me. I know teenagers.'

'Oh, I don't know, Jeffrey. Shel's leaving for school soon and I'm trying to give him as much time as he needs.'

'As much time as he needs, or you need?' Jeffrey questioned in a tone that I found a bit too professional for the setting, and far too insensitive, what with him standing there in Shel's clothes. I turned away from Jeffrey, but not before he saw the tears of indignation? longing? loss? filling my eyes.

'What am I thinking. Of course you should have dinner with your son,' Jeffrey recovered while I retrieved the milk from the refrigerator and the sugar from the cabinet. 'In fact, I'll take you both to dinner tonight. What do you say?'

'I don't know –'

'I won't take no for an answer. After all, I owe him one; he saved me from pneumonia, if not from the Ten Worst Dressed list,' Jeffrey said, holding out the ample legs of Shel's baggy, garish trunks.

We settled on the sofa facing the glass balcony doors, watching the wind and rain blend the dark sky and sea in chaos. Anxious to shrug off the dark mood of my elusive dream, I focused on Jeffrey, looking at him more closely than I'd done before.

He looked a bit like an ape, I thought. But a pleasant looking ape. His eyes were dark and round, his nose small and straight. And his mouth was rather seductive, I noted quite specifically. His chin, almost hidden behind his full beard, was dimpled.

'Have the police talked to you yet . . . about Marjorie Applebaum's death?' I asked, forgetting for a moment the rumours connecting Jeffrey and Marjorie.

'No,' Jeffrey answered in a tone that made me think about what I'd asked.

'Oh, I'm sorry,' leapt from my mouth, bypassing my social censor.

'About what?'

'About Marjorie. Actually about what I asked. It was insensitive . . . considering that you were friends and all . . . you were friends, weren't you?' I fumbled.

'I wouldn't say we were friends,' he said coldly.

'I'm sorry,' I said again, this time for the pain that registered in his eyes.

'So how did your test go the other day?' Jeffrey asked, changing the subject.

'Fine. Actually, I've decided my dizziness is psycho-somatic.'

'Why?'

'Robin thinks so, too.'

'Okay. So what drew you both to that conclusion?'

'I –. Actually, I'd rather not talk about it.'

'I understand,' Jeffrey said, though I was sure he didn't.

'I hardly knew Marjorie at all,' I said, returning to the tragedy, trading my pain for Jeffrey's.

'I don't think anyone did. She certainly took me by surprise – me, the expert.'

'Really?' I said, surprised by his sudden openness.

Pitching his head back, Jeffrey stared at the ceiling and

sighed. 'I can't believe I'm going to tell you this,' he said. 'Are you sure you want to hear it?'

I didn't say a word, but watched him, wide-eyed, as he began to tell me of his unfortunate liaison with Marjorie Applebaum, starting with the day she had come to see him in his office to tell him of the affair between her husband and his wife, and they ended up making love – *just as I imagined!*, I thought to myself as he spoke, as I was once again startled by the predictability of life, and wondered if the scene was as kinky as I'd imagined it.

'. . . And when I left my office that evening I was devastated – certainly about my wife, but even more about the way I'd behaved. I was a professional, acting totally unprofessionally.'

'You're being awfully hard on yourself,' I said, disappointed in the lack of kinky details.

'Oh, it didn't end there. If it had, maybe –. Well, it didn't end there. I saw her again. I wasn't going to, but she called me a few days later, ostensibly to apologise. I was pretty shaken up by then . . . Tiffany had left and all . . . and Marjorie sounded so sincere . . . and I guess I was pretty needy. I told myself that I'd see her once to straighten things out between us, but we ended up making love again. And then I saw her again, and again. I don't understand it, even now. She wasn't even that attractive . . . but there was something.' Jeffrey fell silent.

Although I'd heard the rumours of the affair from Robin – who had heard it from Maggie – and then again from Emma Chankin, hearing the truth of it from Jeffrey, and seeing how closely it fit my fictionalised account was nonetheless shocking to me, a shock that caused me to consider other rumours that I'd dismissed, or had tried to dismiss, but, instead, transformed to fiction where I thought I could deal with them better. Like the seduction of horny young men by the Milfs. Like the seduction of Shel by Brenda Forrester, an idea I could hardly tolerate in fiction, let alone reality. Like the beach boy's smiling mouth beneath his menacing mirrored glasses. A flash of heat overtook me. It wasn't a hot flash of early menopause that caused my skin to burn, it was more like late puberty.

'How could I have been so naïve?' Jeffrey asked, breaking the silence.

'Naïve? About what?' I asked.

That's when he told me about the money, about the fifty dollars Marjorie had borrowed to pay her phone bill, and the two hundred dollars she'd borrowed to pay her plumber's bill, and the eleven hundred dollars for her tax bill, and on and on, totalling more than thirty-five hundred dollars over the past eleven months. 'And I'm supposed to be some kind of expert on human behaviour,' he said.

'We believe what we want to believe, Jeffrey. What we're able to believe,' I said, terrified of what I couldn't believe.

I was almost in a state of panic when he leaned over to kiss me, so I couldn't do anything other than let him. Surprisingly, his kiss was as warm, as comfortable, comforting as it was undemanding. So when our lips parted and he asked again about dinner that night, I agreed.

'So how come the shrink's coming?' Shel asked me when he arrived at the apartment at six-twenty.

'His name's Jeffrey, Shel.'

'So how come he's coming?'

'So how come you sound annoyed? I thought you wanted me to date more.'

'I'm not annoyed. I just asked why he's having dinner with us. No big deal.'

'Precisely. Get the door, Shel. That's probably Jeffrey

now,' I said, packing the last of Shel's laundry into his duffle.

The storm had passed, and the three of us walked into the steamy night, eschewing the Jitney minibus for the boardwalk. Barney's was, after all, only about a mile and a half from the Tower.

'*You're* going to walk?' Shel poked at me as we turned towards the boardwalk, rather than towards the main street. 'Mom takes a cab to the corner to catch a bus at home,' he said to Jeffrey.

'I'm not that bad,' I defended myself needlessly.

'You're worse,' he said.

'Hey! Remember, I'm the one who does your laundry, feeds your hungry belly. How about a little respect?' I scolded, sensing more than the usual playfulness at work.

'That's what mothers are for, short one,' he replied, brushing the top of my head with the palm of his hand.

I could tell by his tone, by his stance, that his attempt at 'cool' had gone beyond cool to rude, and I couldn't for the life of me understand why.

The boardwalk before Albany Avenue – that's where the main streets converge around the monument two blocks inland – is quiet and narrow. Walking between Shel and Jeffrey, I remembered when I was young, walking with my cousins on the boardwalk to the amusement piers at night. It was very quiet around Ascot Place, and dark between the lamp posts. To the right was the beach, to the left huge old homes and empty lots of sand and tough, reedy grass. Now rising up between the homes and lots there were well-lit, twenty-storey buildings.

But the real tumult began past Albany Avenue. Once the embodiment of seaside kitsch, the boardwalk offered hotels and shops with windows full of crystal and gold, fine china and fashionable clothes, along with arcades of skeet ball, photo booths and fortune telling machines. There was the Planter's Peanut store, Steele's Fudge, Fralinger's candy store, and James', where my grandmother always bought me a little silver cardboard suitcase filled with salt water taffy. Between the men demonstrating vegetable slicers and fruit juicers were booths where hot dogs, pizza, chocolate-covered frozen bananas, and cotton candy were sold. On the boardwalk you could buy wind-up walking toys, leashes holding invisible dogs, hula hoops, frisbees, slinkys, and any other fad *de jour*. And, of course there were Million Dollar Pier – with its giant roller coaster that, kids had heard, would one unlucky night dump its riders into the sea – and Steele Pier. The boardwalk was a veritable string of carnivals where there was always something to buy, always something to eat, always something to do.

Walking with Jeffrey and Shel, I noted the crowds milling in and out of the huge, brightly lit casino-hotels that had replaced the grand old hotels and expensive shops. Both piers were gone, too. A giant indoor mall shaped like a ship replaced the amusement rides of Million Dollar Pier, and Steele Pier had burned down years before. Although the honky-tonk remained, it had changed. Like the crowds, it appeared sleazier. You could still buy a tacky ashtray welcoming you to Atlantic City, but the prevalent fare was x-rated tee-shirts.

At Barney's, Shel ate well, but was uncharacteristically quiet. As soon as Jeffrey paid the cheque Shel left, with only a half-hearted thank you to Jeffrey and barely a word to me. Back on the boardwalk, I attempted to apologise to Jeffrey for Shel's behaviour, hoping that he'd understand. I didn't want to have to explain it, because I couldn't.

'That's the second time you've apologised for your son today,' Jeffrey said.

'The second –'

'The message on the answering machine ... this afternoon?'

I smiled and nodded.

'He was fine, Alison, really.'

'He was rude, Jeffrey.'

'He's eighteen.'

'He knows better.'

'He's jealous.'

'Jealous?' I questioned, surprised.

'I'm afraid I invaded his time with you, and he wasn't very happy about it.'

'That's not possible. Shel and I have a very understanding relationship.'

'Maybe you're right. But teenagers can be surprising, you know. They often see things from a different perspective than their sane parents.'

And as we walked I thought about the disparity between Shel's reality and mine, and how I, the sane one, smugly assumed to see the world as it *really* is. I smiled as I remembered the limo affair . . .

Shel was fourteen, and planning to hire a limousine for his eighth-grade graduation dance, he told me. Although somewhat incredulous, I responded, 'Right, Shel,' much in the same way he responds, 'Right, Mom,' finding my assessment of the connection between studying and grades irrational. Perhaps Shel didn't catch the patronising edge to my pat on his overgrown – but *very* clean – crew cut as I mirrored his words, or, perhaps, as he does with so much of *my* reality, he ignored it.

Over the weeks preceding the dance, talk of the limo

faded in and out as, in *my* reality, Shel was playing out the possibilities of a very attractive fantasy.

Of course he asked for a ride *to* the dance. *After* the dance, he explained through the mist of the dream that played on behind his eyes, THE LIMO would arrive to take him and his friends to South Street, To Do The Town.

'Right, Shel,' I said, smiling the lovingly tolerant smile of a teenager's parent.

As I dropped my handsomely suited son at the school the evening of the dance, I reminded him, 'I'll be home. Call me if you need me,' understanding that, in *my* reality, the next call I would get would be for a ride home.

Sure enough, at eleven p.m. the phone rang. It was Shel. 'Hi, Shel! What's up?' I asked, one hand on my car keys.

'Hi, Mom! Just called to say hello,' he answered, drawing me into *his* reality over the noise of traffic and the static of the car-phone. 'I'm calling from the limo!'

... 'Alison?' I heard Jeffrey say through the static of remembrance.

'I'm sorry, Jeffrey. What were you saying?'

'I wasn't saying anything. I was wondering what you were thinking.'

'About Shel when he was little.'

'They do tend to grow up on us when we're not looking, don't they?'

'I don't want to talk about it,' I said, feeling my heart grab my stomach.

'Speaking of little boys, the little boy in me was thinking about a hot fudge Haagendaz ice-cream sundae.'

'Sounds great,' I said, shaking off nostalgia. 'Up another block, right after Madame Zora,' I directed.

'How about if we get our fortunes told first?'

Falling under the spell of the boardwalk – the only place

in the world where I'd eat a hot fudge sundae or get my palm read – I agreed, and we slipped through the beaded doorway below the sign '*Madame Zora – Reader and Adviser*'.

The heavy set woman in a peasant blouse and skirt standing to the right of the entrance pointed to me. 'Just you,' she said, and walked into one of two curtained cubicles in the back of the small room.

Sitting across from her, I noticed the deck of Tarot cards on the table between us. 'Do you use the cards?' I asked.

'No cards for you. Cards can be dangerous,' she replied, taking my right hand in hers.

Suddenly I didn't want to be there.

'You don't have to be afraid,' she said, knowingly. 'There are good things in your hand. You are intelligent, caring, sensitive, a good friend, and intuitive.' Looking into my face she said, 'In two weeks, or two months, or two years you will be married . . .' and then added, '. . . to a man who takes care of people. A doctor.'

I smiled and wondered silently if psychologists counted.

'There is a door in your life. A man is walking out and another walking in. There is another door in your life. It is locked,' she said. Then she looked me right in the eye. 'You have a secret. You look in the mirror and it will be known to you.'

I felt as if she'd draped a cape of chain mail about my shoulders. I looked to her for more, but she let my hand go and put both her hands on the table.

'Now the man,' she said.

Outside the cubicle, Jeffrey was waiting. 'Your turn,' I said, impatiently.

Jeffrey disappeared behind the curtain for a few minutes, then reappeared, followed by Madame Zora. Taking my arm, Jeffrey led me back to the boardwalk, when Madame

Zora called after us, 'Lady. Dreams are the mirrors of our souls.'

'What was that all about?' Jeffrey asked inside the ice-cream parlour.

'I'm not sure. But she'd said something to me about remembering a secret when I looked in a mirror,' I replied. 'And what did she tell you?' I asked, attempting to shake off the odd discomfiture Madame Zora had inflicted upon me.

After ordering two hot fudge sundaes with chocolate ice-cream, whipped cream and dry nuts, Jeffrey told me of the reader's revelations. 'She told me I was kind and intelligent and caring,' he said. 'And she told me that I was going to be married soon.'

'Sounds like she says the same things to everyone.'

'She didn't say anything about secrets to me.'

'When she said that thing about the dreams, I wonder if she meant I'd learn the secret from my dreams . . . because I've been having the oddest dreams lately,' I said.

'I'd love to hear about your dreams.'

'I don't think so.'

'Yes, I would.'

'I mean I don't think I can tell you about them,' I said remembering with a flush my drug-induced erotic dream in the MRI.

'You realise you're tantalising me. Give me a hint.'

'Day-glo umbrellas on the Tower Beach, and Beethoven,' I said, dropping censored images – images that finally jogged my memory about the dream I'd had on the beach that afternoon. Remembering that dream, in turn, triggered something else – an old memory that I couldn't really remember. I must have had a very odd look on my face, because Jeffrey asked if anything was wrong.

'No. It's nothing,' I said, before burying my discomfort

in the intense sweetness of my sundae.

And then, 'Sure you're okay?' Jeffrey asked as we walked home on the boardwalk.

'I was trying to remember something. But the harder I tried, the further away it got from me. Very odd feeling,' I said.

'Memory can be tricky,' Jeffrey said.

'Yes,' I said, and then fell silent, and stayed silent all the way home as Jeffrey chatted on about a variety of unrelated subjects. Or at least they seemed unrelated to me as I had trouble concentrating on anything he was saying, I was so preoccupied with trying to remember whatever it was that I couldn't remember.

'You've been awfully quiet for the last half hour, Alison,' Jeffrey said when we walked into my apartment. 'Thinking about Shel again?'

'No. It's nothing.'

Jeffrey looked puzzled. 'That's what you said in the ice-cream store. Can I help?' he asked, putting his hands on my shoulders.

A barely controllable urge to put my arms around him and press myself close to him swept over me. Taking my hand, he led me to the balcony where my defenses dissolved as we stood side by side leaning on the rail, looking out to the sea.

'Jeffrey, I'm going to try to tell you about something I don't remember.'

Jeffrey looked down at my arms folded across the rail.

'It's a fragment of an elusive, or perhaps illusive memory that sits on the edge of my consciousness, like an optic floater can sit on the edge of your peripheral vision. Do you understand?'

Jeffrey listened silently as I continued. 'You know like that funny little squiggle that can float in and out of your vision and dart away when you try to look at it? Well if you look straight ahead and try not to focus on it, you can see a ghostly form out of the corner of your eye.'

Jeffrey nodded his head slowly.

'That's because the floater is an endogenous bit of matter, you know,' I explained, pulling a definition from my reservoir of medical trivia. 'It's inside your eye, not something *out there*. So although you might forget about it while occupied with other matters, the bit of inner debris remains only out of mind, not out of sight.' Pause. 'Well, I've had a mental floater haunting me for years.'

'What's it like?' Jeffrey questioned gently.

For a moment I thought I couldn't say it, but then I thought of Jeffrey sitting on my sofa that afternoon, looking up at the ceiling. I remembered his deep sigh and his words, '*I can't believe I'm going to tell you this.*' And then I told him.

'I remember a tall man. In my memory I'm not looking at him, but at a green chenille spread on a four-poster bed. He's somewhere beside me, to my right, a little in front of me so I can see his back – the left side of his back. I could say he was wearing a plaid shirt, that I was eye level with his waist, but I could be making that up. It was so long ago. I think I remember him saying, '*Let's take a nap.*' Saying the words precipitated a discrete prickling of my skin, like a mild electric shock. Every hair on my body was standing up.

Jeffrey didn't say a word, but he leaned closer to me, barely touching me. My skin relaxed.

'I could say I remember a stale and familiar smell, and laying down on the bed next to someone with wavy brown hair, who put his arm around me, but I could be making that up, too,' I continued. 'The truth is, I really only remember not remembering something. And I haven't remembered it for years – that is, I remember not remembering it for years, but I'm aware that there *is* something I don't remember.'

'The ghost of your inner eye,' Jeffrey said, putting his arm around my shoulder.

'This afternoon I think I had a dream about it ... or something like it. But it was on the beach ... very strange ... I'm not sure what it meant.'

'Do you remember the dream?'

'Not really,' I said, which was partly a lie. But I didn't want to tell him that I had dreamt about the beach boy. I didn't want him to get the wrong idea.

'Sometimes we remember things the way we want to remember them, Alison, so they fit in with what's going on in our lives at the time. So maybe you don't have to remember what went on in the past. Maybe remembering that you don't remember is enough, and you only have to understand what's on your mind in the present.'

It must have been the telling of my thoughts that lifted my mood, because, although I had no idea what Jeffrey meant, I felt as though a Laingian knot had been severed, if not untied, and the oppressive mantle I'd been wearing since the afternoon dissipated. I felt transported to the pages of *A Stitch in Time*. Was life imitating art, after all? Was Jeffrey Kaufman, a doctor of the mind, not the body, destined to be my love, after stitching together the lost fragments of my life? I turned to embrace him, to kiss him gently, the way he'd kissed me earlier in the day. But when he returned my kiss passionately, I slid from his grasp.

'Did I do something wrong, Alison?' he asked, looking hurt.

'Oh, no, Jeffrey. You're a really special person, but –'

'No, Alison! Please!' he interrupted me, looking positively frantic. 'I've really got to go.'

And he practically ran from the balcony and was out the door of my apartment before I had a chance to say another word, to give him an explanation for my seemingly fickle behaviour, which was probably for the best . . . because I didn't have one.

'I can't imagine what I said,' I told Robin on Saturday morning on the beach.

'I don't think it was so much what you said as what you did . . . or didn't do,' Robin replied.

'No. I think it was something I said,' I insisted, remembering what I'd written in my fiction of Jeffrey Kaufman's life, about how all the women in his life had rejected him with the same words – the words that I uttered to rebuff his ardent advances. Unable, at that point, to separate fiction from reality, I was sure that Jeffrey had fled my presence in dread of hearing the rest of my renunciation, although I had no reason to believe that what I'd written in my fiction was what had actually occurred in his reality.

'Alison, once a woman says "no" to a man, there's no one he'd rather be further from quicker.'

'You're right,' I said to Robin, understanding that no matter what I'd written, or thought, or thought I'd written, the bottom line was all the same: I was going to tell Jeffrey Kaufman that I'd rather talk to him than make love to him. And he knew it.

'Think I'll take a dip before I go in for lunch,' Robin said, standing up, pulling at the bottom of her bathing suit to tuck in exposed white flesh, a gesture that reminded me of my dream of her on the night-beach, touching herself. I felt a dampening between my legs.

God, I must really be horny, I thought. And a picture of myself alone in my apartment, sprawled on my sofa, my hand between my legs obliterated the sea, the sand, the sun. I blinked and flushed, overcome with guilt. Robin headed towards the surf, head high, hands up, elbows swinging out with each step, a gait that reminded me of animated cartoons of chickens. The image dissipated my erotic thoughts. I closed my eyes . . .

Jeffrey. His hurt look, his quick exit flashed before me '*Alison, once a woman says "no" to a man, there's no one he'd rather be further from quicker.*' I knew that.

David. I remembered how tall and lean he was, how exceptionally handsome, even pretty. His hair was silver, but life had left no lines on his face, so he appeared much younger than his thirty-eight years. The night we'd met at the Parents Without Partners meeting was just a month after Shel had graduated from grade school, and I suppose I'd let my mother talk me into going to the singles social because I was feeling guilty about not having a father for Shel at that important pre-teen time of his life. As if it were my fault that Carl had died. As if it were my fault that eight years later I was still a single parent.

The moment I walked into the room I saw David Lawrence. Although his silver hair above the crowd would have been hard to miss, I remember thinking that there was something special about the way I'd spotted him immediately, about the way I found myself standing next to him after the guest speaker had finished his presentation. I remember him talking to me first, but it could have been the other way around. Somehow we ended up sitting together in a corner, talking for over an hour. David was sweet. He seemed naïve. And I remember how he looked in his white shirt, with the sleeves rolled up, his khaki pants, white socks and brown loafers – like a student, not a professor. Except, of course, for the distinctive silver hair. But framing his serene, inexperienced face, his hair appeared not silver as in hair gone grey, but silver as in a shade of blond. His eyes were blue-green, like mine. But when he looked at me warmly and said, '*We have the same eyes,*' I tediously pointed out they weren't really alike, that his eyes were bluer than mine. Not for the first time I could have kicked myself for my insensitive, prosaic, unimaginative response – my discomfort around any man I found attractive.

I was attracted to David Lawrence, but I was wary, too. Beside the fact that he looked too young and unpretentious to be a professor at Princeton, he'd told me that he was at the meeting that night under false pretences: he had no children. But he'd been married for three years, he was quick to point out, and divorced for eight. He didn't like bars and wouldn't date students, he offered in explanation.

We were still talking when the announcement was made that the meeting was over and the doors were about to close. He walked me to my car, we exchanged telephone numbers and made a dinner date for the following Friday evening. On Wednesday I checked him out at the library. Dr David Lawrence was indeed a professor of archaeology at Princeton. Tenured, in fact. It was the first and last time I mistrusted him, as over the next twelve months he disarmed me with his trusting, guileless nature, his uncritical, unconditional acceptance of me and Shel. 'Don't look at me, I look *awful,*' I'd said one night early in our relationship, my skin sallow, my eyes and nose red and runny from a cold. 'You don't look awful, you look sick,' he'd replied without a thought.

'Oh, it's nothing – Shel's just eleven. That's what kids do,' David had said, excusing Shel's balky temperament the first time we all had dinner together. And it wasn't just a polite gesture of largess. David understood eleven year olds because somewhere inside him he was still eleven. Shel could feel that. I could see it, in his wide-eyed, unlined visage. Like a big kid, he enjoyed everything sensual, eating with abandon, relishing every taste, listening to music enrapt, savouring every sound. And his love-making was always like it was the first time – *his* first time. He wanted to try everything, delighted in every part of me, everything we did. When we made love he kept the lights on, his eyes open. He didn't want to miss a thing. 'I love to watch your face when you come,' he'd said to me with more fascination than lust, making me feel like a wondrous toy. And we played games . . . gentle sex games, like follow the leader, and Simon says.

But he had a darker side. He was sometimes moody, occasionally depressed. And, at first, I sensed he was skittish around me, lacking confidence in himself. I'd seen him half a dozen times before he even attempted to kiss me, and another four or five times before we made love. The first time I saw David naked, he'd undressed tentatively, cautiously showing me his scars, graphic reminders of the many illnesses and pains he'd suffered, starting with childhood rheumatic fever at age six. He exposed them one at a time, explaining them, apologising for their presence as one might apologise for embarrassing relatives. But David's scars did not disgust or repel me as he had feared, rather they drew me to him. With each new revelation I felt his old pain; I wanted to somehow free him from it. Kissing each scar, I drew him to me. That first time, he trustingly gave himself to me, and his trust grew quickly within me, pushing aside weeds of doubt and suspicion, providing fertile ground for my trust to grow. With it came the love.

And I almost told him. I almost told him that I loved him. I'd been sick with the flu for almost a week. David came over with Chinese food for Shel and himself, soup from the deli for me, then stayed to oversee Shel's bedtime . . . and mine. Grey-faced and black-eyed like an old raccoon, I languished against my pillow, sapped of colour and strength. David laid down beside me, fully clothed, to watch the eleven-o'clock news on television. I curled close to him, damp and feverish. He kissed me, seeing past the sick to the essence of me. And I felt it well up in me . . . *I love you* . . . open my throat . . . *I love you* . . . press down my tongue and push at the back of my teeth . . . *I love you*. 'What?' he questioned, seeing a statement in my eyes. I swallowed. 'Nothing,' I said, overpowered by a need to close my eyes. That was Tuesday.

By Saturday my body had recovered from the flu. After dropping Shel off at a friend's home for the night, David and I went to dinner, and then returned to my apartment. Standing by the bedroom door, David looked at me with puppy eyes. 'Simon says, kiss David,' he said quietly. It was a familiar opening that made me feel unfamiliarly awkward. 'No,' I said. I wanted him to go. I remember thinking as I turned from him that he was my best friend, but that I'd grown suddenly uncomfortable with him, with his special kind of innocence.

And I sent him home, with no explanation. I didn't have one. He didn't need one. He didn't call again (not until two years later, that is, when he'd seen a shadow of himself in my novel). It was over just like that. Perhaps because '*once a woman says "no" to a man there's no one he'd rather be further from quicker*.' Perhaps not.

. . . In retrospect, I saw the flaws, his and mine. David was as eccentric as he was dear. But, in the end, it wasn't him that had made me uncomfortable, it was me. Lying on the beach I remembered David with affection, and with guilt, for betraying his trust, not once, but twice. He was the only person I'd ever learned to trust completely, but I hadn't learned to trust myself.

CHAPTER 12

White

Back in my apartment, to go to the bathroom (for the second time in an hour) around one-thirty Saturday afternoon, I found the red light on my answering machine blinking. My first thought was of Shel. When I saw that two calls were indicated, I thought of Jeffrey, and his sudden departure the evening before. But my bladder gave me no time to listen to the messages, and I ran to the bathroom, wetting my bathing suit on the way. Incipient urinary tract infection, or too much coffee this morning? I wondered as I peed, ticking off the symptomatology I'd written about for more than one magazine – frequency, urgency, both of which I was experiencing. And then I waited for the classic tweak, the afterburn at the end of my stream, as pictures of patients on dialysis machines flashed through my head. No tweak, no burn, I thought, relieved that my kidneys were safe – for the time being.

By the time I'd changed my suit, I'd made up my mind to tell Jeffrey – who I was sure had called, despite Robin's pronouncement – that I couldn't see him that evening because I was busy with Shel, sure, too, that the other message was another plea for dinner from my son, forgetting that it was Saturday and that the last person in the world a teenage boy would want to be with on a Saturday night was his mother.

Both messages, in fact, were from Ira Pressman. The first was to tell me that my MRI was normal, and to instruct me to call his office Monday to make an appointment. The second message was an invitation to dinner, and a promise that he'd call back at five-thirty. He'd finally remembered where we'd met before, so he felt he should be considered my friend, not just my doctor. '*It was in the supermarket, wasn't it?*' he'd asked. I wondered what else he'd remembered.

Back on the beach in a dry suit, I was happy to see that Elliot had finally arrived. Robin was busy spreading out a lunch of hoagies Elliot had picked up on the way to the Tower, and hadn't seen me approaching.

'Nice to see you, stranger,' I said to Elliot, stopping at the pink umbrella.

He smiled and waved.

Turning when she heard my voice, Robin grinned. 'Alison! Hi! Elliot finally made it,' she said.

'I see. Enjoy your lunch,' I said with a wave, walking to my umbrella.

'*Love* the sweatshirt!' Robin yelled after me, referring to Shel's artfully tattered grey sweatshirt I'd swiped from his laundry.

From under my white umbrella, behind my dark glasses, over the top of my magazine, I watched Elliot and Robin, turning them over in my mind, trying to picture the odd couple *in flagrante delicto*. But the only picture I could conjure was one of bulky Elliot perspiring over Marjorie Applebaum's neat little body, as if what I'd written about them was factual, as if I'd been there to witness his temptation, her manipulation, their deceit. And I was

232

overwhelmed with sadness for Robin, and almost forgave her for her own indiscretions with Marty Steiner, indiscretions that I felt certain were as real as those I'd committed to my computer's memory.

As the fine line between fact and fiction blurred, I felt myself effacing in the serene heat of the afternoon . . .

Ira Pressman's widow's peak rose on the horizon of my beach dream – an inverted mountain of black between pale hillocks of exposed scalp. Then, tip to tip with it, the dark triangle between my pale thighs appeared, like a mirror image. I could feel the warmth of Ira's mouth on me. As the flow started, the internal meltdown preceding orgasm, Ira looked up from between my propped legs. But it was Carl. 'Hi, Mrs Diamond,' he said. How odd that my husband should call me Mrs Diamond, I thought. Then again, he was always such a formal person. 'Mrs Diamond?' I heard again.

. . . 'Mrs Diamond? Are you awake?'

I opened my eyes to find Lieutenant Fiori above me. In one hand was a book with which he shielded his eyes from the sun, in his other were his shoes, his socks stuffed inside. For a moment I felt the confusion of arousal, then embarrassment for allowing him into the very private domain of my dream, remembering at that moment not much more than the feel of it. 'What brings you to the beach today, Lieutenant?' I managed.

'The message you left yesterday, about the notebook. I called, and when your machine answered I took a chance that on a beautiful day like this you'd be on the beach. Hope you don't mind. Besides, I had an ulterior motive.'

I blushed again at the possibilities of his ulterior motive.

'I thought only suspects had ulterior motives,' I teased, trying to gain control of the conversation.

'I guess we're only human after all,' he said, laughing. 'But first things first. Could you tell me about the book you found?'

'There's not much to tell. My son found it in the elevator a few days after Marjorie's death. He was coming to dinner. They grow up, but they still need their mommies,' I digressed wistfully, a little disorientated by sleep. 'It's not just the food, you know, it's –' I caught myself. 'I'm sorry. He's leaving for school soon – in Chicago –' I caught myself again. 'Well, anyway, the book is red leather, the size of a pocket address book, and it has Marjorie Applebaum's name in the front.'

'Funny that the maintenance people would have missed it over the week-end, don't you think?'

'I hadn't thought about it,' I said, thinking about it then . . . how odd it really was . . . if in fact Shel had found it in the elevator as he'd said, rather than in Brenda's apartment as I'd written. 'Teenagers can be odd, don't you think, Lieutenant?' I asked.

'Would it be inconvenient for you to get it for me, Mrs Diamond?' Lieutenant Fiori asked politely, overlooking my eccentric association.

He was so very polite, this very young man. And attractive. Not tanned and muscled like the life-guards and the beach boys, but attractive in a rumpled, sexy sort of way. I wondered how old he really was, if he was as young as he looked – and he looked no more than twenty-five. Was he so polite because I was so much older? Or did he have an ulterior motive? Had he heard of the women of Milfville?

'You mean now?' I asked, afraid that he'd come with me to my apartment . . . to be alone with me . . . in my bathing suit . . . damp from a titillating dream.

'If you don't mind, I'll just wait here and soak in a little sun. We don't get much time for the beach when we're investigating a murder, you know.'

The conflict between the relief and disappointment I was experiencing regarding his non-intentions momentarily eclipsed the shock of his description of Marjorie's demise: *murder*. But not for long. 'Did you say, *murder*?' I asked.

'Well, that's the way we're handling it at this point in time, Mrs Diamond. It appears that suicide is pretty much out of the question.'

And then I remembered what I'd read . . . about the balcony door being locked from the inside. 'I'll get the book,' I said, standing up, pulling a sweatshirt over my bathing suit, picking up my sandals. 'I'll just be a minute. Have a seat . . . and help yourself to some grapes . . . in the bag.'

'Thanks. I'll catch up on my reading,' he said, displaying the cover of the book in his hand: *A Stitch in Time*.

Fifty-some thousand books published each year, and Lieutenant Fiori was reading mine! That's two people I knew reading *A Stitch in Time* this week. What an odd coincidence, I thought as I trotted up the beach and over the boardwalk, stopping only to wipe my feet and slip on my sandals. In my apartment I retrieved the notebook from the top drawer of my desk, and then leafed through it for the last time, jotting down the page headings on a scrap of paper – *yellow, pink, green, orange, turquoise, blue/white, navy, yellow/orange* – along with the first and last date on each page. Then I went over to the balcony door and slammed it shut, to see if the lock would accidentally catch by itself. It didn't. I tried again. Although it still didn't catch, it seemed to move slightly. Maybe if the latch was looser . . . , I was thinking when, sensing pressure in my bladder, I gave up and went to the bathroom again, wondering again if I was getting an infection as I dribbled a mere thimbleful of urine. Once again, no tweak, no burn, and no tell-tale pink stain on the bathroom tissue, I noted, relieved again.

Returning to the beach, I found the Lieutenant comfortably seated on my chair munching on a small bunch of green grapes, reading.

'I didn't think policemen had time to read novels. I'd think this was more down your alley,' I said, handing him the little red book.

'I guess we're only human after all,' he said again, standing up, smiling, taking the red book.

He had a charming smile, I thought. 'I think I've heard that somewhere,' I said. 'By the way, how do you like it? The novel, that is,' I asked, unable to control myself.

'You know, I've read every book by Sloan I. Diamond, and I've come to the conclusion that the author is a woman.'

'Really?'

'You've read Diamond's books, haven't you? Oh, of course you have . . . it's popular stuff, great beach reading.'

'Actually, I never read books on the beach,' I lied, saying the first thing that came into my head, feeling immediately guilty, lying to a police officer – like a criminal.

He paused, smiling askance at me. And then, 'Will you autograph my copy for me?' he asked.

'What?'

'Your book. Will you autograph it for me?'

'I don't understand –'

'You did write it, didn't you? It's well known that Sloan I. Diamond is a *nom de plume*,' he said, displaying his expertise in the world of popular fiction.

I stared at him, nonplussed.

'Now, this story has a medical theme and – the hallmark of Diamond's *œuvre* – a distinctly sexual perspective. It's a mystery. Many of Diamond's books are mysteries, you know.'

He knows! I thought, panicking as I listened to his detailed report.

'Now. Mrs *Diamond*,' he continued, emphasising my name, 'you're a writer; you specialise in medicine. And although you appear to be conservative, maybe even a bit prim –. Well, maybe that's your mystery. Certainly there's no mystery about *Sloan I.* being an anagram of *Alison*.' He looked annoyingly smug.

'Got me,' I said, giving up immediately, intimidated by the authority of his badge. Or so I told myself. In fact, I *wanted* him to know; his discovery excited me. And then it struck me that no one else – no one, that is, other than David Lawrence – had ever seen what Fiori had made appear so obvious. It doesn't take much to hide from those who have no reason to look, I realised, an epiphany that could explain many of life's little mysteries.

'Lieutenant, please, this is between you and me. No one but my agent and publisher knows.'

'Scouts' honour,' Fiori said, running his hand back through his hair, exposing his widow's peak, and then flashing the scouts' hand signal.

Ira Pressman, the boy scout from the supermarket, popped into my head . . . his widow's peak . . . my dream. And I blushed again.

'I wouldn't have thought Sloan I. Diamond would blush so easily,' Fiori said, with what appeared to me to be a leer.

'Well, if that's all, Lieutenant,' I said, turning from him, sitting in my chair, in an effort to dismiss him, so he wouldn't get the wrong idea, whatever the wrong idea might be.

'Just one detail, and that'll wrap it up, Mrs Diamond.'

I stiffened.

'The autograph?' he said, smiling, handing me his book and a black pen.

I opened the book to the title page and wrote *To a 'secret' admirer . . . Best wishes, Sloan I. Diamond*, savouring the glide of the felt tip across the rough grain of the paper. My first autograph . . . and my last, I thought, feeling distinctly uncomfortable with the new way the Lieutenant was looking at me.

'Thanks, Mrs Diamond,' Fiori said, taking the book from me and reading the inscription. Then, flashing the scouts' signal once again, he said, 'It'll be our little secret.'

He was half way to the boardwalk when I experienced a sudden need of warmth, and moved my chair into the sun. Closing my eyes, I saw the image of Fiori before me, his hand raised in the Scouts' signal. *'Our little secret'* echoed in my ears.

My little secret had become *our* little secret, so that it was no longer my secret at all, but *his* secret.

I hated secrets. *Not telling* is an unspoken denial of truth, a lie turned inside out. I'd grown up in a family where everything was a secret, from money to illness, from sex to death, where *Don't tell* were the watchwords of my childhood. Curious, I thought, that I'd created the biggest secret of all – a secret self.

Memories of Evy flooded my consciousness – on the beach, in her house, in my house . . . being lowered into her grave. Her suicide was a secret. Only because the newspapers picked up the story did I find out that Evy hadn't died in a car crash, as I'd been told.

Despite the heat, a cold chill overtook me. Why, I wondered, did I think of Evy now? Perhaps because I'd spoken of her recently . . . then there was Marjorie's fall from the balcony, like Evy's fall from a bridge. Well, Evy had jumped. There was no question of murder. There'd been witnesses.

Sometimes I sensed that I, too, was a witness to Evy's suicide, although I'd been miles away when it happened. I clearly remember feeling a profound sense of guilt when I'd learned the truth about her death. It's a common reaction to suicide, I've read.

And it appeared now that I was the only witness, albeit an imperfect witness, to Marjorie's fall. And, although I hardly knew the woman, I must confess to a certain sense of intuitive cognisance regarding her death. How else to explain the astonishing parallel between my book-in-progress and Marjorie's notebook with its pages of colour. It had to be the umbrellas, I thought. They were all there, as they were in my book: green, blue, yellow, pink. And there were other colours.

Looking around me, I spotted the orange umbrella of Marcie Cobrin (svelte mother of two in camp, wife of an attorney, a man whose first name I couldn't recall but whose physique resembled those seen in the 'before' commercials for diet regimens); the blue and white striped umbrella of Debbie something (blonde, doctor's wife, and mother of three – two in camp, one in Europe – a woman who did aerobic exercises on the beach every day wearing a string bikini, and whose face was so taut from a recent facelift that it looked like a mask sewn on to her face); the navy umbrella of a woman named Cindy or Mindy, who flirted with the life-guards during the week when her handsome husband, Adam, was in the city.

The yellow and orange striped umbrella wasn't on the beach, but I knew it belonged to Lillian Slotkin, a woman about my age who Robin dubbed Diamond Lil because of the expensive jewellery she wore on the beach, including a tennis bracelet of square-cut diamonds, a gold and diamond Piaget watch, a diamond heart necklace, triangular diamond stud earrings, a wedding band of marquis diamonds on her left hand, and, on her right, a huge pear shaped diamond engagement ring. She was married to a very attractive silver-haired man (whose first name I don't know), in real estate – investing not selling – from what I'd heard. Rumour had it that she got a new piece of jewellery every time he had an affair. Her watch was new this year; I wondered if it was for Marjorie.

I noted that the turquoise umbrella wasn't on the beach that day, either. Its owner was among the few year-round residents of the Tower under the age of sixty. Despite her excessive make-up, which made her appear older, she was clearly younger than I. She was only occasionally seen on the beach – in fact, I hadn't seen her at all since I'd started my vacation the week before – but when she did show up she wore a simple black maillot, cut high at the thigh. Her brunette pixie-cut hair and full black brows provided a dramatic frame for her light blue eyes lined with black, her lips stained with pink and lined with fuchsia.

As this young woman was not married, her appearance in Marjorie's book might have given me pause, but for one detail: she was Tish Gordon, Marty Steiner's supposed mistress (according to Robin, who had heard it from Ellen Katz, who had an instinct for that sort of thing), and there was the rumour about the *ménage a trois* –. No, that was something I'd invented in my book.

Well. I had to remember to tell Lieutenant Fiori my theory about the colours.

Looking about me, I saw Brenda Forrester's red umbrella, and I recalled that there was no 'red' page in Marjorie's book. Curious, I thought. After all, though

Brenda wasn't married, it was her apartment in which the little red book was found –. No, that was in my book. But it was a detail that seemed disturbingly real. And, considering the rumour about Brenda's lesbian tendencies –. No, that was something Robin had insinuated in my dream. Then again, it must have come from somewhere for me to have dreamt about it, I thought. Perhaps a rumour I'd half heard and since forgotten. After all, I'm not one to pay much attention to such things. In any case, considering the other rumours about Brenda the Milf, one could imagine her to be capable of just about anything. Like a lesbian liaison with Marjorie.

Like – God forbid! – a liaison with Shel, who, it could then be concluded, might very well have found Marjorie's book in Brenda's apartment . . . on the Friday of Marjorie's demise . . . after Brenda lured him there to soothe her pain over the death of her lover –.

It was truly all too sordid to think about, so I pushed the entire thing out of my head just as I heard my name called.

Looking up, I saw Robin wave to me as she and Elliot headed towards the boardwalk. Probably going back to their apartment to make love, I thought, waving back, feeling a stirring that reminded me of my interrupted erotic daydream of Ira Pressman between my thighs. I closed my eyes and tried to re-enter my fantasy, counting on the special isolation created by the sounds of surf and wind to lull me to sleep in the midst of a crowd. But although I intended to conjure up Ira's image, it was Carl's face that kept appearing below the widow's peak.

When I'd first met Ira, it was his widow's peak that had caught my eye. It was that same dark vee that stayed with me long after I'd forgotten his face. Odd that it hadn't reminded me of Carl. But, then again, it wasn't Carl's hairline, but his mouth that had intrigued me. His full, perfectly delineated lips – lips that he licked often as he spoke – were disturbingly sensual, almost too sensual for his scrubbed-looking face, and too tempting not to kiss. Thinking back, I remembered that it was I who'd initiated not only our first kiss, but most of our love making. The outstanding exception was the first time we'd made love.

I was almost twenty-one, a senior at Temple University, in Philadelphia, majoring in journalism and dating Dr Carl Diamond, an obstetrician/gynaecologist who was thirteen years older than I. We'd met over the summer, during my internship in the public relations department of the University hospital, where he practised.

There wasn't much I remembered about the first few months dating Carl other than how impressed I was with his advanced age, his advanced degree. He was pleasant and took me out nicely, introducing me to the theatre and some of the more sophisticated restaurants in Philadelphia. He didn't drink or smoke and was respectful of my parents, gaining my father's approval. My mother didn't trust him. 'He's too old for you,' she'd said, meaning that he'd want to have sex. But it was several dates before we even kissed – the chaste event initiated by me.

Then, every Saturday night, and sometimes Friday night, we'd go out, now and then with his friend Phil Krausen and his date – occasions when I'd wear my youth uncomfortably – but usually alone. At the end of the evening we'd sit in my parents' living room and I'd listen to him talk softly about his patients and hospital politics until, unable to resist my desire to feel the touch of his lips, I'd reach up and kiss him. He never resisted. His body was warm and smelled good and I began to feel things I'd never felt before. It's not that I'd never kissed a man before. I had. But I was still a virgin. Maybe it was because Carl was older and I expected kissing an older man to feel somehow different that it felt different. Or maybe it was because *he* was different. While younger boyfriends had been demanding, needy, Carl was passive and gentle, a gentleman ... too much of a gentleman, perhaps.

Then one Friday night almost six months after our first date, Carl took me to see his new offices – something he'd been promising to do, but hadn't quite managed. It was an evening I'll always remember, although exactly what I remember may be closer to the fiction I later wrote of how I remembered it, which may be closer to the emotional, if not the actual facts of the event. The story began ...

Pricilla Perkins, television chef of local renown, would never pull a pot roast from the oven again without feeling the hot rush of sexual excitement tear through her body. Every time she'd glimpse the blue and white checkered pot holder mittens hanging innocently from their hook by the stove, she'd blush. For Pricilla, pot holders had taken on a whole new meaning.

... After a few expository pages in which I – or should I say Sloan I. Diamond – introduces the reader to the characters of Pricilla Perkins and her new beau, prominent gynaecologist Dr Stanley Benson, Stanley introduces Pricilla to his office suite, and an unusual experience ...

Stan proudly pointed out the small lab where his technician did some basic urine and blood studies, the two private offices he and his three associates shared on alternate days. Pricilla was impressed, in awe actually, as she pictured Dr Stanley Benson in a white coat behind his desk, below his framed diplomas and credentials. And then Stan led Pricilla to one of the four examination rooms with their forbidding looking stirruped tables. Standing at the door of room number two, she pictured Dr Stanley Benson sitting on the swivel stool between the stirrups of the examination table ... between the legs of a patient ... the legs of a woman. Her heart picked up pace.

'What do you think?' Stan questioned.

'Very impressive.'

'Our equipment is state of the art.'

'So I see,' Pricilla said, chuckling as she recognised the blue and white checkered heel pads covering the foot stirrups for what they were – quilted pot holder mittens, their thumbs sticking out drolly.

'You like our heel cozies?' he asked following her eyes.

'I have mittens like that in my television kitchen,' Pricilla said, pulling one from a stirrup, fitting it on her hand to inspect it further.

'My partner's wife brought them in. The metal can be uncomfortable against a bare foot. But I guess you know that.'

'Actually, no. I've never been to a gynaecologist.'

'Never?'

'No,' she said shyly, placing the mitten back on the stirrup, feeling suddenly very young and inexperienced.

'Well, step right up and I'll give you a preview.'

'No thanks,' she declined, stepping back.

'Not undressed ... just a dry run.'

Although most definitely uncomfortable with the idea, her curiosity was piqued, along with other emotions she didn't take the time to define, so she sat tentatively on the edge of the thickly padded table covered with a white paper runner.

Stan stood in front of her, his hands on her knees. 'Just relax, Pricilla,' he said. 'Let me put your feet –'

'No, I don't think that's necessary,' she interrupted him, having second thoughts.

'It's nothing, really,' he urged, smoothing her long denim skirt down over her legs.

'I really don't think –'

'Here, I'll show you,' Stan insisted, gently removing her sandal and placing her bare left foot in the palm of the kitchen mitt.

Not wanting to make a fuss, to appear foolishly untrusting, overly cautious ... young ... she relaxed against the back of the raised table and allowed Stan to put her right foot in the other stirrup. Her knees knocked together.

'Okay. I think I get the idea,' Pricilla said, pushing her skirt down around her ankles, giggling with embarrassment for her awkward position.

Stan came round to the side of her. 'Here we go,' he said, lowering the back of the table, ignoring her passive plea for release.

'I don't think I like this,' Pricilla said, a little more assertively, feeling ridiculous, and vulnerable. Extremely vulnerable.

But Stan leaned down and kissed her. 'Well, Miss Perkins, what brings you here today?' he asked, playing with her.

Her self-consciousness fell away under the spell of his tender kiss and his intriguing invitation to a fantasy. Forgetting her ungainly posture, she played along. 'I seem to have this funny ache, doctor,' she said.

'Where?' he asked.

'Here,' she answered, putting her fingers to her lips.

'I think we can take care of that,' Stan said kissing Pricilla again, more insistently this time, drawing a quiet sound from her throat, rendering her very centre molten. Slipping his hand into her blouse, touching her breast for the first time, Stan set in motion a sea of feelings, a rip tide pulling all her attention inward, downward.

'I think I have to check you further, Miss Perkins,' he said to her, withdrawing his hand from her blouse, lifting her skirt over her knees. He laid his hand on the inside of her thigh. 'You're warm, Miss Perkins. Perhaps you have a fever,' he said. And then he kissed her again.

Pricilla felt his hand slide under the elastic of her panties where the gentlest of pressure persuaded her to give in to her overwhelming curiosity. Withdrawing her arms from around Stan, she raised her bottom and pushed her panties to her thighs.

'Let me help,' he said, taking his place on the swivel stool between her legs, removing the delicate barrier. 'Just let your knees fall aside,' he said, wedging his hands between them.

Pricilla's face burned, her hands grew cold and began to tremble as Stan coaxed her legs apart with soft strokes, exposing the hidden parts of her to the cool air, heightening her anticipation of Stan's touch, a touch that, when it came, was soft, and satiny, and immutable. And when he put his mouth to her, all of her drained to, focused on a single exquisite point of desire. And then, suddenly, she was driven inward and outward at the same time, towards that point, towards release from a compulsion a thousand times stronger than anything she'd ever experienced in her own bed, with her own hand. Her fingers and toes tingled and burned frosty cold. And the very cells of her body seemed to collapse into the black hole of her passion, pulling in the world around her. She heard herself cry out from another dimension as she erupted in orgasm. And then she felt him moving in her – insistent strokes that reached to the centre of her. The universe was between her legs . . . legs that were supported by her heels sitting in the palms of blue and white checkered quilted pot holders.

* * *

... When I got home I relived every second of that
extraordinary evening by writing it down on sheets of lined
yellow paper with a soft lead pencil. I read what I'd written
over and over the next few weeks, lusting in vain for Carl's
further ministrations, until a missed period threw me into a
guilty panic. That's when I hid the pages away in a folder of
college themes. It was many years later that I found the
narrative and wove my first fiction around it, the title story
of *Appetizers*.

Thinking of it as I sat on the beach, I remembered the
image of Carl's black widow's peak between my white
thighs. Overcome with lust, I luxuriated in its unpretentious power, its straightforward demands. I floated on the
warmth of it, allowed its waves to roll over me, roll me
about. Until my bladder signalled me, again.

Walking back to the Tower, I met Lieutenant Fiori on
the boardwalk putting on his shoes and socks ...

'Mrs Diamond! I was just coming back to see you.'

... Taking *off* his shoes and socks, preparing to return to
the beach, to me.

'Just one more question?' I asked, not being able to resist
the allusion to the television detective's signature line.

'Actually, yes –' he started.

'Well, I'm glad you're still here, Lieutenant, because I
have a theory,' I said, feeling a sudden desire to please him.

'I'm all yours, Mrs Diamond. How about if we sit under
your umbrella and you tell me all about it,' he said, taking
my elbow.

'I was on my way back to my apartment for a minute. Can
you wait?'

'I'll do better than that. I'll come with you. That is, if you
don't mind.'

My nagging bladder gave me no time to object, although

at that point I wasn't sure if I wanted to object. 'This way, Lieutenant,' I said, wiggling into my sandals while he hastily put his shoes on unsocked feet . . .

'Nice apartment,' Lieutenant Fiori said, entering Alison's apartment.

'Thanks. I'll be right with you,' Alison said, heading towards the bathroom.

Lieutenant Fiori walked on to the front balcony where he leaned on the rail and breathed deeply. 'Quite a view from up here,' he said to Alison when she joined him.

'Yes. This is where I was sleeping when Marjorie fell.'

'I know. You told me that the first time we met.'

'I was just setting the scene for you again, because I think I've discovered something important.'

'I'm all yours, Mrs Diamond,' Lieutenant Fiori said with a look that spoke to some part of Alison other than her intellect.

'Look down there, Lieutenant. What do you see?' Alison asked, forcing herself to concentrate on the matter at hand, although what the matter at hand actually was, was growing as fuzzy as the inside of her mouth.

'Unrelenting waves licking the hot shore,' the Lieutenant said, deliberately moving closer to Alison, riveting her with his gaze.

'And on the beach, Lieutenant?' Alison continued in a trembling voice.

'People growing restless beneath the blazing sun,' the Lieutenant pressed on without looking back to the beach, stroking her with the passion of his words.

'What else?'

'I thought I was supposed to be the detective?'

'We all have many roles, Lieutenant. Right now I'm the detective.'

'And who am I?'

'That's one of the things we're going to find out.'

'I'm game.'

'I'm sure.'

For a moment there was silence as each contemplated, assessed the other, until, sure they were each in the *same* game – although not yet knowing if they were on the same side – they smiled.

'What else do you see, Lieutenant?' Alison asked, breaking the silence, but not the mood.

'A beautiful woman,' he answered, taking her lead.

'On the *beach*, Lieutenant,' Alison insisted, reaching out, turning him from her.

'Umbrellas,' he said.

'Yes.'

'Yes?' he questioned.

'Umbrellas,' Alison echoed.

'Am I missing something?'

'I don't think you miss very much, Lieutenant.'

Lieutenant Fiori flushed.

'I wouldn't have thought a police lieutenant would blush so easily,' Alison said in a most definitely, most deliciously flirtatious tone.

The lieutenant cocked his head and smiled a closed lip smile that accentuated the dimple in his right cheek. His dark brown eyes sparked. He said nothing, but nodded slowly, knowingly.

'I'd like you to look at Marjorie's notebook, Lieutenant,' Alison said.

Fiori obediently pulled the little book from his shirt pocket and leafed through its pages.

'And look at the beach again. Now what do you see?' Alison asked.

'Umbrellas,' Fiori reported. '*Coloured* umbrellas –'

'That match the colours in the book, Lieutenant.'

'Yes!'

'I have a theory –'

'So do I,' the Lieutenant said, pulling her to him. 'You're a genius!'

'I'm all yours,' said Alison, surrendering to his embrace.

'I think I've heard that somewhere before,' the Lieutenant said before kissing her on the balcony, above the beach, beyond the call of duty.

She hadn't anticipated his considerable strength, and found the surprise of his sinew as exciting as the fact. And when he held her body flush to his, moving against her, allowing her to know the scope of his intentions, she followed his rhythm until, taking his hand, Alison led him back into her apartment, into her bedroom. There she slowly drew her sweatshirt over her head, and slid out of her bathing suit. The Lieutenant reached out, greedily scooping up her breasts and burying his face in them. Alison wrapped her arms around him and drew him backwards with her until she fell back upon her bed. The lieutenant fell to his knees, putting his mouth to the core of her. His skill surprised her. 'Mrs Diamond,' he called to her from between her white thighs. She smiled at his formality, but, after all, she *was* a much older woman.

. . . 'Mrs Diamond?' I heard Lieutenant Fiori repeat as the elevator stopped at my floor. 'Are you okay? You look a little shaky.'

'Oh? It must be from the elevator. My equilibrium's been a little off lately,' I answered, a bit wobbly from my fantasy.

'Let me help,' he said, taking my elbow, steering me from the elevator to my apartment.

I noted with a twinge of excitement the strength in his hand.

Excusing myself when we entered my apartment, I went to the bathroom, returning in a few minutes to find Lieutenant Fiori on my balcony looking down over the beach.

'Are you alright?' he asked when he turned to me.

'Fine,' I said, although the off-balance feeling was aggravated by a sting of *déjà vu*.

'You were saying that you had a theory?'

'Yes. It has to do with the red book.'

'Tell me about it,' he said, moving closer to me at the rail, giving me his full attention.

'Well, I think it's some kind of log, colour-coded to the umbrellas on the Tower Beach.' I searched Fiori's face for reaction, but he just looked at me, smiling. 'I think Marjorie Applebaum was systematically seducing men,' I ventured further. 'You know her husband left home when Marjorie found out he was having an affair with Tiffany Kaufman, one of the women in the building. And, if you'll note, yellow is the first colour in the red book. Is it only a coincidence that the Kaufman's umbrella is *yellow*?' I asked.

Lieutenant Fiori cocked his head to one side. 'You have a detective's mind,' he said.

'Just a writer's mind. It's only a theory. I could be making this all up,' I said, blushing, wondering if he was flirting with me.

'Why don't you just continue and we'll see where it takes us,' he said. And did he move just a bit closer? I wondered.

'Now, the first date on the *yellow* page is just *before* Tiffany actually left Jeffrey. What if Marjorie found out about her husband's affair with Tiffany Kaufman and seduced Jeffrey Kaufman in retaliation?' I went on without considering the betrayal in my words, the implication of Jeffrey in a most heinous crime, not really clear at that moment whether what I was saying was what I knew for a fact, or what I'd been writing.

The lieutenant was nodding his head slowly.

I continued on enthusiastically like an excited pup, not at all the sexy, sophisticated sleuth of my imagination. 'And what if, after her husband left, Marjorie began to wreak her revenge on all the women on the beach by seducing their husbands, and then blackmailing them?'

'That's certainly an interesting theory,' Fiori finally said, still smiling.

'You're patronising me,' I said, suddenly feeling younger than he.

'Not at all. It's a very interesting theory ... clever, inventive. But do you have any evidence that would tie these men to the victim, or their wives to her husband?' he asked, reaching into his pocket for Marjorie's red book and his own brown notebook.

'As I said, Lieutenant, it's just a theory. But considering that Marjorie's husband was pretty much a sex object on the beach, that he played around a lot before he was married, and that he was having an affair with Tiffany Kaufman when he left Marjorie – or Marjorie threw him out, depending on your point of view – it certainly would be reasonable to imagine him seeing other women, too, keeping in mind the fact that, during the summers, he was alone at the shore all week while Marjorie worked in Philadelphia.'

'A lot to consider there, Mrs Diamond.'

'Well, if I could imagine it, couldn't Marjorie? I mean, it all fits, doesn't it?'

'Seems to. But in my business I've found that there's more than one way to interpret the facts, to fit a puzzle together.' He smiled a questioning smile.

I answered with a smile of my own. There's probably more than one way to interpret his smile, I thought as I watched him watch me, wondering just how he was interpreting *my* smile.

It was he who broke the quizzical silence, the growing tension with a chuckle of abdication. 'By the way, Mrs Diamond, the deceased's apartment is directly above yours, and Mrs Forrester owns the unit above the deceased's . . . right?' he asked.

'Right.'

'And the unit above Mrs Forrester's is the penthouse, belonging to Mr and Mrs Steiner?'

'Right,' I said again, wondering if the lieutenant was thinking what I was thinking – that Marjorie may have fallen from someone else's balcony.

'What colour is the Forrester umbrella?'

'Brenda Forrester's umbrella is red. But there's no *red* page in the book, Lieutenant,' I answered, turning back to him.

'And the Steiners?'

'Green.'

Lieutenant Fiori thumbed through the book and stopped at the page marked 'Green'. He then looked at the calendar on the back of his notebook. Nodding his head slowly, the lieutenant raised his eyebrows – his very finely arched eyebrows.

'What did you find?'

'Give me a minute,' he said, sitting on the foot of a lounge, studying the pages of Marjorie's book, referring back to his own. He nodded some more. 'Fridays and Saturdays,' he finally said, almost to himself.

'Fridays and Saturdays?'

'All the dates on the green page are either Fridays or

253

Saturdays. But the dates on the other pages are Mondays through Thursdays . . . except for the turquoise page. The dates on that page are the same as on the green page. Does that mean anything to you? Who has the turquoise umbrella?' he asked, standing up.

'Tish Gordon, on the seventh floor.'

'She's a single lady, isn't she?'

'Yes.'

'That's interesting.'

'What's more interesting is that it's rumoured that Tish Gordon is Marty Steiner's mistress.'

'Umm.'

'Maybe a *ménage à trois*, Lieutenant?' I suggested, pulling that bit of kink from out of my book.

Fiori laughed. 'Well, it takes a special kind of mind to be able to think up that special kind of thing,' he said, stepping definitely closer to me.

'What special kind of thing?' I asked, coyly, knowing exactly what he meant, feeling a bit naughty, like one of my fictional characters.

'You know. Writerly things. Kinky things, *Ms* Diamond,' he replied.

I warmed as I noted his change in address – *Ms* Diamond, as in *Ms Sloan I. Diamond*. 'There's probably a lot more kink in fact than fiction,' I said, trying to sound writerly, kinky. Turning from him, turning to the sea, resting my hands on the rail, I smiled, as the question of whether I'd said that before or written it buzzed through my mind.

'While we're theorising, who do you think may have murdered Marjorie Applebaum Smith?' the lieutenant asked, a question that startled me.

Looking down, I silently watched the waves of heat rise from the hot sand, wrapping the umbrella-studded beach in corrugated air. Could it have been the Hunk, I wondered, spurred by greed, as Robin had suggested? Or a panic-stricken, guilt-ridden Elliot Crystal? Perhaps it was Marty, or his mistress? Or maybe Marty *and* his mistress? Could a *ménage à trois* be too kinky to consider? That special kind of thing could probably get wildly out of control. And then there was Brenda Forrester, who, capable of just about anything, could have seduced poor Marjorie into a new kind of relationship, another special kind of thing . . . on her own balcony, in the middle of the night, and then . . . what? Marjorie could have threatened to blackmail Brenda about their relationship . . . and Brenda, furious, panic-stricken –.

'How about Dr Kaufman?' Fiori questioned further, interrupting my spiraling train of thought. 'We know for sure his wife had a relationship with the victim's husband –'

'Oh, no. I can't imagine –' I started, turning towards the lieutenant. But there was, in fact, not just in theory, Jeffrey's unfortunate liaison with Marjorie, as well. Jeffrey had told me so, I thought, swallowing the rest of my words, now wondering why I hadn't included him in my mental list of murder suspects.

'Then again, why would Dr Kaufman kill Marjorie and not her husband? It doesn't seem to add up, does it?' Fiori filled in my pause. 'Not unless there's some truth to the rumour that Marjorie and Dr Kaufman were more than just acquaintances, as he's insisted . . .'

No, I could never tell the secret Jeffrey shared with me about Marjorie, I thought, remembering, too, the secret I shared with him – with *only* him. Then again, it's dishonest not to tell, I thought, struggling with the principles of secrets. After all, what if Jeffrey's guilty? I thought. An image of Jeffrey dressed in Shel's flowered shorts popped into my head. No, I couldn't imagine – I wouldn't imagine – Jeffrey doing violence of any kind to anyone.

'. . . Then maybe we'd have a motive. Now, your theory about seduction and blackmail would fit very well in this puzzle, wouldn't it, Mrs Diamond?'

'But, as you said, Lieutenant, there's more than one way to fit a puzzle together,' I said, ruing my previous rash gush of conjecture, protecting my friend, my friend's confidence, my confidant.

Fiori nodded, smiling. 'You pay attention, Mrs Diamond. I like that,' he said. 'You know, maybe you should write a book about this case. You'd probably solve it before we would,' the lieutenant said.

His mention of a possible book – a book, in fact, already in progress – made me flush as I imagined Lieutenant Fiori buying this year's Beach Book next year, reading it, coming across the part where the protagonist has an affair with the sexy police lieutenant (I knew my elevator fantasy would find its way into my computer's memory before the end of the day). And I imagined him thinking of me . . . thinking of me thinking of him in that special kind of way.

'Why, you're blushing, Mrs Diamond. I hope I didn't embarrass you,' the lieutenant said. 'After all, you are a writer, and a very clever writer. Yes, you're a very clever woman with a wonderful imagination. You certainly could come up with something we've missed.'

'Lieutenant, I'm sure your experts –'

'Oh, yes. We have lots of experts, but you've got a fresh, imaginative eye. Now I'm not trying to flatter you, Mrs Diamond – although, I have to admit I am a big fan of yours – but I don't know if we'd ever have figured out the umbrella thing.'

I blushed again.

'Uh-oh. There I go embarrassing you again. I'm sorry. But the facts are the facts.'

'Well, the umbrella *thing* isn't exactly a fact, Lieutenant,'

I said, turning again to the umbrellas on the beach.

'No, but it's interesting, Mrs Diamond. Very interesting. And I hope you don't mind my saying so, but I find you very interesting, Mrs Diamond.'

'You're interesting, too, Lieutenant,' I said, returning the compliment, out of a misguided sense of politeness, really.

But, emboldened by the off-hand remark, or maybe by the way the wind was blowing my dark curls about my head, or the sight of Shel's oversize sweatshirt slipping suggestively off one shoulder, the Lieutenant stepped behind me and put his hands on my arms. 'Actually, when you saw me on the boardwalk, I was coming back to ask you to have dinner with me,' he said close to my ear.

Still looking at the beach, I closed my eyes when the umbrellas began to spin and my heart race in anticipation of his kiss on my shoulder, a kiss that I was as sure of as if I'd written it.

The touch of his lips on my bare skin surprised me nonetheless, and, even more surprising, evoked an image of the little red box that I'd tucked away so long ago in my make-up drawer – just in case. Flushed and tingling, I turned in his arms, opened my eyes . . . and found myself face to face with a stranger . . . a stranger who looked young enough to be my son.

'I'm so sorry, Lieutenant Fiori,' I said, recovering my balance with incredible *savoir-faire*. 'I think I've given you the wrong idea.'

His arms dropped to his sides and his face flamed red.

'Perhaps in another time, another place we're lovers, but here, now, we're strangers,' I heard myself say as I turned back to the sea, astounded by my ability to retrieve that pulpy, enigmatic statement from my reservoir of literary allusions.

'Thank you for that,' said the lieutenant, who was young enough to mistake my pretension for wisdom.

I felt like a Milf.

Sitting on a chair after he'd gone, I propped my feet up on the rail and smiled incredulously at my almost adventure. Attempting to recapture the aura of unrealism – or was it hyper-realism? – that had surrounded Fiori and myself on my balcony, I thought of Borges' story of the garden of forking paths, where all things were possible, where all possible things happened, but in different spheres of existence reached by turning down different paths. Perhaps fiction is a window into the different spheres of an author's life, I thought, jumping up to retrieve my computer from the living room.

Back on the balcony I began to enter into my *Notes* file my fantasised affair, my alternate relationship with Tony Fiori, a relationship down another path in my garden, where Tony and I were lovers not strangers. Maybe a little too ethereal an affair for some, but in these days of venereal warts, herpes and AIDS, a lot safer, I thought, sterile passion burning through the tips of my fingers.

At five-thirty the phone rang, dragging me from the arms of Tony Fiori. Not answering the phone wasn't an option, I decided, putting down my computer, leaping from my seat, reasoning that the events of this sphere of existence must be attended to as they happen, while other worlds can be put on hold. In short, it might be Shel.

It was Ira Pressman.

'I'm sorry, but I can't tonight,' I replied to his invitation to dinner, after a bit of chit chat, before thanking him for his call, for his previous call, for letting me know the results of my MRI. I promised to take a rain cheque for dinner, and I said goodbye.

A bit disorientated in time and place, I stood by the phone and looked blankly out of the balcony door to my laptop computer sitting on my chair. At that moment there seemed to be more reality on the balcony than where I was standing. Untethered from the earth is how I felt. And Shel hadn't even left yet. It pained me to imagine that, once he was gone, he might feel as lost as I was already feeling.

CHAPTER 13

Black

When I was six years old, I'd sit on the front porch of my grandmother's summer home with cousin Evy and chant, 'I'm Alison Ellis. I'm at 23 Ascot Place.' Then Evy would say, 'Atlantic City.' Then I'd say, 'New Jersey.' Then she'd say, 'America.' And then we'd both say, 'Earth,' which was as far as we could go. I never felt diminished by our game. To the contrary, it was an exercise in egocentrism.

Looking down at the beach from my balcony on the seventeenth floor of the Ivory Tower Condominium more than thirty years later, however, I realised how insignificant an individual is in the whole scheme of things – like a grain of sand spun off from a shell or a rock thrashing around in the sea ... a rock that was once part of a mountain, which was part of a continent, which is part of the earth ... the earth, a planet among other planets and moons, all spinning around one another, pulling at each other, holding each other, turning about a glorious star called Sun. And this giant relationship called a solar system is but a speck in a galaxy of billions of stars called the Milky Way, itself pirouetting among other galaxies in a grand dance of the universe. All under the black umbrella of space. And space itself, perhaps, spinning in an unbounded abstraction called Time.

It is quite remarkable, then, how really insignificant a single person is – except when that person is a mother's son, a fact driven home just minutes after I'd declined Ira Pressman's dinner invitation, when the phone rang again, and, again, I thought of Shel. And this time I was right.

'I was just thinking of you,' I said, fooling us both into feeling it was an extraordinary feat of extra-sensory perception instead of the very ordinary coincidence it really was, a coincidence that was, in fact, inevitable considering that, these days, I thought of Shel whenever the phone rang.

And when he told me he had the week-end off, that he was going to Great Adventure animal preserve and amusement park on Sunday with his friends and he was short on cash, I asked him to have dinner with me, and told him that I'd give him a few dollars. 'I have plans for tonight,' he said, 'but I *will* stop by to pick up some cash.'

And my heart sank because I didn't want to eat alone, and I knew that he didn't like me to eat alone, but I didn't dare tell him that if he didn't have dinner with me I'd have to eat alone, because I didn't want to make him feel guilty, cause him distress, disturb his psyche, perhaps injure it ... maybe permanently ... forgetting that children's psyches are fairly well set by the age of six. So I said, 'Fine.'

Barely had I replaced the receiver when the phone rang again. It was Jeffrey Kaufman. And when he said he wanted to talk to me I asked him if he'd like to make it over dinner, momentarily forgetting my suspicion of him as a possible murderer earlier in the day.

The image of a baby monkey clinging to an ersatz mother of wire and cloth – a psychology experiment I'd seen on public television – came to mind. It's something deeper than lack of experience that allows us our surrogates, I thought.

'Bear,' I said aloud, staring at the clouds from my balcony a little after six. 'Rabbit . . . eagle . . . butterfly –'

'Two-toed sloth,' I heard behind me. It was Shel.

'You've got to get a little more imaginative, Mom. I mean, *rabbit*? How boring,' Shel said, grabbing my shoulders from behind and shaking me before dropping into a lounge.

I thought of telling him about the filet of sole and the fish cakes I'd seen days earlier, but I decided it wouldn't sound all that clever in the telling. 'So what's the plan?' I asked, turning to him.

'Well, I'm going to con you out of fifty dollars, and then the guys are getting hoagies from the White House, and then we're probably going to smoke, drink, do drugs, pick up hookers and stay up all night until its time to go to Great Adventure tomorrow to see the giraffes copulating.'

'Ten,' I said, starting low.

'As I said, first I'm going to con you out of forty dollars, and then –'

'Fifteen.'

'Thirty-five.'

'Twenty, tops. I'm sure you have money. Mr Fishbein does pay you, I trust.'

'Twenty-five . . . please,' he implored.

'Sold. And who's driving?' I asked, ignoring his baiting, fully aware that Shel rarely drank more than beer, *one*

beer. And I was as sure as any parent could be that
he didn't use other drugs, although I wouldn't say for
certain he'd *never* tried pot. Then again, he didn't smoke
cigarettes, I thought, looking at my handsome son,
smiling the self-satisfied smile of one surveying a job well
done. Of course, there was still sex. Sex. That's what
separates the men from the boys, I thought. From *my*
little boy. Except that Shel wasn't little any more, I
admitted fleetingly, pushing the subject from my mind.

'Drive carefully, there'll be a lot of people on the road,'
I said.

'I always drive carefully, Mother dear.'

'And when you get there, make sure you keep your
windows closed so the animals can't get in. And don't feed
them ... and don't tease them. And what ever you do,
don't get out of the car –'

'Hey! I'm not a child.'

'Well, you're still *my* child,' I retorted, more literally
than either of us would care to acknowledge.

'Yes, Mommy,' he teased me.

'Look, honey, I just don't want you to do anything
crazy,' I said, picturing Shel being grabbed by a gorilla,
run over by a rhino, falling fifty storeys in a derailed roller
coaster car.

'Forty bucks and you got a deal.'

'It's twenty-five, and don't push your luck or it'll be
fifteen. Get me my pocketbook.'

Shel retrieved my wallet from the apartment and then
fell again into the lounge.

'By the way, how come you're not working this week-
end?' I asked as I handed him three tens.

'Since next week-end is my last, Fishbein gave me a
break.'

'That was nice of him. By the way, if we leave the shore

a week from Monday, you'll only have four days to pack for school. Are you sure that's enough time?'

'More than enough. I packed my stereo, television and stuff for shipping before I left home. All I have left is clothes.'

'Our plane takes off sometime in the morning that Friday, and –'

'Why are we going over this now? We've got loads of time.'

'It's just two weeks away, Shel. I want you to think about it now so you remember everything you have to do before it's too late.'

'It's never too late for anything, Mom. Remember that.'

I smiled indulgingly.

'So what are you up to tonight? You're dressed for company,' Shel questioned.

'I'm having dinner with Jeffrey Kaufman.'

'The shrink, again?'

'You had your chance,' I said, surprised at the hostility in my voice, hoping that Shel wouldn't pick it up.

'A little touchy, aren't we?'

He had.

'It wasn't directed at you,' I lied. 'It's just been a long day.'

'Why? What's going on? You feeling okay or are you dizzy again?'

'I'm fine, Shel.' Pause. 'Lieutenant Fiori was here to pick up the book you found. In the elevator ... on Tuesday? Right?'

'That's right.'

'Don't you think it's odd that maintenance hadn't found it over the week-end?'

Shel was suggestively silent.

'Shel?'

'What?'

'Don't you think it's odd that –'

'Hey, maybe Marjorie didn't drop it. Maybe someone *else* dropped it after the week-end – like the murderer. Did you think of that possibility?' he snapped.

He was right. I *hadn't* thought of that possibility. Of course, it was only another possibility. There were so many possibilities –

'So where're you going tonight?' Shel asked, derailing my train of thought.

'We haven't decided yet.'

'Sure you don't need a chaperone?'

'Last night, when you were invited, you didn't seem too happy to be with us. Besides, I thought you said you had plans with the guys.'

'Well I certainly know when I'm not wanted,' Shel said, feigning a sulk.

I bit. 'You're always wanted, Shel. We'd love to have you join us.'

'No, no. I'll just have an oily, unhealthful hoagie with my friends. At least I know they care about me.'

'Shel, stop that. You really can come if you want to.'

'No. I'll be fine. Just go and have a great time without me,' he said, jumping up, heading for the door. '. . . And thanks for the cash,' he added, showing me his beautiful, straight, white teeth.

As much as I knew he'd been teasing me, I couldn't help but feel there was some grain of truth to his hurt demeanour. With the bang of the front door I heard the plaintive squawk of the mother gull.

'By the way, I think you're right, about Shel being jealous of other men . . . or whatever it was you said,' I was saying to Jeffrey over a hamburger at *Michael's* on the

boardwalk. Our conversation had been politely imper-
sonal until then, neither of us alluding to the evening
before.

'Mothers and sons. Complicated relationship,' Jeffrey
responded. And then, 'I was close to my mom,' he began,
relating his own story. 'My dad left when I was about
seven. Mom never remarried, and, although my sister is a
year older than me, Mom relied on me to take care of
things, to take care of her and my sister.'

'At seven?' I asked, thinking how unrealistic demands
of responsibility on a young child could lead to a warped
personality. Warped enough to be homicidal? I wondered
fleetingly, pushing the thought away as absurd, thinking
that Shel, too, had an unusual childhood ... probably
feeling responsible for me since he was three.

'Well, it seemed that way at the time. Certainly when I
was older it was a fact,' Jeffrey was saying as I reined in
my galloping imagination.

'Are you still close to your mother?' I asked, feeling the
florid surge in my face slowly subside.

'She died, about eight years ago,' Jeffrey answered, not
noticing my fluctuating complexion. 'The year before I got
married, actually. But until then we were very close. She
lived with me in my Germantown home.'

'And your sister?'

'She's married, two kids ... moved to Washington
when her husband was transferred.'

'Are you close?'

'In a way. I'm more like a father to her than a younger
brother. But that's the way we grew up. I was the
caretaker.'

Listening to Jeffrey, I realised that although his
background was completely different from what I'd
imagined, I hadn't been far off the mark in the way I'd

portrayed his basic psychological make-up in *Beach Book-91* – a man in search of a mother not a lover. Certainly not a killer, I judged.

'About last night,' I heard him say, pulling me from my ruminations over his lost childhood, his found innocence. 'I just want to say I'm sorry about the way I ran out.'

'No, Jeffrey. I should be apologising to you,' I said, thinking of my near betrayal of him.

'No. *I* apologise. I'm afraid I was taking advantage of a vulnerable time for you. I should know better than that,' Jeffrey insisted.

'Well, I guess I was feeling a bit vulnerable,' I said, taking the out, knowing that I couldn't tell him of Fiori's suspicions, the seeds of which I may have inadvertently helped to cultivate.

'Your friendship is valuable to me. I feel I can share things with you. It's usually the other way around, you know . . . people sharing their feelings with me. I find this very comfortable,' Jeffrey said in flawless psycho-cant.

'Of course we'll be friends,' I replied, *comfortable* with the idea that Jeffrey had finally found someone he'd rather talk to than make love to.

So. We were in agreement after all.

Walking on the boards after dinner, I felt an urge to urinate and I wondered, for the third time that day, if I had a urinary tract infection. As we walked I remembered the last time I had cystitis, two years ago, and that I'd reacted badly to the sulfa medication. Possibly a mild nephrotic syndrome – an Untoward Effect of the sulfa – the doctor had told me in response to my inventory of symptoms, some of which I may have exaggerated to make sure he took me seriously. Perhaps the sulfa had damaged my kidneys, I thought, picturing myself – for the second time that day – bound to a dialysis machine by coils

of tubes, awaiting a kidney transplant, understanding that
if I survived the transplant surgery – optimistically
assuming a matching kidney could be found – I'd probably
spend the rest of my life on steroids to prevent tissue
rejection, which would result in a hideously bloated face
and brittle bones, leading to a series of fractures and
surgery in my later years – if I had any later years.
'Jeffrey, I'd like to find a bathroom,' I said, trying to
sound unconcerned.

'We'll go into a casino,' he said, stopping in front of
Atlantic City's quintessential house of fantasy, the Taj
Mahal. A gaudy, colourised cartoon of Agra's magnificent
structure, it looked like a monstrous plastic toy.

I wondered at its garish purple, aqua, and gold
minarets, its sheer size. I'd sworn I'd never enter the
building that, in my mind, stood for everything that had
gone wrong with Atlantic City. But, I did have to go to the
bathroom.

'Well, it'll be an adventure to see the inside of a casino,'
I acquiesced, climbing the tiers of white steps.

'You've never been in one?'

'Hard to believe, isn't it? But I hate to lose money.'

'Casinos aren't just about money, they're about the
suspension of reality,' Jeffrey said.

After hitting the reality of the bathroom, where I found
to my relief once again that I had a bladder full of clear
urine – suspending for the moment my horrific renal
fantasy – we hit the unreality of the casino.

The noise is what I noticed first, the clanging and
chinging and ringing, a cacophony of coins and bells – the
sound of fortunes being made and lost.

Then there were the lights, the crowds, and the vastness
of that cavernous, windowless interior. Windowlessness –
another particularly noticeable condition, especially for a

room so large. Most of the casinos are windowless, Jeffrey informed me. Windowlessness creates timelessness and weatherlessness, essential ingredients for the illusion of endlessness that keeps players at their games saying, *Just one more time*.

Walking up and down the aisles, I noted the blackjack tables, craps tables, the wheels . . . of fortune, roulette . . . and, of course, the hundreds of slot machines responsible for the overwhelming metallic din.

'Don't you find it a bit ironic that the real Taj Mahal is a mausoleum?' I asked Jeffrey rhetorically, feeling somewhat stifled, although, in fact, the air was conditioned cool beyond comfort.

Jeffrey didn't hear me as he pulled on the arm of a dollar slot machine and watched the oranges, cherries and plums spin into expensive fruit salad.

'Well, I think I've had enough,' I said, having seen my fill of empty change cups and vacant eyes.

Although my plea didn't register with Jeffrey, a zealous shout from a craps table across the room did.

'Sounds like a hot table, Alison. Let's get in . . . for just a minute.'

Following him following the cheers, I stayed a step or two behind and watched as he wedged himself into the chain of players hugging the hot table. But in no time – or at least it seemed like no time in that timeless place – the triumphant cries died down and, one by one, the links of the chain fell away until only two players were left.

I stepped close to Jeffrey. 'I think I've had enough,' I tried again.

'Just one more roll, Alison,' he said without turning around.

The croupier smiled and winked at me as Jeffrey picked up the dice.

'SEVEN ... OUT,' the croupier called after only four rolls, raking in small stacks of chips from the table.

Jeffrey relinquished the dice to the only other player, an elderly man wearing baggy pants, a floral shirt and a baseball hat.

'SEVEN ... OUT,' the croupier called after a short time.

The elderly man muttered something, pocketing his few remaining chips, and walked away, leaving only Jeffrey at the table. Before picking up the dice again, Jeffrey signed a marker, and was given a fresh stack of twenty-five dollar green chips. Watching Jeffrey roll again and again, I saw something in him I hadn't seen before: a willingness to lose all in an unwillingness to lose. And I began to wonder how he had dealt with losing his wife to Marjorie's husband ... what he may have gambled in an attempt to come out a winner ... what more he may have lost in the effort. My God, I thought, could Jeffrey Kaufman have murdered Marjorie Applebaum? Although I hadn't figured out the plot line, I was sure a motive could be insinuated.

Standing next to him in that huge, noisy vault amidst a pressing crowd of disparate – and desperate? – people, I felt estranged. A now familiar gnaw in my stomach and lightness in my head overtook me as my skin registered hot and cold, my centre of gravity shifted uncomfortably to one side.

'SEVEN ... OUT,' the croupier called, as he swept the table clean of Jeffrey's chips.

'Can we leave now?' I asked Jeffrey.

'Just one more roll and then we'll go,' he replied. 'I promise.'

'Now. Please,' I insisted, 'I'm dizzy.'

On the boardwalk I breathed easier. It was warm and moist, and, once we passed the glitter and shine of the casinos, dark – like a womb, I thought, feeling comforted, noting that my inner gyroscope had almost righted itself.

'I won't ask how much you lost, because I believe you told me that casinos are more about fantasy than money,' I said, feeling a bit testy.

'Sometimes fantasy can be more expensive than reality,' Jeffrey replied, smiling guiltily, shaking his head. 'So. Back to reality. When does Shel leave for school?' he asked, turning to my weakness.

'A week from Friday, the sixteenth. But we're leaving the shore the Monday before to get everything in order.'

'That's just ten days away, Alison. Will that be the end of the summer for you? At the shore, I mean.'

'Oh, no. I'm going to Chicago with Shel to get him set up in his dorm, make sure he has everything, and then I'm coming back for another week or so. I just hope I'm not getting sick.'

'Why would you think that?'

'I don't know. I've had some symptoms of a urinary tract infection. Peeing a lot. More than I should.'

'I don't know much about urinary pathology, but I do know that stress can do that.'

'Really?' I said, mentally trading in my dialysis machine for a shrink.

Sunday morning I found myself on a bridge headed towards Philadelphia. It was dark – pre-dawn – and foggy. I was driving fast ... maybe too fast. When I was about halfway across the bridge, I saw the flashing red lights of a police car in my rear view mirror. Looking at my speedometer, I was relieved to see that I hadn't been speeding, but I pulled over to the side of the bridge anyway. While waiting for the policeman, something far ahead on the bridge caught my attention. It looked like a person, a woman, walking.

'Mrs Diamond? Your licence and registration please,' I heard Lieutenant Fiori demand through my open window.

'There's someone on the bridge,' I tried to tell him.

But all he said was, 'Your licence and registration?' as he wrote on his pad of tickets.

'Up ahead ... someone climbing on the rail!' I said in a growing panic.

'It's too late, Mrs Diamond. Can't save her now,' he said nonchalantly as we watched the woman plummet from the bridge and disappear into the fog. 'You should have told sooner.'

'I didn't know,' I cried, handing him my identification.

'You're smart about this special kind of thing,' he said, scanning my cards. 'You should have figured it out, *Ms* Diamond.'

'But I promised not to tell,' I sobbed.

Ignoring my plea, the Lieutenant handed me a ticket. 'See you in court,' he said, leering through my window.

Just then the radio in my car started blaring.

... My clock radio, which I kept set for nine-thirty in case I overslept, had gone off. Fumbling to stop the penetrating noise, I lost sight of my disturbing dream. But after a quick, hot shower, while standing in front of my fogged mirror brushing my teeth, the bridge suddenly loomed before me. Gagging on my toothbrush, my ears clogged, my eyes watered, and through my tears, my own image in the mirror appeared to be Evy. And through my momentary deafness I heard her voice: 'Don't tell.'

Shaking, I washed the toothpaste out of my mouth, then sat on the closed toilet seat and wept.

* * *

It was a resplendent morning. The sun shone hot and crisp in a clear, azure sky that went on forever. A cool ocean breeze mounded the grey-green ocean water into graceful rollers that glistened in the sunlight to the delight of swimmers, waders and spectators alike. I, however, was not feeling so sanguine. Though I was on the beach, a part of me was still in my dream. I felt captured, encapsulated in it. I looked around for Robin, for someone to talk to. Not finding her or her pink umbrella I remembered that Elliot had come. *Probably still in bed*, I thought. Enviously.

I moved my chair out of the shade of my umbrella and took off my dark glasses in an attempt to brighten my mood. But all I felt was hot, and the glare of the sun hurt my eyes. Squinting painfully, I spotted Jeffrey's cheerful yellow umbrella three or four parties to my right. It was enough to move me.

I'd forgotten my suspicions of the previous evening, that Jeffrey could be a killer, until I stood up and started towards the yellow umbrella. Remembering, I slowed my approach and studied the pleasantly apish body sprawled on a towel. In the radiant light of day, however, he appeared blissfully free of guilt, or perhaps I needed him to appear so, my mood being heavy and dark.

'Good morning, Jeffrey,' I greeted him, feigning a light-hearted demeanour. I must have startled him because he sat bolt upright, making an odd little catching sound in his throat.

'Alison! Well, good morning. I looked for you when I came down, but I didn't see you,' he said, recovering his voice.

'I overslept. I've only just come down.'

'How can you oversleep on vacation?'

'I feel logy if I sleep too late in the morning, so I set my alarm.'

'That's very controlled of you.'

'Yes. Well, I don't feel much in control this morning.'

'Want to talk about it? Here, sit,' he said, moving to one end of his oversized yellow and white striped towel.

'No,' I lied, sitting next to him, slipping my dark glasses back on.

We sat for a time, allowing the noise of the wind and ocean to fill the conversational void.

'Ices, fudge bars, ice-cream sandwiches!' a vendor called out as he walked nearby.

I put my hand up and waved to him. 'Want a fudgsicle?' I asked Jeffrey.

'A little early, isn't it?'

'Chocolate helps.'

'Helps what?'

'Whatever,' I said as the vendor dropped his white ice chest on the sand in front of us.

'What'll it be folks?' he asked.

'Two fudge bars,' Jeffrey said, reaching into his beach bag for loose bills.

'Two fudgies,' the vendor repeated, opening the chest and pulling the bars through a fog of dry ice vapours.

'Thanks, Jeffrey,' I said, stripping the paper from my fudge bar, watching the brown ice turn frosty white. 'I needed this.'

I'd learned that there's an art to eating a fudge bar on the beach. Initially, your lips and tongue can stick to the frost, so it's best to bite the first bits off the top edge with your teeth. After a minute or two the frost melts . . . but so does the fudge, so you have to start licking the drips from the bottom of the bar. The most satisfying part is when the bar is small enough to fit in your mouth and you can shave the melting chocolate down a little at a time with your lips and teeth. But you must be mindful of the danger of the last thin layer of fudge breaking away from one side of the stick, leaving you with a mouthful of too cold chocolate and the choice of quickly stuffing your already frozen mouth with the rest of the bar, or letting it fall into the sand. And, of course, there's the aftershock – teeth that ache from the cold. Attempting to warm them with your tongue only intensifies the pain. The trick is to pull your lips back, exposing your clenched teeth, and quickly inhale through your teeth to wash them with cool air, which is what I was doing when Jeffrey started to laugh.

'What's so funny?' I asked.

'You are. I've never seen anyone eat a fudgsicle with such precision.'

'Wait a minute, my teeth are still aching,' I said, clenching them again and inhaling sharply.

Jeffrey laughed again.

Then, 'I had a really strange dream this morning, Jeffrey,' I said, braced by the pain, and the infusion of sugar.

'More Beethoven and day-glo umbrellas?'

'No. Bridges and falling bodies.' Pause. 'Jeffrey, do you remember what the fortune teller said, about learning a secret in a dream?'

'Actually, she said a mirror. Then you asked me if I thought dreams were like mirrors.'

'You really listen, don't you?'

'Just doing my job, Ma'am,' he said, smiling.

'I think I dreamt about my cousin Evy jumping from the Tacony Bridge.'

'That must have been unsettling.'

'But that's not all. *I* was there. And so was Tony Fiori – you know, the lieutenant investigating Marjorie's death?

He was patrolling the bridge and stopped me for speeding–. No. I wasn't speeding. But he stopped me and gave me a ticket anyway.'

'For what?'

'I don't remember. I was more concerned with the woman I saw about to jump from the bridge. I tried to tell him, but he told me it was too late.'

'Too late for what?'

'I don't know, but he said I should have figured it out and told him sooner. That's when he gave me the ticket.'

I could feel Jeffrey's eyes on me, probing for more.

'So. What do you think?' I asked, not turning to look at him.

'What do *you* think?' he threw back at me.

'That's a typical shrink answer,' I replied, annoyed.

Silence.

'I think that for some reason I feel responsible for Evy's death,' I then answered, my need to talk overwhelming my need to be in control.

'Why would you think that?'

'I haven't a clue.'

'What did he mean when he said you should have told sooner? Did he mean about seeing her on the bridge?'

'No,' I said instinctively, only that instant aware of what he did mean.

Flushing hot, then cold, I shivered ... and I remembered our secret hideout, a tiny grotto in a dense section of hedge in the back of my parents' home. Evy and I would slip in there with a handful of my mother's homemade chocolate chip cookies and tell secrets to each other, deep dark secrets that we swore never to reveal to anyone. It was there that I told her about the time I took a comic book from Perchick's drugstore and forgot to pay for it ... how I courageously took it back the next day, although I was terrified the police would be there waiting to arrest me. They weren't.

It was there, too, that I told Evy about my first orgasm. I couldn't have been more than six or seven, and I had no idea what I'd done to myself late one night in bed, only that whatever it was, it was something I made happen over and over again. I told Evy she should try it because it felt so good, and I started to show her how I'd made this secret thing happen. 'Watch me, Evy, watch me,' I said. But she wouldn't watch, she didn't want to know, and she ran out, leaving all her chocolate chip cookies behind, leaving me drenched in shame. I had thought I must have done something really evil to myself for Evy to have run from me like that . . . and leave her cookies.

Then it was a long time before we met in our secret grotto again, or it seemed like a long time. It may really have been only a few days. That's when she told me *her* deepest, darkest secret. That's when she told me '*Don't tell . . . don't ever tell*,' even though not telling was a given in that secret place. But she said it over and over – '*Don't tell*' – while she told me about her father . . . and the games he played with her in the park . . . and in her bed . . . when he'd wake her with touches that pleasured and frightened her, when he'd tell her, '*Don't tell . . . don't ever tell*.'

'He meant I should have told someone about Evy's father long before . . . that maybe I could have saved her,' I heard myself telling Jeffrey, tears running down my face from behind my dark glasses.

Jeffrey wrapped his arm around me, instantly understanding my words and my distress.

'I never told,' I sobbed. 'I never, ever told. And then I forgot. And then we were grown and Evy was into boys and I wasn't. And then she was gone. And I could have saved her if I'd told.'

'You don't know that. You were just a little girl, Alison. You had no idea what it all meant.'

'In my dream the lieutenant said that I should have known what it all meant, that I knew about this special kind of thing.'

'Why would he say that to you?'

That was something I couldn't answer without revealing my secret self. So I didn't answer, but pulled away from him and wiped my face with a corner of the towel.

'Remember, we create our own dreams, Alison,' I heard Jeffrey say, and I began to think about the dream I'd created in Sloan I. Diamond. I remembered Tony Fiori's leer in my dream . . . on my balcony. I wondered what he was thinking of me, what others might think of me . . .

'I can't believe it!' Robin cried, throwing a copy of *A Stitch in Time* in the middle of my beach blanket. 'I've always worried about saying something a little off-colour to you, when all along you were pecking away on your computer getting off on lurid little tales of sexual depravity. I'm absolutely shocked. *You* finally shocked *me*!'

It amused me that people are so sure of their own perceptions. I enjoyed watching Robin's perception of my innocence blasted, knocking her a little off-centre. No doubt it made her wonder just what else about me she had misperceived.

'I wonder what else I've gotten wrong,' she said. 'I don't know who you are any more.'

'The same person you've known for . . . how many years now?'

'Not quite.'

'Exactly the same.'

'But–'

'What I write comes from a part of me that even I'm not completely familiar with, Robin. More often than not, what leaves my fingertips is a surprise.'

'Very glib.'

It was the best explanation I could come up with that was as close to the truth as I dared to get.

... And what might Shel think of me ... if he knew ... if he knew who I really was ...

'I don't know you, Mom. I *never* knew who you really were,' Shel said angrily, throwing a copy of *A Stitch in Time* in the middle of his laundry on the kitchen table. 'I can't believe *my mom* could write such stuff, could *think* such things. You've always acted the innocent, but you're a fake! You're not my mom. I've lost my mom forever!' he said, turning from me, walking towards the door.

'And you! Who do you think you're kidding? You're not so innocent, either,' I admonished my son, running after him, like the mother gull. 'I know about you and Brenda Forrester, that ... that Milf! Do you think I can think about you the same way now that you've indulged in such ... in such special kinds of things?'

... *Do I know who he really is? Do I know who anyone really is?* I wondered silently, emerging from my day-dream.

'Let's walk,' I said, jumping to my feet, heading towards the water. Jeffrey – the shrink, the cuckold, the possible murderer, my possible friend – followed obediently behind.

That night as I sat alone on my balcony looking up at the

sky, I thought of the incomprehensible vastness of the great black umbrella of space, where all things are possible, where all possible things can happen, and I chanted, 'I'm in the universe . . . the Local Group . . . the Milky Way . . . the Solar System . . . Earth . . . America . . . New Jersey . . . Kent . . . Ascot Place . . . the Ivory Tower Condominium . . . apartment 1701. Who am I?'

CHAPTER 14

Purple

I was the Purple Butterfly, the star of the second grade Spring play. But I never remembered it quite that way.

Wearing white tutus and gossamer wings fashioned of coat hanger wire and cheesecloth, my classmates and I were the magic butterflies of spring, distinguished by our sashes and paint pails of red, blue, and white. I was the White Butterfly.

'I'm a colourless butterfly in a season of colours,' I cried to the audience of mothers, as the Red and Blue butterflies flitted about with their brushes and pails, pretending to paint the paper flowers adorning the classroom.

'Don't cry, White Butterfly, we'll change you into a Purple Butterfly!' they said, tipping their red and blue pails towards my white pail. 'Just dip your sash into the magic purple paint we made for you.'

Much to my embarrassment, when I attempted to exchange my white sash for the purple one hidden in my pail I retrieved instead only the white one. Returning it to the pail and struggling to free the purple sash caught beneath the false bottom, I spilled them both to the floor.

The colourful butterflies tittered; the mothers were breathlessly quiet. Driven by mortification, I picked up the purple sash and, tying it around my waist, joined the Red and Blue Butterflies in a dance. The mothers, clapping their hands vigorously, let out a collective sigh of relief.

Decades later I would recall the hushed sigh but not the applause. And I'd still remember myself as the White Butterfly.

Perception is everything, I was thinking as I leafed through a copy of the Smithsonian magazine on Monday morning on the beach, gazing at photographs of gorgeous butterflies, images that had raked up the tragic little episode from my childhood that was spinning around in my head, when Jeffrey dropped on to a towel in front of me, seemingly from nowhere. He was dripping wet from the sea.

'Good morning. Feeling better today?'

'Jeffrey! You startled me.'

'I was a little concerned about you yesterday. I know you were upset and –'

'You know, Jeffrey, perception is everything,' I blurted out. 'So sometimes it's hard to know what's really real. I mean, how do you sort it all out? Isn't that what psychologists do? help people sort out their perceptions? And how do you deal with your own perceptions while you're doing it. Don't they get in the way?'

'Wow. Big questions for so early in the morning, Alison. But I'll let you in on a trick of the trade. We do it all with mirrors.' He smiled until I smiled. Then he said, 'Alison, if you think it would help, I could give you the name of a couple of top notch colleagues who I'm sure you'd be comfortable with.'

'Do *you* think I need a shrink?' I asked, cocking my head, smiling askance at Jeffrey.

Without a moment's hesitation, Jeffrey said, 'I think you need to trust yourself.'

He paused, and in that quiet moment I felt a subtle shimmering of my skin, like the top layer had some-how loosened, allowing fresh air to wash over me. My whole body relaxed and I looked at Jeffrey Kaufman, the big, warm, fuzzy man who, at that moment, I would have loved to love. But I knew that in this sphere we were meant to be friends. In another world, another time, perhaps, we'd be more than friends. Maybe some day I'd write it. 'Thanks, Jeffrey. I needed that,' I said.

'Anytime, Alison. I'd hug you, but I'm soaked from my swim,' he said, getting up, pulling his towel with him.

'Wet is okay,' I said, standing, giving him a long hard hug. The cool of his body seemed to stick to mine. And when he let go, it stayed with me.

'And now I've got to go. I've got some stuff to do ... some people to see. Just wanted to touch base. See you tomorrow.'

Settling back into my chair, I watched Jeffrey as he made his way across the beach, stopped to slip on his sneakers, climbed the stairs to the boardwalk and dis-appeared down the ramp to the street on the other side. How could I have ever considered such a kind man to be a murderer? I thought to myself. Then I closed my eyes and thought about what he'd said – that I had to trust myself.

I took a deep breath and focused my inner eye on the green chenille bedspread in my aunt's guest room, the room where I'd slept when I was a child. I kept looking at the spread until the image of a man appeared in the corner of my eye. *Let's take a nap*, the man said. I think he said it. And then I was lying on the bed rolling a bit of green chenille between my fingers, and there was a presence behind me. I think I remember that. And at that moment I believed that I would never really know if I remembered it or made it up. Or, even if what I'd remembered was real, whether or not there was any more to it than I'd actually remembered. What I did know was that, at that moment, remembering it caused me no particular discomfort. At that moment I believed it didn't matter whether it was real or not. And I remembered what Jeffrey had said to me Friday night, . . . *Maybe you don't have to remember what went on in the past. Maybe remembering that you don't remember is enough, and you only have to understand what's on your mind in the present.* What was on my mind now was the guilt I felt about Evy's death. And had I taken on some of the guilt she'd felt, as well? adopted it as my own? I'd have to ask Jeffrey about the possible psychological realities of such a *guilt by association*, I thought.

The vague sense of something *wrong* I'd felt for years was finally making sense. There was nothing wrong with me. The *wrong* was with Evy's family. Remembering her secret, my secret, had changed me. Lying on the beach on Monday morning I imagined the film that had loosened on the surface of my skin was drying in the heat of the sun. I imagined it breaking away . . . a chrysalis, falling away, leaving me new and acutely sensitive to the reality of the world around me.

After lunch, after grocery shopping Monday afternoon, I returned to the beach and found Robin sitting under my umbrella, looking forlorn.

'Lost, little girl?' I teased her.

She looked up at me with a rueful smile.

'So, Elliot left,' I said, interpreting her demeanour.

'About six this morning.' After building a tiny mountain of sand on her right foot, Robin said, 'Lieutenant Fiori knocked at my door at nine.'

'Oh?' I said, sitting down, trying not to show disproportionate interest in news of the lieutenant.

'He was looking for Elliot. He wanted to know how well Elliot knew Marjorie Applebaum.' She paused. 'Remember, last summer – the end of the summer – I told you I thought something was going on with Elliot ... that he wasn't himself?'

'I'm not sure,' I said, thrown guiltily off balance by her question, not sure if what I *was* remembering was what she'd told me or what I'd written in *Beach Book-91*.

'Well, I was concerned that Elliot might be having an affair.'

'You don't think Elliot and Marjorie –'

'I know that Elliot saw Marjorie professionally about that time. At least he said it was professional,' Robin continued.

'Why would he lie, Robin?' I asked, although I'd already created both the rhyme and reason in my fiction.

'And Lieutenant Fiori's visit clinches it. Why else would he want to talk to Elliot? He must know about their affair.'

'I don't buy that,' I said, having bought and wrapped it long before.

'There's more, Alison. There's Marty Steiner,' she said.

Uh-oh! I thought, startled again by my incredible acumen, sure that Robin was about to confirm yet another fragment of my fiction – the giant crab I'd invented, reflected in the mirrored skylight that was a known fact, the talk of the Tower, in fact, when Marty had it installed above his whirlpool tub. 'So what about Marty Steiner?' I asked.

'Well ... Tish Gordon isn't the only woman Marty entertains when Maggie's off visiting their daughter,' Robin said, finally admitting knowledge of Marty's involvement with Tish, an admission obviously – obvious to me, that is – prompted by the weight of her own guilty affair with Marty.

My God, she did it! She really did it! I thought, the dovetailing of fiction and reality overwhelming me, setting my heart apace, my face aflush.

'Alison, why are you blushing?'

'Erythema,' I blurted out, trying to distract Robin with medical jargon.

'Era-what?'

'A flush ... in response to the heat.'

Robin stared at me, looking puzzled.

'I'm *hot*, Robin.'

'For Marty!? Alison, you and *Marty*!?,' Robin exclaimed, smiling for the first time since she'd sat down.

'Me!'

'No?'

'Of course not!'

'Well, it appeared he was trying to screw everyone else on the Tower beach,' she said with a snicker, which seemed to me particularly inappropriate considering that *everyone else* included her.

'What do you mean by *everyone*?' I dared to ask.

'Well, as I said, there's Tish –'

'A couple of days ago you said it was just a rumour.'

'I didn't want to break a confidence. Marty told me about her himself.'

'Why would Marty tell you –'

'Maggie's been away so much, Alison . . . and I told you Elliot's been distant . . . so Marty and I . . . well, we talk.'

'And?'

'And what?'

'And what else?'

'Nothing else!' Now it was Robin's turn to flush. '*You* think Marty and *me* . . . ?'

'No?' I asked.

'No!'

'So who else?'

'Marjorie Applebaum.'

'Marty and *Marjorie*?'

Robin was quiet for a moment and then she leaned closer to me, and in a most conspiratorial way she said, 'Just for the record, I did think about it . . . about sleeping with Marty.'

I blinked at her.

'Not that he ever actually propositioned me, but . . . well, I did let him kiss me once.'

I blinked again, which was terribly disingenuous of me, considering that I probably had them in bed long before either of them had considered it.

'Don't look so stricken, Alison. We didn't do anything else. I swear.'

'So what's all this got to do with *Elliot* and Marjorie?' I asked, lost.

'Don't you think it's bizarre that Marjorie Applebaum – mousy Marjorie Applebaum – would get involved with Marty Steiner?'

Bizarre enough for me to have already rendered it in fiction, I thought. 'I'm lost, Robin.'

'You're not listening, Alison. Now. There's also Marjorie

and Jeffrey Kaufman, a rumour that was more or less confirmed by Emma Chankin,' Robin continued.

'So?' I asked, knowing full well that it was fact, not rumour, although I never told Robin that Jeffrey had *absolutely* confirmed it to me.

'Well?' she questioned back, waiting for me to catch on ... to understand that it was *Marjorie* who was screwing everything on the Tower beach.

'But why?' I asked, having already answered that question, too, in *Beach Book-91*.

'Who knows? Who cares? I only care that she got her hands on Elliot. I just wish I knew how Fiori connected Marjorie to Elliot.'

'For what it's worth, I think you're completely wrong about the whole thing. It's too unreal,' I said, sure that she was right, and feeling again guilty about the little red book that *I'd* handed over to Fiori, along with my theory.

'You okay, Alison? You look a little unfocused.'

'No. I'm fine.'

'You sure? What does Ira Pressman have to say? Has he come up with a diagnosis for your dizzy spells yet?'

'Actually, he called this morning to tell that me that the rest of the test results came in – all negative. So he concluded it must have been a viral infection of my inner ear, and it could take a long time for my equilibrium to stabilise.'

'Typical. When they don't understand something they call it a virus. So what else did he say?'

'What do you mean, *what else*?'

'Dinner, maybe? Didn't you tell me –'

'I told you I took a rain check. He didn't ask again.'

'I don't believe –'

'How about a fudgie wudgie?' I asked.

'Sure, but –'

'Ice-cream!' I shouted, jumping up and waving to Bill who was passing nearby.

'So what do you think about mousy Marjorie Applebaum now, Alison?' Robin asked in a rather nasty tone.

A sigh escaped my lips. 'Maybe she had a virus.'

By about eleven-thirty that night, I'd given up on hearing from Shel, although I'd left two messages on his answering machine, and one at the deli. If the phone rang before morning, I decided, it would be the police telling me that Shel had been in an accident coming home from Great Adventure on Sunday, that they had trouble identifying him because of the wallet full of false IDs found in his possession. They'd say he'd been seriously injured, but they'd mean he was dead. And I'd be too hysterical to drive to the hospital to see him – to identify his body – so I'd have to call Robin, or maybe Jeffrey to drive me there, and it would be so horribly, overwhelmingly grotesque, so inconceivably sad.

Tears were pouring down my face when I pushed the macabre thoughts from my head and turned out my light, muttering a quick prayer to the telephone god . . . that the phone shouldn't ring in the middle of the night – which could only mean disaster – but that nine o'clock in the morning would be fine.

It was eight-thirty when Shel called on Tuesday morning before he left for work.

'Did you see the paper?' he asked right off.

'You're home? Where were you yesterday?' I asked, grateful that he was alive and well enough to use the telephone.

'Yep, I'm home . . . went to work late yesterday. But

look at the paper, Mom. We've got a real live scandal at the Ivory Tower! Gotta go. Talk to you later . . . and sorry I didn't get a chance to call back yesterday. Bye.' And he hung up.

'Love you, Shel,' I said into the receiver, even though I'd already heard a click.

Outside my door the daily paper pulsated with headlines of sex, blackmail and death: '*Little Red Book Tells All . . . Sex and Money May Have Helped Push Tower Resident Over the Edge.*'

Quickly scanning the article, it became obvious to me that it was a leaked story, and a pretty shoddy one. Suspects weren't named, but reference was made to the colours listed in the book and their possible connection to the umbrellas of the Tower beach. Blackmail and murder were insinuated. '*Witnesses are being sought for questioning,*' the paper stated. Lieutenant Fiori was quoted: '*No comment.*'

On the beach an hour later, Robin and I were under my umbrella, poring over the article in her paper and mine. Looking around, I saw newspapers up under every umbrella as people read in shock a barely plausible story some reporter had concocted from the most meagre of facts. And they were reading it as truth. On a day when colour could be incriminating, I was content to remain colourless.

'He called Elliot,' Robin said quietly over the top of her paper.

'Fiori?' I questioned, lowering my paper.

'Yep. And Elliot called me last night very shaken up. He said he has to talk to me, that he has something to tell me. He's coming down tonight.'

Silence.

'I'm sure he's going to tell me about his affair with Marjorie.'

'What will you say?' I asked, no longer protesting his innocence.

'I don't know,' Robin answered, putting her paper down, leaning her head back.

As she stared at the corroding metal ribs of my umbrella, I watched tiny spasms pull the corners of her mouth downwards, scrunch her eyes into a squint. A trickle of tears ran down her temples. 'You okay, Rob?'

'Sure,' she said, sitting upright, reaching into her beach bag for a tissue. 'This is just horrible.'

'Don't jump to conclusions, Robin. You don't know what Elliot has to say.'

'Only *you* wouldn't believe it, Alison,' she said, making me feel consummately guilty, because not only did I believe it, I'd *invented* it. Sniffing again, she said, 'It's all rather obvious you know.' Pause. 'Maybe it's even worse.'

'Worse?'

'Maybe he's involved in her murder.'

'You can't be serious –'

'How do I know where he was Thursday night? For all I know he came to see Marjorie. Maybe she threatened to tell me about their affair. He'd panic, you know. He'd definitely panic.'

Spurred on by Fiori's visit, by Robin's revelations, by the end of the week I had my story – well, the bare bones and vital organs of my story. The mystery was established, the characters formed.

Who murdered Marjorie Applebaum? was the obvious question, and I certainly had a wide range of suspects from which to choose. But I decided to leave the murder mystery to Tony Fiori. Murder seemed so trite. I wanted to give my readers something different. In my book Marjorie's death would turn out to be random, an accident, one so far from probability – but not possibility – that it would make my readers think about how much we don't know about others' beginnings, how much we can learn from their ends, how very different a life can be from what it appears . . . how random life is . . .

She'd played the game so many times before, it had become ritual. But this time, before she even had time to spread her wings, let alone fly, Marjorie Applebaum was falling, stark naked, on to the boardwalk below, passing Alison Diamond lying half asleep on her balcony.

. . . Sitting on the beach that Thursday morning constructing the final scene of *Beach Book-91*, I must confess, I wondered how different from the *real* story my fiction would end up being.

Friday morning I got my answer, because, by the end of the week the media had their story, too: '*After systematically seducing and blackmailing a number of married men who were summer residents at the Ivory Tower Condominium, Marjorie Applebaum Smith, a twenty-six year old Philadelphia accountant, ended up in a* ménage à trois *of dangerous, and finally fatal, sex games with fifty-six year old Martin Steiner and thirty-seven year old Patricia Gordon, both residents of the Ivory Tower. Accidentally slipping free from a rope in the early morning hours of July 26, Smith plunged from the balcony of Steiner's penthouse apartment in the Ivory Tower Condominium, in Kent, New Jersey, to her death on the boardwalk below.*'

I could have written the newspaper story; I already *had*

written it, in *Beach Book-91*, I thought incredulously, reading the newspaper account for at least the tenth time. The story was a bomb exploding in the centre of peace, blowing away half its population. Looking down from my balcony I saw that, although it was a perfect beach day, Robin and Elliot's pink umbrella was missing (I hadn't heard from Robin since I'd seen her on the beach on Tuesday morning, and later found out that Elliot and Robin had left the shore on Wednesday morning). Jeffrey's yellow umbrella, too, was absent (he'd cut his vacation short and returned to Philadelphia sometime on Wednesday, too – after several calls from the media) – as were the orange umbrella of Marcie Cobrin (the pudgy attorney's wife), the blue and white striped umbrella of Debbie (the doctor's wife), Cindy's (or was it Mindy's?) navy umbrella, and Diamond Lil's yellow and orange striped umbrella. Of course, the Steiner's green umbrella and Tish Gordon's turquoise umbrella were nowhere to be seen.

'. . . *First break in the case came from a colour coded diary of the deceased's sexual liaisons . . . found in the elevator the afternoon following her death by Sheldon Diamond, the eighteen-year-old son of Ivory Tower resident, Alison Diamond,*' I read further down.

They didn't have to use his name, I was thinking, furious that Shel had been involved in the sordid affair in even such an oblique manner, when my eyes shot back to the words, *found in the elevator the afternoon following her death*. The afternoon following her death – that is, *Friday*, not *Tuesday*, as Shel had told me. Of course, newspapers were notorious for getting that kind of detail wrong, I thought. But if the paper had it *right*, what was Shel doing in the elevator on Friday afternoon?

My eyes focused on Brenda Forrester's red umbrella

and I thought about what Shel and Robin had said about Brenda ... what I'd written about Brenda and Shel. Could that possibly be true, too, I wondered in horror.

I tried Shel at his house, but his machine answered. When I called the deli, I was told he wasn't due in until one. I called his machine back and left a message for him to call me as soon as he got in, then I started to organise my things for our trip home on Monday in preparation for our trip to Chicago on Friday, and, while I was at it, I cleaned the kitchen, including the oven, and the bathrooms, and then I started cleaning out my bedroom closet. If Shel had been there he'd have known I was upset. I always cleaned when I was upset. And when I cleaned closets, it was serious.

Sex was serious. Sex and Shel was serious. Sex between Shel and Brenda Forrester was very serious. I cleaned more closets.

When Shel walked in at eleven-thirty, I was deep in the hall storage closet weeding out dozens of bare wire hangers from the back rung, finally convinced that paper clips – I could *never* find a paper clip when I needed one – were indeed the larval stage of wire hangers.

'Uh-oh. Mom's cleaning closets. What happened?' I heard from the hall.

'I saw your name in the newspaper,' I said, emerging from the overstuffed little room with a handful of the black and silver closet pests.

'How about that story!'

'So when did you find the book? Friday or Tuesday?' I spat out as I walked past Shel to dump the hangers in the kitchen trash can.

'What did the papers say?'

'Friday.'

'Then I guess it was Friday.'

'You told me it was Tuesday.'

'Guess I was wrong.'

'So what were you doing here on Friday?' I interrogated.

'I must have been coming to see you.'

'Wrong. You didn't even know I was at the shore.'

'So what was I doing, Mom?'

'You tell me.'

'I *told* you. I was looking for you,' Shel insisted, sticking to his story.

'Why would you have been looking for me when you didn't expect me to be here until Saturday?' I asked, my voice rising.

'Because when I called you in Philly on Thursday night my call was forwarded to your machine here. Different message than your Philly machine,' he explained quietly, carefully.

Too carefully, I thought, wondering why he was even answering my irrational questions. 'But I was here all night. What time did you call?' I asked, losing some steam.

'About eleven.'

'I guess I could have been asleep . . . but I didn't see any messages in the morning,' I persisted lamely.

'Didn't leave one. Thought I'd surprise you on Friday.'

'Well, your friends found me on the beach, how come you didn't?'

'Can't answer that one, Mom.'

'Maybe you were visiting someone else?'

'Like who?' he asked, becoming irritated.

'That's what I'm asking *you*.'

'I wasn't visiting anyone else. I went back to the beach, couldn't find you or the guys, so I walked for a while and then went home.'

'And you didn't call me until Saturday morning. Shel, that makes no sense at all.'

'Give me a break, Mom. I tried to see you. You weren't in. What's so serious, anyway?'

SEX is serious! Sex between you and BRENDA FORRESTER is very serious! screamed in my head. Of course I couldn't tell him about that ... about my neurotic ruminations over my own imaginings ... about my friend's suppositions about my son – my baby – based on vicious rumours about a woman none of us really knew and a few off-hand comments Shel had made in an attempt to shock me. And I wondered if rumour is different from perception ... if perception is really so different from fantasy ... or even close to THE TRUTH. And the more I thought, the dizzier I got, and the dizzier I got, the less sense any of it made.

'Hey, Mom, you okay?' Shel said lunging forward to grab my arm as I started to visibly sway.

'Just a little dizzy. I'll be fine,' I said, holding on to the sink.

'You're white.'

'Too much sunscreen,' I said, trying to lighten up.

'You sure you're not sick, Mom?' Shel asked, looking so concerned I thought my heart would break.

'I'm fine. It's just my inner ear ... in shock – a virus, the doctor said.'

'Maybe you shouldn't fly with me next week,' he suggested.

'I already asked. The doctor said I'm allowed to fly,' I said, wondering if he'd brought that up because he didn't *want* me to go with him.

'You sure?' he pressed.

'Don't you *want* me to go with you?'

'I give up! I've got to go to work. See you Monday

morning,' he said, walking to the door, out the door, down the hall.

'Love you, Shel,' I said to his back, angry at myself for upsetting him, pushing aside the fact that he'd upset me. Well, pushing aside the fact that I'd been upset ... by facts or fiction. It appeared now that I'd never know for sure. Which was probably for the best.

'Bat. Dragon. Two-toed sloth,' I said aloud, staring at the sky from my balcony at the Ivory Tower the Tuesday morning after returning the night before from Chicago, after settling Shel into his dorm at the University, after spending what seemed at once an interminable and all too short week in Philadelphia sorting and shopping and packing and bickering ... like the pair of gulls, I thought.

Leaning on the rail, I closed my eyes, breathed in the hot salty air. But peace eluded me as I thought about Shel in a strange place among strangers, as I worried about his ability to cope, reflecting, of course, on my ability to teach him how to cope, *my* ability to cope. How *had* I coped all these years? I considered. *Clumsily*, I thought. I'd been thoughtless, selfish, and, sometimes, downright mean. I'd been insensitive, harsh, and ineffectual. I'll pay for his shrink, I thought, full of remorse. I'll even go with him if he asks. And I'll tell his shrink that his inability to cope with the world stems from my inability to provide him with the proper tools. I'd let him down, made him feel insecure. I should have found a father for him, made a proper home for him. Maybe my mother was right, after all.

I felt the heat rise up in me until my face burned with the guilt of poor mothering, until the pressure of contrition squeezed burning tears from my eyes. I was hard on myself, but probably not as hard as Shel would be when he began to understand how I'd failed him. Maybe he already knows, I thought, understanding that there had to be a reason why he never told me that he loved me.

I was seized with a need to be near him, to touch him, to apologise to him. But he was so far away. I only hoped I'd have the chance to explain before some random accident took me, or worse, took him from this life ... from me. And then I remembered the folder of papers I'd packed hastily just as I was walking out the door to head down the shore. Shel had left it on the kitchen counter along with a library book on the Shakers he'd never returned, an empty six-pack of glass Coca Cola bottles, and a lined yellow legal tablet, unused except for a couple of old telephone messages I don't remember him ever telling me about scrawled in the upper left hand corner. A quick peek inside the folder had revealed one of his report cards from the year and some pictures he'd taken for his photography class, so I'd scooped it up and stuffed it into my overnight bag.

Retrieving the folder from the bedroom, I sat on the balcony to explore it, to touch some small part of my son, who was surely otherwise lost to me. Two close-up photos of my left eye – looking terribly old and tired, I thought – fell out. I couldn't imagine why he'd kept them. They were part of an unsuccessful photography class experiment, as was a photo of my silhouette against an open window, although I rather liked that one. No wrinkles. There were a couple of French quizzes he'd aced, and his ten page term paper on the Shakers – marked with an *A*. I didn't bother reading it because I knew every word of it. I'd typed it for him in the wee hours of the morning the day it was due.

In the very back of the folder was a two-page, handwritten paper for English lab I'd never seen, entitled, *Making a Difference*. My breath caught in my throat as I read the first sentence: '*Not many people can make a difference in a man's life, but let me tell you about my Mom.*' My world disappeared as I read about our relationship – from *his* perspective – about the unqualified love he'd seen behind my clumsy actions. '. . . *She always protected me . . .*' Tears ran from my eyes, squeezed from the very bottom of my heart. '. . . *sometimes overprotected me. But isn't that the way a Mom's supposed to be?*' he wrote. And I remembered the thousands of times I wondered how a Mom *was* supposed to be. And then, '. . . *She never says goodbye without telling me she loves me.*' And I had thought he hadn't heard, or didn't care, or worse. By the time I'd reached the end I was sobbing and had to wipe my eyes on the bottom of my tee-shirt before I could read, '*My Mom: parent, teacher, friend – the one person who has made a difference in my life.*'

I laid the pages in my lap and smoothed them with my hand, the way I used to run my hand over Shel's silky baby skin so many years ago, the way I ran my hand over his clothes when I packed them just days before.

Looking over the rail, out to sea, the distance from Shel had become unbearable. I left the balcony, picked up the phone in the living room and punched in his new phone number, which I'd already committed to memory.

'Hey!' he answered from another universe.

'Just called to make sure you're okay,' I said, trying to sound bright, supportive.

'I was just gonna call you.'

'You were?' I said. *He misses me!* I thought.

'Yeah. Forgot to pack my lucky sweatshirt. Can you send it to me?'

He missed his sweatshirt.

'The grungy one with the holes?' I said, knowingly.

'Mom, it's a work of art!'

'I'll UPS it when I get home.'

'You down the shore?'

'Yes. And it's a beautiful day.'

'It's nice here too, but I'm off to physics lab. So . . . I got to go. Don't forget my sweatshirt.'

'Anything else, Shel?'

'Of course! Send money!'

Of course. 'I seem to remember quite a sizable monetary transaction before you left –'

'Okay, okay. Got to run. Call me later.'

'Have a good day. Hope you like your classes. Love you, Shel.'

'I love you, too, Mom.'

Overwhelmed, I continued to hold the receiver to my ear . . . past the click, to the dial tone. But all I heard was, '*I love you, too, Mom*' . . . until a loud *beep, beep, beep*, signalling *phone-off-the-hook*, shattered my reverie, and I lowered the phone gently back into its cradle. I returned to my computer on the balcony, pulled up the *Notes* file and began to write . . .

'Have a good day. Hope you like your classes. Love you, Shel,' Alison said, her heart full of longing.

'I love you, too, Mom,' he responded.

. . . *overwhelming her*, I thought, but could not write. I was too overwhelmed to write. There are some things that are too precious, too fragile to write, to try and hold in the memory of a machine, I thought, turning off my computer. I looked up and saw a pair of sea gulls flying gracefully, beautifully free. And I imagined myself lightened, aloft on wings of equanimity, understanding at last the difference between *to have* and *to hold*.

'Hey! Mrs D.,' the young man in the wraparound mirrored sun-glasses greeted me on the beach the next morning. 'You're gonna love this! It'll give you a whole new perspective,' he said, retrieving from his aluminium and canvas mountain the bright purple umbrella I'd requested the afternoon before.

EPILOGUE

Beach Book

It was like a new baby. Created from bits and pieces of others' lives, *Beach Book-91*'s original incarnation had been subsumed by the uniqueness of its final form. Sitting under my purple umbrella on the Ivory Tower Beach, a new mother, I inspected my progeny, counting its pages, checking for imperfections. Running my fingers across my novel's shiny embossed cover, I felt a rush of pride. So maybe it wouldn't receive a Pulitzer, but it was mine, and I loved it.

It was hard to believe that a year had passed since the death of Marjorie Applebaum, since Shel had gone away to school and I'd begun the painstaking task of transforming last summer's *Beach Book-91* notes and vignettes into a complete work of fiction.

This year's *Beach Book-92* – about the murder of a female body builder in Sweden (an idea that came to me while sweating on the Stair Master at my fitness centre in Philadelphia) – is well under way. In it, the protagonist, doing research in Sweden as a correspondent for a health magazine, lands the murderer (a psychotic, lesbian, male impersonator) after barely escaping being murdered herself. Following a passionate but doomed affair with a psychologist with whom she consults regarding serial killers – he confesses that he's trapped in a loveless marriage to the woman who saved his life at the expense of her health in a boating accident when they were twenty-two – she ends up marrying a nice radiologist at the MRI lab where she goes to find the cause of her frightening dizzy spells. Next August, I'm confident, I'll be reading the published book and writing *Beach Book-93*.

August: the final gestational period, when my Beach Book is meticulously filled out and toned ... vital connections made, life breathed into its lungs ... when the strokes of my fingers on the keyboard of my laptop assures the heart of my new novel a good, solid beat. Then it's scrubbed and brushed, manicured and coiffed. There'd be no dirt under the fingernails, no split ends, no unsightly stubble evident when I'd mail this year's completed manuscript to my agent on September 1. I learned early on in my writing career that polish sells. But, as Robin had so succinctly pointed out to me (or had I written it?), in real life there's a lot more spit than polish.

And so, while in the book I held in my hands the character inspired by Marty Steiner learns a lesson or two and gives up his mistresses, but not the mirrored ceiling in his bathroom, giving his wife more diversion than she'd ever dreamed possible ..., in fact, Maggie Steiner ran off with the bass recorder player with whom she'd been having an affair during her visits with her daughter. Marty's mistress, Tish, left him, too, being utterly unnerved by Marjorie's death. All this I learned from Emma Chankin, who I saw in the elevator with her new live-in gentleman friend, Morris Grossman, the first week-end of this summer season. Marty, I noted a few days later, had gained about thirty pounds and had taken to wearing boxer trunks.

Robin's and Elliot's facsimiles also fared better in fiction than in fact. In *Beach Book-91* he confessed his affair to her, and she confessed her affair to him. And, of course, she had a baby (although she wasn't sure whether it was Elliot's or her former lover's, a mystery she chose to keep to herself). In fact, when I'd called Robin this past fall, she told me that Elliot had indeed confessed his affair with Marjorie Applebaum to her and they'd entered into family therapy. Although I spoke with her answering machine several times after that conversation, Robin never returned my calls, and it wasn't until this summer that I learned that Elliot and Robin had separated in January and that their unit at the Tower was up for sale. This Marty had related when he'd approached me for information about Robin – he wanted to date her – not knowing that he already knew more than I knew, which didn't surprise me a bit.

The characters modelled after the Hunk and Tiffany Kaufman were killed off in a fiery helicopter accident fairly early in the plot, as they were no longer needed. Real life, however, is seldom as neat as a novel, and usually more banal. While walking along the beach towards Atlantic City, I saw Doug 'The Hunk' Smith in his lifeguard stand, surrounded by bikinied young women. Emma told me that there's a nasty legal dispute between Doug and Marjorie's mother over ownership of Marjorie's unit at the Tower.

Brenda Forrester, looking younger than ever (rumour has it that she had a face-life . . . or was it *another* facelift?) is wearing her thick, jet black (dyed?) hair pulled back taut in a sleek bun this summer. An inordinate number of young men, I note, continue to visit under her red umbrella. I do my best to avoid her.

Of course the 'Jeffrey' and 'Alison' characters end up together in the book, she providing the perfect wife for him – a woman who loves to sleep with him as much as she loves

to listen to him – and he, transmogrified into a derma-
tologist, providing the perfect mate for her – a man who
loves her son (the son he never had) almost as much as he
loves her. The son finds in his mother's new husband a
confessor for his liaison with the older woman, learning
from him that the woman probably suffered from self-
image problems stemming from alopecia universalis, a
condition characterised by total body baldness (which,
incidentally, was the subject of a non-fiction article I'd
written for a women's magazine a couple of years ago). The
young man goes off to college with a clear conscience and a
mind towards medical school.

Jeffrey Kaufman, in fact, didn't return to the Ivory
Tower this year. He'd called me once last fall, while I was
still at the shore, to see how I was doing. He'd sounded
strained. We promised to keep in touch. But we didn't.
According to Marty, who'd heard it from Emma, whose
source was undetermined, Jeffrey was dating his ex-wife,
Tiffany, in Philadelphia.

And me? Well, I've been dating Ira Pressman since last
September when I finally collected on his rain check for
dinner . . .

I'd been back at the Tower for almost a week after leaving
Shel at school in Chicago and was sitting on the balcony,
working on *Beach Book-91*, when I'd gotten a call from
Lieutenant Fiori. The quake of events surrounding the
death of Marjorie Applebaum had abated, leaving only
minor aftershocks of self-righteous tongue clacking. But
with the mystery solved and all the players gone from the
scene, the scandal quickly ebbed and the Tower beach had
become quieter than ever. Hearing the lieutenant's voice
on the other end of the phone that morning was therefore
jolting.

First he apologised for calling, then he apologised for not calling sooner, and then he invited me to dinner.

I declined without a moment's hesitation, remembering his advances on my balcony . . . his very young face.

After promising to send him a signed copy of my latest book when it was published, I said goodbye. And that would be the end of it. No matter how much I'd anxiously ruminate on how he'd probably keep pestering me, how he'd spill my secret identity, the vapid reality was, a simple *goodbye* would be the end of it.

Returning to my laptop on the balcony I searched the *Notes* file for the scene with Fiori I'd invented . . .

She hadn't anticipated his considerable strength, and found the surprise of his sinew as exciting as the fact. And when he held her body flush to his, moving against her, allowing her to know the scope of his intentions, she followed his rhythm until, taking his hand, Alison led him back into her apartment, into her bedroom.

. . . Too bad. It could have been an adventure, I thought, feeling a small prickle run through me. Remembering his actual kiss, on my shoulder, on the balcony, remembering how I'd considered that the little red box in the drawer of my dressing table might actually see the light of day, I started to laugh, at Fiori's lust, at my own, and at the old box of condoms still sitting unopened in the drawer.

I left the laptop on the balcony and sat down in front of the mirror at my dressing table. Staring past the reflection of my grown up self, I succumbed to an irresistible desire. Withdrawing the small red box from the back of the make-up drawer, I removed a rubber and carried it into the bathroom, where I fitted it over the sink tap, turned on the water and watched the pallid pouch slowly fill, becoming the great white whale of my youth. This time I wouldn't be daunted, I thought, not thinking about the consequences of courage. Steadfast, both hands gripping the sheathed tap, I observed the latex skin swell and thin until it was as transparent as the water distending it – a tense, tenuous membrane staying the drowning-beast. Remembering Larry, I gripped the tap more firmly until, stretched beyond its generous limits, the rubber ruptured.

Drenched but victorious, I went to the phone and called Ira Pressman.

. . . As I said, it was after Shel had left for school that I began in earnest the task of whipping *Beach Book-91* into existence. I'd chosen a foreign venue – a mountain-top luxury condominium overlooking the sea, on St Kitts, a small island in the Dutch West Indies – and surrounded my American protagonists with characters from Italy, France and Morocco, adding the spice of foreign intrigue to the barrel of pickled red herrings.

The extra week I was going to spend at the Tower turned into a month as I laboured furiously to write my story. The days grew cool and then warm again.

Sitting on a deserted beach beneath my purple umbrella, I'd just finished reading the last chapter of the first draft of the completed manuscript, the final scene graphically depicting a woman's accidental fall from her balcony to her death in the sea below. Putting the pages aside, I found myself unsettled. I wasn't finished with my tale. There were too many questions buzzing around in my head. A freak accident might be acceptable in reality, but, I decided after all, it was too random for fiction. I learned in high school physics that every action has a reaction; I was still learning that every reaction is the result of an action. In real life there are reasons for everything, even for events that appear to be random. As creator and ruler of my fictional universe, I had to provide patent grounds for the behaviour of my characters.

The sun was low in the sky, and a cool nip had cut through the humid heat of the day. Leaving my chair and the shade of my umbrella, I laid face down on a towel, closed my eyes and ran the story backward in my head, starting with the answer to find the questions, the reaction to find the action . . . but I fell asleep . . .

And then I was in my car, stopped on the bridge from Atlantic City to Philadelphia, with Fiori writing me a ticket. I knew I was dreaming because I'd been there before, a fact that didn't relieve my horror at my inability to get Fiori to pay attention to the woman about to jump into the river. But this time she didn't jump. After handing me a ticket I couldn't read – it was too dark, or the writing was too light – Fiori drove away, and the right rear door of my car opened. The woman from the bridge got in and sat on the floor, wedging herself between the front and back seat.

'Come on. I have a secret,' she whispered.

Squeezing through the front bucket seats, I sat on the floor with her. The tight space grew roomy as the woman and I became little girls, Evy and I as children, and we were in our secret hideout in the hedges, and she was telling me her deepest, darkest secret – about her father, my uncle . . . about how he had touched her. And then she burst into tears and made me swear never, never, ever to tell anyone.

I swore, crossing my heart, hoping to die.

And then we were standing on the bridge above the dark river. We were all grown up. 'I didn't tell! I never told!' I was crying to Evy. Turning to me, she said, 'It's never too late for anything.' And then she jumped.

311

* * *

. . . I awoke on the beach before she hit the water.

That evening, on my balcony, I began the final draft of *Beach Book-91*.

By the end of the following week I'd finished the manuscript.

. . . And now, here I sit reading the last few pages of last summer's *Beach Book-91*, published this past May under its own unique name, and this dedication: *For Evy – A grain of truth* . . .

Against the perfect silver-gold disk of the full moon, she turned slowly on the slim cord binding her ankles, holding her aloft two hundred feet above the Caribbean shore. Blood pounded in her ears. Her stomach weighed upon her heart. Opening her eyes, she saw the diamond-peaked black sea tossing and churning above her, the lucid sky below. As she moved, her buttocks flashed in the moonlight, her white breasts peeked out from behind her arms crossed against her chest. Her red hair hung down from her head like a flag.

She was imagining a cocoon about her, a metamorphosis within. Hanging from the silken thread, she could feel her body expanding, pushing out wings as she transformed before her inner eye.

'Now,' she said aloud.

Grasping the cord, the man in the balcony above her pressed it gently to his left and then released it. She swayed back and forth slowly, excitement growing in her as the to and fro of her flight played havoc with her equilibrium.

She remembered when she was a child, on the swing in her back yard, and her father pushing her higher and higher. Closing her eyes, she would lean back as far as she could. Then she'd pitch her head back, inducing a sensation so acute, it would reach to her private parts, causing her to gasp. 'Faster, Daddy. Faster!' she'd cry. And he'd push her faster and faster until she'd scream from the overwhelming sensation.

'Faster, *faster*,' she cried, and the man pushed the rope harder.

And then, she remembered, her father would grab her from the swing, hold her close to his body and swing her around and around until they fell on the ground together and he'd tickle her all over, and she'd giggle and squirm and he'd call her his little caterpillar. 'Make me a butterfly,' she'd implore. And he'd spread her arms out wide. 'You're a butterfly,' he'd say, pinning her to the ground. And then, straddling her body with his knees, holding her arms out by her wrists, he'd kiss her full on her mouth. And she'd soar.

Spreading her arms slowly outward, the woman moaned softly. As she waved her gossamer wings, glimmers of moonlight reflected off the small blade in her hand and into her eyes, into the night.

'Yes!' she called.

She'd played the game so many times before, it had become ritual. But this time, severing the silken cord with the blade, she slipped the bonds of her secrets, away from the man who would pull her up, to bed, to mount her in a reality that, although tangible, was no more real than her wings of air, no more sustaining than the air through which she spiraled. She flew past the moon over the sea, away from memory, away from the trident of fear, desire and shame that had pierced her soul. She fell from their reach as she soared free on the cool, clean air. And all memory ended as she struck the tranquil waters of eternity.

. . . It's hard to believe that a year has passed . . . that a lifetime has passed, I thought, closing my book, touching the embossed letters of its cover:

A TELLING TALE
by
ALISON DIAMOND